THE TREASURE OF RIGMORE HOUSE

BETWIXT THE SEA AND SHORE
BOOK 3

THE TREASURE OF RIGMORE HOUSE

Betwixt the Sea and Shore Book 3

CLAIRE KOHLER

Cover by MoorBooks Design
Editing by Sarah Everest

This book is a work of fiction. Names, characters, places, and incidents are either the product of the author's imagination or are used fictitiously.

ISBN: 979-8-9855674-2-7

To Peter:
For having the courage to say "no."

Thank you for your love and support as I chase my dreams.

Acknowledgments

I couldn't have completed this work without the generosity and kindness of my wonderful Lord and Savior, Jesus Christ. All my creativity is a gift from the Creator.

Thank you to my lovely friend and editor, Sarah Everest, for the quick and thorough job she did on this book. She is amazing!

Special thanks goes to my ARC team as well, who took the time to read and review this labor of love. Thank you to Stephanie Ascough, Peace Asuzu, Rainelle Barrett, Maria Anne Bollmann, Becky Briggs, Lydia Brown, Emily Bueckert, Carrie, Patsy Case, Catey Chew, Stephanie Cotta, Isa Deal, Kelly Demers, Angel Dotson, Slavka Edelmayer, Heather Hackney, Sophia Harlow, Brooke Hickman, Karla Holdier, Kristi Horton, Hunter, Suze Hurzner, Ami Jacobs, Amanda Keller, Tina Kohler, Nicole Lam, Abigail Langton, Rebel Lee, Simone Lindberg, Naomi Longoria, Lia Lorimer, Sherry Marlowe, Pat Martin, Kim Moore, Fiona Muliett, Darleen Nelson, Sarah Nolan, Lynda Osborne, Anastasia Ouzounidou, Jay Que, Candice Lee Rawe, Roisin Robbins, Chantal Rogers, Nevaeh Ruegger, Amber Severns, Danielle Smith, Hope Stiles, Iris Maya Tommack, Janelly Valdez, Summer Vaselovic, Patricia Webb, and Tami Willard.

And thank you finally to my husband and children for supporting their quirky neurodivergent wife/mom in my latest creative endeavor!

Prologue

Orkney Islands[1], 1748

What a fascinating shade o' red the laird's face turns when he's angry,
Vincent thought to himself.

Vincent McLaren had a knack for noticing the things no
one else did. When Lady Oliver's best dress had gone missing,
no one else had picked up on how Alysett Brown, the Olivers'
new maid, barely looked anyone in the eye for weeks despite
having been quite sociable when she'd first arrived. When hoof
prints had appeared near the local loch around the same time
children had started disappearing, he'd been quick to urge
everyone not to go fishing after dark. And when his neighbors
had been so concerned over the bad luck trailing the Martins
one summer, Vincent had been the only one with the sense to
tell them to get rid of their new iron heuk[2].

He'd also noticed that Laird Oliver was quickly losing his
patience.

"Good evening, my dear neighbors," Joseph Oliver said
from his spot behind the church pulpit. This was, in fact, the
third time he'd spoken these words, but almost no one was
paying him any mind. The town meeting should have started

---

[1] An archipelago in the Northern Isles of Scotland.

[2] A sickle.

fifteen minutes ago, but with Yule[3] almost upon them, the children were so excited they hadn't stopped chattering long enough for the laird's voice to be heard beyond the first pew.

The majority of Everton's residents were seated near the front of the church, huddled close together to keep warm against the icy blast that blew in every time someone opened the door. A few neighbors hadn't arrived yet.

Where is Bethany? Vincent wondered. *I hope she and Briony are well.* It had snowed the night before, and since the Fairborns' cottage was a good distance from the rest of Everton, it was possible Bethany hadn't deemed it safe for them to come tonight.

Still, I don' think she has ever skipped a meeting before.

Almost as if his thoughts had conjured them up, the Fairborns slipped in the door and took their seats at the back. The mad fisherman smiled. *Now the meeting can begin.*

He rose to his feet and stole over to the laird's side. "Allow me," he offered.

The laird stiffened in recognition. Joseph often reacted like that—as if he could barely stand to be in Vincent's presence. Maybe it was because the scent of fish followed him wherever he went. Maybe it was because Vincent was one of the few fishermen Laird Oliver didn't have complete control over. Or maybe it was because everyone thought the "mad" fisherman was just that—mentally unstable.

Vincent didn't know and didn't particularly care.

He didn't usually offer the laird help—one, because Vincent didn't like the fellow and two, because the laird didn't like to admit when he needed it. Conflict appeared on Joseph's face, and the mad fisherman waited patiently to see which side would win out: Joseph's pride or his desire for attention.

"If you think you can establish some semblance o' order, by all means," the laird said finally, putting his hands over his ears and marching off to join his wife in the first pew. As he sat down, he grumbled, "I can' handle much more o' this."

---

[3] Orkney's midwinter festival.

Mr. McLaren slid behind the pulpit and raised a finger to his lips. "Listen here, and listen well, as I tell you a tale that will make the hairs o' yer arms stand affright."

The children ceased their talking, save for a few giggles, and turned to the fisherman. The adults raised their eyebrows, both impressed and amused by Mr. McLaren's methods.

"This is the story selkies don' dare whisper. The story o' reclaiming what was once lost, though it came at a terrible cost. I warn you now that you may na sleep tonight if you hear it, so the faint o' heart best cover their ears."

Laird Oliver, who hadn't yet put his hands down, dropped them before someone could claim he was cowardly. Meanwhile, the lads and lasses glanced at each other, the nervousness in their friends' eyes mirroring their own, though none would admit it.

After a pause, Vincent smiled. "Excellent. Then let me begin. Long ago, a selkie by the name o' Evander visited a maiden on this very shore. This young woman, scorned by her community fer a scar marring her face, had wept seven tears into the ocean. Why? Because she, as well as everyone else, knows when the sea catches those tears, a fair selkie will come to comfort her.

"She did this three times, and three times, mighty Evander did come to her, though he never stayed long fer fear o' her fisherman father. But despite her efforts to conceal their tryst, the woman's father eventually discovered the truth. There were some things which couldn' be concealed fer long."

"How did he find out?" interrupted a small redhead named Muireall. She was a curious sort, eager to understand the world in all its facets. Vincent very much enjoyed her questions and always encouraged her to keep asking them.

"Never you mind that," Laura Oliver called, sending the mad fisherman a deathly glare. "Let him finish his story."

The young girl's lower lip quivered, as it often did when her mother scolded her, but she ducked her head and obeyed.

Vincent continued, "The fourth time Evander came to his lover, her father was prepared. He waited silently on the shore, and when a lone seal shed its pelt, he crept up and snatched the skin."

"But didn' Evander get angry?" asked the Martins' boy, Gregor.

Vincent McLaren shook his head with a barely concealed grin. "Nay, he—"

"You told us before that selkies could call down storms. He should have struck him dead with a lightning bolt. Yer story doesn' make sense, Mr. McLaren," little Muireall pointed out, her forehead wrinkled in confusion.

"Daughter, what did I tell you? Yer old enough now to know that 'tis na proper fer a young lady to behave in such a repugnant manner. Apologize at once," Laura snapped.

The mad fisherman's heart clenched at the tears that formed in Muireall's eyes. The poor girl was so upset she could barely squeak, "I'm sorry, Mr. McLaren."

"That's quite all right, lass," Vincent said softly, then raised his voice for his eager audience. "Anyway, Evander didn' know the pelt had been stolen until a great heat came over his body, as if the sun itself had swallowed him up. He realized then that his sealskin was burning.

"Evander cried out to the sky fer help, trying to summon lightning to destroy his enemy, but 'twas too late. His selkie magic was already fading, leaving him practically human."

Vincent dramatically waved his hand. "But that wasn' the end fer Evander. Nay, he wasn' about to give up his beloved ocean so easily. He lay in wait fer his fellow selkies on a moonlit beach, and when they shed their skins to dance, he made his move. He stole the nearest pelt, thinking he could claim it fer himself. Except the skin would na fit properly, fer it belonged to someone else. What do you think he did then?" Mr. McLaren eyed each child in turn.

"He gave up?" offered Ewan Sherwin, the young son of the village doctor.

"O' course he didn', Ewan. Don' be foolish," said Matthew Levins, elbowing the other lad. Ewan shrank into himself at the slight, but Matthew didn't notice. "Tell us already, Mr. McLaren."

"Well, that was when Evander did something truly horrible." Vincent lowered his gaze to the floor. "He took a stone and attacked the sealskin's true owner, beating him until his life-force fled. And as the sand ran red with blood, Evander again put on the skin, this time with success."

"He . . . he killed the other selkie?" Elspet Milligan whispered, her blue eyes wide with horror.

"Aye." Mr. McLaren nodded his head solemnly. "And what's worse, 'twas his own brother he'd murdered. His lust fer the ocean had grown too great, and he could na see the sin o' his actions."

"What did the other selkies do when they found out?" Elspet's little brother, Henry, asked.

The fisherman tapped the boy's nose. "Fer that part o' the story, you'll have to wait until the adults finish their meeting."

A chorus of groans erupted, but the children knew better than to argue. Vincent McLaren leaped from the pulpit and spun in a circle. "And if I forget, may the selkies strike me down."

The children chuckled at his theatrics, and Laird Oliver returned to his place, nodding to Mr. McLaren with a condescending grin. "Thank you, Mr. McLaren fer the . . . interesting story." He turned to address the crowd. "Let's go ahead and talk about more pressing matters. Mr. Buchanan, yer crops didn' do very well this year. I have a grand idea fer something you could do instead. It seems people on Mainland have started burning seaweed and . . ."

Mr. McLaren ignored the laird's words as he made his way to an empty spot. He knew most of what would be shared now wouldn't be worth listening to. But right before he sat down, someone caught his attention.

Little Muireall, just shy of eight, was mumbling to herself. ". . . have to behave better. No more crying. No more crying." Then she wiped her face, straightened her back, and pressed her lips into a firm line.

The mad fisherman turned away, sad but not surprised. Ever since Muireall's older brother had died last summer, a great shadow had fallen over the Oliver household. And though Laird and Lady Oliver might not realize it, their daughter's fire was dying a little bit more each day.

Vincent glanced at the child one more time and said under his breath, "I fear that won' fix it, lass. You'll just snuff yerself out."

Wolves in Sheep's Clothing

Eleven years later

"I'm almost finished, my lady." Anne wound another iron rod into Muireall's red locks.

The laird's daughter held back a sigh. Getting ready was her least favorite part of the day, and today her morning ritual was even worse than normal. Today she was going to a wedding, and that meant letting a maidservant curl her naturally wavy tresses into perfect ringlets, a tedious task Muireall loathed with a passion.

"What do you think, my lady?" the young maid asked after a moment, glancing at the woman in the mirror.

Muireall didn't answer, but that was to be expected. The laird's daughter didn't talk to servants unless absolutely necessary.

"As you should," her mother had reminded her on many occasions. "And servants must na speak to their employers unless spoken to, and then only in dulcet tones with as few words as possible."

Apparently, no one had shared that rule of etiquette with Anne, for she always jabbered incessantly while she was helping Muireall get dressed. Most of what the young maid said was of little consequence, for she was a dreadful gossip, but Muireall silently stored away anything that seemed like it might be useful.

Anne took another rod off the stove. *The last one*, Muireall realized with relief.

"Isn' it so exciting having a wedding here in Everton?" the maid chirped.

"Hamish and Bridget wed na that long ago," Muireall pointed out, forgetting to stay silent in the face of inaccuracy.

"Oh, that's right. I completely forgot." Anne giggled. "This wedding will be grander than Hamish and Bridget's though. Why, Adaira is one o' the most loved people in town, and Mr. Burgess is so handsome. . . ."

Searing pain erupted at the nape of Muireall's neck as the rod in Anne's hand slipped. The redhead shrieked and jerked away before giving the careless maid a sharp glower.

"I'm so sorry!" Anne stuttered, eying the rod with dismay before placing it back in the fire. "I wasn' paying attention!"

"You could have seriously injured me," Muireall snapped, running her fingers along the singed area. It was hot to the touch, and when she checked in the mirror, a telltale red line had formed below her right ear.

"Forgive me," the maid begged, throwing her small body onto the floor. The teenager was trembling so badly she looked like she was about to fall apart. "Please, don' tell her ladyship. My family needs my income."

The absolute terror on Anne's face made Muireall's chest seize up, for the maid's fear was all too reminiscent of her own, but she kept any sympathy from showing on her face. "Get off the floor," she ordered coldly.

Anne sniffled but did as she'd been told, tears dripping down her blotchy cheeks.

"If you *ever* do something like this again, yer job will be the least o' yer worries. There will na be another chance. Na fer you nor fer the rest o' yer family. Do you understand?"

The maid's eyes widened, and she slowly nodded.

Muireall gestured to the door. "You may leave now."

"But Lady Oliver said na to miss a single—"

"Do you want to keep working here or na?"

The maid clammed up and darted to the door. Just before she left, though, Muireall said, "One more thing—never cry in front o' me again, Anne. Learn to hide yer weakness better."

Once the laird's daughter was alone, she let out a deep groan and turned back to her reflection. While others would have seen a beautiful young woman with wavy red hair, bright-green eyes, and a spattering of freckles, Muireall saw only a girl who still couldn't control herself no matter how hard she tried. *I should have told her she was done here, na given her a second chance. Why am I so pathetic? After all this time, I should be able to hide my weakness better, too.*

She glanced at the clock over the fireplace. Half past nine. It wasn't as late as she'd thought. *I'm sure Mother isn' ready yet.* Muireall's full lips lifted into a smile.

A short while later, the girl was creeping toward the garden, hot rods still in her hair. Lilies, azaleas, and rhododendrons gazed up at her as she strolled past, their petals as heartwarming as an embrace. She came out here as often as she could, though she made sure her parents only knew she liked to visit the flowers, not tend to them. It wouldn't do for them to find out she did something as dirty as gardening. They thought their gardener was responsible for the beautiful flowers, and Muireall was happy to let them believe that.

If only I had as much say over my own life as I do this garden, I'd be the most joyful woman in Everton. She paused and breathed in the scent of a nearby rose, but she didn't stop for long. She had a specific destination in mind, and she might not have much time before her mother came looking for her. *I just need to see if there are any buds,* she told herself. *Then I'll go back inside.*

Are you sure yer na just stalling? asked a cynical voice in her head. *You still have to attend the wedding, regardless o' how much you wish you didn'.*

The young woman sighed. She definitely wasn't looking forward to that. Adaira Stubbins's wedding was all her mother had talked about for the past several weeks. Ever since the date had been announced, in fact. Adaira was Muireall's first cousin, once removed, but Muireall would have had to attend even if she wasn't family. The laird's daughter was expected at such gatherings. *Far be it fer me na to do my duty.*

It wasn't that Muireall disliked Adaira. The pretty brunette was pleasant, helpful, and got along with everyone, exactly the sort of person Muireall wished she could be friends with. The laird's daughter just wasn't in the mood to hear her mother complain about why Muireall wasn't the one getting married right now. She'd been hearing that since the wedding announcement, too. It wasn't that Muireall opposed marriage itself, but the man she'd been betrothed to since infancy— Lord Carmichael of Lanarkshire—wasn't in any hurry to wed, and Muireall didn't feel ready to start a new life hundreds of miles away from her home.

When the redhead reached the middle of the garden, she squealed with glee. Small pink buds peeked out from the tips of the geraniums she'd planted earlier in the year. This was the first year Muireall had grown them, and she was delighted that they were starting to thrive.

She gently touched the nearest bud. *Everything looks healthy.* They'd had an especially rainy summer thus far, and Muireall had been worried that the flowers were getting too much water.

"Mistress Oliver?" asked a voice.

Muireall looked to her right, her eyes landing on Bernard Buchanan, the family gardener. He was a tall, unassuming fellow with a weathered face and compassionate spirit. He'd been working at Rigmore House since before Muireall was born and had an avuncular way about him, though Muireall was careful to make sure he always remembered she was his superior.

"Bernard, hello," she said pleasantly. "I came to check on the geraniums, and they look like they're doing very well, thanks to yer good work."

The older man shook his head with a grin. "Nay, mistress. You know I hardly did anything. All this is because o' you, na me."

Muireall smirked. It had been many years now since she and Bernard had made their arrangement. The man had a bad leg and couldn't keep up with the other servants' pace, so

Muireall had offered him a deal: if he volunteered for the recently vacant gardener position, she would happily do most of the work and let him get paid for it. "Be that as it may, I couldn' have done it without you being here, so that means you deserve some credit as well."

Bernard's kind brown eyes crinkled, then he looked away sheepishly. "That's actually something I've been meaning to talk to you about, mistress. I don' think I'll be able to continue doing this much longer. Even walking around the garden has become challenging o' late, and I've saved up enough money to live comfortably fer the next several years. My son has been saying I need to slow down fer the sake o' my health fer over a year now."

Muireall drew in a quick breath. *But that means I'll have to bring someone else on. Someone who may nu be as good at keeping my secret.*

The girl's hands shook, both with anger and fear. Her fear was directed at the future, but most of her anger was directed at herself. *Why am I so surprised? I should have expected this. Everyone leaves. 'Tis my fault fer allowing him to get close enough that it hurts.*

"If that's what you want, then that's yer choice. It makes no difference to me," she said in a hard voice, tucking her pain into the corner of her heart, so she could deal with it later.

The servant ducked his head. "I'm sorry, mistress. I know how much this garden means to you. I'll try to stay a wee bit longer fer yer sake."

Muireall didn't respond. *If he's done with this garden, he's na going to get another word out o' me.* After a few seconds of awkward silence, Bernard bid her farewell before tramping off.

She stood motionless, trying to digest all that his departure would mean for her. A footstep sounded nearby. She spun around. *Did Bernard change his mind?*

But instead of her servant, a thin, dark-haired figure was walking just outside the garden, heading straight for Rigmore House. *What in the world?*

No one should have been on the property besides her parents and the hired workers. Muireall didn't pay much attention to the servants, but this man's rumpled clothing made it obvious he didn't work for the Olivers. Muireall's mother wouldn't have stood for such messy attire.

"Hey!" Muireall called, hurrying after him. "Just who do you think you are, traipsing across my property?"

The man stopped and whirled toward her with a fierce scowl. "What?"

Muireall stumbled, unused to such a rude response. Most people lowered their heads around her, for fear of Laird Oliver's wrath if they gave her even the slightest offense.

The stranger's face softened. He was younger than she'd realized, perhaps only a year or two more than her eighteen years. Damp black hair hung almost to his shoulders, contrasting with his smooth pale skin. His handsome smile drew Muireall in, but there was a pain lurking in his dark eyes that made her wary. People in pain often hurt others. Muireall knew that all too well. "I'm looking fer Laird Oliver. Is he at home?"

Muireall started to nod, then stopped. "Wait. You didn' answer me. Who are you, and where did you come from?"

The man's eyes darted to the left for a split second before returning to hers. Muireall followed his glance, but that direction only led to the beach.

"My apologies," he said, claiming her attention once more. "I'm Niall Moreland. I stayed at Everton Inn a couple o' months ago. Do you live here? I'm surprised we haven' met before."

The name rang a bell in Muireall's mind, but she couldn't recall where she'd heard it. "Aye, I'm Mistress Muireall Oliver, Maid[4] o' Harray, and daughter o' The Much Honored Joseph Oliver, Laird o' Harray. Why are you looking fer him?"

"Ah, his daughter. I believe I do see the resemblance." He eyed her up and down, raising his eyebrows at the rods in her hair.

Muireall drew back, cheeks blazing. It was entirely inappropriate for her to be outside in such a state. *If this man was decent, though, he wouldn' try to shame me fer it.*

---

[4] A title for the eldest daughter of a laird.

"As fer yer question, I wanted to ask if he'd take me on as a hired hand. I'm sure I'll be seeing you often if he says aye." He winked.

Muireall's face grew even hotter. Disrespectful behavior didn't intimidate her, but flirtation was something she had no experience with. "W-We're about to leave fer a wedding, so you'll need to wait to speak with him until afterwar—"

"It won' take long. I'd be much obliged if you'd tell me where to find him."

Muireall blinked a few times, her embarrassment giving way to indignation. *Did he just interrupt me?*

The man cocked his head. "Muireall? Are you all right?"

The redhead's mouth fell open. Only her parents and a select few individuals addressed her by her given name. Everyone else knew not to be so informal, for it implied either intimacy with her or superiority over her. As this man should have known.

"O' course I'm na all right, you *fool*," she said once she'd regained her composure. "And if you have any sense at all, you'll refrain from speaking to me in such a familiar manner the next time we meet." She lifted her chin and sashayed off to the house.

Once she was back in her bedroom, Muireall began to pace. *How dare he act like that around me. I'm na some commoner. I'm Muireall Oliver, heiress o' Rigmore House. No one disrespects me. No one.*

She remembered then that the rods were still in her hair, so she angrily ripped them out. She smoothed down her wild red waves, waves that should have been curls, then gasped. *How could I have been so stupid! Anne is always the one who takes the rods out, na me. Is there time to call her back before—*

"Muireall? Are you ready yet?" came a shrill voice.

The young woman opened the door with a grin that belied the anxiety hovering in her stomach. In the hallway stood Lady Laura Oliver, Muireall's mother and mistress of Rigmore House. Today she wore a blue dress that emphasized her curvaceous figure, a figure she often pointed out that Muireall hadn't inherited.

"O' course, Mother. Shall we go?"

Laura Oliver curled her lip at her daughter's unruly hair but simply said, "Aye, let's." Muireall almost commented on the lack of criticism, but she stopped herself at the last moment. Silence was nicer than harsh words.

The two women made their way downstairs, Muireall running her hand along the rail. When she'd been a child, the stair's barley twist spindles had seemed to stretch on forever, but now that she was on her way to the wedding, they seemed to end far too quickly. When they arrived at the front door, Muireall expected her father to be waiting for them, but only the butler, Hamish Dunnet, stood there.

"Where's Father?" Muireall asked her mother.

Laura's lip curled even farther. It was her signature expression of disgust, an expression Muireall was on the receiving end of far too often. "A young man came to the door and asked if he might have a word with him. Said he ran into you earlier, and you told him we were in need o' a new manservant."

"He what?"

"Honestly, Muireall," her mother scoffed. A wisp of gray hair flew free from her updo. "You should have said we were too busy today. Adaira's wedding will be starting soon, and you know how yer father feels about tardiness."

"But I didn'. . ." Muireall trailed off, for her mother was already talking about the time they'd been late for church a few months ago, and her father had made the vicar start his sermon over.

". . . 'Twas so humiliating I would have thought you'd remember." Laura glanced down at the glistening rings on her fingers. "I suppose we'd better go ahead by ourselves. Better to have *some* Olivers at the event than none at all. Even if they're . . ." She eyed her daughter distastefully.

Muireall slumped a bit, wishing her mother's words didn't pierce so deeply. Laura often made jabs such as this, and though she hadn't said it directly, Muireall knew what she'd meant: "I wish yer brother was here. He wouldn' disappoint me as you do. Why can' you be more like Alastair?"

I have to be strong. I can' let it get to me. Her emotions started to spiral, but then a thought sparked in her mind. *Wait. I'm na the one responsible fer Mother's foul mood this time.*

Her eyes narrowed. *Aye, that's right. Niall Moreland is the one to blame. But if he thinks he can use me in his deception, he's sorely mistaken.*

"Mother, I've changed my mind," Muireall said. "Would it be all right if I stayed behind to fix my hair? I can come along with Father."

Relief flooded Laura's features. "Oh, thank goodness. I'm glad you noticed it needed more work."

Once her mother was gone, Muireall marched off. Rather than going upstairs to her room, though, the young woman turned down the hallway. When she reached the study, she gave the door a quick knock and stepped inside.

Laird Oliver and Niall Moreland stood within, their conversation halting as she entered. Her father's jaw clenched at the sight of her, for though he loved his daughter in his own way, he always seemed irritated when she interrupted him from his work.

Muireall, on the other hand, usually looked on her father with pity. Between his wife's nagging and his son's death, the years hadn't been kind to Joseph Oliver. What had once been thick black hair atop his head was now thin gray strands that looked like they could blow off in a gust of wind. Wrinkles ran along his face and hands like map lines, clearly displaying both the man's heartaches and disappointments. He may have seemed like he had everything a person could want, but Muireall knew losing his son had broken something inside him. Something inside both of her parents.

Niall Moreland, on the other hand, was paler than before. Almost as if he was nervous.

As well he should be.

"Daughter, you don' need to wait fer me. I told yer mother I'd be along in due time," Laird Oliver said curtly.

Muireall stuck out her lower lip in a well-practiced pout. "Father, I just missed you," she replied, her voice syrupy sweet. "You've been so busy o' late that I hardly get to spend time with you anymore."

Laird Oliver's sour expression melted like snow in the spring. "Aw, I'm sorry I made you feel that way, freck[5]. That wasn't my intent at all." He took one of her hands and gave it a consoling pat. "I was just telling Niall here that I'm sure there's room fer another set o' hands at our *humble* abode."

The laird chuckled at his own joke, and Muireall resisted the urge to roll her eyes. She turned to Niall with a patronizing grin. "Then let me just say welcome to Rigmore House."

The man slowly nodded, suspicion dancing in his gaze. "Thank you, mistress." He gave a small bow. "I'm honored to be here. Laird Oliver was just telling me about the wedding. I'm afraid he didn' mention the lucky couple's names though."

"Did I na?" Joseph asked. "Why, Adaira Stubbins and John Burgess. You must know them from when you stayed here in the past."

Niall's expression faltered, just for a moment, but long enough for Muireall to realize his goodwill was a mere facade. *Hmm, doesn' like them, does he? Or at least isn' happy they're getting married. I should remember that.*

"Truly? How delightful. I should very much like to attend, so I can celebrate this happy occasion with them." The man's smile was bright but didn't reach his eyes.

Laird Oliver nodded and took a breath to reply, but his daughter spoke up first.

"Oh, my father must na have told you," she said. "Many o' our servants will be taking care o' guests at the wedding. Adaira is our relative and recently lost her father, so we wanted to ease her burdens in this small way. The only problem is, we'll hardly have anyone here to keep Rigmore House in working order. You should go find Hamish, our butler, and ask where yer most needed. You want to make a good impression, don' you?" Muireall grinned innocently.

"Astute thinking, daughter." Laird Oliver returned his attention to the young man. "Go back down the hallway and out the front door. Then go to the building on the left. You'll find Hamish there, I'm sure."

---

[5] A child or animal that wants attention.

Niall seemed at a loss for words, though his mouth opened and closed several times before he bowed in acquiescence.

As he turned to leave, though, he threw a subtle glare in Muireall's direction. She grinned wider. *Those who slight me always regret it. If you want to survive at Rigmore House, you better learn that quickly.*

Second Chances

"Quite a good-looking fellow, wasn' he?"

Muireall jumped at her mother's unexpected words. The wedding still hadn't started yet; apparently, the fiddler was frantically searching for his instrument in Torin Woods since his young son had gotten hold of it and left it there. The groom and best man had run off to help once they'd found out, which left the vicar and all the guests waiting awkwardly outside Everton Inn. The bride and her best maid hadn't come out yet for the wedding walk[6], so Muireall assumed they were still getting ready.

"Whoever do you mean?" Muireall twisted around to face her mother.

"That Niall fellow. His skin looked like it hadn' seen a day in the sun," Lady Oliver said tartly next to Muireall. The woman's eyes weren't on her daughter though—they were on the crowd, which was growing more impatient by the minute. It seemed the entire town had shown up. Even miserly old Steven McLaren, who had barely left his house in weeks, was standing off from the main group with Angus Dunnet and Phillip McGuff, two of his surly friends.

"Did he?" Muireall said vaguely, not wanting to discuss Niall Moreland. Especially when she was probably going to have to see him on a regular basis now. *Maybe he'll be assigned somewhere I won' have to cross paths with him.*

---

[6] The wedding party's traditional walk to the church, led by a fiddler.

"Don' pretend you didn' notice. You'd have to be blind. Too bad his inferior blood will keep him from amounting to anything."

Muireall didn't respond, for she was used to such comments. It was difficult for Laura to pay anyone a compliment without coupling it with an insult.

"If he'd been born a noble, I would have set the two o' you up together," the older woman continued. "No doubt you'd have produced lovely heirs."

The redhead blanched as she tried not to gag. *More marriage talk. Please let this end once the wedding is over.* "Mother, please don' say things like th—"

"—But I suppose I'll just have to settle on Matthew Levins instead," Laura finished, raising her voice until it drowned out her daughter's.

Matthew Levins? Anxiety pressed against Muireall's chest. "What are you saying?"

"Exactly what you think I'm saying." Laura inclined her head toward the Levinses, who were standing close to the inn door. Nathaniel Levins, an ornery old man, came from one of Everton's two tacksman families. His wife, Elizabeth, originally a McGuff, came from the other.

And their only child, twenty-four-year-old Matthew, stood between them.

"But I've been betrothed to the earl o' Hyndford's son since we were babes," Muireall pointed out. She'd only met Thomas Carmichael a few times. They knew each other through their mothers, and the arrangement was one of mutual benefit for the families: a rise in social standing for Muireall and an expansion of wealth for the young Lord Carmichael. Truth be told, though, Muireall didn't much care for the man. In the little time she'd spent with him, he'd made it clear Muireall would have no voice as his wife and would merely be a pretty trinket to show off to his friends.

Still, it wasn't right to break off an engagement without due cause.

Laura's face darkened. "That insufferable sot has turned his attentions elsewhere. I received word a few weeks ago that he is ending yer betrothal, though he wishes us all the best."

Ah, so that's why Mother has been talking about marriage so much lately. Muireall couldn't say she was disappointed that Lord Carmichael had made other arrangements. However, she wasn't particularly happy with the alternative her mother had come up with.

"We've already spoken with Nathaniel and Elizabeth, and they're delighted at the match," Laura added.

"We?" Muireall turned to Joseph, who stood on her left. "Father, you didn'."

Guilt passed over Joseph's face for a split second before he brushed it aside. "Yer almost nineteen, Muireall. Most women yer age already have families o' their own."

"What about Br—"

"Don' you dare bring up Briony Fairborn," Mother spat. "Comparing yerself to that strumpet[7] will na do you any good."

Laird and Lady Oliver held a special dislike for Briony Fairborn, Everton's only midwife, since the woman's illegitimacy put a stain on their otherwise wholesome village. Luckily for Briony, her medical skills were invaluable. Especially now that she'd taken on all of the late Dr. Sherwin's duties until Laird Oliver could convince a replacement doctor to move out to Everton.

"But Matthew?" It was no secret Muireall despised the tacksman. Ever since he'd thrown her into the ocean when they were bairns[8], she'd maintained a special enmity for young Mr. Levins. It didn't matter that he'd apologized when he'd seen how upset she was; the damage had already been done. "You don' like him either, Father."

Laird Oliver, too, had a problem with Matthew, though his only spanned the last few months. Muireall didn't understand exactly what it was about, but it had something to do with her father's push to build up the town's kelping[9] business. Muireall had never been privy to much information about her father's affairs, but if this latest endeavor was anything like his last one,

---

[7] A promiscuous woman.

[8] Children.

[9] An Orcadian practice of burning seaweed carried out from the early eighteenth century until the early nineteenth century.

it wouldn't amount to much. Joseph Oliver was full of grandiose ideas, most of which never came to fruition.

Her father bristled. "Aye, yer right about that. Can barely stand the sight o'—"

"Joseph," Laura cut in, "we talked about this already. Matthew is the only unmarried man in Everton who's even close to Muireall in social status, remember? Don' let yer personal feelings cloud yer judgment. We must do our part to ensure the Oliver line . . ."

As Muireall's mother continued, the young woman watched her father deflate. It was slow at first, just a slight drooping of his shoulders, a downward tilting of his chin, but by the time Laura had finished scolding him, all Laird Oliver's bluster had dissipated. And it was clear he was sorry he'd bothered protesting at all.

Laura turned back to Muireall. "So, even though Matthew isn' yer equal in rank, yer going to give this a chance."

The young woman's gaze flicked toward the man in question. Matthew was handsome, she'd give him that. He towered over most of their neighbors, and his light-brown eyes reminded her of the juniper trees in Torin Woods. She'd seen the other village lasses gawking at him as he passed, no doubt wishing he would give them the time of day.

But his gruff personality thoroughly negated any attraction Muireall had to his physical attributes. The man was ruthless, exacting exorbitant amounts of interest from his tenant farmers if they fell behind on their payments, regardless of the farmers' circumstances. He'd even almost thrown the Martins out of their home a couple of months ago right after they'd just had their first baby.

At that moment, Matthew's muscular arms were crossed as if he'd rather be anywhere else. Muireall shook her head with contempt. *I thought he and Adaira were—na quite friends—but friendly, at least. Can' he show her a wee bit o' support on her wedding day?*

Her brow furrowed as she reconsidered. *Maybe I'm wrong about Matthew. Maybe he could be a good husband. Besides, all Mother wants me to do is give the man a chance. If he proves he's inadequate, I'll simply walk away.*

A few minutes later, Donal McGuff appeared on the path that led from Torin Woods, Mr. Burgess and his son, William, on either side of him. Mr. McGuff triumphantly raised his fiddle in the air, and then the three of them jogged down the hill toward the group.

Laura snorted as her eyes homed in on William. *"He's* the best man? That lad is too young fer—"

"Mr. Burgess insisted on it," Laird Oliver stated, his tone light.

As Laura turned away with a humph, Muireall could have sworn her father smirked before schooling his face into a neutral line.

When Mr. McGuff and the Burgesses reached the inn, several men clapped them on the back and made jokes about getting lost in the woods to keep the wedding from happening. Mr. Burgess laughed and said that was nonsense, but a tremble in his voice caught Muireall's attention.

Must be nerves. Hamish was the same way at his wedding, she reminded herself. The fiddler knocked on the door, and Briony Fairborn, Adaira's best maid, opened it with a grin.

"Mr. McGuff, you have perfect timing. I have yer pudding[10] right here." The midwife held out a dish.

Once the fiddler had eaten his food, he launched into a merry tune to signal the start of the wedding walk. With a spring in his step, Mr. McGuff led everyone away from the inn. Mr. Burgess escorted Briony, as was customary, while William escorted Adaira. The guests trailed after them while the Martins, the designated tail sweepers[11], covered everyone's tracks with their heather broom.

Townsfolk sang and clapped in time with Mr. McGuff's fiddle, Muireall among them, but her mind wasn't on the song. She was paying attention to Mr. Burgess. Unlike most grooms on their wedding day, he wasn't watching his bride. He was glancing around as if he was looking for something. Or someone.

---

[10] It was customary for the fiddler to receive a special pudding prior to the wedding march.

[11] The couple whose job it was to drag a heather broom behind the guests during the wedding walk.

"Does Mr. Burgess have any other family?" Muireall asked her parents as everyone paraded into the church and took their seats. The best man and best maid stepped away from the bride and groom, allowing the vicar to begin the ceremony.

"Just a cousin from Hollandstoun. That's him there." Laird Oliver pointed to a lanky gentleman in the front pew.

Muireall frowned. *He can' be the person Mr. Burgess is looking fer.* That man had been in the crowd earlier when the walk had started. Muireall surveyed the room, but she recognized all the other faces as Everton natives. *Whomever Mr. Burgess is looking fer isn' here. I wonder whom it could be. . . .*

She didn't get an answer during the ceremony, and by the time the feasting and dancing were underway, she'd quite forgotten Mr. Burgess's odd behavior. She had bigger things to worry about.

Like dealing with Matthew Levins.

***

Niall scrubbed and scrubbed the pots until his arms felt like they would fall off. Everyone else had already completed their work in the kitchen for the evening, but Niall had been strictly told he couldn't stop until all the cookware was spotless. It was a good thing the rest of the servants had left him to do the task alone because, by the time Niall had finished, he'd called down just about every curse he could think of on the horrid humans responsible for his suffering.

Be patient, reminded a voice that sounded like his father's. *If you keep yer head down, then everything will be worth it.*

He glanced up at the clock on the wall. Niall didn't yet understand what it meant, but the head servant, Hamish, had pointed at the symbol at the bottom when he'd been talking about duties for the following day. The markings had something to do with time—Niall had figured that out, at least. Sunrise had always been enough of a marker for him when he was a selkie. *Why must humans complicate things so much?*

He shook his head and rose to his feet, his muscles aching after being in the same position for hours. He longed to dip

18

into the water and drift off to sleep as he had so many times before.

Grief shot through him as Niall remembered that was in the past now. No longer could he wrap himself in his sealskin and lean into the sea's cool embrace. Oftentimes now, he'd wake in a rage and realize he'd clawed at his own flesh while sleeping. But the horrors of his dreams couldn't compare with the nightmare of reality.

Niall had always enjoyed being in human form; it afforded greater mobility and strength than he had as a seal. Now it was both a prison and a betrayal. To walk among his enemies as one of them, to smile and speak as if his greatest desire wasn't to destroy them all—such torture was almost physically painful.

But if that was the price Niall had to pay for vengeance, then so be it.

Niall slipped out the door into the main hallway. Rather than making his way to the servants' quarters in the rear of the manor, though, the young man veered in the opposite direction. *I might as well have a wee bit o' fun before turning in.*

Hamish had mentioned that the wedding celebration was taking place on Mary's Hill. With any luck, the happy couple might still be up there. *Seeing me will be such a wonderful way to end their big day.*

Niall scurried up the path, trying not to think about what had happened the last time he'd been to Mary's Hill. But the more he pushed, the more the memories pushed back.

He'd held Briony so close that night, their shared love of dancing guiding their movements, energizing them as they'd twirled and leaped in time with the music. Her eyes had glowed like the fires around them, igniting such love in Niall's heart he'd thought it would consume him.

Briony . . . Regret moistened the man's eyes, but he took a deep breath and pressed onward. There was no sense in reliving the past; it might shake his resolve. And that was simply unacceptable.

So focused was he on his introspection that he almost didn't spot the couple at the gate to Everton Inn. A woman in a white dress with flowers in her hair stood next to a man kneeling in front of a small pile of rocks. Normally, Niall would have just chalked the strange behavior up to typical human idiocy and not given them a second thought. He almost did, in fact, until he recognized his brother-in-law's bright-red hair.

John and Adaira Burgess.

Just the people I was looking fer. A sneer spread over his lips as he crept up behind them. "Did I miss it?" he whispered.

The couple whirled around with a start. Both of them gaped at him in shock, but John had the presence of mind to move in front of his bride.

As if you can protect her.

"I was trying so hard to make it on time," Niall continued, positively beaming. "After all, 'tis frightfully inconsiderate to miss a family wedding."

Before he had time to react, John grabbed the front of his shirt, making him remember just how strong the farmer was. "After all you've done, you should have thought twice before coming back here."

"Easy there. Easy." Niall gently put his hand on top of his brother-in-law's. "I come in peace. Let my past sins be forgiven. Family is forever, right?"

The farmer's grip tightened. "Yer no family to me."

"John, that's na what you said the last time I saw you. I'm sure Elene wouldn' have wanted us to fight."

"She wouldn' have wanted a lot o' things, but they happened, anyway."

"Why are you here, Niall?" Adaira drew the men's attention away from each other.

Niall smirked at the pretty brunette, reveling in the terror in her eyes. *She's trying so hard to hide it, but 'tis still plain as day.*

"'Tis like I said, I'm here to congratulate you. What? Am I na good enough to be here? Too much o' a reminder o' yer new husband's first love?"

He should have seen John's fist coming.

"You don' speak to my wife that way," the farmer said as Niall picked himself up off the ground. Pain emanated from his left cheek where the blow had landed, but Niall kept the smile on his face.

"The truth this time," John demanded.

Niall sighed dramatically. "Oh, all right. The truth is . . ." He sniffled. "My father has exiled me."

"What?" Adaira's eyebrows drew together. "Why would he do that?"

"Because I'm na a selkie anymore," Niall replied, real emotion seeping into his voice. "I don' belong in the sea. I don' belong on land. I don' belong anywhere." He glanced at the ocean beyond the inn, his heart swelling with anguish.

"Then why come to Everton?" John growled.

"Because . . ." In times like these, Niall wished he still held his selkie powers of persuasion. Back then, it would have been all too easy to fool the humans with a simple lie. He hung his head to look more pitiful. "Because I didn' want to lose the only family I had left."

Adaira gasped, and it took all of Niall's self-control not to laugh. *Just as gullible as ever. I didn' even need my selkie powers. Now to convince the other.*

"William saved me when I didn' deserve it, whereas my father turned me away as soon as I was well enough to survive on my own." Niall placed a hand over his chest. "I've done a lot o' self-reflection since I left, and if I'm ever going to make things right by William—by Elene—I need to be here to do it. What do you say, John? Will you give me a chance?"

The farmer took a quick breath, but before he could respond, footsteps caught everyone's attention.

"What are you doing here?" snipped an angry voice.

The hairs on the back of Niall's neck stood up as he swung around. *Oh, great. Here we go again.*

Dancing and Disgrace

"Are you hiding, Muircall? Stop that at once!" Lady Oliver demanded, her nostrils flaring with anger.

Muireall rose from her crouched position and faced her mother. The two of them stood at the edge of Torin Woods, not far from where many of the wedding guests were dancing.

"I wasn' hiding; I was studying." The younger woman pointed to the large tree behind her. "Did you know birch trees symbolize new life?" She tried to smile, but her lips twitched so badly she gave up and settled for a neutral expression. She wasn't about to admit her mother had been right—she had been hiding. Not from Matthew specifically but the party in general. Socializing wasn't exactly Muireall's strong suit.

I should have just gone back home.

But you would have been spotted straight away if you'd done that, her common sense reminded her.

Laura patted her elaborate braided updo and sighed. "Daughter, how many times have I told you, you must forgo these absurd interests and focus on yer future?"

Muireall scratched at her arm. "Umm . . ."

"And you can start by dancing with Matthew," Laura chirped, grabbing the girl's wrist and wrenching her back toward the crowd.

Muireall allowed her mother to tug her along, anxiety building within her. When they reached the nearest bonfire, Laura clucked her tongue expectantly. "Well?"

The young woman's mind zipped through a host of excuses she could make: pain in her ankle, nausea, needing to check on the servants back at Rigmore House. . . . She settled on what she hoped was the most believable. "I'm quite tired, Mother. I doubt I'd be very good company."

It wasn't that far from the truth. She'd played several songs on her clàrsach[12] before scurrying off to the presumed safety of the trees. *I should have insisted on playing a few more. Perhaps then Mother would have been more sympathetic.*

"Nonsense, Muireall. You were exercising yer fingers, na yer legs. What will Matthew think? He has been waiting so patiently fer you." The older woman gestured to the tacksman, who, to Muireall's surprise, was standing only a short distance away with his parents.

Muireall's breath hitched. "Has he truly been waiting all this time?" She'd avoided eye contact with the man while she was playing her instrument, for she hadn't wanted to give him the impression she was happy about their parents' arrangement.

He couldn' be happy about it either, right? Muireall took another peek, but as soon as she did, her stomach dropped. Matthew was staring straight at her, his gaze as sharp as a knife. She ducked her head and tried to look busy brushing off her green gown.

"Aye, he has," Lady Oliver pressed. "And as his future bride, dancing with him is the least you can do. You don' want to disgrace the Oliver name, do you?"

Muireall huffed, her throat burning at the word "bride." "I hardly think refusing to dance would disgrace the—" She broke off at her mother's withering expression. "I'm sorry, Mother. O' course, yer right."

Muireall steeled herself and sashayed over to the Levins family, knowing Laura was scrutinizing her every move. There would be no escaping now.

Matthew's parents were engaged in a heated discussion about how much ale Nathaniel had drunk tonight, so they

---

[12] A small Scottish harp.

didn't notice her arrival. Their son, on the other hand, watched her like a hawk, his gaze never wavering. *Is that good or bad?*

"Good evening, Mr. Levins," Muireall greeted, smiling like she wasn't dying to be anywhere but here.

The tacksman didn't smile back. "Mistress Oliver."

Muireall gulped. She'd never been so intimidated by Matthew's taciturn personality before. *He wasn' my intended before, though, was he? Could I be content with him?* She did her best to meet the man's brown eyes, searching for any trace of warmth within them, any sign that would give her hope for their future together.

All she got in return was a glare, so she looked away. "I was told you wished to dance with me," she said tartly.

"Hmm, 'wish' is a strong word." Before she could react to his statement, he extended his hand. "Shall we?"

Muireall's palm was clammy as they made their way toward the other dancers. She glanced back at her mother, who was eying them approvingly. Happiness cascaded over Muireall like a gentle rain; pleasing Mother was a challenging task.

But even that wasn't strong enough to quench the dread in her stomach.

***

"Everyone seems so merry tonight. The last time I saw this much cheer was back on Johnsmas[13], I believe," Muireall remarked, trying to keep up the conversation. This was the third song they'd danced to, and she was beginning to run out of topics to discuss.

This would be far easier if Mr. Levins put forth some effort as well. The tacksman hadn't initiated any small talk, and every time Muireall had spoken, he'd responded with either a grunt or nothing at all.

Again, Matthew made no comment, though his jaw stiffened ever so slightly.

Muireall caught sight of Adaira kissing her new husband as they swayed nearby. Such overt displays of affection normally

---

[13] Orkney's midsummer celebration.

sickened Muireall, but tonight, a tendril of envy sprang up in her heart. *Perhaps 'twould be nice fer someone to care fer me like that. . . .* She'd never been one to daydream about such things—she knew what her parents' marriage was like behind closed doors—but maybe, just maybe, not all marriages were that way. Maybe real love did exist. The Burgesses certainly seemed to think so.

"Johnsmas was when Mr. Burgess proposed, wasn' it?" Muireall continued, smiling up at her partner. "I was so focused on playing my clàrsach that night that I didn' see it. Were you nearby when he asked Adaira to marry him?"

"Nay, I wasn'," Matthew snapped, his tone icy.

Muireall raised her eyebrows. *Hmm, that at least got a response. Na the one I was aiming fer though.* "I heard 'twas quite romantic, something about how he couldn' bear the thought o' losing her."

When the man's face darkened, Muireall added, "Oh, don' worry; you don' need to bother with such sentimental rubbish. I'm sure my mother will insist on a proposal—she's too formal na to—but you can keep it simple and straightforward. I'm na Adaira."

Muireall waited for relief to flood the tacksman's face, for no other woman in Everton would be so practical. They all wanted their lovers to sweep them off their feet and whisper sweet nothings in their ears, whereas Muireall would be happiest when given the freedom to explore her own interests.

And since marrying Matthew means I'll be able to stay here, that shall be much easier. I'll be able to continue working in the garden and won' have to deal with as many responsibilities as I would have if I'd married Lord Carmichael. Suddenly, the prospect of marrying Matthew seemed much more appealing, and a genuine smile spread across the woman's cheeks.

Instead of beaming in return, though, Matthew released her hands and stepped back.

"Mr. Levins?" Muireall asked, trying to read his stony expression. The townsfolk around them turned their heads, their ears perked for gossip.

"What are you doing?" she said through her teeth, keeping her smile in place to hide her annoyance from her nosy neighbors.

"I don' feel like dancing anymore," Matthew grumbled. He wiped his hands on his trousers as if touching her had sullied them. "Have a good evening, Mistress Oliver."

"But, Mr. Levins, you . . ." Muireall trailed off, for the tacksman was already storming down the hill.

What just happened? Why is he leaving? It couldn' be that he actually wanted me to be sentimental. . . . Muireall's mind ran back through their conversation. *I must have been right. This was all because his parents want him to marry me, na because he does. He did imply he hadn' wanted to dance with me, but I thought agreeing to it meant he'd accepted our engagement.*

The other dancers started whispering, reminding Muireall of the humiliating position she now found herself in. The position Matthew had put her in. She looked down her nose at everyone watching her, staring hard enough that they all turned away in embarrassment and pretended like they hadn't been eavesdropping. Many were so intoxicated they probably wouldn't remember this moment in the morning, but those who did would blather about it for weeks. Then Muireall would have to hear about it all over again from Anne.

She glanced at her intended's retreating figure again. *If Matthew didn' want to marry me, he should have just said so directly.*

Muireall sighed. *Fine, I'll take care o' this myself. Mother won' be happy, but it can' be avoided. And if Matthew possesses any ounce o' decorum, he'll thank me fer saving him the trouble.* She spun on her heel and marched off, her chin held high as she made her way over to her parents.

Laird Oliver was in the midst of an animated conversation about his piano with Donal McGuff, who didn't appear nearly as interested but was far too courteous to say so. Laura stood beside her husband, her features pinched yet refined.

The older woman frowned as Muireall approached. "Daughter, I didn' expect you to be back so soon. Can' you handle a wee bit more time with Mr. Levins? Yer going to have to see him quite often, you know."

The men stopped chattering and turned to the younger woman as well; Laird Oliver's face was littered with annoyance, but Mr. McGuff simply looked curious.

"*I'm* na the one who couldn' handle it, Mother. It seems Mr. Levins has had enough o' me." Muireall inclined her head toward the figure disappearing down the hill. "In fact, I believe he'd prefer if we put a halt to the wedding plans entirely."

The laird's daughter tried not to look too eager as she spoke; otherwise, her mother might misinterpret Muireall's words and think *she* was the one trying to end things. *But I'm na. Matthew is. He may na have said it aloud, but his actions were almost screaming it. Really, I'm just being helpful.*

Laura's thin eyebrows knitted together. "Hmm, he knows better than to behave so impertinently. This marriage is quite advantageous fer him since 'twill allow him to assume the laird title." She turned back to Muireall. "What did you do to upset him?"

Muireall's mouth fell open. "Why do you think 'twas something I did?"

"I wouldn' put it past you to try to sabotage this union."

The young woman's eyes flicked to the men watching their exchange, her cheeks flaming with embarrassment. Father's mouth was turned down in disapproval; he was clearly in agreement with Mother. Mr. McGuff, on the other hand, was more difficult to read.

"I wasn' trying to do that, Mother. I was *trying* to get along with him."

"Hmm . . ." Laura drummed her fingers against her lips, her facial wrinkles settling in deeper. "Well, regardless o' the reason fer his departure, you'll be seeing him again morn[14]. His parents have invited you over fer dinner."

Muireall held back a grimace. *Did you na hear what I just said? Matthew doesn' want to marry me. Why are you trying to force this when it clearly isn' working?* "O-Oh, how . . . lovely."

Laura glared in a way that said Muireall wasn't fooling anyone. "If yer na going to be pleasant, you can run along

---

[14] Tomorrow.

home, lass. I know that's what you'd prefer, anyway, rather than doing what's best fer the family."

Muireall shriveled a little more. This wasn't going the way she'd intended. *Maybe if I talk to Mother alone, I can make her understand.*

She reached for Laura's arm. "But, Mother, I need to talk to you about—"

Laura stepped out of reach. "I don' want to hear it.

Muireall slowly turned away, more humiliated now than she'd been over Matthew's abandonment. Despite that, her mind was already moving, trying to come up with alternative measures to escape her predicament. *If I can' convince Mother, I'll just talk to Father in the morneen. He may be on Mother's side right now, but once he's alone, he'll be more open to my thoughts on the matter.*

Her heart rate began to slow. *Aye, that's what I'll do. Nothing to worry about.* She started to leave, then paused. *Ah, I didn' congratulate Adaira and Mr. Burgess yet. I better do that; otherwise, Mother is bound to scold me once she finds out.*

She glanced around Mary's Hill. Many of the other townsfolk had already left for the evening; only a scattering of adults remained, some dancing, a few laughing and talking together. Mr. Burgess's son, William, was leaving with the Martins, who had offered to keep the boy at their house while the newlyweds spent a few days by themselves. Anne stood a short distance off with some of the other servants; Muireall debated going over to greet the maid for the briefest of instances before shaking her head at the silly notion.

Well, if they're already gone, I guess there's nothing left to do but go home. As she passed through Cramer's Field, though, she caught sight of Adaira and Mr. Burgess at the entrance to Everton Inn. *Oh, they've na gone inside yet. Are they talking to someone?*

She veered toward the couple, but her hands clenched into fists when she recognized the man with them. *Why is Niall Moreland here? Shouldn' he be back at Rigmore House? He's trying to go around me again, isn' he?*

The servant's back was to her, but she could see the newlyweds' faces fairly well in the moonlight. And they almost looked frightened. *Is Niall bothering them?*

I'll put a stop to that.

"What are you doing here?" Muireall snapped, cutting off whatever conversation had been taking place.

The black-haired man flinched before spinning around. Annoyance flashed across his face before he expertly concealed it behind a dashing grin. "Mistress Oliver, how lovely to see you again. I was just telling my dear friends congratulations on their nuptials."

He's good. If na fer Mr. Burgess, I'd probably believe him. The newlywed farmer was not nearly as adept at schooling his features. His fingers were trembling at his sides like it was taking all his self-control not to hit Niall in the jaw.

Actually . . . She scrutinized the servant's face. His left cheek was slightly redder than the other. *What have I walked into?*

Everyone's expression was guarded; Muireall was clearly the outsider. *I doubt they'll be fully honest with me, but perhaps I can at least learn if I have good reason to dismiss Niall.*

"*Was* he just congratulating you, Mr. Burgess?" Muireall asked. He seemed more likely to let something slip. If someone had hit Niall in the face, it had to have been the farmer. Adaira would never have done something so improper. "Niall has already shown himself na the most trustworthy o' servants"— she threw the man a sharp look before meeting Mr. Burgess's gaze—"so if he's lying again, I'd be glad to know."

Please give me a reason to dismiss him. 'Twould make this awful evening so much better.

"Servant?" Mr. Burgess's eyes widened in alarm. He turned to Niall. "You work at Rigmore House now?"

"Aye, that I do." Niall smirked.

Muireall narrowed her eyes. *Stop smiling. Don' you understand his answer may get you thrown out o' Everton?*

The servant just blinked at her like he hadn't a clue what was going on, but Muireall could tell he was secretly taunting her. And that just infuriated her more.

"So, is he or isn' he, Mr. Burgess?" Muireall pressed, trying to keep her voice from rising above an acceptable level. "Telling the truth, I mean."

The farmer started to reply, but Adaira placed a hand on her husband's arm and squeaked, "He is, Muireall." She nodded to Niall. "Thank you kindly."

The servant's smirk spread, and he nodded back.

Muireall frowned and waited to see if Mr. Burgess would refute his wife's claim. Indecision darted across the man's blue eyes, and for a moment, he looked like he was about to speak, but then, for whatever reason, he held his tongue.

When the silence stretched into awkwardness, Muireall said sweetly, "In that case, let me also extend my congratulations, fer I didn' get a chance to do so earlier."

Adaira thanked her, still gripping Mr. Burgess's arm, but the farmer said nothing.

Muireall turned to her wayward servant. "Niall, I believe I told you na to come fer the festivities and instead to ask Hamish what needed to be done tonight."

"Ah, I did speak to Hamish."

"Then why do I find you here now?"

"I completed my duties fer the evening, so I thought I was free to go where I pleased until work resumed in the morneen[15]. Or was I wrong and I'm to be treated as a slave, rather than a servant? Confined to Rigmore House until told otherwise?"

Muireall's blood boiled. "You insolent—"

Adaira jumped forward and grabbed Muireall's hand. "Cousin, I pray you forgive him. He's na used to our customs and sometimes speaks without thinking." Adaira released her hand and gave the servant a stern glare. "Apologize."

He wrinkled his nose, but then he dipped his head. "She's right. Forgive me, my lady."

The way he said "my lady" sounded like a thinly veiled insult, so Muireall quipped, "Don' call me that."

"What would you prefer, then?" His black eyes flashed as he smiled up at her. "Princess?"

Muireall sucked her teeth. "Are you trying to anger me?"

"O' course na. 'Tis as my brother-in-law's new wife said, I'm still learning the customs o' the town." This time, he

---

[15] Morning.

seemed humble and sincere, holding up his palms as if he posed no threat.

The effect was fairly disconcerting, leaving Muireall to wonder exactly whom she was dealing with. "Where are you from that you don' know how to temper yer words?"

"Oh, far away from here." He squeezed his lips together as if he were holding back laughter.

"Well, in *Everton*, servants don' question their betters. That's something you'd better get into yer thick head fast, or you won' be welcome at Rigmore anymore. Understand?"

"Perfectly," he whispered, lowering his eyes.

"Excellent. Then we should get going. I'm sure Mr. Burgess and Adaira would like some time to themselves. That is, unless there's someone else you planned on visiting tonight?" The sarcasm dripping from her words was unmistakable, even for someone as foolish as Niall Moreland.

He shook his head and bid the Burgesses goodbye before skirting down the road, not even waiting for Muireall to follow.

She rolled her eyes, about to bark out an order for him to stop, but Adaira blurted, "Muireall."

"Hmm?" She turned back to her cousin.

Adaira bit her lip, her eyes sliding back and forth before meeting Muireall's. "I know this isn' my place to say, but please, try to stay away from him."

"What? Why?" Muireall peered into the brunette's face, searching for answers.

"Niall has suffered a great deal o' loss, and he has more reason fer bitterness than you can imagine. He may even—"

"He's na to be trusted, mistress," Mr. Burgess rumbled from Adaira's side. "You already knew that though."

"Aye . . . that I did," Muireall replied. *What are you na telling me? What sort o' loss?*

"If he does anything suspicious, come find me right away," the man continued.

Muireall's mind snapped back to something Niall had said, something she'd missed before. "Wait. He said you were his brother-in-law. That means he's . . ."

"My first wife's brother," Mr. Burgess said stiffly.

"And what exactly do you think he's going to do?"

"Nothing," Adaira exclaimed, glancing toward the dark-haired man as he disappeared in the distance. "We hope."

Threats and Treachery

The following day, Muireall tried to get a moment alone with her father, but Laird Oliver was suspiciously absent from breakfast. And lunch. Her mother said he was just terribly busy, but the glimmer in the older woman's eye told Muireall the truth: Father was deliberately avoiding her.

Muireall didn't bother trying to talk to her mother again about Matthew; she knew it would do no good. Instead, she fussed with her hair, her clothes, her makeup, everything she could think of to put off dinner. Eventually, though, Laura came to her room and told her she'd better depart before it got too late.

Muireall took a deep breath as she walked out the door. *I can do this. 'Tis only a few hours.*

The Levinses' home was on the other side of the village, so she took her time as she ambled up the road. She passed the market, so loud and full of life during the day, but quiet as the grave now. She normally avoided it because of her parents' desire to protect her ears from the commoners' uncivilized talk.

As Muireall strolled by the late Dr. Sherwin's office, a strange sense of loss billowed up within her. It truly was a shame he'd lost his life in the recent storm. She hadn't been overly fond of the fellow, but she'd respected his skills as a doctor. And he'd been one of the few people who hadn't tried to push his way into her life because of her social standing.

Many of the older villagers had tried to use Muireall for their own ends over the years, but a few of the younger generation had also attempted to befriend her: Henry and Elspet Milligan, Adaira Stubbins, Bridget Calhoun. Whether their efforts had stemmed from sincere desires for friendship or not, Muireall still wasn't sure. She occasionally wondered, though, how different things would have been if Alastair hadn't died.

"A lady knows whose company to keep and whose to avoid," her mother had told her the last day she'd come home from playing with the Milligans. It had been a few weeks since Muireall's brother had passed, and Laura had been hinting at her disapproval of the girl's choice in friends for several days. "Our neighbors are only after what they can get out o' you, Muireall. Don' be foolish enough to let them close."

After that conversation, the young heiress had distanced herself from everyone, instead throwing herself into her studies. Her governess had made sure Muireall knew everything a lass of her station should, but Muireall had spent as much time as she could poring over the topics she found most interesting. First, it had been the clàrsach, then, gardening.

She'd wanted to learn how to manage the estate, but her father had insisted that was her future husband's job. When he'd later caught her perusing the documents in his study, he'd threatened to take away her clàrsach if it ever happened again. Muireall had made the wise decision to stay out of her father's affairs from that point on.

When she arrived at the Levinses' house, she stopped short. She'd passed this building countless times, but now she couldn't remember the last time she'd gone inside. Sweat stuck to the undersides of her arms as she tried to work up the nerve to enter.

Do I really have to do this?

Before she could turn around, the door flew open. There stood Elizabeth Levins, her brown eyes twinkling with joy. She was a short, heavy-set woman with curly brown hair that always seemed to fall out of its pins. A thick curl was already resting against her neck, and before the evening was over, more would likely follow. "Muireall, come in, come in!"

Muireall smiled back, relieved that at least one person was happy to see her. It wasn't entirely appropriate for this woman to use her given name yet, but Muireall found herself not minding as much as she should. Elizabeth had always been kind to her over the years. If only she had a more pleasant son.

"Matthew, Nathaniel, Muireall is here," Elizabeth called as she ushered Muireall into the dining room. A beautiful wooden table awaited them, already bursting with food and drink. Only the Olivers kept on servants, so Elizabeth must have prepared all of this on her own. Six chairs sat around the table, and Muireall had a passing thought of whether or not the Levinses had ever wanted more children.

So much expectation lies on an only child. Muireall knew from firsthand experience how heavy the burden could be. *Maybe Matthew and I aren' so very different. . . .*

Heavy footsteps clomped down the stairs, then Nathaniel and Matthew appeared. The older man barely acknowledged Muireall as he entered, simply nodding his bald head before settling into his chair with a closed expression. Matthew, on the other hand, grimaced when their eyes met.

I guess he's still just as unhappy about this arrangement as he was the other night, Muireall thought as she slid into the seat across from her intended.

Elizabeth sat down beside Muireall, pointedly ignoring the cold atmosphere in the room as she offered up the blessing. Once that was done, she turned to the younger woman. "Muireall, I can' tell you how elated we are about this betrothal. 'Tis all we've talked about since yer mother suggested it a couple o' weeks ago."

A couple o' weeks ago? They've known about it fer that long? Why didn' Mother tell me sooner?

"More like 'tis all *you've* talked about," Nathaniel muttered as he stuffed a spoonful of potatoes into his mouth.

The man's grumpy attitude reminded Muireall of her father's opinion on her betrothal. *Mother probably didn' tell me until now because it took a while to convince Father to go along with it.*

When no one else said anything, Muireall's cheeks reddened. "I . . . I'm flattered you think so highly o' me."

"O' course we do," Elizabeth replied. "You come from the very best family in Everton."

Muireall's warm feelings toward her hostess began to evaporate. *Just as I suspected. She wants her son to marry me simply because o' my title.* She took a swig of ale, hoping the cool liquid would wash away the bile rising in her stomach.

She peeked at Matthew, who was clenching his utensils like he wanted to break them in half. *Strange that he doesn' seem to care about raising his station. . . .*

Her eyes widened. *I've been going about this all wrong. Matthew isn' my enemy; he's my ally.*

"I'd love to take a stroll with you once we finish." Muireall looked expectantly at her betrothed.

Matthew shifted in his chair but said nothing.

"With yer parents as chaperones, o' course," she added, nodding to Mrs. Levins.

"That sounds wonderful. I'm sure Matthew will enjoy that," Elizabeth replied, shooting daggers at her silent son.

The tacksman cleared his throat. "Aye, let's do that," he said, his voice so pained it sounded like he'd just agreed to his own murder.

Once dinner was over, the four of them stood. Nathaniel muttered a weak excuse of being too tired for a walk, so the others made their way outside without him. Elizabeth left some space between herself and the couple to give them the illusion of privacy as they meandered down the road. Most betrothed couples would have been upset not to have the time alone, but all Muireall desired was enough room not to be overheard.

"Listen, I know yer just as dissatisfied with this arrangement as I am," she started, "so, rather than oppose each other, why na work together to end it?"

For the first time that evening, Matthew's frown softened. "I don' fight battles I know I'll lose."

"How do you know we'll lose when we haven' even tried yet?"

Matthew's eyes flicked back toward his mother. "Oh, I know."

Muireall huffed. "But—"

The tacksman shook his head. "You may believe you can reason a way out o' this if you think about it long enough, but yer just wasting yer time. Whether we like it or na, we're going to be husband and wife before the year ends." He groaned. "Which means we should make the best o' it."

"I'm sorry 'tis *such* a hardship fer you," Muireall mocked. At some point, the two had stopped walking, but Elizabeth politely remained the same distance away. "I know why I don' want this marriage, but why are you so against it?"

"Hmm, I'm sure you can figure it out."

"As far as I can see, there are only benefits fer you."

"Na if I want to avoid marriage entirely"—Matthew stepped nearer until his face hovered just above hers— "especially to someone as disagreeable as you. In fact, when Mother told me about our betrothal, I felt physically ill. As any man would in my position. But, like I said, that's out o' our hands. Now, I suggest you stop discussing things you don' know *anything* about before you regret it."

Muireall trembled, too afraid to say another word in the face of such untempered malice. He may not have stated it directly, but she knew a threat when she heard one.

"Matthew, you may be betrothed, but that's hardly proper," Elizabeth called.

The tacksman stepped back, his gaze still ominous. "Shall we continue our stroll?"

Muireall silently assented, keeping more distance from her companion than society deemed necessary. She didn't try to engage him in further conversation, for she'd heard all she needed to. And when their walk was over, she was all too glad to depart.

It was only as she made her way home that she allowed her intended's hurtful words to really sink in. *He was lying. He had to be lying.* Tears started to brim in her eyes, but she blinked them back. *Control yerself, Muireall. Crying is weakness. You have to be strong.*

***

Meanwhile, Niall was on his way to Drulea Cottage, his heart hammering in his chest. He'd had a difficult day, too, though for starkly different reasons.

When he'd risen early that morning, he'd already regretted his choice to work at Rigmore House. The strange, uncomfortable box[16] he'd squirmed in had kept him from getting any decent amount of sleep. The beds at Everton Inn had been simple; his new bed had a sliding door that jammed nearly as often as it worked and a pillow that smelled like it hadn't been washed in decades. All that aside, the bed wasn't really what had made Niall's night miserable. That honor belonged to Gilbert Rendall.

The short, curly-haired fellow hadn't looked like a troublemaker when he'd introduced himself as Niall's new roommate. That was before Niall had known the man's snoring was worse than a whole herd of seals. Niall had hardly slept a wink, a fact which hadn't helped his mood when he'd been forced to rise before the sun was up.

Gilbert had happily showed Niall around Rigmore House, explaining where servants were and weren't allowed to go and what sorts of duties Niall would be expected to complete. Then they'd proceeded to clean the fireplaces, polish the silver, and dust the rooms. Niall had barely listened to his companion's chatter, but Gilbert was good at carrying a conversation on his own, so that hadn't mattered much. From what Niall could remember, he wasn't going to have a specific position for now; he would just have to go wherever Hamish told him to go.

And Niall could already tell he and the butler were not going to get along. Not only had he scolded Niall for being late to breakfast but he'd also reprimanded him for doing a "shameful" job cleaning the dishes. *I think I did a wonderful job on them, considering I've never washed a dish before in my life. They looked perfectly fine to me.*

---

16 A traditional Scottish bed built into a recess.

Niall's stomach rumbled as he continued up the path. The measly porridge he'd eaten at dinner hadn't been enough to sate his appetite. He started to tell himself he could just get more food when he returned, then he caught himself. Humans only ate at specific times of the day, not whenever they wished as selkies did. And Hamish seemed like he was just waiting to see what else Niall would do wrong.

'Twould be fun to upset him though. . . . Niall sighed and threw out the thought, appealing as it was. He reminded himself he wanted to be overlooked, not singled out. He'd just have to wait until morning. That is, unless Briony was generous enough to give him something.

He shook his head. *I'll be lucky if she even lets me in the house.* But after what he'd just heard at dinner, he had to try. He arrived at his destination and rapped his knuckles against the door.

Surely John and Adaira already told her about my change o' heart. She won' kill me . . . right? Anxiety dripped down his forehead. *If she knew the truth, she'd strike me down in an instant.*

The door opened. "Aye, how can I help"—the woman's golden eyes narrowed in recognition—"you." A gust of wind pushed Briony's long black hair away from her face, her expression full of rage.

Niall stepped forward. "Wait, I just wanted to—"

"Stay back," she warned.

"I know I've hurt you deeply—"

"Hurt me? You tried to kill me. Then when you couldn', you killed Mr. McLaren and tried to drown Santiago." Lightning crackled overhead, a flagrant reminder of the power imbalance between them.

Niall winced. *This is going to be harder than I thought.* "Killing the fisherman was simple justice fer Einar's death," he explained.

"And Santiago?" Briony raised an eyebrow in challenge.

"That was . . . wrong o' me to do." He eagerly changed the subject. "Speaking o' yer precious Mr. Mendes, I heard he's returned to Everton."

Niall had nearly spat out his porridge when Gilbert had mentioned that Mr. Mendes was back in town. He'd thought that infernal foreigner had left for his own country; he'd even confirmed it with Laird Oliver before agreeing to become the man's servant.

If Mr. Mendes was here, that meant he might be planning to take Briony away. And that would ruin Niall's whole scheme. *Has he truly returned, Briony?*

"What o' it? He has just as much right to be here as you do. Nay, more so since he didn' try to destroy the entire town."

Niall's hands curled into fists. If he still had his powers, the sky wouldn't have been able to contain his fury. Mr. Mendes, the one who'd stolen Briony's heart, the one who'd helped her rip away Niall's very identity, was waltzing around the same town Niall was and thought he could get away with it. *He's soon going to learn just how wrong he is. When I get my hands on him, I'll—*

"*Na yet,*" his father's voice whispered in the back of his mind. "*If you wait fer the right moment, you'll have yer revenge. Move too fast, and everything yer striving fer will escape yer reach.*"

Niall took a heavy breath and gave Briony a thin smile. His father, Callum, had always tried to teach Niall the value of patience. Probably because Niall had never been very good at it. The last time he'd been to Everton, he hadn't even lasted a week before he'd not only told Briony the truth of their shared heritage but had also tried to raze the village to the ground in a fit of anger.

But this time, he was going to do it how Callum would have. Patiently. And when Niall finally earned the right to rejoin his herd, his father would be proud of him once more.

"Can' we talk civilly? Like we used to?" he asked softly. If Niall was calm in the face of such terrible news, perhaps it would curb her anger.

"You've got a lot o' nerve, bringing up the past," Briony replied, still upset but slightly more restrained.

"Isn' that what yer doing?" He kept his voice low despite his true feelings. "I'm here because I want to move on from the past, but you seem content to keep us both stuck in it."

Niall tried not to flinch, fearing his words would trigger another outburst, but instead, Briony's glare faltered.

"What is it you want to say?" Suspicion shone in the woman's eyes, but even a sliver of uncertainty was enough for hope to flare in Niall's chest.

"May I come in?"

She nodded and moved back. Niall followed her inside, trying to ignore the way his breath caught as he stepped over the spot where she'd destroyed his sealskin. It felt like an age had passed since that moment. The moment when his life as a selkie had gone up in smoke.

As they sat down at a small table, Niall's eyes swept over the cottage's interior. It was a modest home, large enough to comfortably accommodate two—perhaps three—people. The kitchen, dining area, and sitting room were all in one connected space, and what appeared to be two bedrooms were off to the left side.

"So?" Briony prompted.

Niall cleared his throat. "I wanted to ask if Mr. Mendes has made you an offer o' marriage."

The young woman lifted her chin. "I don' see how that's any concern o' yers." Her tone wasn't hostile anymore, though, so Niall kept silent, waiting to see if she would give him a more satisfying response.

She sighed and let her gaze drift to the floor. "Na yet." A small smile lifted her cheeks. "I'm hopeful 'twill be soon though."

"And then you'll return to Portugal?" he asked, his voice coming out a little too strained.

Briony's eyes homed in on his; she'd picked up on his concern, though she didn't seem to know where it was coming from. Niall controlled his expression, hoping he could keep it together for the rest of their conversation. He raised his eyebrows to show he was still waiting for an answer.

"Nay," she finally replied, "Santiago sold his ship. He wants to stay here."

A weight lifted off Niall's chest. *Then I can take all the time I need.*

"*Why* do you want to know?" Briony drew him out of his thoughts. Her expression was pensive, wary, as if she was just waiting for him to attack her.

The old Niall would have, too. But now I know better. "I assume the Burgesses told you why I've returned?"

"They told me what you claimed; that doesn' mean I believe you."

Niall nodded. "I didn' expect you to right away. With enough time, though, I hope all o' you will realize I'm na the person I once was. Besides, my being here is actually beneficial fer you."

Briony snorted. "And why is that?"

"Because I have knowledge you and William don' have. Selkies spend years honing their gifts under a mentor. I can train you to control yer powers."

"You already showed me how to control them."

Niall bristled. "You mean when you almost let the ocean's rage consume you?"

A bright blush spread over Briony's face.

"If I hadn't been there that day, you would have died," Niall continued, trying to make her understand just how ill-equipped she truly was.

When he'd helped her access her abilities that day, he hadn't expected her to display such raw strength. He'd thought she'd be able to summon a few clouds or a bit of rain, and that would be it. Instead, she'd created a storm so powerful it would have killed her if Niall hadn't stepped in and convinced her to release it. For while selkies could harness the ocean's energy for their own ends, channeling too much at once could prove deadly.

"And there are other things you need to learn, too," he added.

"Like what?"

"Like how to handle the other *beings* you may come across. Which ones to be respectful o'. Which ones to avoid."

Briony leaned forward, her eyes piqued with curiosity.

Perfect. Now, to get what I want out o' it. "But I don' have a lot o' time since I'm working fer the Olivers. You'll have to be patient. I believe I get Fridays off, so perhaps you and William could meet me then to discuss this more." Niall threw William's name out nonchalantly, hoping Briony wouldn't notice how eager he was for her to agree.

"Is it that essential fer you to be at Rigmore House? Why na just leave?"

Niall crossed his arms. "I have nowhere to live, and I seriously doubt John will let me stay at the inn again. Besides, being at Rigmore House offers me protection."

"Protection from what?"

"From you, should you decide 'tis better to kill me. At least by working there, people will notice if I disappear one day. So, I don' plan to leave any time soon."

Na until I get what I came fer, that is.

"Hmm . . ." The woman mulled it over. "I suppose Mr. Burgess might agree to that, as long as I'm present." She tapped her lower lip, still thinking.

What Briony didn't seem to realize was that bringing attention to her mouth made it impossible for Niall to focus on anything else.

She's so close. Close enough to reach out and touch. Close enough to kiss—

He drew in a quick breath, his thoughts pricking at the memories he'd been trying so hard to suppress: Dancing together in the firelight. Briony's mouth pressing against his as he pulled her to his chest. Howling in pain as his sealskin turned to ash—

Waves of emotion passed through him, and in their wake, a question blazed through Niall's mind: *If I'd known she would betray me, would I still have saved her?* He peered at the midwife's haunting visage, searching his feelings for an answer.

And, to his surprise, his heart whispered an emphatic, "yes."

What? That can' be right. . . . I tried to kill her; why would I—

Niall stumbled out of his chair and onto the floor, unable to accept what his heart was telling him.

"Are you all right?" Briony rose to her feet.

He jumped up. "I better get going." He darted out the door without waiting for her answer, for he feared the consequences if he stayed much longer.

I can' allow myself to fall back in love with her. I can'. Niall didn't pay attention to where he was running; all he cared about was putting as much distance between himself and Briony as he could.

When he glimpsed the sea up ahead, he bolted toward it without a second thought and dove straight in, hoping he could drown out his feelings in the crashing waves.

Time became meaningless as Niall swam farther and farther from the surface, light and sound fading until he couldn't hear anything anymore. Not even his own heart. The darkness was a balm to his weary soul; within it, he could almost forget what he was running from.

Whom he was running from.

Only when his lungs were bursting did he return to the surface. As much as he wished he was still a selkie, his body was apt to remind him that that wasn't the case. He gasped as his head broke through the water, the fresh air sharpening his senses once more.

Niall glanced toward the small cottage at the top of the cliffs nearby, bitterness coating his tongue. He'd thought he could handle seeing Briony again, but his traitorous heart had proven otherwise. *If I can' even talk to her without almost losing my resolve, how am I going to do what I must when the time comes?*

An Unlikely Proposal

Muireall's next few weeks passed in a repetitive blur. In the beginning, she sought out her father, but each time she did, he was busy in some way or another. Whether it was overseeing farmers' crops, discussing new potential trade partners with the local merchants, or investigating the village's recent fish shortage, Laird Oliver had absolutely no time to talk with her about personal matters. In fact, the only occasions when she got to see him for any considerable amount of time were when Matthew came for dinner once or twice a week, and such a setting wasn't conducive for sharing misgivings about the tacksman. Especially since Matthew and Laird Oliver struggled to get along in any conversation that extended beyond the most droll of subjects.

She saw Mr. Burgess's strange brother-in-law every so often during this time, as he completed various chores around the estate with his fellow servants. Her curiosity about him remained, but since she lacked any appropriate reason to speak to him, she ignored him whenever he was near.

Muireall also had the great displeasure of eating in the Levins's home every Saturday night before being forced to stroll through the village afterward with her suitor. Matthew proved just as disagreeable as ever, though he put on a courteous front whenever their parents were within earshot. Muireall did what she could to keep their private conversations as short as possible, the man's threat still clinging to her thoughts. She may have been higher in rank than him, but as a woman, her voice held only as much weight as her father gave it. And even though Laird Oliver didn't like Matthew personally, he respected the man's position as a tacksman.

Maybe even more than he loved his daughter.

Muireall hadn't wanted to believe such a thing was possible, but each day her father resisted her attempts to speak with him, her doubts grew stronger. Eventually, she concluded it was foolish to keep trying to reach him when the man was determined to shut her out.

He's just doing what he thinks is best fer me, she told herself, but such words couldn't quench the sense of betrayal in her heart. Mother had always dismissed Muireall's opinions, but until now, Father had at least been somewhat open to what she'd had to say. She wondered if she'd only been fooling herself, that perhaps this was how life had always been and she'd just never noticed before.

A great melancholy fell over her soul, broken only when she was out in her garden or playing her clàrsach. She focused all her attention on those two areas, learning and practicing as much as she could without arousing her mother's anger. But as time went on, even those pastimes couldn't fully restrain her sorrow.

Especially when Bernard moved out of Rigmore House, leaving not only a gaping hole in Muireall's already withering heart but also an empty position in the household.

Muireall didn't reply when Anne told her the tragic news about the gardener. *There goes my time in the garden since he was the only one I could trust with my secret; next, I'll lose my clàrsach. Is this to be my lot in life? Muireall Oliver—nay, Muireall Levins—wife to a man who despises me, friend to no one, purposeless, joyless, empty.*

Anne said little after her announcement, but Muireall barely noticed. The maid had been speaking less and less since the day of the Burgesses' wedding, at least in her mistress's presence. The redhead suspected this was due to how cold she'd been of late, but she hadn't the energy to care.

Once Muireall was ready, she walked sluggishly down the hall to the dining room, her footsteps echoing off the walls. When she stepped into the room, she stopped mid-stride, her eyes flicking back and forth. There sat Joseph and Laura, chatting happily together with tea and porridge. Father wasn't rushing to consume his food as quickly as possible, and Mother was actually smiling. *What's going on?*

"Ah, Muireall! Come join us," Mother called, her grin even larger than before.

She hesitantly made her way to the table and sat down beside her father. A bowl of porridge and a steaming cup of tea were already prepared for her. "Good morneen?" She hadn't meant for the phrase to come out as a question, but she was so bewildered she didn't know how to respond.

Mother said, "You'll never guess what yer father and I decided last night. We"—

Muireall tensed. *Is she going to say something else about how I need to maintain the family's dignity? I haven' done anything to upset her in weeks. Did Mr. Levins say something?*

—"decided we've been too forceful about this whole betrothal to Matthew Levins. You really should have some say in all this."

Muireall's eyes bulged. *W-What? Am I still asleep?* She turned to her father.

"Don' look so surprised, daughter," Joseph said, just as upbeat as Lady Oliver. "Yer mother and I only want what's best fer you."

Wait, this is real, isn' it? I'm na dreaming? Real happiness filled her for what felt like the first time in over a month, and she wanted to cry, scream, and laugh all at once. "I don' have to get married?"

Father held up his hand. "Wait a moment. We didn' say that."

Muireall's joy petered away. "Then . . . what are you saying?"

Laura clasped her hands together atop the table. "As you know, yer birthday will be here soon. Yer father and I want to host a ball in yer honor. 'Twill also be a wonderful opportunity to formally announce yer engagement . . . to the man o' yer choice."

Muireall's mouth went slack. *My choice?*

"So, I don' have to marry Mr. Levins; I just have to choose *someone* by my birthday?"

Her parents nodded.

"But there's no one else in Everton you would approve o'. All our neighbors are commoners." She couldn't keep the disgust out of her voice as she said the final word. *This makes no sense. Mother and Father would never let me choose someone like that. I would never choose someone like that either.*

Or would I? Marrying a commoner might still be better than marrying Matthew Levins.

Muireall peered at her parents. *Nay, there must be some catch to all o' this. There must be something I missed. . . .*

Hope began to rise within her. It started out small, and she tried to tamp it down, but the emotion was too slippery, escaping her grip before she could squelch it. Then, once free, it ran wild through her mind, conjuring visions of a bright and joyous future. *What would it be like to work in the garden without fear o' reprimand? To play all the songs I wish without having to cater to Mother's wishes anymore? To visit the places I've only read about in books? Maybe I could even be lucky enough to experience a love like the Burgesses'.*

Laura giggled, dissipating her daughter's daydream. She raised her eyebrows conspiratorially at her husband. "Do you want to tell her or should I?"

Muireall almost groaned. *This is my life we're talking about. Must you act like 'tis just a game?* But such behavior didn't befit a woman of her station, so she kept herself composed and waited for them to explain.

"I learned something fascinating yesterday about Mr. Mendes," Father said. "He——"

"What does he matter? He's just a merchant," Muireall blurted, surprise overtaking her tongue.

Joseph narrowed his eyes at his daughter's rude behavior. An apology spilled from her lips, and she urged him to continue.

"*As* I was saying, Mr. Mendes is na just a merchant. He's also a viscount. And he is very wealthy. The tight-lipped lad wouldn' say exactly how much, but it sounds like his estate is worth more than double all o' Rigmore House."

Muireall blinked a few times. *A viscount? Really?* She hadn't spent much time in the man's company since he'd returned to

Everton, but he hardly carried himself like a nobleman. *Why would a viscount be working as a merchant?*

"Isn' he betrothed to Briony Fairborn though?" When the man had first arrived here after a dreadful storm, he and Briony had been together constantly. Initially, everyone had said it was just because she was helping him recover from the injury he'd incurred during his voyage, but it hadn't taken long before rumors had begun of a secret relationship between the charming merchant and the beautiful midwife.

"Nay, he is na," Joseph replied with confidence. "I asked him that specifically. However, he implied he's going to change that very soon."

"Then that means he's na an option fer me, doesn' it?"

"Tsk, tsk." Laura wagged a finger. "Until the man makes a formal proposal, you still have a chance to win him over. Which I imagine won' be difficult since you have so much more to offer." She gestured to the room.

Muireall tucked her shoulders inward, the hope in her chest shrinking in turn. *They may say they're giving me a choice, but in truth, they've already decided fer me, haven' they?*

"If I married Mr. Mendes, I'd have to move to Portugal, wouldn' I?" she pointed out. She at least knew what to expect in Everton. *Everything is different in Portugal: the environment, the customs, the language. What if I couldn' handle it?*

Father patted her hand. "There, there, freck. You'll be all right. I'm sure you can get along fine without us."

"*That's* na what I'm worried about," Muireall said under her breath.

"And we'll come and visit," Mother cooed. "I'm simply ecstatic at the thought o' getting to see . . ." She turned to Father. "What was the name o' the city he's from?"

Joseph scratched the top of his head. "Ave— . . . Something with an *A*. I can' recall."

Laura shifted her gaze back to her daughter. "So, what do you think? Would you like to be a viscountess?"

With her mother's wolf-like stare on her, Muireall's first instinct was to comply. It would be so easy, just a single word, then she could retreat back into the fog she'd been in for the last few weeks. Back to mindlessly allowing her parents to make the decisions they'd have forced her to comply with, anyway. "I . . ."

An unexpected resistance stilled her tongue. *Nay. I can' just agree because Mother and Father want me to. Na on something this important. I need to make sure Mr. Mendes is a worthy husband first. He could be just as bad as Mr. Levins—or worse.*

Or what if he isn' even open to marrying me? Mr. Levins certainly isn' doing it because he wishes to.

But will rejecting Mr. Mendes mean I'm stuck with Mr. Levins again? Such thoughts and more ran rampant through her mind, threatening to overwhelm her with the great emotions attached to them.

Muireall couldn't bear to look either of her parents in the eye, so she kept her gaze on the table. "May I have some time to think about it?"

Every second of the pause that followed was like an eternity.

"O' course," Father supplied finally.

Muireall's eyes flicked up to his, blazing with gratitude. "Thank you."

"But na too long," Mother clarified, her nose wrinkled with displeasure. "Remember, an engagement will be announced on yer birthday."

My birthday. That's only . . . She counted the days in her head. *A month away!*

Muireall picked up her spoon and took some porridge, but as soon as she swallowed it, her stomach lurched in protest. She leaped to her feet. "Forgive me. I—I need to excuse myself."

The young woman fled the room, too distraught to wait for her parents to give her permission to leave. She went out to the garden and took a deep breath of the fragrant air.

Muireall wasn't good at situations like these, at dealing with so many emotions at once. Oftentimes, she wondered if it would be easier not to have them at all; they were such troublesome things. If only she could examine them from a distance, maybe then she could make sense of them.

The world of facts was a much more comfortable place to dwell. Facts were steady, unchanging, and never messy. People solved problems with their minds, not their hearts.

That was how Muireall was going to solve this problem, too. She just needed to figure out how. And for the life of her, she had to stop crying.

A rustle drew a gasp from her lips, and she whirled toward the sound.

***

Niall silently glared at the young man on his left at the servants' dining table. It was completely unfair for Gilbert to look so rested after his snoring had kept Niall awake for half the night. Again. *I don' know how much longer I can endure this.*

Since his arrival, he'd spent his days running from one end of Rigmore House to the other, performing every task—and torture—Hamish could think of. Whether it was polishing silver, dusting furniture, washing sheets, or arranging Laird Oliver's clothes, no undertaking was too humble for Niall to carry out. He'd even had the misfortune of having to empty the chamber pots on several occasions.

At the start of his stay, Niall had nearly had to drag himself to bed every night, unaccustomed to such arduous labor. But as the time had passed, his muscles had grown stronger, and he'd learned how to complete his duties with ever increasing efficiency.

Fridays were different. Fridays were the days when he didn't have to grit his teeth every time one of the Olivers turned up their nose at him or complained about the temperature of their tea. Instead, he got to do as he liked, and so far, that had translated to hours spent teaching Briony and William.

Niall's thoughts drifted to their first session together. Briony had taken the three of them to a small outcrop just beyond her home, an ideal place to practice since it was tucked behind several large stones, effectively concealing them from the village below.

Niall had told them to demonstrate their storm summoning first. As expected, Briony called down rain and lightning like it was child's play, but for William, the task was much more difficult. It took him several minutes just to summon a small cloud, and even that only produced a light drizzle. Niall could tell the boy was frustrated, but he encouraged him that it was normal for young selkies to struggle at first. It sometimes took months of practice before they could create anything of real significance.

They moved next to raising their body temperatures, a task both Briony and William performed easily once they focused on something that made them angry. Niall didn't ask Briony what she was thinking of, but from the way she scowled at him, he had a pretty good idea what it was.

When they'd shifted to charmsong, things had gotten . . . complicated. Once Niall had explained to William what it was, the lad had eagerly lifted his voice in a beautiful rendition of "Wondrous Foaming Waves," a song Niall never would have expected to pass over the boy's lips.

"W-Where did you hear that?" Niall demanded, unable to hide the pain in his voice.

William jumped behind Briony. "Mother used to sing it at home all the time." He peeped around the midwife's back. "What is it?"

"'Tis an old selkie ballad." Niall paused. "'Twas yer mother's favorite song."

The lad's face lit up, but Niall immediately changed topics after that, focusing instead on teaching them about the magical folk they could run into in the area.

As Niall dwelt on the memory now, he wondered why he'd been so quick to shift the conversation away from Elene. It would have been an excellent opportunity to strengthen his bond with the boy. *And isn' that the reason I wanted to train them in the first place? To earn William's trust?*

But the fact that Elene had taught the boy something from her childhood didn't sit well with Niall, for it didn't align with what his father had told him.

"She's fallen in love with a human," Callum had said the day Elene had disappeared, his lips trembling with despair.

"Somehow, he's tricked her into hating us. I'm so sorry, son." The entire herd had grieved the terrible loss that day, then had done so a second time when both Niall's sister and mother had perished seven months ago.

Did Father lie to me? Did Elene na hate us, after all? Shame pricked Niall's heart, for he'd never doubted his father before.

Focus on the prize, Niall. Don' waste time on meaningless thoughts.

For his plan to work, he needed to convince Briony he could be trusted. Then she could persuade John to let him spend time with William alone. But that goal still seemed far away, for while the midwife no longer glowered every time Niall was near, she was definitely still keeping her guard up.

That's na completely a bad thing, he reminded himself. At least he hadn't had any more troublesome urges to kiss her.

It also meant she didn't trust him enough to reveal where she stored her sealskin.

So far, Niall had been extremely careful in his search, only perusing one or two places at a time when he'd gotten a few seconds alone in Drulea Cottage. But since moments like that were few and far between, he'd only concluded that the sealskin wasn't anywhere in the kitchen or dining area. That still left many hiding places, and Briony could always move it if she wished.

Perhaps I need to think o' something else, something that will force her to bring the pelt into the open. He glanced around the dining hall. *If I was to plant something on Briony and frame her fer theft, the Olivers would surely throw her out o' town. Then she'd have to find a new home and take her sealskin with her, giving me the perfect opportunity to strike.*

He tapped his fingers against his leg. The idea held merit, but there were many things that could go wrong. *What if someone catches me stealing? What if Briony finds the item and returns it before I can frame her?* He groaned inwardly. *Too many potential problems. Still, I might as well see if I can figure out where the Olivers store their valuables.*

"Are you ready to get started?" Gilbert interrupted Niall's musings. The servant wiped some food off his round face before lifting his freckled cheeks into a smile.

"I suppose so," he replied, grinning in return. "Where will I be working today?" Over the past few weeks, he and his roommate had struck up a fairly decent friendship. The fellow was amiable, hardworking, and remarkably naive. Traits Niall would be happy to exploit if the need arose.

"The two o' us will be working together again today. I'll show you where. Come along."

Niall resisted the urge to roll his eyes. *Great. Still na trusted enough to be on my own.*

Even though he'd been working there for almost a month, Hamish had yet to assign him any solitary tasks. Gilbert was his usual companion, though he'd also worked alongside a few of the other servants from time to time. Most of them were just as kindhearted as Gilbert, though Jeane Martin, the cook, seemed to find him particularly unlikeable. But she seemed to find everyone unlikeable, so Niall wasn't too worried.

Gilbert led him out of the dining room, through the foyer, and down a long hallway. They passed several grand rooms, each with its own specific name and purpose yet seeming to carry out relatively the same function. Niall had spent enough time in them to identify the sitting room and drawing room, but the others' names still escaped his memory.

Gilbert stopped at an ornate wooden door Niall hadn't been through before and turned around.

"Thank you fer helping me so much," Niall said with a tight nod, "but don' you think 'tis time I did some o' these things on my own?"

Gilbert shrugged. "Perhaps, but there's still a lot you haven' learned yet, and I know what 'tis like to be new. What I would have given fer someone to help me out when I was first getting started."

"Why is that?"

"I made quite a few mistakes when I first came here. I'm sure you've noticed by now that the Olivers have high . . . expectations o' their staff."

"Which is another way o' saying they're demanding," Niall ventured.

Gilbert's lips twisted like he was holding back a laugh. "Perhaps," he hedged. His eyes swept around the empty corridor. "But like I've warned you before, don' let anyone else catch you talking like that. If word got back to Laird Oliver, you'd be dismissed in no time. And you'd have no chance o' getting a job anywhere else in town."

"Laird Oliver is that influential, is he?" From what Niall had seen, the laird was a puffed-up buffoon who was only tolerated because of the humans' ridiculous social hierarchy.

In selkie herds, leaders were chosen by their wisdom and strength. Bloodlines only mattered as far as increasing the potential for powerful offspring. Someone like Laird Oliver never would have held sway.

His wife, on the other hand, bore a much keener mind. Anytime Niall was in her presence, he was especially diligent in his duties; she always noticed even the smallest misstep. And severely punished the offender. If only she wasn't so waspish, Niall might have actually respected her.

"Oh, that's fer sure. Anyone he wants out o' Everton, you can guarantee they'll be gone within a week . . . except fer the Fairborns, that is."

A tremor went through Niall's hands, so he shoved them in his pockets. "The Fairborns? He tried to get rid o' them?"

Gilbert babbled on, oblivious to his friend's unease. "Aye, 'twas over a year ago now. Briony Fairborn's mother had just passed away, and Laird Oliver wanted to get the young midwife out o' town. She's illegitimate, you see. The whole family is like that, always has been."

"But about what happened?" Niall prompted.

Gilbert chuckled. "You should have heard the fuss Adaira Stubbins—oh, I guess she's Adaira Burgess now—put up about it. She shut down all o' Everton Inn—refused to bake, take in guests, everything. The Olivers called a town meeting over it, and Adaira made such a strong argument about Briony staying that the mistress backed down. No one's ever kept the Olivers from what they wanted before."

Hmm, seems Adaira has been influential since long before she stole William from me. He grimaced at the memory.

"Anyway, let's go in," Gilbert said, opening the door. He stepped inside and threw out his arms as if he was presenting something glorious, but all Niall could see was a big, empty room covered in dust and cobwebs.

When he didn't react, Gilbert lowered his arms, his eyebrows squished together in confusion. "Don' you know what this place is?"

"A room with strange windows?" The back wall was covered in colored glass the likes of which Niall had never seen before.

"Haven' you heard o' stained glass windows before?" Gilbert sighed. "This is the ballroom. And we're going to clean it." He pointed to an assortment of tools in the corner.

"Oh. And that's . . . a good thing?"

"'Tis a wonderful thing!" Gilbert squealed, his tone so shrill it hurt Niall's ears. "This room hasn' been used since the Olivers' son passed away eleven years ago. If we're supposed to clean it, that means they'll be opening it up again soon. We usually have our dances on Mary's Hill since there's so much space. I wonder what special reason the Olivers might have fer using this room again. . . ." The man turned away, lost in thought.

"Ah!" Gilbert whirled back, beaming with excitement. "Perhaps 'tis fer their daughter's betrothal."

"Mistress Oliver is betrothed?" Niall tried not to look too surprised. He avoided her as much as he could, but from what he could tell, his first impression of the haughty redhead had been correct. She'd demonstrated time and again how little she thought of the people below her. Her demands were insouciant, often coming when the servants were busy doing other things, though she expected her wishes to be carried out immediately. And she seemed especially disgusted any time she saw Niall, for she always turned away from him like he wasn't even worthy of her gaze. The other servants had many nicknames for her, none of which were good. And from what he'd heard in the village, it wasn't just the household that despised her—everyone but her parents either avoided the young mistress or at least spoke poorly of her behind her back. As the bearer of so much disdain, it hardly seemed possible someone would agree to put up with her for a lifetime.

"Haven' you been paying attention? Why did you think Mr. Levins has been coming fer dinner so often?"

He didn't respond. Such trivial matters weren't worth noticing. Mr. Levins was just another human who thought himself something; if he'd been privileged enough to know anything of magic folk, he'd have quickly realized he was just a fool, striving for wealth and power in a world where humans were barely above the animals.

"It may be a bit premature to celebrate," Gilbert muttered to himself.

"Why is that?" Niall asked.

His friend's eyes widened; he didn't seem to have realized he'd spoken aloud. After a moment, he admitted, "Mistress Oliver and Mr. Levins have na been on speaking terms fer years. I don' know all the details, but apparently, there was an incident when they were bairns—" Gilbert cleared his throat. "Anyway, let's start working. We need to get these floors shiny if anyone's going to want to dance on them."

Niall slowly nodded. "Right . . ." The young man followed Gilbert's lead, picking up an identical tool and dipping it in a nearby bucket of water.

The pair spent the next several minutes cleaning in silence, but then Niall remembered something his father had said just before he'd returned: *"Gather all the information you can before you make yer move. Don' dismiss something that might end up helping you."*

Niall scowled. Gossiping with a human felt beneath him, but—

"Why would they be betrothed if they dislike each other?" he asked.

Even if this doesn' help me with my plans, maybe I'll be able to use it against Mistress Oliver. A rush of pleasure went through him at the thought of tormenting that irksome woman. Her arrogance practically demanded it.

"Their parents want the match," Gilbert explained, keeping his eyes trained on the floor as he washed with both speed and precision. "The Olivers are the highest ranking family in the village, and the Levinses are just below them. By marrying, Mr. Levins will become the next laird o' Everton and owner o' Rigmore House."

"And what does Mistress Oliver get out o' the marriage?"

Gilbert looked up at Niall with a frown. "What do you mean?"

"You just said Mr. Levins has a lot to gain from the union. What about Mistress Oliver?"

"She—she gets—she gets a husband to look after the estate, that's what," Gilbert said with an emphatic nod. "And someone to raise bairns with."

Niall pursed his lips, not understanding how these were good things if Mr. Levins wasn't someone Mistress Oliver even liked. *Humans are very odd, indeed.*

The conversation faded after that, and soon, Niall's mind wandered back to his mission. He hadn't been in the study since Laird Oliver had agreed to hire him. *Perhaps the old fool has something in there worth stealing.*

"Gilbert, would you mind if I got some fresh air?" He coughed a few times as if the dust was getting to him.

"I suppose, but be quick about it. If Hamish catches you na working, he won' be pleased."

"I'll keep that in mind," Niall said before departing. He roamed down the hall, peeking his head into each room he passed. Most were fairly dull, and their redundancies made him again wonder at the intellect of human beings. *Why do they need so many chairs? Every room seems to have at least three.*

Niall was fairly used to the estate's layout now, so he was confident he could find the study on his own. But just as he was about to reach it, he spotted Hamish coming down the hall from the opposite direction.

I have to get out o' here! Niall jumped backward, opened the nearest door, and threw himself out.

A beam of sunlight hit him straight in the eyes, blinding him. Niall shielded his face and staggered to the left, wincing at the pain charging across his skull. He shut his eyes and pressed his hands to his temples as he waited for his vision to return. *That was far too close. I can' afford to let anyone see—*

But he was too late, for someone already had seen him. And when she gasped, Niall's eyes shot open.

He'd unintentionally wandered into the garden. Niall didn't care much for plants, but even he couldn't deny the beauty of this place. It was an explosion of color, ranging from soft oranges and whites to brilliant reds and yellows. Whoever had chosen and arranged these flowers had certainly known what they were doing, for it felt like walking into another world. A world of joy and peace and magic, where nothing bad could touch you.

Of course, Niall knew it was foolish to believe evil could ever truly be kept at bay, and this place would almost certainly be ruined by the time he was done exacting vengeance, but Niall could still respect artistry when he saw it.

And what was by far the most exquisite flower sat a few feet away at the fountain, her red hair hanging limply over her shoulders. Niall had thought the young mistress fairly pretty when he'd first laid eyes on her, but her snobbish attitude had been so appalling that he'd almost forgotten. Sitting there now, though, tears glistening on her sharp cheeks, Muireall Oliver looked almost ethereal.

Until she started talking.

"Servant, you shouldn' be out here. Get back to yer duties," she commanded, her voice cracking on the last word.

Niall's brow knitted with curiosity. "I came to get some fresh air, na to disturb you. Are you . . ." He took a small step forward and cocked his head to the side.

Muireall pulled back, shifting her body as though she was about to flee. Yet she didn't rise from her seat. "Am I what?"

Niall closed the rest of the distance between them, walking slowly so as not to frighten her. He sat down beside her. "Are you well?"

She broke eye contact and ran her hands along her arms. After a moment, she let out a humorless chuckle. "I'm na, am I? If even someone as daft as you can see it."

Anger rose in his stomach at the insult, but he kept his temper in check. This woman didn't often show weakness—he could tell that much. That meant an opportunity like this wouldn't come along again any time soon.

"I know I'm just a servant, and we didn' meet on the best o' terms, but if there's anything I can do to help . . ." He rubbed the back of his neck and looked away, hoping she wouldn't reject him again.

When she didn't answer, he stole a peek at her from the corner of his eye. She was staring out, away from the garden, toward the wild heather in the field just beyond. But her gaze was distant, unfocused. More tears rested in her eyelashes.

"Mistress?"

"Are you in earnest?" she asked. Niall had thought she was looking at the heather, but now he realized her gaze went past it. To the sea.

His chest tightened. *I'll return to you soon. I promise.*

"About what?" he asked, swallowing the longing in his throat.

Mistress Oliver's deep green eyes zeroed in on his. "About helping me."

"Oh. Aye, I am. Just tell me what you need."

A weak smile tugged at her lips, then her expression turned cold. She rose from her seat and brushed off her dress. "I've just been told I have until my birthday to choose a husband."

Ah, so that's what this is about. That's a bit different from what Gilbert told me. I thought she was already betrothed to Mr. Levins. . . .

"I fail to see the problem."

Mistress Oliver huffed. "Then I suppose you and my parents would be in agreement." She threw her hands in the air. "Everyone in Everton would be in agreement!"

"If you get to choose, why na just choose someone you *want* to marry?"

She laughed again, a bitter, disjointed sound, and lowered her hands. "That's the problem. There's no one I want to marry. And even if there was, I'm na sure I'm ready fer that yet."

"So, you need a way to change yer parents' minds about yer marriage entirely."

"What I *need* is a miracle." She groaned. "I don' know why I'm even telling you this. Yer the last person who could help me."

She started to walk off, but as she passed a group of roses, an idea struck Niall like lightning.

"If you slowed down long enough to realize you don' know everything, Princess, you might find out I'm more useful than you think."

That got the reaction he was hoping for, and when she
turned back with a glower, he smirked.

"What did you just say?" She stomped over and planted
herself right in front of him.

Niall crossed his arms, loving the way her nose scrunched
up when she was angry. "I said, I know a way to help you. But
only if you help me in return."

Mistress Oliver gritted her teeth. "What do you want?" she
hissed.

"Nothing much. A wee favor, that's all."

*With any luck, she'll think I want to use her social standing fer my
own ends.* He chuckled to himself. *In a way, I suppose that is true.*

She pursed her lips, thinking it over. "I could arrange that
but only if you do what you say you can."

Niall's smile stretched over his whole face. "Excellent."

The woman leaned closer. "So? What is yer great plan?
How are you going to change my fate?" Despite her haughty
tone, eagerness sparked in her eyes.

He laughed. "Simple. We're going to use magic."

Utter Foolishness

Muireall gaped, certain he must be jesting. But as the seconds stretched between them and he didn't take back his words, she realized she'd been wrong. This man wasn't mocking her.

He was insane.

She closed her mouth and tried to smile as if nothing were wrong, but inside, her heart was racing. *When he finds out I don' believe him, he's na going to hurt me, is he?*

Niall frowned. "Why are you—" He moved slightly closer, and she couldn't help but recoil. "Are you frightened o' me?"

"O' course na." Muireall chuckled. "Don' be absurd."

He wasn't fooled. "You are. You think I've lost my mind, don' you?" The man's nostrils flared. "The world isn' nearly as small as you think 'tis. You humans have no ide—" He broke off and ran his fingers through his hair.

"You humans"? He really is mad. Maybe I can sneak away while he's na looking. She slowly lifted her foot, but Niall's eyes caught the movement.

"Wait!" he cried, his voice straining as if he was barely keeping his emotions in check.

Muireall's legs tensed as she prepared to run.

"Please," he said, his tone softer. "Wait."

She paused, his desperation catching her attention. "Why should I?"

"I'm na mad, truly," Niall insisted, clasping his hands together in front of him. "Even though . . ." He grimaced. "Yer na the first person to think so. Just let me explain."

She ran her tongue along the inside of her cheek as she mulled over his words. He seemed perfectly reasonable now. "A-All right. How exactly are we going to use magic?"

When Niall strode over to one of her beautiful red roses and broke it off, she tried not to flinch. Normally, she would be outraged that he'd taken one of her flowers without permission, but right then, she was afraid of provoking him further. *If I made him angry enough, would he snap me in two like that stem?*

"Well, we're na going to use it *ourselves*," the man clarified. "We're going to get help from the fairies."

"Are you in earnest?"

He peered over his shoulder at her. "What? You don' believe they're real?"

Tales of the Fair Folk skittered across Muireall's thoughts. She'd heard plenty about them over the years. Most of her neighbors could cite strange events they attributed to the fairies' handiwork—some of them boons but others misfortunes. The small, spiteful beings known as fairies would just as soon curse a human as bless them. And if someone made the great mistake of offending one, he might as well just accept that misery was bound to follow him for the rest of his life.

But fairies weren't the only supernatural beings her neighbors told tales of. Vincent McLaren, the recently deceased son of Steven McLaren, had filled children's ears with fantastical yarns for decades before his untimely death. Tales of banshees[17], kelpies[18], trows[19], and other such creatures had been on the lips of every village child at one point or another, Muireall included.

Not everyone in Everton gave much credence to the stories, however. Her parents had always told her not to

---

[17] Female spirits whose appearance or wailing meant that someone was going to die soon.

[18] Water spirits that could shapeshift between human and horse form.

[19] Orcadian trolls.

believe in such nonsense, that those were just tales invented for the simple-minded. That hadn't stopped them from warning her to stay away from the haugr[20] at the edge of their estate though, where rumor claimed a hogboon[21] resided.

The laird's daughter should have easily dismissed the tales as utter foolishness. If such beings truly existed, they would have already been captured and studied by now. She knew this in her head, yet a small part of her wondered if Niall might be telling the truth. After what she'd seen—

Dizziness hit her as an unwelcome memory started to emerge. "I-I never said that."

Niall turned back to her and stared deep into her eyes. "Then you don' think I'm mad?"

There it was again, that same trace of insecurity she'd heard before. Muireall didn't trust this man for a second; for all she knew, he would turn on her the instant an opportunity arose. But that tremor in his voice—that, she did trust. He'd mentioned that someone else had called him mad once before. Whoever that someone was hadn't just offended him; they'd left him bleeding.

But she wasn't about to help him heal.

"Let's na play games with each other," she said with a note of disdain. "You don' really care what I think, so long as you get out o' yer duties, right?"

The man's expression—so open a moment ago—disappeared behind the veil of arrogance he seemed to reserve especially for her. *Or is this his true face, and what I saw before was the mask?*

"Yer smarter than I expected."

"What Adaira said before about you na understanding our customs—that was a lie, wasn' it?"

He shrugged, his lips twitching with amusement.

"And where would we go to find them—the fairies, I mean?"

"Meet me here in two days just after sunset, and I'll show you."

---

[20] A burial mound.

[21] The spirit of a deceased ancestor who lived in the haugr and watched over its family's land.

"Yer na going to tell me now?"

"Better to keep a few things to myself."

Muireall sighed. "Are you even sure this is going to work?"

"Oh, 'twill work. I've no doubt o' that." He waggled his eyebrows, taunting her.

"How do you know? Have you ever seen a fairy, servant?" she threw back, trying to throw him off balance. *He needs to remember he's below me, na the other way around.*

"I've seen more than you can imagine," he replied, his eyes glazing over for a second before homing in on her once more, "which is why when we meet them, I'm going to do the talking. Fairies are very particular, and I don' want you ruining things."

Muireall opened her mouth to protest, but Niall spoke again before she could.

"So, Princess, what do you say? Are you brave enough to take a chance on this? Or are you too *noble* to consort with a servant?"

His expression was so smug she wanted to slap it right off his handsome face. "I'll be here."

***

Niall sauntered back into Rigmore House with a spring in his step. *What a wonderful turn o' events. I couldn' have planned that better myself. Soon, I'll have Mistress Oliver's influence to use as I see fit.* He would need some time to figure out exactly *how* he was going to use it, but several delightful possibilities were already forming in his mind.

Now, to get back to the ballroom. He'd gone through the door by the garden, which had taken him back into the hallway he'd been in before. A series of giggles hit his ears, and Niall looked over as two young maids came out of a nearby room.

"Hello, ladies," Niall greeted. "I was hoping I'd run into you today."

"Oh, hello," said the taller one. She smiled and batted her eyelashes. "I wondered how long 'twould take you to start making yer rounds. Being so handsome and all."

Niall smirked; he'd always known his popularity among human women hadn't been solely due to his charmsong. "I'm sorry to admit I don't recall yer names. Would you be so kind as to share them? Then I'll know who I'm dreaming about tonight."

"Bessie, Anne, what are you doing?" called a cross voice.

The three servants turned to Hamish, who stood a short distance down the hall, arms folded over his chest.

"You all should be working," he said to the maids.

"We were just leaving," replied the taller girl.

Hamish strode up to the group, his expression stern. "It didn' sound like that to me, Bessie. It sounded like you were having an inappropriate conversation with Niall here."

Bessie's tray rattled as she trembled under Hamish's gaze. Anne seemed just as nervous, her elbows pressed into her sides as if she was trying to make herself as small as possible.

"'Twas my fault," Niall said. "They've done nothing wrong."

Hamish's head jerked toward him, his face contorting in anger. "As fer *you*, I thought you were cleaning the ballroom with Gilbert."

"I was, but Mistress Oliver wanted my help," Niall replied. *'Tis na exactly a lie.*

Hamish leaned toward him. "That doesn' explain why yer here. Besides, Mistress Oliver doesn' ask servants fer help."

"Well, she did this time," he retorted, pushing out his chest. "Then I . . . got lost when I tried to find my way back."

"You've been here fer weeks, yet you still don' know yer way around?"

Niall smiled helplessly, hoping the man would accept his flimsy excuse.

Hamish said nothing for a long moment, his face still riddled with suspicion. Finally, he gestured to the corridor behind him. "After you cross the foyer, the ballroom is the second room on the right. Don' get lost again. There's more to be done, and until I hear it directly from one o' the Olivers' lips, yer expected to do every task I give you. Is that clear?"

Niall bit his tongue to keep from snarling. He gave the man a sharp nod and scurried off, leaving the maids to deal with any further reprimand the butler had in store.

"Niall, where have you been?" Gilbert asked when he spotted his wayward partner. "I thought you just wanted a quick break."

"I'm sorry, Gilbert. I got . . . distracted."

"Well, don' do that again. Yer going to get us both in trouble if word gets back to Hamish."

Niall picked up where he'd left off cleaning the floor, his thoughts soon drifting back to his upcoming meeting with the laird's daughter. This time, he quickly recognized the stupidity of his actions.

What has yer impulsive behavior gotten you into now? asked the voice of reason in his head, still sounding remarkably like his father. *Reveal the existence o' other magical folk to a human? How could that possibly be a good idea?*

Plenty o' humans already know we exist, so 'tis na like I'm doing something that terrible, Niall argued with himself. *Besides, I'm sure the fairies will want her to complete some impossible challenge in exchange fer their favor.*

And yer just going to let her fail?

The redhead's face appeared in his mind again. Not the pinched, arrogant one he encountered most of the time—the sad, desperate one he'd seen today. The one that had looked so pitiful he'd wished he could do something to ease her burdens.

Maybe I could help her get the fairies' magic. She certainly seemed like she'd be miserable if she had to go through with her marria—

She's the enemy, you idiot! Did you forget her brother tried to kill you? Niall froze, water sloshing out of his pail, much to Gilbert's displeasure. But Niall heard none of his companion's complaints; all he heard was Alastair's horrible laughter. The dead boy's face hovered in his mind's eye, blotting out any ounce of compassion he might have felt for the laird's daughter.

She may na be the one who did it, but she's still human. And humans don' deserve kindness.

Stained Glass

Two nights later, Muireall crept downstairs and went out to the garden, her steps light and her heart pounding. Mother had commented on her nervousness at dinner, but she had claimed she was just anxious to make the right choice of husband. The real reason for her nerves, though, was that she was trying to hold back the growing excitement inside her.

What if Niall was telling the truth? Is he really going to take me to see fairies? Are they as powerful as the stories say?

When she reached the fountain and found no one there, she pressed her palm to her heart. *Good, he isn' waiting fer me.* She always preferred to be the one someone was coming to; it felt less vulnerable for some reason. She sat down and spread her fingers over the fountain's cool stone, her thoughts soon starting to wander.

What if, instead o' asking the fairies to change my parents' minds, I asked them to bring me a husband I actually could love? A silhouette began to form in her mind, its features shadowy and uncertain. Muireall didn't care much for physical appearances, so she didn't spend time considering what he would look like. She had more important qualifications for an ideal husband. *He'd have to be very intelligent, witty perhaps. Someone who isn' afraid o' social expectations, like Matthew is. Someone who can stand up fer himself and his loved ones.*

And I don' want a husband who just caves to my every wish like Father does with Mother. Nay, he needs to be my equal in an argument. She smiled. *Aye, that sounds amusing. A duel o' minds. A man who can handle my sarcasm and throw it back at me. And at the end o' it, we would both come out understanding one another a bit better.*

But no such man really exists. Na in Everton, na in all o' Orkney. Na when women aren' allowed to be curious or have interests beyond taking care o' their homes. Interests like that are "absurd," as Mother says.

She groaned. *What am I doing? I shouldn' be allowing such useless thoughts to cloud my mind. I don' need a husband. I don' even want one!*

Even as she told herself that, she remembered Adaira's joy as the new bride had danced in Mr. Burgess's arms. Muireall's heart stirred with longing.

Where is Niall? She'd been waiting for a while now, but the servant had yet to appear. *Did he get held up by someone?*

Muireall jumped to her feet. *Did Mother catch him sneaking around?* She didn't want him to have to face her mother's wrath. *If that's what happened, I need to help him. He won' know what to say, and then she'll assume the worst and have him thrown out.*

She started to walk back to the main part of the house, then stopped herself. *If I come to his rescue, who knows what Mother will think . . . and she'll punish both o' us. Then what will I have accomplished? Niall will be in worse trouble than he would have been without my involvement, and this opportunity will have slipped right through my fingers.* She returned to her seat and shook out her hands, wishing she could just as easily shake off her worries.

A while later, soft footsteps approached. Muireall shot up, only realizing then how suspicious she must look. *If that isn' Niall, how am I going to explain my presence? I've no good reason to be out here. . . .*

Muireall breathed more easily when the figure appeared, for the man's clothes and long dark hair made it obvious it was Niall. She scowled as their eyes met. "What took you so long?"

Niall put his hands in his pockets, a lazy smile coming onto his face. "'Tis much harder fer me to sneak out than you since I have to share my room. But I'm here now, and that's the important thing." He clapped his hands together. "Are you ready?"

"That depends on where we're going," Muireall said tartly, still a bit upset that he hadn't told her their destination. She liked details, not mysteries.

The servant's eyes twinkled. "Follow me." Niall led Muireall north through town, and as they walked, Muireall was reminded of her stroll with Matthew. Spending time with unmarried men used to be a rarity for her, yet here she was, walking with another one in less than a week. This time, without the watchful eye of a chaperone.

"So, Niall, tell me about yerself," Muireall said as they entered the market. The Burgesses' cryptic comments about the man the other night had left her eager to know what they were concealing. *What kind o' suffering has Niall gone through? I know his sister—Mr. Burgess's first wife—died several months ago, but there seemed to be more to it than that.*

"There's na much to tell," he replied in a clipped tone.

Muireall frowned. *What an odd response. Is he just opposed to polite conversation? He certainly seemed quick enough to talk when it meant getting to insult me. Perhaps I'll try a more direct approach.*

"How do you know so much about the Fair Folk?"

"Same as you. I've heard stories."

"But before you said you'd seen them, didn' you?"

Niall turned, their eyes meeting for the first time since they'd left Rigmore House. The man's black orbs were wistful as he said, "Nay, I said I've seen more than you could imagine."

"Which implies that you've seen fairies," Muireall argued.

"Does it imply that?" He smirked. "Well, since you've got me all figured out, what else have you discovered? I'd love to hear it."

Muireall swallowed and looked down at the road. "Uhhh . . ."

This isn' how the conversation was supposed to go. What do I say now? Yer an insufferable—possibly mad—miscreant whose lack o' respect is so brazen it unnerves me?

"What's wrong? Na so sure o' yerself anymore, Princess?"

Her anger flared up, and she said coldly, "You need to stop calling me that."

Niall tilted his head as though he was confused, which merely infuriated her more. "I just didn' want to make the same mistake I made when we first met. After all, you didn' want me to speak informally with you. And yer basically the Princess o' Everton, aren' you?"

"Nay, I'm na. I'm just—"

"The most powerful woman in town aside from yer mother? Heir to the Oliver fortune?" His tone was cruel, mocking. His eyes cut away from hers. "Or perhaps you prefer what everyone calls you behind yer back—a living statue?"

Muireall stopped walking, her heart slamming against her ribcage. *How dare he! I should dismiss him from Rigmore House this instant.*

But as she took a breath, Matthew Levins's harsh words came back to her: *"When Mother told me about our betrothal, I felt physically ill. As any man would in my position."*

The fire in her chest died away, replaced by an all-consuming dread. *Are they right? Am I really so cold I drive everyone away?*

She didn't want to believe it, but far too much evidence lay before her. The depression she'd struggled with these last weeks hovered over her, threatening to take control once more, but before it could, her lips moved in desperation. "And what do you say? Do you agree with them?"

"That yer a living statue?" The man spun toward her with a chuckle. "Nay, mistress. If anything, yer a stained-glass window—completely untouchable."

***

Niall's laughter died away, for the moisture on his mistress's face was unmistakable. He'd thought she'd find his comment flattering, for the noblewoman was always so quick to point out their difference in social status. But now, staring into the green expanse of her eyes, he realized just how accurate his words had been. While a stained-glass window was distant, beautiful, and cold, it was also easily broken. *She doesn' want to be untouchable, does she? She may be the Princess o' Everton, but all that money and power hasn' made her happy. It has made her lonely.*

Niall bristled at the compassion welling up inside him. *It does no good to pity them. Humans will turn on you in an instant. They're false, fickle creatures.*

Even so, the compassion lingered.

Niall didn't know how to handle such a treacherous feeling, so he broke eye contact and said softly, "I'm sure my opinion isn' worth very much."

His gaze darted back to her face, but she ducked her head before he could see her expression. "Aye, that's true. 'Tis worth nothing at all."

"Glad we've established that." His tone was sharp. "And yers is worth nothing to me as well."

A pregnant silence settled over them as they hastened up the road, but Niall didn't dare break it for fear he might take back what he'd said. Even though that didn't make any sense.

When they reached Mary's Hill, Niall tried not to think about all that had transpired the last time he'd been up here. But memories still pressed against his mind like hungry rats, seeking even the smallest opening to get inside.

"Yer mad," Briony whispered.

"After everything I've said, that's yer response? To deny everything you know is true? What o' the connection between us? You yerself said 'twas there."

Niall shook off the thoughts and tried to refocus. He'd spotted a fairy ring up here before; he was sure of it. He just needed to keep looking until he found it. His eyes swept over clumps of marigold, thistle, and shrubs amidst the thick grass.

There! A perfect circle of mushrooms sat at the base of the hill on the eastern side, right at the edge of Torin Woods. He imagined quite a few unlucky villagers had probably stumbled into it over the years, never to be heard from again.

But Niall knew how to handle fairies. He'd run across quite a few, so he was well-versed in their tricks. As long as he and Muireall didn't eat or drink anything or accidentally indebt themselves, they would be fine. Fairies couldn't resist a deal.

"Do you see that?" Niall pointed to the ring. "Once we step into it, we'll pass through the Veil separating the human world from the fairies'. You must stay right with me the whole time; do you understand?"

Wariness flickered across the woman's face, but she gave him a swift nod.

"Good. Take my hand."

Mistress Oliver's nose wrinkled. "Is that necessary?"

Niall rolled his eyes and grabbed her hand, grinning at her intake of breath.

Together, they walked into the fairy ring and, as far as the human world was concerned, vanished without a trace.

Dangerous Deals

Muireall stood at the edge of an unfamiliar clearing, this one teeming with life. It appeared to be a huge party, the likes of which she'd never beheld. The grandeur dripping from everything—and everyone—was incredible. Dresses and suits of the finest silk in every color imaginable, beautiful delicacies on long white tables, large crackling bonfires, all bathed in a magical glow of moonlight that seemed to pulse with energy.

The dancers, themselves, were breathtaking, their every movement like the stroke of a master painter. Their heights and coloring varied, but all were exceptionally beautiful. They wove in and out from one another in perfect harmony, following the rhythms of a hypnotic tune that was altogether unfamiliar yet called to Muireall's soul as if she'd known it from her first breath.

Despite their beauty, two of the strangers' features sent a tremor of unease through her. The first was their ears, which swept upward into delicate points at the tips. A subtle reminder that these weren't humans she was amongst. The second was far less subtle—each bore a pair of large, iridescent, butterfly-like wings that stretched from their shoulder blades.

Their most irresistible trait, though, was that no one knew who she was. That meant Muireall could behave in whatever manner she saw fit without fear of repercussions from her parents. She was free to do as she pleased.

If not for Niall.

Niall's hand in hers was the only thing keeping her from leaping into the fray of dancers and joining the merriment. She couldn't fathom why he would keep her from such enjoyment. In fact, she saw no reason to continue holding his hand at all, now that they'd passed through the Veil safely.

Muireall released her grip and took off toward the fairies, but a sharp tug on her wrist pulled her back.

She looked down at Niall's hand in indignation. "Unhand me, servant." She gave him a burning, reproachful glare.

The man didn't respond with anger; instead, his eyes widened with concern. He swung her into the circle of his arms and whispered in her ear, "Don' be fooled, mistress. Much o' what you see is but an illusion designed to entrap you. Stay with me, and you'll be safe. Please."

Muireall's heart fluttered; he seemed to earnestly be trying to protect her, though she didn't understand why she needed it. No one here wished her ill. Most seemed so caught up in their revelry they'd barely noticed her presence, and those who had were smiling at her in such an inviting manner Muireall couldn't believe they had sinister intentions.

No matter. If he wants me to stay with him, he can just come along. She stepped out of Niall's embrace but grabbed his hand and pulled him toward the center of the dance. The servant was surprised at first, but when Muireall grinned and placed her other hand on his shoulder, he slowly began to sway with the music. Soon, the two of them were spinning, leaping, flying with exhilaration as one song drifted into the next. The other dancers spurred them on, never tiring in their graceful movements.

But Niall's smile was the most exhilarating part of all. Muireall didn't think she'd ever seen him smile like this before. There was no condescension, no contempt in the liquid pool of his eyes, just an infectious vitality that sent Muireall's spirit soaring. She laughed as the two of them moved back and forth, something unspoken growing between them.

A handsome fairy with long blond hair and eyes of purest silver twirled closer and took Muireall's hand. She spun away from Niall with her new partner, barely caring about the worried look in her servant's eye.

I can dance with whomever I like, she told herself. *I'll come back to Niall later, and we can do what we came fer then. There's no need to rush. We have all the time in the world.*

Muireall took a closer look at the man she was dancing with. His face was youthful, but his eyes held the wisdom of great age. Fairies were masters of deception—she knew that, yet she felt no fear in his arms. When the music faded into the next song, he whirled her into a new partner's arms, this one with dark hair like Niall's.

"Have a drink, my love," the fairy whispered, pressing a goblet into her hands. Muireall stared down at the cup—filled to the brim with a sparkling liquid—and took in its heady aroma. The scent of roses overwhelmed her, so potent she longed to drink the entire glass.

Yet something held her back.

"Why do you hesitate, dearest one?" The dark-haired man's voice was like the song of a dove.

Aye, why? she wondered, still looking into the cup. The lights from the bonfires around them shimmered in the liquid, begging her to tip the goblet and consume its contents.

She tilted the glass, but before she got a taste, someone knocked it out of her hand.

"Stop!" Niall roared, moving between her and the fairy. Anger rolled off him in waves. "Don' touch her. She's with me."

The music and dancing stopped at once, and all the fairies around them watched curiously.

Muireall cowered against Niall's back. Now that the music had ended, her good sense had returned, and she realized just how stupid she'd been. These fairies weren't docile. They were predators who'd very nearly made Muireall their prey.

She recalled what Vincent McLaren had told the children about fairy food and drink: *"If you so much as let a single drop pass yer lips, you'll be trapped in the Fairy Realm forever."*

Niall just saved me. A warm, inexplicable feeling built up in her chest.

"And who are you?" the dark-haired fairy demanded, his tone no longer soft and seductive. Now it rumbled with an unspoken threat.

The warmth Muireall had been feeling vanished in an instant. She glanced at the strangers surrounding them, her stomach folding in on itself. *How could Niall bring me to a place such as this? I should never have agreed to come.*

"I'm Niall, a leannan na mara," Niall replied.

The fairies whispered amongst each other as if this held great significance. Muireall recognized "leannan na mara" as Scots Gaelic, but in her slightly addled state, she couldn't recall its meaning.

"Callum's son?" boomed a new voice, emanating with power and fury.

Muireall trembled as she peeked out from behind her servant.

A figure she hadn't noticed before sat on a tall wooden throne, a sparkling crown atop his head. Flowers, vines, and thorns extended from his chair, draping over the man's arms like a blanket. His clothes were much the same as the other fairies', but where theirs bore bright splashes of color, his were a deep raven black. White hair cascaded beyond his shoulders, but no signs of age touched his surprisingly human face.

Except this was no human. Raw, untethered energy radiated off the strikingly handsome stranger, and a pair of silver wings hung from his shoulder blades.

"Aye, yer Highness," Niall replied.

Highness? Then that crown isn' just fer show. He's royalty—a prince perhaps. Sweat trickled down Muireall's brow. *And he knows Niall's father—this Callum?*

She glanced curiously at her companion. *Just how important are you?*

"Yer taller than the last time I saw you. And a leannan na mara now? I'm sure yer father is so disappointed." The fairy lord sneered, and Muireall felt Niall stiffen. "I seem to recall my father saying something about granting a request fer Callum recently. That couldn' have been anything to do with you?"

"That's na why I'm here right now," Niall hissed.

Muireall swatted the man's back. Whatever his personal feelings toward this fairy were, he couldn't let them ruin this opportunity. Muireall still needed the Fair Folk's help.

"Then what are you here fer?" the fairy asked, seemingly unaffected by the servant's rude behavior. "Na to bother my sister again, I imagine? After what happened last time, I would have thought you were smarter than that."

His sister?

"We've come to make a deal," Niall proclaimed, his voice belting across the field without fear.

Though it still seemed foolhardy for them to be here at all, a sense of calm swept over Muireall. If Niall wasn't afraid, maybe she didn't need to be either.

The fairy lord bridged his long fingers together, and the left side of his mouth twisted into a hungry half-smile. "A deal? What is it you wish fer?"

I should probably speak up since I'm the one who needs the help. She slowly stepped around Niall and came up on his right side, watching her companion anxiously.

Niall's eyebrows knitted, and he swiftly inclined his head for her to go back behind him. Muireall remembered then what he'd told her before they'd come: "Let me do the talking."

She gulped and did as he'd bidden, happy to let Niall take the lead here. To say she was out of her element was an understatement, and she was not so prideful as to allow herself to be killed.

"Great Prince Aodhàn, my mistress needs to rid herself o' the burden o' marriage, so she may inherit her parents' estate and conduct herself as she pleases."

"Ah, I see," the Prince replied, his tone vague.

What does that mean? Is he going to help me or na? Muireall subtly tugged at the back of Niall's shirt.

"And what reward would you have in exchange fer such a favor?" Niall asked, ignoring Muireall's touch.

The Prince rose from his seat in a single fluid motion. Niall bowed his head respectfully, and Muireall did the same. Fairies were easy to insult, and she didn't want to think about what sort of punishment fairy royalty might bestow.

"Three things you must obtain to achieve yer heart's desire, three treasures o' great price: a fiddle from the earth, a bridle from the waters, and a cloak from the rocks. Only with these in hand shall you receive yer due reward."

Muireall listened attentively to the fairy lord's words, but his riddles left her confused. *What sort o' . . .* She hoped Niall understood the Prince's terms, for she was too befuddled to know if they were even real things.

"Do you accept?" The Prince's eyes swam with avarice.

"Aye," Niall replied. He stepped away from Muireall and gave her a look.

"Aye," she hastily added, her voice barely above a whisper.

"We shall return here once we've collected them," Niall told the Prince.

The fairy wagged his finger. "Nay, you must return on the first night o' the next full moon, na a day sooner or later. Otherwise"—his eyes homed in on Muireall—"yer deal is forfeit."

"Agreed," she said.

Prince Aodhàn nodded and returned to his throne as if Niall and Muireall held no more interest to him. He gestured to the other Fair Folk. "Resume the festivities."

"Let's go," Niall whispered, taking Muireall's hand as the music started up again. He led her back to the fairy ring, but just before they entered it once more, she glanced over her shoulder. She committed the scene to memory, overcome with both awe and horror.

How close did I come to death tonight?

Before she could hazard a guess, Niall pulled them back into the ring, and the scene around them disappeared.

***

In an instant, they were back at the base of Mary's Hill. Niall shook his head a few times to get his bearings. It had been a while since he'd gone through the Veil, and it could be pretty disorienting. Mistress Oliver's hand trembled, making him remember he was still holding it. He turned to the laird's daughter and said, "Still think I'm the last person who could help you?"

Mistress Oliver's ashen face was concerning; their encounter with the Fair Folk seemed to have shaken her up quite a bit. She dropped Niall's hand and looked away. "What about the three treasures? Are those even things we can acquire in the time given?"

Niall's mouth turned up in a half-smile. "Aye, but 'twill be very dangerous. And will require some hunting to find. Do you have a map o' the area?"

The young woman grimaced but nodded. "I'll bring it to you in the morneen."

"Am I correct in assuming, then, that you agree to our deal?" Niall asked. He kept his expression neutral, but his voice betrayed his inner excitement. As a leannan na mara, he possessed no power of his own, making him human in all the ways that mattered. But his father had given him a final gift before sending him away, something that tipped the scales in Niall's favor.

"I went to King Daegan and convinced him to part with a bit o' magic," Callum had said. "Now, you can make one fairy deal with the person o' yer choice. Use it wisely."

Niall felt the magic's tug now, just beneath the surface of his skin. Unlike most magical folk, selkie bargains possessed no inherent power. A deal with one of them could be broken without harm to either party. But since Callum had gifted Niall a fairy deal, whomever Niall bound to it would be compelled to fulfill their end of the bargain.

Without exception.

Mistress Oliver crossed her arms and shot him a cold glare. "Aye, I do."

"Excellent. Now, as fer that favor, I'd like—"

She held up a hand. "I decide the terms, na you."

Niall narrowed his eyes but waited for her to continue.

"Only after we obtain all three treasures and exchange them fer the fairies' magic will I grant you yer favor. Understand?"

Niall bit back a growl. That would delay things, but he could work with it. *Now I suppose I really will have to help her with her search.* "Can I trust you'll keep yer word once you've gotten what you want?" he quipped.

Mistress Oliver's eyes flashed, and for a second, Niall almost thought lightning was about to rip open the sky. *She's na Briony, you idiot,* he reminded himself.

"You don' need to worry about that," she grumbled. "Whatever 'tis you wish fer, I promise to do all in my power to give it to you."

As soon as the words left her lips, magic sparked across Niall's veins, signifying the contract's binding.

Mistress Oliver turned to walk off but stumbled a bit, and Niall reached out to steady her. "I'm fine." She pushed his hands away, but her voice was weak. "Just fi—" Before she could finish, her eyelids closed, and her legs gave out.

Niall caught her as she fell, her head landing on his chest. The scent of lavender tickled his nose, so faint it was barely perceptible. When she didn't move, he put his fingers to her neck and felt her pulse. *Just asleep. After making a deal with Prince Aodhàn, making another one with me must have been more than her body could handle.*

He lifted the woman in his arms but paused as he glanced toward town. There was no way he had the strength to take her the whole distance. *And how am I going to get her inside without anyone noticing?*

I don' have to. He turned and headed east, straight to Drulea Cottage. He hoped his intuition would prove right and he wasn't making a terrible mistake. He knocked on the door.

"You better have a great reason fer waking me at this time o' night," Briony called as she opened the door. When her gaze landed on the unconscious woman in his arms, her eyes narrowed to slits. "What did you do?"

"I—"

"Come inside quickly." The midwife cut him off before he could explain. She motioned for him to follow her, then led him to a small bedroom. The bed was still made, so he could only assume this was her mother's former room.

Would Briony keep her sealskin in here? He didn't have time to ruminate on the passing thought, though, for she shooed him out of the room as soon as he'd put Mistress Oliver down.

Briony covered the redhead with blankets, then spun around with a scowl. "Now, tell me what happened, so I know what she needs."

"All she needs is rest. She probably spent more energy than she realized dancing—"

"Dancing? Why on earth would she be dancing in the middle o' the night?"

"Calm down, and let me speak." Niall tried to keep the irritation out of his tone. At this rate, the sky would start storming soon. "I took her to a fairy dance"—he ignored Briony's gasp—"and *nothing* bad happened. I made sure o' it. She simply tired herself out; that's all."

The midwife pressed her lips together, shaking with emotion. "That's all? *That's all?*" Lightning struck right outside the window, blinding Niall for a few seconds.

Briony took a deep breath before continuing. "You told me there were other beings out there, but you neglected"—her volume rose as she seemed to lose her battle to contain herself—"to tell me there were any in Everton. And are these ones to be respected or avoided?"

"Both, actually," Niall admitted.

The midwife growled before squeezing the bridge of her nose. "Niall, you are testing my patience."

Niall shrugged, unable to keep a tiny smile off his face.

"Don' act like this is funny!" She waved her finger in front of him. "If fairies are supposed to be avoided, why would you take Mistress Oliver to them?"

"Because she—"

Mistress Oliver groaned in her sleep. Briony and Niall's heads turned to her reflexively, but when it became clear she wasn't going to wake, the midwife indicated for Niall to finish his sentence.

He hesitated, then said, "That's Mistress Oliver's story to tell, should she choose to divulge it."

Briony's brow wrinkled. "'Tis surprisingly virtuous o' you to keep her secrets. Does that mean she's also aware o' yers?"

"I've put that life behind me, so there was no reason to bring it up."

"Yet 'tis that very life that put her in danger tonight."

Niall didn't respond to her accusation. *Tonight wasn' the real danger. What she'll have to face fer her deal with Prince Aodhàn is much worse.*

"Thank you fer taking care o' her."

He looked at the sleeping heiress once more. *Will she be able to handle it?*

". . . Niall."

"Hmm?" He turned to Briony, who was watching him curiously.

"I was just saying that you, o' all people, should know the past is never truly gone. And even if you've put it behind you as you claim, that doesn' mean she has."

"What does that have to do with anything?" he asked, his tone approaching acerbic.

Briony glared. "If Mistress Oliver finds out yer the one who killed her brother, do you honestly think she'll still want anything to do with you?"

A Witch and a Gardener

Sunlight roused Muireall from her strange dream. Most of its details were hazy, but she recalled something about stepping through the Veil into the Fairy Realm and dancing for hours before coming face to face with the Prince himself.

What was it he said? Three treasures o' great price . . . a fiddle, a bridle, and what was the third thing? Muireall pressed her fingers to her temple. Her pounding headache made her wish she could return to unconsciousness.

Mother and Father will want me to have an answer fer them, but I still haven' decided. If only that dream o' the Fair Folk had been real. She opened her eyes and stretched. *Then I could—*

Muireall's head swung from side to side in confusion. *This isn' my room. Where am I?*

Old, worn-out blankets covered her on the small, uncomfortable bed where she lay. Small was the word she would use to describe everything in this room—small and incredibly plain. A half-burned candle lay on a wooden table on the opposite side of the room, with a single chair beside it. The walls themselves bore no decoration other than a pair of faded green curtains that did little to block the sunlight streaming into the room.

She slowly pulled back the covers and rose to her feet, racking her brain for a memory of coming here. But all that flooded her mind was the peculiar dream of the Prince, the dance, and—

Muireall gasped. *Niall! Was it na a dream? Did we actually visit the Fair Folk last night and make a bargain with them?* She surveyed the room again. *But that doesn' explain where I am now. The last thing I remember is my head spinning. . . .*

The door opened. "Yer awake!" In walked a smiling Briony Fairborn with two cups of tea. "How are you feeling?"

Muireall took a step back from the midwife, her hands shaking. "Are we at yer house? How did I get here?" If this was the midwife's home, it was no wonder she didn't recognize her surroundings. Mother had made sure Muireall knew to stay away from the Fairborns from an early age, so Muireall had never been inside the midwife's modest home.

Briony nodded, a touch of sadness coming into her eyes. "Aye, this is my room. Niall brought you here last night after you passed out."

Then the dream I had was real. Fear shot through Muireall's body, but she tried not to let it show. "I see."

"Why don' you have a seat and drink this?" Briony held out the cup in her right hand.

Muireall accepted the tea and sat down on the bed while the midwife took the chair.

"Niall told me he took you to a fairy dance, and you fainted because you tired yerself out. Is that true?"

She was so surprised she slurped her tea in a manner most unladylike. "He told you?"

Briony chuckled a bit. "Aye, but he refused to share why you were there in the first place."

A tiny bubble of relief rose in Muireall's chest. *He didn' tell her about our deal, then.*

"Will *you* tell me?" the midwife pressed. There was an urgency in the woman's tone that raised Muireall's defenses.

"'Tis none o' yer concern."

Briony rolled her eyes. "Mistress Oliver, I'm only trying to help you. I don' want you getting involved in things you can' handle. And fairies are undoubtedly beyond yer capabilities."

How can she say that so calmly? As if talking about fairies is completely ordinary. Are the rumors about the Fairborns really true? Muireall had never put much stock in the dark tales surrounding Briony's family. Many villagers thought they were secretly witches, but the Fairborns' skills at midwifery had always made them too valuable to dismiss. For all its faults, Everton was a village that—at its heart—loved its children more than it feared sorcery.

A witch wouldn' have any trouble believing in the existence o' fairies. She might even have regular dealings with them.

She stared down at her teacup. *Could she have tainted this somehow? What if my memories o' last night are just the result o' a spell she placed on me?*

"Don' worry; I didn' poison it," Briony said cheerily.

Muireall's gaze snapped to the midwife, who was watching her with a bitter smile.

"I don' know what you mean." She took a quick sip to demonstrate that she hadn't been considering that very thing.

Briony raised her eyebrows, clearly not fooled. "I know what our neighbors say about me behind my back. That I'm a witch? Yer mother and father are bold enough to say it to my face." She took a sip of her drink and sighed.

"Fer yer own peace o' mind, rest assured that I'm na what they think I am." Her gaze zoomed to Muireall's, her golden eyes piercing. "But that doesn' mean I'm na dangerous."

The laird's daughter tried not to flinch. *If she's na a witch, why would she be dangerous?* She scrutinized the woman before her. Pretty, aloof, disliked by most, and quick-tempered— Briony and Muireall shared more traits than she cared to admit.

But we also differ in two very important ways. The first is that my birthright forces the townsfolk to tolerate me, whereas her illegitimacy guarantees she will never be fully accepted. The second is . . . she's brave enough to speak her mind, regardless o' the consequences.

As much as Muireall didn't want to acknowledge it, she actually admired the young midwife for saying the things she really believed. And she'd noticed that ever since Briony had taken up Dr. Sherwin's work, she'd been even more prone to do so than before. *What would it be like na to be tied down by crippling expectations?*

"If yer trying to frighten me, Briony, you'll need to do better than that."

"Oh, I know. You grew up in a world where you were taught everyone was beneath you, so why should you be afraid?" The midwife rose to her feet. "I only said it to make you aware. And while *I* may na frighten you, I'm sure last night's experience was quite jarring. Now you know the world yer parents showed you is only a fraction o' what's out there. The real world is full o' dangers. . . ." Her gaze left Muireall's for a moment, as though as she was remembering something. She lifted her eyes back to the laird's daughter, pinning her down with an earnest look. "Should you need an ally at any point, know you can come to me."

She's . . . offering me protection? Muireall blinked a few times. *Just who are you, Briony Fairborn, that you think you can protect me from magic?*

Muireall lifted her chin, defying the dread trying to slither into her bones. "Thank you, but that won' be necessary."

The midwife slowly nodded, pity shining in her eyes. As though she knew far more than Muireall did. And had seen far more than a woman of her age should have. "I'm baking some bread. Yer welcome to have some once 'tis ready." She turned to leave.

"Nay, that's all right. My parents must be wondering where I am. What time is it?" Muireall asked. *When they find out I stayed out all night, they're going to be so upset. They may na let me leave home fer a while either. If that happens, how will I gather the treasures the Fairy Prince spoke o'?*

The midwife glanced over her shoulder. "'Tis nine o' clock, but you needn' worry about yer parents. When Niall brought you here last night, I asked him to go to them first thing this morneen and let them know you were here because o' a headache"—

Muireall sucked in a sharp breath. That answer wouldn't be enough to keep her out of trouble. Mother would still demand to know why she'd been out so late in the first place.

—"and I told him to say you left just as the sun was rising, so they won' know you stayed out last night."

Her nerves relaxed even as her forehead wrinkled in confusion. *Why is she helping me so much? Is she trying to gain my favor, or is there some other reason behind all this?*

She bristled when Briony's mouth stretched into an arrogant smirk. *She thinks she has this all figured out, does she?*

She gestured down to her dress. "What about my clothes? Won' it be obvious that Niall lied once they see I'm wearing the same dress from yesterday?"

Briony's smile remained. "If you managed to get out o' Rigmore House without being noticed, I'm sure you can get back in."

Muireall huffed as she broke eye contact. She didn't like losing a verbal spar, but it wasn't worth continuing to argue at this point. Her thoughts turned to how she might successfully sneak back into her room. *If I went in through the back, could I get upstairs unseen?*

"Oh, and Mistress Oliver?" Muireall looked up at her hostess. "Don' be so ungrateful. Niall and I didn' have to help you at all, you know."

Without waiting for a response, the midwife marched out, leaving Muireall alone with her thoughts.

***

Niall tried to ignore the worry pressing against his shoulders as he washed the hall floor. Gilbert mopped close by, his strokes smoother and more precise than Niall's.

Not that Niall cared about having good form right now. Ever since he'd left Mistress Oliver last night, the laird's daughter had been all he could think about. *Will she change her mind about our deal once she wakes up? What if there's something wrong with her beyond what I thought? What if the fairies injured her in some way without me realizing?*

Niall caught Gilbert staring at him from the corner of his eye. "What?" he snarled. This was the fourth time he'd noticed Gilbert watching him. At first, Niall had thought he was imagining it, but now he was just getting annoyed.

Gilbert flinched and looked away. "N-Nothing."

Niall softened his expression and tried again. "Gilbert? I can tell something is amiss. What is it?"

The other servant sighed. "Hamish threatened to have my head if I let you out o' my sight again."

"Really? Does he have that kind o' power?"

Gilbert frowned. "What are you—oh, was that meant to be funny? He probably just means he'll make sure I can no longer stay here. I work hard at this job, though, and I'm na keen on leaving it, so I'm going to do all I can to make sure that doesn' happen." He grinned and punched Niall's arm. "And yer going to help me, right?"

"O' course." The lie rolled off Niall's tongue with ease. "I'd hate to cause yer dismissal."

Soon after they'd finished the hallway floor and had started cleaning the foyer, they received word that Niall was needed. What made it even more fun, though, was that Hamish was the messenger.

"Mistress Oliver has requested yer presence in the garden," the butler said, his body rigid and professional.

Oh, good, she's all right, Niall thought, holding back a sigh of relief. A cruel sneer came over his face. "Looks like she needs my help, after all, hmm?"

Hamish said nothing, but his jaw clenched tighter.

Gilbert mumbled to Niall, "Stop baiting him. He'll find a way to get you back."

Niall coughed to cover up a laugh. He was sure the veins in the butler's neck didn't normally look like that. *How much o' a push would it take to send him into a rage?*

"Thank you so much fer informing me, Hamish. I guess Gilbert doesn' need to keep an eye on me this time."

The butler's lip curled back like he wanted to say something unpleasant, but all he said was, "Report to the garden immediately."

Niall winked at Gilbert, then sauntered out of the foyer and made his way to the garden. When he reached the fountain, there stood the beautiful redhead, a piece of parchment in her hand.

"I'm glad to see yer looking well," Niall remarked. "After you passed out last night, I wondered if the fairies had done something to you without my noticing."

Mistress Oliver threw a finger over her lips. "Shh!" She glanced around, and only when she was satisfied that they were alone, she whispered, "You can' be so careless with yer words. Someone might overhear us."

He shrugged, but he knew she was right. This mission was much too important to jeopardize over mere foolishness. "Is that the map?"

Mistress Oliver unrolled the parchment and held it out. "This is Everton." She pointed to a group of buildings in the bottom-right corner. "It starts down here at Rigmore House"—she moved her finger over several houses scattered along the village's winding roads, then stopped at a green area in the top-left section—"and ends here, at Mary's Hill."

Niall studied the drawings with interest. "Where does this lead?" He pointed at the spot where the road disappeared off the edge of the map.

The young woman frowned. "That goes to Hollandstoun. It says so right—" She broke off with a grimace. "Oh, I wasn' thinking. Can you read?"

Niall didn't appreciate the pity shining in her eyes. He said curtly, "Does it matter?"

Mistress Oliver bit her lip. "I suppose na."

Niall stepped away from her. "Shall we get started, then? I have a few ideas fer where we might find a banshee."

Mistress Oliver shook her head. "I can' be seen wandering around the village with a servant. What will people say?"

Niall rolled his eyes. *So many rules.* "Then how do you propose we find what you need?"

"I think you should check out the areas where we think the items are on yer own first, then—"

"These aren' just trinkets, you know. The creatures guarding them won' give them up easily. I may na be able to get them by myself." This was true enough. It would be helpful to have a partner, especially when it came to dealing with a banshee. The fairy woman's cries could be deafening, so he had a better chance of success if he wasn't working alone. "Besides, why should I risk my life on something yer unwilling to risk yers fer?"

"'Tis na that I'm unwilling," she argued. "'Tis just that there's no way my parents would let me spend time alone with a man, much less a servant. I'm taking a big chance even talking to you right now."

"Well, then, I guess this arrangement isn' going to work." Niall turned to leave.

"Wait!"

He stopped and spun around. "Aye, Princess?"

"What if . . ." The woman's brow furrowed. "What if I gave you a position that would make it easier to be alone together? We would still have to be cautious, but as long as we didn' meet up too often, I don' think anyone would suspect anything inappropriate was going on."

"And what position would that be?"

Mistress Oliver hesitated, her gaze trailing away from his as if she didn't want to tell him. "How would you like to be responsible fer all this?" She gestured to the flowers around them.

"The gardener?" He snorted in disgust. "I don' know the first thing about taking care o' plants."

Her face darkened. "There's nothing wrong with gardening. 'Tis a wonderful thing, tending to something to help it flourish."

"Hmm . . ." Niall glanced at the flowers. "I do admit 'tis a beautiful place. Who normally takes care o' it?"

"I do."

"What? But I thought a servant—"

"Aye, and that's what I want everyone to keep thinking," Mistress Oliver said. "Bernard Buchanan mostly just walked the grounds to make it look like he was taking care o' everything. I'm the one who chose where to put the plants, made sure they were getting enough water and sunlight, and trimmed them back when they got out o' hand."

Niall pursed his lips. He could appreciate the subterfuge, but he failed to understand the purpose behind it. *What kind o' princess would choose to work in the dirt?*

He thought back to a run-in he'd had with an actual princess several years ago. While she'd been a fairy, he couldn't help but note the many similarities between her and his new mistress. Each had a grossly exaggerated sense of self-importance, and while they didn't look anything alike, both were exceptionally beautiful.

But Princess Aoife would have dropped dead before getting her hands dirty.

"So, yer just going to give his position to me? Mistress Oliver, have you no compassion?" He put his hand over his chest dramatically.

She crossed her arms. "Mr. Buchanan left Rigmore House a few days ago, so I'm na hurting him in the slightest." She said the words nonchalantly, but her voice held a slight tremor that made Niall wonder if the man's departure had been more significant than she wanted him to believe.

Niall considered the offer again. "Family gardener, huh? I suppose I could make that work since 'tis mostly just fer appearances."

Mistress Oliver's shoulders fell. "Unfortunately, that won' be the case. Now that I have two suitors to visit, I fear I won' have nearly as much time to spend out here. You'll have to carry most o' the load."

Niall's gut churned with annoyance. It would have been nice to have a job that didn't require much work. Before he could voice his thoughts, though, the young woman bent down and touched a nearby flower, her expression full of regret.

His own feelings dimmed in importance, and before he knew what he was doing, he said, "That will only be fer a short while though."

She jerked her head back, waiting for him to continue.

"Once we collect all the items we need and give them to the Prince, you won' have to worry about yer parents trying to make you marry anymore. You'll be free."

Hope flared in her eyes, but it quickly vanished behind a veil of skepticism. "Yer certain the Fair Folk are powerful enough to change my fate?"

"Aye, I have no doubt o' that."

Mistress Oliver's cheeks lifted into a grateful smile that sent warmth skittering through Niall's chest.

He cleared his throat and held out his hand. "Leave the map here with me, and I'll figure out the best places to look. If you come back in the morneen, we can start our search fer the treasures then."

She nodded and handed over the parchment. Niall tucked the map into his clothes and waited for her to leave, but when she didn't, he said, "Don' you have suitors to meet?"

Mistress Oliver placed her hands on her hips. "Aye, but if I'm going to be leaving the garden in yer care, I need to make sure yer na going to kill all my plants as soon as I'm na around. Wait a moment." She marched off, only to reappear a few minutes later with a shovel in hand. "Are you ready fer yer first lesson?"

Niall frowned as he took the shovel. "Why do I need this? The garden is finished."

Her green eyes twinkled. "Oh, Niall. Don' you know? A garden is never finished."

A Puzzle Most Vexing

Muireall spent the next few hours teaching her servant all she could think of to keep her flowers in the best condition possible. She showed him how to tell when a plant needed more sunshine, rain, or room to grow. Which plants could be used for healing and which ones were poisonous. The ones that needed the most care and the ones that flourished with hardly any attention at all. Niall was a fast learner, and it was nice to talk about something she loved with a person who listened attentively for once; she'd tried discussing plants with her mother and father, but they had always shut down the conversation before she'd gotten more than a few sentences out.

"And these are my favorite," she said when they reached a rosebush on the far side of the garden.

"White?" The man's tone was light but curious.

Muireall spun around with a grin. "What?" She raised her eyebrows. "Did you think I'd prefer red simply because o' my hair?"

Niall didn't answer, instead stepping up to the roses to examine them more closely. "They are beautiful," he said quietly. "I should probably get those." He pointed to a few flowers that had wilted.

When the young woman nodded, Niall pulled at the dead petals, then yelped in surprise.

"Oh, I forgot to warn you about the thorns," Muireall exclaimed, taking the man's hand. His skin was warm to the touch and smooth as silk. Much smoother than she'd expected for a commoner with a livelihood built on toil. A pinprick of blood had welled up on his index finger, so she pulled out her handkerchief.

As she dabbed at the wound, her eyes landed on a thin pink line peeking out from under the man's sleeve. Muireall seized the cloth and drew it back so quickly neither she nor Niall realized what she was doing. But at the sight of what lay beneath, the young woman gasped in horror: jagged scratch marks stretched across the man's wrist in all directions, weaving over and under each other like scarlet threads. Some were light enough that they hadn't broken the skin while others went much deeper. Several had scabbed over, but a few looked fresh.

"How did you come by these?" Muireall whispered, one hand gingerly clutching the servant's wrist while the other held his sleeve back. Compassion flooded through her as she lifted her gaze.

Niall's dark eyes bored into hers, much closer than she'd expected. But oddly enough, the proximity didn't bother her. In fact, it was just the opposite, and Muireall had the strangest inclination to lean closer.

"I . . ." Indecision flickered in the man's expression. He tore his eyes away and stepped back. "'Twas nothing. Just an accident." His voice was low, vulnerable, and—if Muireall wasn't mistaken—ashamed.

She moved toward him, overcome by both intrigue and the urge to comfort him. She didn't know what reason he had to be ashamed, but she was well-versed in the feeling.

And bearing it alone made it so much worse.

A branch snapped nearby, and the two of them whirled toward the sound. Movement caught Muireall's eye, but it was gone before she could identify it. *Probably just an animal.*

She turned back to Niall, eyes widening as she became cognizant of how inappropriate this was. "I better get going before my parents come looking fer me," she said, then hastily retreated to the house.

It wasn't that far from the truth. Father's insistence on punctuality bordered on ridiculous at times, so it truly was in her best interest not to delay going to lunch.

Her steps were light as she sashayed down the hall. She had a plan now; life wasn't as out of control as she'd thought. Granted, that plan involved several challenges she'd never come across before, but she was confident she would rise to the occasion and overcome them.

The only thing that wasn't sitting well with her was Niall himself. The man was a puzzle, and the more she got to know him, the less she understood her bizarre servant. On one hand, he was incredibly vexing, disrespecting her at every turn. On the other hand, he'd also offered to help her with what had seemed an impossible dilemma, all in exchange for just one small favor.

Why would he want a favor from me when he could have made a deal with the Fair Folk anytime? They're much more powerful than I am.

And how does he know so much about them? The man seemed more knowledgeable about magical beings than anyone she'd ever encountered—even the mad fisherman. Muireall recalled the strange title he'd given the fairy lord when asked who he was. *Leannan na mara. Lover o' the sea. I wonder what that means. . . .*

Her stomach quivered. *Is that why Niall said that about humans when I upset him the other day? Because he isn' one?*

When Muireall entered the dining room, her parents were waiting for her with fairly pleasant expressions, though Laura's lip seemed on the brink of curling.

Still unhappy I haven' made a decision yet, I see. Normally, that would have stressed Muireall, but she pushed her anxiety away and reminded herself that as soon as the Fair Folk fulfilled their end of the bargain, her mother would see things her way for once.

The meal passed quickly; the family made their usual small talk, falling into patterns that were so familiar Muireall almost forgot about suitors, fairies, and favors.

I should very much like to go practice on my clàrsach. She hadn't had much time alone in the past few days, and her fingers itched to strum the instrument again. She dabbled in songwriting and had recently composed a rather beautiful song in honor of her brother. Nearly one, anyway. The ending was still missing something.

"... I'm sure he'll be delighted to get to know you better," Mother said, her eyes twinkling.

"What?" Muireall turned to Laura in alarm. "Whom are we discussing?"

Laura released a throaty laugh and patted her daughter's hand. "No need to look so frightened." Her eyes hardened. "But do pay better attention. I was just saying you should go visit Viscount Mendes at the tavern once we're finished, and invite him fer dinner next Saturday. He can' be enjoying his time there, what with all the commoners around and"—her nose wrinkled at the female servant pouring more tea into Laird Oliver's cup—"having to serve them. I don' understand why he would do such a preposterous thing. Truly, you better get down there as quickly as possible, so you can talk him out o' this madness. Why on earth would a viscount choose to work at a tavern? Or want to be with someone like Briony Fairborn?"

Muireall's gaze flicked to the servant, whose polite expression seemed a little more forced than before. She didn't know the young woman's name, had never believed it mattered before this moment, but now she studied her with curiosity. *How do you really feel when Mother talks about you like that?*

Discomfort squeezed her shoulders, and she shoved the question away. *Perhaps I've been spending too much time with Niall.*

"Now, now, Laura, do remember 'tis his very madness that has given us this opportunity." Father took a sip of tea. "If he wasn' insisting on staying here to be with the Fairborn wench, Muireall wouldn' have the chance to convince him o' his folly and win him over."

Mother eyed him with distaste. "Indeed." She turned to Muireall. "Daughter, you must do all you can to show him how silly this is. He's a nobleman. And if he's going to be yer husband, he needs to act like one."

But he's na, Muireall wanted to say. *Why bother him when I already know that?*

The look in Lady Oliver's eyes left no room for dispute though.

The young woman nodded her consent. "I shall take my leave, then." She rose from her seat, giving the servant one last glance before gliding out of the room.

"Before you go, make sure Anne freshens yer makeup," Laura called after her.

"O' course, Mother," she said over her shoulder.

***

Muireall reluctantly made her way to the tavern. She didn't usually go there; according to her mother, it wasn't a suitable place for a lady, but she supposed that rule no longer mattered now that Mr. Mendes owned it.

She didn't enjoy gossip, but since her parents were so set on her marrying the young viscount, she'd asked her maid what she knew about him before she'd left. According to Anne, Mr. Mendes had originally wanted to buy Vincent McLaren's fishing boat, but Tam, Vincent McLaren's brother, hadn't approved. Muireall's father, in one of his wiser moods, had suggested for Mr. Mendes to purchase Tam's tavern and Tam to take up his deceased brother's fishing business instead.

Mr. Mendes wasn't nearly as fast as Tam when it came to getting people their drinks, but he was such a charming fellow that most people were being gracious so far. Aside from Philip McGuff, who had given Mr. Mendes all manner of insults for serving him the wrong drink the other day. Tam would have thrown the old fool out, but Mr. Mendes had smoothly handled the situation with a drink on the house and the promise of a second one the next time the man came in.

It was about one o' clock when Muireall arrived. A few villagers were inside—Angus Dunnet, St. John Peterson, Gregor Martin—but the place wasn't overly crowded. Muireall ignored the shocked expressions on her neighbors' faces as she entered and walked straight to the counter where Mr. Mendes was pouring a drink.

The man was exceedingly handsome with his neatly trimmed beard and light-green eyes. His most attractive feature, though, had to be the smile on his face. Muireall had yet to see Mr. Levins smile around her, and since he'd made his feelings toward her very clear the other night, she doubted she ever would. This Mr. Mendes, on the other hand, seemed much more at ease.

When the young man noticed her, he turned his smile in her direction. "Good afternoon, senhorita[22]. I'll be with you in just a moment."

Muireall nodded and sat down in the nearest chair as he took the drink in his hand over to St. John.

"What would you like today?" Mr. Mendes asked once he returned.

"An ale, please."

"Of course." The man grabbed a glass and carefully poured her a drink.

Beyond his good looks, he seems so ordinary. Is he truly a nobleman? "Sir, I've just learned the most surprising information about you," she said slowly. "It seems yer a viscount?"

The man flushed. "Ah, did Laird Oliver tell you? I wasn't expecting him to share that. In fact, if you could keep it to yourself, I'd be much obliged."

Muireall frowned. "Whatever fer?"

"I enjoy the friendliness of the common folk here." He lifted his eyes to the tavern's patrons with a soft sigh. "I wouldn't want them to put on airs simply because they find out I'm not one of them. It's hard enough being a foreigner in your midst."

Someone asked for a refill, so Mr. Mendes hurried off. Muireall watched him go, bewildered by his strange behavior. As he interacted with Mr. Dunnet, though, a touch of envy stirred within her. *Is it truly that easy to get along with other people? If the rest o' Everton didn' know I was a noblewoman, would they treat me with the same warmth?*

Almost as soon as the thought appeared, though, she threw it out. *I'm na nearly as likable as Mr. Mendes. Nor do I wish to be.*

The gentleman returned after a few minutes to ask if there was anything else she needed.

---

[22] Portuguese title for an unmarried woman.

Muireall took a deep breath. *I suppose I'll just be direct about my reason fer being here. Na much point in skirting around the issue, especially considering it won' matter anymore in a few weeks.* "Since yer a viscount, my parents are determined that the two o' us wed."

Mr. Mendes's eyes widened, but he hid his surprise behind a thin smile. "Oh, are they? I thought I told Laird Oliver I intend to propose to Mistress Fairborn in the near future. Did I not?"

"You did, but until that's formally announced, my parents aren' giving up on the idea o' making their daughter a viscountess."

"You don't sound like you approve."

She grabbed her glass. "I'm na ready to marry anyone right now, much less a man who's in love with someone else."

He nodded in understanding. "And do your parents know this?"

"Na everyone has the freedom to express their desires openly," she admitted, a hint of sadness coming into her voice.

"Then would you like me to tell them for you?"

Muireall shook her head. "I appreciate the offer, but I doubt 'twould do much good. My parents would simply continue to press me to change yer mind. But I have plans o' my own, so I'm na worried."

"O' course."

The discerning look in Mr. Mendes's eyes was unnerving, so she quickly swallowed some ale. *If only I was as confident as I pretend to be. All my hope depends on being able to get things from creatures that shouldn' even exist.*

And what if Niall and I can' even find them in time?

The door creaked open.

"What, may I ask, are you . . ." Mr. Mendes looked over her shoulder. "Excuse me." He walked off.

Muireall leaned back to see who'd taken his attention away. She scowled. *Briony Fairborn. I should have known.*

She watched the two of them talk. Mr. Mendes's smile was wider than before, and Briony laughed—actually laughed—at what the man was saying. The love between them couldn't have been more evident.

Muireall lowered her eyes to her glass. *What am I doing here? This was a mistake.* She reached for her cup and took another sip before standing up. She placed some money on the counter and turned to leave.

"Mistress Oliver? What brings you to the tavern?" Briony asked, thwarting her attempt to skirt by the happy couple.

She winced before looking over with a tight grin. "Briony, hello." She hadn't wanted to run into the midwife again so soon. After their conversation this morning, Muireall wasn't sure what to think of the strange woman who lived not only on the outskirts of the village but also mostly on the outskirts of her notice. Briony Fairborn had always been a bit of a mystery, but her reputation had kept Muireall from ever getting too close. Until now.

"I came fer a drink," she lied. There was no way she was going to tell the midwife the true purpose of her visit. Briony would surely rescind her offer of protection if she shared that little tidbit.

Muireall nodded to Mr. Mendes. "Thank you."

As she tried to scoot out the door again, another person entered the tavern, and it was all Muireall could do to stop herself from walking straight into him.

"Mistress Oliver. How . . . unexpected," breathed a voice in her ear.

She shivered as she tilted her face up, suddenly cold all over. "Mr. Levins."

The tacksman's body language was relaxed, but she knew better than to let her guard down. "I heard recently that Laird and Lady Oliver aren' as supportive o' a union between us. Something about better opportunities elsewhere?"

Before she could answer, his eyes trailed from hers to Mr. Mendes. "I must say, you don' look much like a nobleman."

Muireall spun around, her gaze shooting between Mr. Mendes and Briony. The first kept his face fairly neutral, though the slight twitch of his lips suggested he didn't care for Matthew's tone. The midwife's expression, though, snapped from puzzlement to angry understanding in the space of two seconds. She turned to Muireall.

"Now, Briony, wait." Muireall raised her hands defensively. "'Tis na what you think."

"Then that's na why you came here?" The bite in the midwife's words was unmistakable.

"I . . . I only came to talk. I actually . . ." Muireall's cheeks heated. Normally, she wouldn't care if Briony was upset with her, but not knowing what this woman was capable of made her want to err on the side of caution.

She looked helplessly from Mr. Mendes to Mr. Levins, the only two men her parents deemed acceptable suitors.

Neither of whom she wanted.

What can I say? I can' publicly announce that I don' intend to marry either o' them. Briony may be able to keep a secret, but Mr. Levins has no reason to. If he discovers the truth, he'll make sure word gets back to my parents. Once that happens, they'll choose my husband fer me and will watch me so closely I won' have time to slip away and find the three treasures.

Sweat beaded at the back of Muireall's neck as she scanned the room. Everyone had stopped talking and now stared at them with open interest. "I actually have been wanting to talk to you, Mr. Levins."

Matthew's brown eyes narrowed, but he said nothing. Briony and Mr. Mendes also looked suspicious, but they, too, waited for her to continue.

Muireall lifted her lips into a smile. "And now that I've found you, 'twould be my honor to invite you to Rigmore House fer dinner next Saturday."

An Irresistible Challenge

The following day, Muireall skipped down to the garden as soon as breakfast was finished. After hearing about Niall's extensive gardening experience—courtesy of a convincing lie—Muireall's parents had easily agreed to give Niall the vacant position, so now there would be no questions asked if she and her servant were seen alone together.

At least, that was what she hoped.

The young woman hadn't told her parents that Mr. Levins, rather than Viscount Mendes, would be Saturday's dinner guest, but that was for the best. Mother wouldn't be happy about the surprise, but good manners would keep her from turning the gentleman away. Muireall would simply tell Mother afterward that Mr. Mendes had been busy, so she had asked Matthew to come instead.

Eventually, Mother would demand the viscount join them for a meal, but Muireall would figure that problem out later. For right now, she needed to focus all her wits on her most pressing dilemma: obtaining the three items for the Fairy Prince.

When Niall heard her approach, he whirled around with her map in his hand and a brilliant smile on his face. "Mistress Oliver, you'll be glad to know I've found two likely spots fer our search."

Muireall's expression was pensive. "That's wonderful, but first, how are my plants this morneen?" She scanned the area, pleased to see everything looking just as good as it had the day before. *Except—*

She pointed to a small plant nestled in the dirt. "What's this?" She kept very good track of all the flowers in the garden, and this one had definitely not been there yesterday.

"Oh, that." Niall rubbed the map against his leg. "You mentioned that you didn' know what to put there, and I thought a few wildflowers might be nice. Gilbert said these will be a pretty purple, and you didn' have any purple ones."

"Ah, 'tis probably Scottish primrose, then." She squatted down and examined the plant. A few buds had sprouted, but it was too early to tell what color they'd turn. She stood back up with a grin. "Thank you fer thinking o' me."

The man's eyes crinkled up at the corners for the briefest second before he cleared his throat and gestured to a spot on the map. "I'd like to go to Loch Isla to hunt fer the kelpie. One o' the other servants said a few bairns went missing near there several years ago, and kelpies are known fer stealing bairns." He moved his finger to one of the islets off Everton's shore. "And banshees prefer desolate areas when they aren' giving their grim omens. An islet like this would be the perfect place to find one."

"What about the trow?"

He scratched the back of his neck. "That's the one I'm struggling with. Trows usually like caves, but from what I've heard, there aren' any caves in Everton. We may na be able to find one around here."

Muireall peered at the map, letting her mind wander until it snagged on something relevant. "Wait . . . I remember a story Mr. McLaren used to tell us about trows visiting the well up near Drulea Cottage." She pointed to a spot near the edge of Torin Woods. "Do you think there's any truth to it?"

"Only one way to find out. Let's go there first." The man's grin returned, and a shot of pleasure went through her. *He should smile like that more often. 'Tis much nicer than the annoying smirks he normally gives me.*

Muireall grabbed hold of her errant thoughts, her lips turning down into a frown. "Shouldn' we make a plan first?"

Niall made a dismissive motion. "I know what I'm doing. We'll be fine."

"But what about—"

"I took care o' you at the fairy dance, didn' I?"

She peered into her servant's black eyes, his words at the dance coming back to her: *"Stay with me, and you'll be safe. Please."*

"Aye . . . I suppose you did," she whispered. The smile tugging at her mouth smoothed out as they began walking again. "But you didn' warn me how exhausted I'd be afterward. If I'd known that, I wouldn' have danced fer so long."

He raised his eyebrows but didn't challenge her words. Both of them well knew Muireall hadn't been herself that night and that she'd been so entranced by the fairies' illusions that she wouldn't have listened to him, anyway.

As the two of them made their way through town, Muireall tried to mentally prepare herself for what they were about to do. She knew little of trows except that they were small, ugly creatures who came out at night and weren't overly fond of humans.

Niall didn't seem concerned, but she doubted he would tell her even if he was. *He did fine with the fairies. Maybe being a leannan na mara gives him a certain level o' protection? The Fairy Prince knew exactly who Niall's father was.*

She studied her companion more closely. Now that she thought about it, he was as handsome as one of the Fair Folk, yet they'd clearly identified him as something "other" than them. *I should have asked Briony when I was with her. Maybe she would have told me.*

She chewed on her lip. *Or perhaps I should stop speculating about it and just ask the source himself.* "So, Niall, are you going to tell me what a leannan na mara is?"

The man stiffened for the slightest instance before he looked over at her. "Ah, I was wondering if you would ask me. After everything that happened at the fairy dance, I thought you might have forgotten that wee detail."

When Muireall's eyes narrowed in impatience, he continued, "It simply means lover o' the sea. I am but a shadow o' a memory, one amongst countless lovers the sea has rejected."

What does that mean? She opened her mouth to ask but stopped when Niall cast a glance toward the ocean, just visible between the buildings.

The grief on his face was all too real—and all too similar to her own. *He looks at the sea as if he were looking at a family member's grave. Could he have loved the ocean like I loved my brother?*

Of its own accord, Muireall's hand reached out and touched his wrist. "I'm sorry."

Niall lurched away from her so quickly it was as if she'd burned him. He clasped his hands behind his back, not meeting her eye.

She slowly closed her fingers, unsure what had made him react so viscerally to what had only been an attempt to give comfort.

"Thank you, but there's no need fer sympathy," he said. "I'm fine. Shall we continue?"

Muireall followed Niall's lead as they passed the church, the inn, and finally, the McGuffs' cottage. That was the last building they would pass, and soon, they would be at Torin Woods.

She wrung her hands, wishing she could ask for more details about the man's past but not wanting to cause him further pain.

As the forest came into view, though, other questions flooded Muireall's mind, and the strange emotion simmering in her chest fizzled out before she could identify it. "What are we going to do if we find a trow? How will we get its fiddle? We won' have to fight it, will we?" If there was one thing Muireall hated, it was walking into something blind.

"Trows don' socialize much with other magical folk, but they're fairly reasonable, so I doubt 'twill come to a fight. However, they love music above all else, so they won' part with one o' their beloved instruments easily. Like many magical beings, they're very proud o' their own abilities though. If I challenge one to a battle o' musical skill, I've no doubt they'll agree."

"But you don' have an instrument," Muireall pointed out.

"Or do I?" Niall winked. "Now, which way do we go from here?" His head rotated from left to right. Drulea Cottage sat at the end of the path in the distance, but the well wasn't visible from the road.

She took the lead, stepping into the shade of the trees with new eyes. No longer was the forest just the home of simple creatures, like voles, hedgehogs, and hares; now it was also the home of magic. Anything could be lurking just out of view.

Before long, the small well appeared, but Muireall was tentative as she approached. It seemed deserted, but that didn't mean anything. Not when dealing with creatures that could disappear and reappear at will.

Niall came up beside her and scanned the area, presumably for holes where a trow could hide away. They were just barely past the tree line, meaning anyone passing by on the road would hear their footfalls. Muireall worried that Briony might notice them out here. If someone else saw them, she could claim they were just searching for plants, but she doubted the midwife would believe that.

After a few minutes, Niall exclaimed, "Here!"

Muireall hurried over to where he stood beside a small, unassuming knoll.

"Truly?" she asked, making no effort to hide her doubts. "But where's the entrance?"

Niall raised his finger in the air. "Ah, and that's yer first problem. Why would a trow make his home visible to human eyes?" He turned from her and squatted down. "Madainn mhath, a charaid. Tha sinn an seo gus iarraidh air luchd-èisteachd còmhla riut co-dhùnadh a bheil do chomas ciùil cho math 's a chanas daoine.[23]"

Muireall understood the words, though she frowned at Niall's use of the word "friend." *Does he know the trow who lives here?*

A strange shimmering passed over the knoll, blinding Muireall for a few seconds. When she could see again, a small door stood at the knoll's base. The door opened and out came a short, ugly creature with bulbous gray skin and stringy white hair. It appeared male, based on the green tunic and pants it wore, but Muireall couldn't be sure. She was more focused on

---

[23] Good morning, my friend. We are here to ask an audience with you to decide if your musical ability is as good as people say.

its eyes, which were undoubtedly its most unsettling feature. Unlike those of a human, there was no white surrounding the irises. Instead, they were almost entirely red with only pinpricks for pupils. Like a raven's.

When the trow spotted his unexpected guests, he drew back in terror and shrieked, "Boireannach daonna agus leannan na mara? Chan urrainn dhut a bhith an seo! Cò am fear agaibh a bha gòrach gu leòr airson mo ghairm?[24]"

"That would be me," Niall replied in Scots English, stepping in front of Muireall and placing a hand over his heart. His voice was calm and soft, almost melodious.

The trow's beady eyes narrowed, but he didn't retreat back into his home. He clenched his small fists and said, "Just who are you that you think you can come to my home without an invitation?"

"I'm no one. Merely a traveler who heard a trow lived here. I simply wanted to test my skills against yers."

"And her?"

"She's my . . ." Niall peered over his shoulder, his searching gaze making Muireall's stomach tense.

Why are you looking at me? You told me you knew what you were doing!

" . . . beloved," he finished, his head swiveling back around.

Muireall watched Niall carefully, her cheeks a blazing red. *Are you mad?! I understand the value o' anonymity, but no one in their right mind would mistake us fer a couple. I don' even find you attractive—*

Niall flashed her a smile that seemed to say, *Don' worry. This will turn out fine.*

Muireall's heart skipped a beat, then she groaned inwardly. *All right, I suppose he's attractive when he isn' vexing me. Na that that matters.*

"Yer beloved, eh?" The trow crossed his arms.

"She just came along to see if you can best me," Niall added.

---

[24] A human woman and a leannan na mara? You can't be here! Which one of you was stupid enough to call me?

The creature snorted in disbelief. "Do you take me fer a fool?" He sniffed the air, then glared. "No human has disturbed me in almost ten years. Vincent made sure o' it. That means you can only be the leannan na mara I heard about." He leaned around Niall toward Muireall. "And you must be the human lass he helped to make a bargain with Prince Aodhàn."

Muireall stepped out from behind Niall and nodded.

"Which means yer actually here fer this." The trow ducked back into his home and returned with a small fiddle. He gazed lovingly at the instrument. "This fiddle saved my life once. . . ." His expression hardened as he looked up at the pair. "Give me one good reason why I should risk parting with it."

Niall, ever the quick-witted one, opened his mouth to speak what Muireall was certain would be another lie. "Because—"

"Because I need it now to save mine," the girl blurted.

"And yer life is at risk because yer parents are forcing you to wed against yer will?" the trow asked, his tone skeptical.

Muireall glanced at Niall, who was watching her with wide, panicked eyes as if she'd just made a terrible mistake. Maybe she had. Maybe this trow was incapable of pity and trying to appeal to his compassion would be fruitless. But the creature had already proven he was both intelligent and informed enough to see through Niall's facade. And his reference to "Vincent" must have meant Vincent McLaren, the mad fisherman. If this trow had trusted one human, perhaps he could trust another.

If she told the truth.

"I suppose na. But even so, I'm asking—nay, begging— that you would consider my servant's challenge. All I want is a chance to win yer fiddle, that I may make my own path in the world rather than allow someone else to make it fer me."

The trow's nose wrinkled, and Muireall knew without a shadow of a doubt that she hadn't convinced him. But as her shoulders sagged with defeat, a new thought blazed across her consciousness. "And if you help me, I also promise to do what I can to continue where Vincent left off."

The creature faltered, something akin to worry appearing in his red eyes. "Left off? What do you mean?"

Muireall pressed her lips together. "Vincent McLaren—that's who you were talking about before, right?" At the trow's swift nod, she continued, "He . . . passed away recently."

The creature took a sharp breath. "Are you certain o' this?"

She nodded.

"How? When?"

"About a month and a half ago, there was a terrible storm. He—and two other villagers—died as a result o' it."

The trow's gaze shot to Niall, rage shining in his eyes. "A tragic accident, then?"

"Aye," Muireall replied, though the trow seemed to have lost all interest in her as he stared her companion down.

Now that she thought about it, Vincent McLaren's death had been different from the others'. It was customary for family members to stand guard over a corpse until it had lain in its house for eight days, but Briony Fairborn had insisted on watching over Vincent's body alone. Vincent's father and older brother had been incensed, but Briony had used her newfound authority as the village's only medical expert to get her way. The whole thing had been so bizarre that new rumors had sprung up about both the Fairborns and the mad fisherman. Whispers of everything from an illicit relationship between Vincent and Briony's mother to attempted necromancy.

As far as Muireall knew, no one but Briony had even seen the mad fisherman's body. *Was there something she didn' want anyone to find out about him? Could Mr. McLaren na have been human? Or perhaps his death wasn' an accident at all.*

Briony did say she was dangerous. Could she have had something to do with the man's passing?

She discarded the notion as she recalled Briony's tears at the fisherman's funeral. The midwife's grief had been so visceral that Muireall had almost choked up herself.

"So, what say you, trow?" Niall's question brought her back to the present. "Do you accept my challenge?"

"My name is Lachlan," the creature retorted, "and I've yet to hear the terms o' yer proposal."

He wants to hear the terms. He's considering it. Muireall held back a hopeful smile.

"If I win, the prize shall be yer fiddle," Niall replied.

"And if I win?" Lachlan said. "What do you have to offer?"

Niall glanced at Muireall expectantly. She narrowed her eyes. *Oh, surely you jest. You must have something in mind as a reward in the event that you fail.*

But when the servant continued to wait, she realized exactly what he'd had in mind. *Just because I'm a laird's daughter, he assumes I must have something desirable to offer? I have no idea what a trow would even wa—*

An idea skittered through her mind, and she spoke up with confidence. "You'll have my clàrsach."

The trow's mouth lifted into a smile that displayed two rows of pointed teeth. "A fine offer."

"Then you accept?" Niall pressed.

Muireall glared at him. His impatience could very well cost them this bargain.

But Lachlan nodded. "Aye, I do, except"—he held up his palm—"I won' compete against you. A musical contest with a leannan na mara is no contest at all. I wish to compete against her." The trow pointed a knobby finger at Muireall.

Her mouth fell open. "Me? But I—"

"Yer the most talented musician in Everton, are you na, Muireall Oliver?"

She took a step back, fear gripping her. "How do you know my name?"

"I've heard tell from the bravest among us who have crept close enough to listen at yer gatherings. A fair lass with hair red as fire and fingers faster than wind. Beat me, and you'll have yer fiddle."

"But I don' have my clàrsach with me right now."

Lachlan snapped his fingers, and the instrument manifested in her hands.

"That's na—" Niall tried to protest, but the trow cut him off with a growl.

"What's it to be, lass?" Lachlan cocked his head to the side.

Muireall ran her hands over the clàrsach, feeling a familiar stirring in her soul as her fingers grazed its strings. She'd never competed against someone before. She might not be as skilled as she believed.

Yet, the chance to find out was too tempting to resist.

Muireall met the creature's eye. "I accept."

A Worthy Opponent

Niall watched the two competitors with trepidation. This trow was far smarter than he'd predicted; he'd been sure it would make the mistake of allowing Niall to compete. That would have guaranteed their victory. He might not have the ability to control others with a melody anymore, but a leannan na mara's song was still a thing of exceptional beauty.

He had no idea if Mistress Oliver was skilled enough to rival the trow. He vaguely remembered seeing her with a few other musicians at the Johnsmas celebration, but his mind had been too focused on Briony to notice if she bore any real talent.

Outplaying a trow would require a great deal.

His mistress held herself confidently, but Niall was certain that was only an act. Inside, she had to be feeling even more nervous than he was.

When she glanced his way, anxiety flashed in her eyes for a split second, proving his assumption correct. He folded his arms over his chest, refusing to offer her any support when she was the one who'd been stupid enough to agree to this.

Be reasonable, Niall, his conscience argued. *Did she have much choice? The trow refused to compete with you—fer good reason—and 'tis imperative we get that fiddle. She did the only thing she could have done.*

Niall drummed his fingers along his arm, not liking the way his thoughts had been softening toward his mistress. *She's simply a means to an end. Nothing more.* And once this charade was over, he was never going to see her again, anyway.

"I'll start," Lachlan said, tucking his fiddle under his chin. An eerie, shrill sound sprang forth from the instrument, creeping over Niall's skin like spider limbs. It was slow at first, but just as it seemed to settle into a consistent rhythm, the tempo surged forward, the notes almost leaping into existence. Niall didn't recognize the song, but his soul understood its meaning. It was a requiem to the ground beneath their feet, the rocks that had withstood the test of time, carrying treasures and secrets the likes of which the world would never know.

His gaze darted to Mistress Oliver. Wonder filled her green eyes, and her smile was like starlight, radiating with beauty. The last time he'd seen her so unguarded had been when she'd wept in the garden, but in that moment, sorrow had been billowing off her in waves. Now, she was pure joy. A laugh bubbled up from inside her, and without meaning to, Niall drifted closer, like a moth to a flame.

She turned his way, her eyes lighting even further. As if the moment were somehow better because he was there to share it.

Niall's hand twitched at his side, his fingers suddenly eager to clasp hers.

All too soon, the music died away, and Lachlan lowered his fiddle. Mistress Oliver leaned away, breaking the strange connection between them.

"That was the most amazing thing I've heard in all my life," she told the trow, her voice earnest and appreciative. "Did you compose it?"

Lachlan smiled shyly, and if it had been possible, Niall was sure he would have blushed. "Aye, I did. Thank you fer yer praise, lass. Now"—he pointed to her instrument—"let's see if you can outdo me."

The glow emanating from the young woman faded, but she threw her shoulders back with determination. "All right." She lowered herself to the ground, crossed her legs, and placed the clàrsach on her lap. "This is a song fer my deceased brother."

Niall sucked in a quick breath and looked away, ice enclosing his heart before she had strummed the first note. Alastair Oliver didn't deserve to be remembered, and he certainly didn't deserve anything done in his honor. Niall tried not to listen, unwilling to give that fiend any modicum of respect.

Despite his efforts, it wasn't long before soft, tinkling notes filled Niall's ears. His jaw dropped, and though he wanted to ignore the song, a lightness filled his body and compelled him to turn back to the enthralling musician.

Mistress Oliver's fingers danced upon the strings, her eyelids fluttering closed as she became one with the song. Niall forgot his anger as her haunting music wrapped around him like the sweet whispers of the sea. Tears spilled down his cheeks as he felt the emotions she'd woven into the song as deeply as if they were his own. Grief, soul-numbing grief, pressed against his spirit, showing him that though he and Muireall were different, her sense of loss was just as powerful as his own.

And that humanity wasn't as monstrous as he wanted to believe.

Niall's heart squeezed against his ribcage, but he did nothing to resist the emotions funneling through him. Muireall's music was too exquisite to resist, and if he hadn't known better, he would have sworn she was casting a spell on him.

The song swelled, morphing from a theme of grief to happiness. Happiness from moments shared, moments remembered. Niall saw his mother and sister in his mind's eye, heard their laughter as they danced together by the light of the moon. Their time together had been short, far too short. Yet, even in its brevity, it had been full of love.

As Muireall's song came to a close, Niall couldn't help but wonder if even a beast like Alastair hadn't been as wicked as Niall had thought. *How else could she create something so beautiful in his memory?*

When the ache in his chest intensified, he took a few shaky breaths to steady himself and swiped at the moisture on his face before anyone could notice he'd been crying.

Mistress Oliver opened her eyes slowly, her cheeks dotted with scarlet as she assessed her audience's reaction. Niall kept his expression neutral, but he nodded to show his approval.

Both of them turned to Lachlan to see what the trow would say next.

If he doesn' have the dignity to admit defeat after that performance, I'm going to slam his tiny head in the dirt.

***

Once Muireall was done with the song, she glanced at Niall to see what he'd thought of her performance. *Was I good enough?*

The servant didn't say anything, but a light shone from his dark eyes, warming her soul and sending her heart pattering. He gave her a swift nod, and in that one motion, she knew she had succeeded.

She turned to the trow, who was scratching his head as if he couldn't get a handle on what he'd just heard. After a moment, the small gray figure lowered his hand and bowed. "A worthier opponent ne'er have I met." He stood back up and held out his instrument. "The fiddle is yers."

Muireall took the fiddle, then peeked at Niall, who was outright beaming at her now. She smiled in return before looking down at the little creature before her. "I quite enjoyed our competition. 'Tis na often I meet someone with yer incredible skill. Perhaps we shall meet again," she said, meaning every word. She never would have predicted it, but somehow she felt more at ease with this bizarre, magical being she'd only just met than she ever had with the neighbors she'd grown up with. Perhaps it was because of the trow's affinity for music, or—more likely—it was because, with Lachlan, she was free to be herself without society's expectations weighing her down.

And 'tis all thanks to Niall that I got to meet him. . . . A pleasant sensation swept through her again, and she had the strangest urge to throw her arms around her servant in thanks.

The trow raised an eyebrow at her. "I should hope na. I don' wish to lose all my treasures." He chuckled, then his face became somber. "Lass, do be careful. Should you break yer contract with the Prince, the consequences will be dire."

Muireall's cheerful mood faded. "What do you mean? Won' I just na get the favor I asked fer?"

120

Lachlan grimaced. "I'm afraid 'tis more serious than that. Yer contract magically binds you to Prince Aodhàn. Break it, and you'll be in his debt."

Muireall paled. *What? Niall never mentioned that.* Her eyes flicked to her servant, but he was suspiciously staring at the ground.

"But after the way you handled yerself today, I'm confident you'll uphold yer end o' the deal," Lachlan added, his tone soothing. He grabbed her hand and whispered, "If you get into any trouble, though, you know where to find me."

Muireall barely felt his hand leave hers as she nodded woodenly. Fears swirled around her mind, but she forced herself to keep a straight face as the trow stepped back and lifted his hand in farewell.

A sparkling light encompassed the knoll once more, and within moments, both the trow and the entrance to his home had vanished.

Muireall and her companion returned the way they had come, neither saying anything until they were back on the road. Once there, she let out a huge sigh. "That was the most . . ."

"Thrilling thing you've ever done?"

She whirled toward Niall, eyes blazing. "More like terrifying," she snapped. "Why didn' you tell me about the consequences o' breaking a magical contract?"

He shrugged nonchalantly, but his words bore a hard edge as he said, "You told me you needed a miracle. I gave you one."

"If I were to fail, though, what sort o' payment would the Prince want?"

Niall smiled, but the expression seemed forced. "Oh, something trivial. I'm sure you've got plenty o' things at home that would do, so don' worry about it. As long as we collect what we need and cross back through the Veil on the full moon, all will be well."

"'All will be well'?" Muireall's voice was piercing. "We only have a few more weeks, and so many things could happen between now and then."

He jerked his chin toward the fiddle. "You already have the first treasure; we need but two more."

Muireall threw her hands in the air, utterly disgusted. "Perhaps I should have simply asked Lachlan to help me find them. He certainly seemed willing to do so and without requiring anything in return."

The servant gestured back in the direction they'd just come from. "You think you can trust a trow? Most o' them are greedy, thieving liars who would sooner stab you in the back than do anything to help you."

She huffed. *But Lachlan isn' the one keeping secrets from me, is he? Why wouldn' Lachlan compete against a leannan na mara? Just what else are you hiding, Niall Moreland?*

She inhaled a breath to ask, but Niall spoke up first.

"I don' understand why yer so upset. You had a problem. I gave you a solution. And na only that but I also agreed to help you reach yer goal. If anything, you should be grateful."

"Grateful that you didn' tell me what I was really getting into?" Muireall shook her head, sarcasm adding bite to her words. "Aye, I can' imagine why gratitude *isn'* the emotion I'm feeling right now."

"You impossible, infuriating—" He broke off, an odd expression coming over his face. "Are you . . . Mistress Oliver, don' tell me yer angry because you thought I *cared* about you."

She drew back, apprehension coursing through her. "O' course that's na why. I just would have liked to have known exactly what I was agreeing to *before* I agreed to it."

Niall nodded slowly, but a trace of skepticism lingered in his face. "Well, I assure you I'll let you know next time, so you can be fully informed before you make any decisions. Satisfied?"

She nodded, and the two began walking again, the silence heavier than before.

Is that really why I got so angry? I knew from the start o' this arrangement that he was only using me to get what he wanted. Just as I'm using him. There's nothing more to it than that.

Muireall twisted a strand of hair between her fingers, still uneasy. *Why do I feel like that's na the whole truth?*

The enigmatic tune Lachlan had played flitted through her thoughts once more, and an echo of the happiness she'd felt earlier came back to her.

"That was rather thrilling," she said, hoping to lighten the mood. "I hadn' quite finished writing that song, but when I started to play, the ending just came to me." Her eyes darted to her companion's face, where a pleasant half-smile teased the corner of his mouth.

"'Twas truly lovely," he whispered.

Muireall's heart swelled at the compliment, and the two of them stared at each other for a long moment, the animosity from earlier only a distant memory now.

"I'm glad the trow didn' frighten you off, Princess," Niall said.

"Are you ever going to stop calling me that?"

"Nay, I don' think so," he quipped, his voice full of mischief.

Her cheeks warmed, something delightfully unsettling shooting through her stomach. She cleared her throat and looked away. "Anyway, where will we be traveling next? I won' be able to go today, but we can make a plan still. You said you thought the kelpie could be near Loch Isla?"

"I admire yer focus, but before we go after the kelpie, there's something we need to get from the market."

"The market?" She winced. "I . . . I don' know if 'twould be a good idea to be seen with you there."

No one had said anything so far, but the more time they spent together—especially in public—the greater likelihood there was of whispers.

Niall shook his head, exasperated. "I thought you said being the gardener would allow us to spend time alone together. Do you want my help or na?"

"O' course I do. I just—" She sighed. "All right, I'll go."

The pair agreed to meet in two days, then chatted amicably for the rest of the journey home. When they reached Rigmore House, though, Muireall hesitated.

"I don' suppose you know o' a way fer me to get out o' trying on ball dresses?"

She hung her head at the thought of all that would entail, but Niall's answering laugh had her snapping her head back up with a scowl. "Hey, you don' know how awful 'tis. Mother purchased six different dresses, and I'll have to try on all o' them more than once before she decides which one is the best. 'Twill take several hours, I'm sure."

Niall raised his eyebrows teasingly. "You just bested a trow and claimed his most prized possession. I'd be surprised if there's anything you can' handle."

Blazing Brightly

The following morning, Niall happily rose and dressed for the day. He didn't worry about getting to work as quickly as possible or about avoiding Hamish's judgmental stare. Today was *his* day, and he was going to spend it how he liked.

He frowned. *If 'twas entirely up to me, I wouldn' be seeing Briony today at all. But since she's the only way to get to William, I suppose I'll deal with her.* He strolled through town at a leisurely pace, inhaling deep breaths of fresh air.

When he knocked on Briony's door, she opened it with an aloof expression. "Hello, Niall."

"Good morneen," he replied, unfazed by her cool attitude. "Is William here yet? I'd like to do something new today—"

"Uncle Niall!" William appeared in the doorway, his arms open for an embrace.

Niall stepped forward eagerly, but just before he reached the boy, Briony moved in between them. "Na so fast." She turned to William. "Are you forgetting what yer father told you?"

The lad grimaced. "Oh . . ." He scratched at his arm before meeting Niall's eye. "Da' still wants me to be careful around you because he thinks yer na safe."

Niall held back a groan. *We've been meeting fer weeks now. How long is this going to take?*

Instead of voicing his frustration, though, he asked calmly, "Do you agree with him?"

"It doesn' matter if he agrees," Briony cut in. "He needs to obey his father's wishes."

Niall ignored her and waited for William's answer. The boy peered into his uncle's dark eyes—identical to his own—and said, "I'm na sure. You weren' very nice to me after I saved you, but you've been kind since you came back."

Regret squeezed Niall's chest. If it hadn't been for William, he would have drowned in the aftermath of his fight with Briony and Mr. Mendes. William had only barely gotten to him in time, and Niall's wounds had left him too weak to escape when John and Adaira had found the two of them lying on the beach.

But, as luck would have it, John and Adaira had made the mistake of going to search for Briony, leaving William and Niall alone once again. As soon as Niall had been able to, he'd knocked the boy out and made his escape.

Niall bent down to his nephew's level. "Fer what I did before, I'm deeply sorry. Can you forgive me?"

Forgive me fer only having the strength to rescue myself that day. If only I could have taken you with me. . .

William pursed his lips as he mulled it over. His eyes darted to Briony, who was gracious enough to stay silent.

As well she should. She may be standing in fer John, but she's na William's family. Besides, this is the lad's choice, na anyone else's.

"I don' know yet," William said.

Niall smiled and stood back up. "That's all right. You don' have to make any decisions right away. With some more time, you'll see that you can trust me again."

Briony rolled her eyes. "Anyway, shall we get started?"

He nodded. "Today, we're going to do something different. I'm going to teach you about magical creatures."

William's face lit up. "Really? Are we going to see any?"

Niall chuckled. "Let's take a stroll."

The group spent the rest of the morning tramping around the northern end of Everton. Niall considered taking them to see Lachlan, but the trow hadn't been very keen on visitors last time, so he decided not to. They didn't come across any magical folk, but Niall had a great time teaching his nephew what creatures might live in the area, which ones were friendly, and what to do if you offended one. William found it all fascinating, but Briony's shrewd gaze stayed vigilant. Niall tried to tell her most of the creatures around here posed little threat to humans, but the midwife remained skeptical.

What Niall didn't say was that he was also hunting for clues to help in Muireall's quest. And as they walked along the western side of Loch Isla, he found just the evidence he'd been hoping for.

"Does anyone in Everton own horses?" he remarked, his tone casual.

Briony's brow wrinkled. "Nay, why would you ask that?"

"Oh, no reason," he said with a smile, careful not to glance back at the hoof prints they'd just passed.

If no one in Everton owned a horse, then prints like those could only belong to a kelpie.

***

Around noon, the three of them returned to Drulea Cottage for lunch. Briony quickly urged her guests to sit down while she went to prepare the meal.

"You told me about a lot o' magical folk, uncle, but there's one you left out," William said.

"Oh, did I?" Niall grinned. "What's that?"

"Fairies."

"Aye, you should definitely tell us about them," Briony called from the kitchen, a note of bitterness in her voice. "I'm curious about their dances since you were so eager to take Mistress Oliver to one."

William clapped his hands. "Oh, please do!"

Niall nodded. "All right. Well, fairy dances are unlike any dance you've ever been to. To attend one, you must first pass through the Veil separating this world from theirs . . ."

William sat enraptured as Niall told of the exciting—and perilous—realm of the Fair Folk. Niall had had several encounters with their kind over the years, and he'd learned firsthand just how important it was to avoid their anger.

"What happens if you make them angry?" William asked.

Niall's eyes twinkled. "Well, let me tell you what happened to me when I was fifteen years old."

He launched into an exciting tale of the time he'd offended a fairy princess and she'd stolen his voice as punishment. It was merely through his father's pleading with the king that Niall's voice had been returned—and that had only been after he had promised to stay away from Princess Aoife.

But as he spoke, a worrisome thought passed through his mind: *I hope Aodhàn didn' mention me to her. There's no telling what she might do to me if she finds out I've lost my powers.*

By the time the story was finished, Briony had brought over tea, fish, and vegetables. The group blessed the meal and ate heartily, though they all agreed the fish was much more delectable than the vegetables.

As everyone laughed, a sense of camaraderie rose up in Niall's heart. It wasn't quite the same feeling as the kinship bonds he'd shared with his herd, but it was nice to be amongst his own kind again.

At least, almost his own kind.

Have you forgotten why yer really here in Everton? asked a dark voice in the back of his mind.

Niall's hand shook as awareness came over him. He swallowed, throat suddenly thick. *I've gotten so lax I almost fell fer my own lie. Keep it together, Niall. Yer na here to enjoy yerself.*

He glanced around the room, eyes peeled for any compartments where one might store a sealskin. Briony probably put it in her bedroom when she didn't have it on her person. *Hmm . . .*

"Briony," Niall said during the next lull in conversation, "I hope you've been wise enough to keep yer sealskin well hidden."

She looked up from her food, her expression guarded. "Aye, I usually have it with me."

"And when you don'?" Niall asked, but William spoke up at the exact same moment.

"You do?" The boy scrutinized the midwife. "I don' see it anywhere."

Briony ignored Niall's question—on purpose, Niall was sure—and instead turned to William. She giggled and shook her head. "'Tis under my clothes, you goose."

The lad's cheeks flushed, then he stuck out his lips in a pout. "I wish I could do that with my sealskin."

Niall couldn't help but chuckle at the boy's ridiculous statement, which set the other two off so badly it seemed the entire cottage was shaking with laughter.

Once everyone had caught their breath, William said, "So, what's it like working at Rigmore House?"

"Oh, well, 'tis . . ." Niall glanced at Briony, who was watching him with raised eyebrows. "'Tis good work, I suppose. Better than when I was kelping with Mr. Calhoun. That was exhausting."

"What do you do fer work?" William asked.

"I take care o' the garden."

Briony let out what sounded like a snicker, which quickly morphed into a loud cough.

Niall scowled at her. "Don' think I didn' hear that. What's so funny?"

She had the decency to look sheepish. "You? In a garden? I'm sorry, but 'tis very difficult fer me to imagine."

Niall puffed out his chest a bit. "I'll have you know I'm quite adept at it. Mistress Oliver was very impressed by how well I could recall the names and medicinal purposes fer the flowers at Rigmore House. Why, I—"

"Mistress Oliver? She's teaching you how to take care o' the garden?"

Niall winced. *How could I be so careless!*

"Please, keep that to yerself. I wasn' supposed to say anything. She doesn' want people to know."

Briony frowned, then took a bite of fish. When she set her fork back down, she said slowly, "You care fer her, don' you?"

He dropped his knife, grimacing when it clattered against the floor. He bent down to retrieve it, unsure why he'd reacted like that. When he got back up, his lips were pressed into a tight smile.

"What an odd thing to say. She's my mistress. 'Tis my duty to care fer her needs."

Briony tilted her head. "I didn' say care fer her needs. I said care fer *her*."

"Isn' that the same thing?" William asked.

The midwife shook her head. "On the contrary, lad, they're two very different things."

"I'm quite sure I don' know what you mean," Niall said sharply, his tone making it clear he didn't want to continue talking about this.

Briony met his gaze with a fire of her own, but he quickly added, "I need to take my leave. All this talk o' gardening reminded me that I left some work unfinished yesterday. I should do it before it gets late." He rose from his chair.

"Yer leaving already?" William whimpered. "But there's still so much I want to ask you." His shoulders slumped.

Niall ruffled his nephew's hair. "Don' worry, lad. We'll see each other again soon." He looked pointedly at Briony. "So long as we can stay focused on the right things."

Her eyes narrowed even as the lad replied, "Um, I think so?" William looked between the two of them.

"Great," Niall said. "I'll see you later, then."

"I'll walk you out." Briony jumped to her feet.

"Nay, that's really na necessar—"

"I insist."

Niall turned to leave, hurrying so he could avoid whatever Briony was so eager to discuss with him alone.

"Thank you fer the food," he said as she opened the door. "Now, I really must—"

"I may be wrong about yer feelings toward Mistress Oliver"—she leaned against the door—"but know this: if you hurt her in any way, you'll have me to answer to."

"I didn' think the two o' you were friends."

"We don' need to be. She's a part o' the village, and that puts her under my protection."

Niall scoffed. "You don' need to worry about Mistress Oliver. I wouldn' hurt her."

She crossed her arms. "Mhmm. I wasn' just talking about physical harm." When Niall didn't respond, she raised her hands and groaned in frustration. "I know you know what I'm talking about. Why must you be so stubborn?"

"*I'm* the one who's stubborn?"

Briony's lips twitched with amusement for a brief second. "Fine, I'll just say it, then. Muireall Oliver doesn' let anyone close to her. Na friends, na family. Na even Adaira has been able to get through that thick shell o' hers, and everyone loves Adaira."

"But you think I have?"

She gave him a flat look. "She's been personally teaching you how to garden? And you went to a dance together? If anyone else in Everton heard about that, they'd think you were—that you were . . ." Her cheeks pinked as she trailed off.

Niall's answering smile was mocking. "I'm na in love with her if that's what yer trying to say."

Briony shook her head. "Nay, that's na it. People would think yer trying to take advantage o' her."

All traces of entertainment slid off his face. "How ridiculous. That's na even close to . . ."

But 'tis, isn' it? his conscience argued. *You took her to Prince Aodhàn, knowing she'd be given a task she could never complete. If she hadn' changed the terms o' yer agreement with her, you would have already used her to help you get Briony's sealskin, then left her behind to deal with the Prince's challenge on her own. Yer only helping her now because you have no choice.*

Something unpleasant pooled in Niall's gut, catching him off guard. *What is this?*

Mistress Oliver annoyed and confused him like no other. She was a spoiled princess who treated her servants like they were worthless. There was nothing wrong with using someone who was so wretched.

But that's na all o' who she is, is it?

His mind turned to her reaction when she'd discovered the scars on his wrist. While the woman was usually self-seeking, no pretense had guided her when she'd asked—nearly weeping—how he'd come by his injuries. She'd been so tender, so unlike the cold, unfeeling mistress he'd come to know. Her behavior in the garden had been genuine, driven by nothing but concern—Niall was certain of it.

Yet yer planning to destroy everything she loves once you regain yer powers. She might even die in the process. Is vengeance worth risking her life?

Niall bristled, not wanting to answer the question. The ache he'd felt when he'd heard her song reappeared in his chest, taunting him.

Except this time, he recognized it for what it was: guilt.

As much as Niall disliked Mistress Oliver, she didn't deserve to die. Even though she was human and even though she was irritating, she deserved better than that.

And Niall couldn't deny it any longer.

So, are you going to risk her life to get revenge on the people who stole yers? his conscience pressed.

Nay, I'm na.

The answer lit up his mind like a candle in the night, burning steadily despite the darkness surrounding it. It should have winked out, just like every other kind thought he'd had for his mistress.

But the more he tried to extinguish it, the brighter it blazed.

Once Niall realized there was no getting rid of this newfound benevolence toward the young mistress of Rigmore House, he resolved that instead of destroying Everton as he'd intended, he'd exact vengeance solely on those responsible for his undoing. He would ensure that Briony, John, Adaira, and Mr. Mendes all met their end.

The rest of the village, however, would be safe.

He lifted his head and met Briony's eye. "I'm na taking advantage o' her," he said firmly, "and I'm na going to hurt her. If you don' believe anything else I've told you, believe that."

Mr. Park

"Well, you seem to have survived the other day," Niall said as he and Mistress Oliver meandered down to the market. The sky was gray this morning, so they kept a brisk pace in case it started to rain.

"Survived?"

Niall pantomimed putting on a dress, moving his hands in an exaggerated fashion.

Mistress Oliver clamped her lips together, somehow resisting the urge to smile even as his motions became more elaborate.

But he was determined. From the way her mouth was quivering, she wouldn't be able to hold back much longer.

"Something wrong with you, lad?" called Steven McLaren from across the road. The old fellow had been walking in the opposite direction, but he'd since stopped to stare at them.

Niall stiffened, then tried to subtly duck behind Mistress Oliver, which was a difficult feat since she was a good deal shorter than him.

"Are you all right, mistress? He's na bothering you, is he?" Steven took a few steps toward them, then stopped before he'd fully crossed to their side of the road.

"I'm fine, Mr. McLaren," Mistress Oliver replied, her tone sharp and dismissive. Niall peeked around her shoulder just as the old man opened his mouth. He seemed to reconsider whatever he'd been about to say, though, then scuttled off down the road.

Once he was gone, Niall's companion swiveled toward him and let out a giggle that quickly turned into a snort.

Niall glowered for a moment, but the sound of her laugh and sight of her breathtaking smile were too heartwarming for his embarrassment to last. He rubbed the back of his neck, a smile creeping onto his face.

When the pair reached the market, Niall wasted no time pretending to peruse the various stalls. He veered to the left, stopping right in front of a stall with several wooden sculptures spread out on the table. A merchant squatted behind it, presumably gathering more items to put out on display.

"Niall, what are you—"

A small gasp behind the stall stole the rest of Mistress Oliver's question. The merchant jumped up, his wares forgotten on the ground. He looked between the two of them cautiously, fear clouding his brown eyes.

The man was young, perhaps Niall and Muireall's age, but that was where the similarities between them ended. From his warm beige skin to the almond shape of his eyes, it was clear this man wasn't native to Scotland. A long yellow robe with billowy sleeves hung from his thin frame, and an ornate gold pin held his hair in place atop his head. A large black hat with a string of colorful beads sat on the table.

Niall glanced at the merchant's feet, as he always did when he met someone new, and noted the man's soft white shoes. Most people around here went barefoot. The only exceptions were the Olivers, who were too noble to expose their toes, and those with selkie blood, like Niall himself, whose webbed feet would have stirred up too many questions.

Is he hiding something, or is it just normal to cover one's feet wherever he's from? Niall wondered, openly scrutinizing the fellow.

"I'm closed for the day," Mr. Park stuttered. His voice bore an unusual accent, each word enunciated very distinctly.

Niall shook his head. He'd heard from Anne and Gilbert that Mr. Park—for that was the merchant's name—always kept his stall open until noon. He had never approached the man specifically before, but he had a feeling this foreigner possessed the very item he needed. "I'd like to buy an iron knife."

Mr. Park's eyes narrowed, irritation and the tiniest fleck of curiosity replacing his fear. "And what makes you think I have one? As you can see"—he gestured to the table—"I sell sculptures." The man's reply was curt, but a tremor in his voice told Niall he was lying.

Niall propped his elbow on the table, leaning close to the tradesman with a wry grin. "Aye, but what sort o' sculptures?" He picked up the nearest one, relishing the way Mr. Park grimaced like he'd been caught.

The carving was of a small female figure with delicate features and long curly hair. Her slender arms and legs were stretched out, her dress curling upward as though she was mid-twirl. A beatific smile graced her lips, and her eyes almost glowed with silent joy. The artwork was masterful, no doubt, but that wasn't what drew Niall's attention.

It was the gossamer wings upon her back.

Niall had spotted the sculpture over a week ago, but he'd never taken the time to examine it up close. Now that he had the opportunity to study it, though, he was certain: whoever carved this hadn't just imagined what the Fair Folk might look like. They had actually seen them.

"Did you make this?"

Mr. Park swallowed, no longer making eye contact with his guests. "All of this is my work."

Niall's eyes drifted over the wooden figures once more. Some he recognized at once, but others were unfamiliar: dolphins with strangely shaped fins on their backs, creatures possessing the features of multiple animals, foxes with more than one tail, monsters that sent a shot of fear through even him. *If the fairy was crafted from memory, does that mean the rest were, too?*

Niall bared his teeth in a smile too wide to be inviting. "Then yer definitely the person who can help me."

Mistress Oliver, who had been silent up to this point, tugged on Niall's sleeve and said softly, "Why do we need a knife?"

"Because"—Niall looked straight at Mr. Park—"'tis just the tool we'll need to kill a kelpie."

Muireall didn't miss the way the merchant's fingers clenched his robe, recognition sparking in his eyes.

But just as suddenly, the fire fizzled out, and he looked away. "I can't help you. Like I said, I'm closed for the day." He picked up a basket from the ground and started collecting the sculptures.

Niall leaned forward, but Muireall grabbed his wrist and gave him a look that said, *Wait. Trust me.*

When he gave her a slight nod, she asked, "What if I were to purchase all yer inventory?"

The merchant stiffened, then continued putting away the carvings. "A pretty offer, but I doubt you can back it u—"

She shoved one of her rings under his nose. "Will this cover it?" The ring was made of gold, with tiny rubies encircling a sapphire in the center—a leftover betrothal gift from Lord Carmichael.

The merchant's eyes glittered, but still, he hesitated. "Is such a treasure yours to give?"

She nodded, then withdrew her hand, noting how he watched the ring until it disappeared in her fist. "Do we have a deal, then?"

The foreigner took a deep breath, then let it out in a great whoosh. "Fine. I haven't sold anything for several days. It will be nice to clear everything out, so I can work on something new." He extended the basket of sculptures to her.

Niall held up his hand. "I believe the lady said *all* yer inventory."

The merchant huffed, then set down the basket. He reached into one of his sleeves and pulled out a long knife. "This is the last of it." His hand trembled as he held it out.

As Muireall's fingers wrapped around it, the foreigner leaned forward and whispered, "Be careful whom you trust, agassi[25]." His eyes darted pointedly to Niall.

Muireall took the knife, hating the fear his words stirred within her.

---

[25] Korean title for a young, unmarried woman.

"Thank you, sir," Niall said, his smile full of triumph. He took the basket before turning to Muireall. "We best get going, mistress."

Muireall nodded, turning away from the foreigner. But the man's concerned expression lingered in her mind. *What could he have meant?*

"Was that wise, telling him what we plan to do with the knife?" Muireall asked as they trekked back to Rigmore House.

Niall had been quiet up until now, his expression pensive. He turned to her sharply, then his features softened. "Oh, you don' need to worry about him. He's clearly had dealings with magical folk before. 'Twas obvious he knew I was a leannan na mara as soon as he saw me"—his voice deepened—"which means he knows better than to trifle with me."

A shiver went down Muireall's spine, and she started to ask what he meant by that, but then the mansion came into view.

"Ah, here we are. I'm sure yer mother is wondering where you are," Niall remarked. "Yer dinner with Mr. Mendes is all the servants have been talking about fer the last several days."

Muireall gulped. "Except 'tis na Mr. Mendes who'll be joining us this evening."

Niall raised an eyebrow. "What do you mean?"

"I haven' told anyone yet, but I invited Mr. Levins instead."

The servant's jaw tightened, something dangerous flashing in his eyes. "Is he a problem?"

Muireall shook her head, smiling despite the anxiety tearing through her veins. "Nay, o' course na. I shall be fine."

Slipping Facades

"What do you mean, *I* have to help? I'm just the gardener. I don' take care o' dinner." Niall's tone bordered on disrespectful.

Lunch had just concluded in the servants' dining hall, meaning it was almost time to prepare the Olivers' dinner, and Hamish stood at the front of the room with his arms crossed. He had just told everyone they needed to listen for evening chore assignments, then he'd started barking orders.

Up until now, Niall hadn't had to take care of the Olivers at dinner. He—along with most of the other servants—had gotten the rest of the evening to himself to spend how he pleased.

And he wasn't keen on giving it up.

A vein in the butler's forehead popped out at Niall's disregard for his authority. "This isn' just any dinner. Viscount Mendes is coming over, and if you kept abreast o' the state o' the house, you'd know that."

Niall hid a smirk at the man's error. *Are you sure I'm the one who's in the dark? I'd love to see yer face when you open the front door, and Mr. Levins is the one standing there.*

"But instead," Hamish continued, "yer outside all the time, probably na even putting forth much effort at that position yer so proud o'. How did you convince Mistress Oliver to make you the gardener, anyway?" His tone was insinuating, as if Niall had used some nefarious means to seduce the young mistress.

Briony's words rang in Niall's mind: *"People would think yer trying to take advantage o' her."*

Niall leaned back, his jaw tight. *This man may pretend to know everything about this household, but he's an idiot if he thinks Mistress Oliver would fall fer something like that.*

"I've always had a tremendous amount o' interest in plants," he replied. "Mistress Oliver simply noticed my appreciation o' them."

Hamish scoffed. "In other words, she saw you playing with the flowers rather than doing what you were supposed to do. Is that it?"

Niall scowled, ready to refute the man's claim, but Gilbert jumped in first.

"Shouldn' we be focused on dinner right now? I'm sure the Olivers won' appreciate if we're late." As soon as he said the words, the curly-haired servant flinched and gave Hamish a nervous smile.

"I wasn' talking to you, lad," the butler said with a glare. He paused. "But I suppose yer right. We should be getting on with things. As I would have if *someone*"—he eyed Niall—"hadn' interrupted me earlier."

Hamish nodded to two female servants. "You shall be in charge o' beverages. Make sure no one's glass is empty, no matter what."

Next, he gestured to a manservant. "You go help Jeane in the kitchen. I don' want her to run out o' ingredients."

Finally, he slammed one hand on Niall's shoulder and the other on Gilbert's. "And you two shall serve the food."

Niall refused to wince even though the man's grip was painful. Gilbert, on the other hand, cowered and looked close to tears. He turned to Niall with pleading eyes.

Fine, but only fer yer sake, Gilbert. Niall lowered his head in submission.

Hamish grinned in triumph, then shoved the men toward the exit. "Now, go."

Once the two servants were alone, Niall let out all the pent-up anger he'd been suppressing. "Who does he think he is, the laird o' Rigmore? He may be the butler, but he's no better than the rest o' us. How did someone like him even get to be butler? I bet he got it through his father, didn' he?"

Gilbert, whose eyes had been growing wider and wider the longer Niall's tirade had continued, clapped a hand over Niall's mouth. "Are you mad? You can' say things like that!"

Niall rolled his eyes and pushed Gilbert's hand away. "Don't fret, Gilbert. No one can hear us."

The other servant glanced around nervously, not placated by his friend's words.

Niall wrapped an arm around his shoulder. "Relax. 'Tis all right."

"I wouldn' be so sure with yer hearing skills," said a nearby voice.

Niall and Gilbert whirled toward the sound, the latter squealing in fright.

Anne stood a short distance away with an amused glint in her eyes. "No need to worry. 'Tis just me, and I don' gossip about my friends." She winked. "What were you two talking about?"

"Nothing." Gilbert's voice was much too high.

"Nothing worth repeating." Niall sent his friend a sharp look to hush him up. "Will you be working with us this evening?"

"I'm afraid na. I have to help Mistress Oliver get dressed. I just came by to wish everyone luck." Anne stepped closer, her voice dropping to a whisper. "And remind you that last time, Lady Oliver was very upset when Beth didn' light the candles *before* the family sat down. Don' want to make the same mistake twice."

Niall's head swiveled to his friend. "Did Hamish assign someone that task?"

"I don' think so. . . . I better go ask him." Gilbert scampered off.

Anne started to excuse herself, but Niall stopped her. "Before you go, may I ask you something?"

The maid giggled. "O' course." There was no denying the interest in her eyes.

"You probably know more about Mistress Oliver than any o' the other servants, right?"

Anne blinked a few times, seemingly confused by his question. "I suppose."

"Were she and her brother close?"

Niall usually tried not to think about Alastair, but ever since he'd listened to Mistress Oliver's song, he'd been unable to shake a fierce curiosity about the boy who'd shown him firsthand how cruel humans could be. Part of him was disgusted that he would even bother to ask. He should have already known all he needed to.

But doubt had a funny way of creeping in when one least expected it.

"The young master?" Anne's previous friendliness vanished, and she suddenly seemed eager to leave. "Aye, I suppose they were."

"What can you tell me about him?"

"Oh, I wasn' working here then, so I couldn' rightly tell you."

"But you've lived here all yer life, haven' you?"

"Aye, I have. The young Mr. Oliver wasn' someone I had much contact with though. After all, I'm just a servant."

"This is a small village. You must know something," Niall pressed, giving her his most winning smile.

Anne exhaled. "All right. This is the truth. I know 'tis impolite to speak ill o' the dead, but Alastair Oliver was one o' the worst folk you could come across, even as a child. After he broke Hamish's foot fer beating him at a race, I did all I could to stay away from him. You should be glad you never met him."

If only I'd been that fortunate. Sounds like my initial impression o' the lad was correct. He deserved to die.

"Wait, he broke Hamish's foot? As in, the same Hamish who's now the butler?"

"The very same."

Interesting . . .

"But you said Alastair and Mistress Oliver were close. Did he treat her the same way as everyone else?"

The maid started to answer, but then footsteps sounded behind them.

Bessie came up and grabbed Anne's arm. "I've been looking everywhere fer you."

Anne smiled apologetically at Niall, then the two of them scurried off, leaving Niall to wonder how his mistress could have crafted such a lovely song for someone so horrible.

He was just about to go look for Gilbert when raised voices caught his attention. *Mistress Oliver?*

***

Before Muireall knew it, it was time to go to the dining room. She glided down the stairs with all the grace of a queen, though inwardly she was shaking like a leaf. She may have told Niall she would be fine, but that didn't mean she believed it.

Mr. Levins's threat whispered in her mind, *"I suggest you stop discussing things you don' know anything about before you regret it."*

She took a few steadying breaths. *All I have to do is get through tonight, and then I can focus on other things. Like how I'm going to get the kelpie's bridle once I find it.*

I should go ahead and make a plan fer that. From what Muireall knew of kelpies, they frequented water and were notorious for stealing any children who were stupid enough to climb on their backs.

Or was it beautiful lasses? Ideas began forming in her mind, connecting and disconnecting—

"There you are!" Laura sashayed toward her from the direction of the dining room. Her eyes flashed with anger.

"Mother, what's wrong?"

The older woman ran her tongue along her top teeth before hissing, "Oh, why would something be wrong? It couldn' be because there's something you forgot to tell me, could it?"

What? What did I forget? Muireall laughed nervously, her smile tight as her mother continued.

"Imagine my surprise when I went to the front door and found Matthew Levins standing there." Mother raised a critical eyebrow. "And then to discover he'd been personally invited by none other than you, daughter. I can' fathom why I'm feeling upset right now. Can you?"

143

Fear trickled down the back of Muireall's neck. She'd been so focused on seeing Matthew that she'd forgotten she hadn't told Mother about the change in plans.

"I . . ." She fidgeted with her dress sleeve. "I simply wanted to keep my options open, and the Levinses were gracious enough to invite me over fer a meal last time. Good manners dictate 'tis our turn next."

"Keep yer options open?" Laura rubbed her forehead. "I thought yer father and I made it clear that Viscount Mendes is by far the *better* option. Why would you string Matthew along?"

"Mother, anything could happen between now and my birthday. I need to be smart about this."

As soon as the words tumbled out of her mouth, Muireall wished she could swallow them back. *Oh, well done. You've just proven how little intelligence you actually possess. Now Mother is going to kill you.*

Laura's face reddened, and she took a step closer. "What did you just say? Are you trying to tell me I'm na smart?"

Muireall shook her head. "Nay, I'm so sorry. I didn' mean to say it like that. I simply meant—"

Her mother's slap reverberated off the walls and sent Muireall reeling backward. The girl touched her stinging cheek and stared at her mother in shock. It had been many years since Laura had laid a hand on her.

She had nearly forgotten what it felt like.

The memory flashed through Muireall's mind. She had been six years old at the time, and she'd just witnessed something terrible.

"Mum, I need to talk to you! 'Tis about Alastair," little Muireall said, panting between words. She'd just found Mother after running all the way home from Everton Inn. She knew it was a bad idea to interrupt when Mother was playing the piano, but this was too important to keep to herself.

Laura looked up, concern raising her dark eyebrows. "What about Alastair?"

Muireall shrank under her mother's gaze, uncomfortable being the focus of Laura's attention. "He's at the inn with Ewan. I was just going up there to see Adaira—I didn' mean to eavesdrop!"

"You heard something, I take it?"

"I . . ." She fidgeted with her fingers. *"I heard him tell Ewan he was going to put spiders in his bed if Ewan didn' do what he wanted. I couldn' hear the next part too well, but Alastair said something about stealing money from the tavern and—"*

"How dare you make such an outrageous claim," Mother cut in, practically spitting with anger.

"But, Mum, 'tis the truth."

Laura slammed the piano shut and rose to her feet. "Stop. Don' say any more. When yer brother gets back, I'll let him tell me what really happened."

"But Alastair won'—"

The rest of what Muireall had been about to say died on her lips the moment Laura's hand made contact with her jaw. She fell to the floor, too frightened to move. Too frightened to breathe.

Laura pointed at the staircase, jolting Muireall back to the present. "Go cover up yer face and get back here as quickly as you can. Matthew has already been waiting fer ten minutes."

Muireall fled to her room without hesitation, tears flooding her eyes.

Anne was no doubt busy with other duties now, so she set to work concealing the bright-red handprint on her left cheek. *Put back on the mask, Muireall. It wasn' on firmly enough before. Make sure you get it right this time.*

Once everything was covered, she reapplied the makeup that had smeared from her tears, sat up straight, and assessed her reflection. *There. Now no one will know. No one will ever know. The real Muireall is safely hidden away behind the layers o' what society demands o' me.*

She shook her head. *Nay, what Mother and Father demand o' me. Would the rest o' Everton care if I wasn' the "perfect noblewoman" they all expect?*

She rose from her seat and turned to the door. *I suppose we'll find out once the fairies grant my request, and my parents stop pushing me to find a husband. Then I'll be free.*

Strangely Breathless

Muireall swept into the dining room with her head high, just as her mother had taught her. She met Matthew's brown eyes and smiled, just as she was expected to. She flowed gracefully into her chair and politely greeted everyone—even Mother—just as she knew she should.

And all the while, no one saw the misery building up inside her. They couldn't, not when she played her part so perfectly.

After a few minutes of small talk, Muireall took a sip of water, set down her glass, and wiped her mouth with a napkin. The first course of the evening, a rather bland soup, had already been on the table when she'd arrived; now it was time to move on to the next course.

Everything will be fine, she told herself, barely noticing as servants came in to attend to them.

"Are you all right?" whispered a voice at her ear.

Muireall's knee collided with the table as she nearly leaped out of her chair.

Mother shot her a quick frown before returning to a conversation with Matthew.

Once she'd looked away, Muireall turned to the left, eyes wide. "Niall? What are you doing here?"

The dark-haired servant gestured to the tray in his hand. The three mostly empty soup bowls on the tray wobbled, dangerously close to slipping onto the floor. "I think 'tis fairly obvious." He reached down and added her bowl to the tray. "But I'm still waiting fer yer answer. Are you all right?"

He brushed his thumb against her cheek. The very one her mother had struck.

Muireall trembled under his touch, her heart thumping in her chest. *He saw Mother slap me?*

She pulled away, glancing around the room. No one was paying them any attention. For now. She turned back to Niall. "O' course I'm all right. There's no reason na to be."

The servant gave her a withering expression. "Don' lie to me, Muireall. You may fool everyone else but na me," he said, his tone gentle but scolding.

Heat rose in her face as he stared deeply into her eyes, searching for the truth.

Am I lying? I'm na even sure I know.

She wet her lips, drawing the man's gaze to her mouth. "Niall, I—"

"Lad, hurry up," Father called.

Niall stepped away and bowed apologetically before dashing out with his tray.

Muireall watched him depart, strangely breathless. *What was that? Why did it feel like we were the only two people in the room?*

"Mistress Oliver?" Mr. Levins called, breaking into her puzzling thoughts.

"Hmm?"

"I just wanted to compliment you on how lovely you look this evening." He gestured to her blue dress.

Muireall took a quick drink, unsure how to respond to his remark when she knew how he really felt about her. Her eyes drifted back to the doorway.

Wait . . . Niall called me by my first name just a moment ago. That insufferable man! Why, I'll—

Then she remembered how nice the pad of his thumb had felt on her cheek. She lifted her fingers to the spot, a soft smile playing at her lips.

She shook her head. *What is wrong with me? I should be angry right now, na—*

"Daughter, yer being rude," Laura chided from across the table, cutting off her daughter's train of thought. "Thank the gentleman."

Muireall turned to Matthew and said woodenly, "I apologize, Mr. Levins. Thank you fer yer kind words."

A question hovered in Matthew's eyes as he glanced at the door, then back at her. She followed his line of sight, wondering what he was thinking. *Did he notice what Niall just did?*

The door opened, and the two servants returned with the next course. Muireall made a point not to look at Niall, just in case Matthew was still watching her. She wasn't about to let herself get accused of giving a servant undue attention. Instead, she folded her hands in her lap and resumed her role of a demure noblewoman.

When she caught sight of the tacksman's unpleasant smile, though, she suspected she wasn't succeeding.

As Niall placed Muireall's plate on the table, Matthew said, "Mistress Oliver, I also wanted to tell you I've been quite impressed with yer . . . dedication to Rigmore House o' late."

"Dedication?" Laura asked, arching one thin eyebrow. "What on earth do you mean?"

Muireall grabbed her glass of water and took another swallow, ignoring the slight tremble in her hands. She felt Niall looking at her, but she refused to meet his eye. *Go on. Don' just stand there.*

Mr. Levins's gaze went from Muireall to Niall, a smirk spreading over his face.

What's he playing at? Muireall wondered, dread gathering inside her.

Niall moved to serve Mr. Levins, pointedly avoiding the tacksman's hard stare.

Matthew spoke to Lady Oliver, but he continued watching the servant. "I recently heard yer daughter has been working very hard to make sure the grounds are in pique condition. Specifically the garden."

"Ah, Muireall loves walking out there," Mother said, the confusion draining from her eyes. "She has many ideas fer how to arrange the flowers. She's quite good at it and often speaks to the gardener about making improvements."

Muireall's heart swelled at the praise until Mother added, "I always had a talent fer such things, too."

"I wasn' talking about giving the gardener ideas," Matthew said. "I was talking about something more . . . direct."

Muireall's stomach dropped, and it took all her willpower not to turn to Niall. *Someone must have seen us out there.*

Her mind went back to the flash of movement the other day when she'd taken Niall's hand. *It wasn' an animal retreating in fear; 'twas a spy hurrying back to Mr. Levins!*

Muireall's gaze flew to her parents. If Mr. Levins said something that could sully Muireall's reputation—regardless of how true it was—they'd lock her up so tightly all chance of freedom would be lost forever.

To say nothing of what they'd do to Niall.

Guilt and dread mingled in her gut, spurring her to action. She rose to her feet. "I—"

Matthew's plate wobbled in Niall's hands before falling to the floor with a great crash.

"I'm so sorry," the servant exclaimed, rushing to clean up the mess as the other servant came over to assist him.

"You clumsy oaf!" Laird Oliver shook a thick finger. "Get out o' here, and find someone more capable to take yer place."

The servants bowed and apologized several times before scurrying away, but just as Niall passed Muireall, he gave her a subtle nod.

She took a bite of food to hide her smirk, grateful for his distraction. She'd have to thank him later for his quick thinking. "Mr. Levins, I was hoping to give you a performance on my clàrsach after we've finished dinner. I just composed a—"

"About what we were discussing before," Matthew interrupted. "I'd really like to talk about this further, specifically what you've been *doing* in the garden."

Muireall ground her teeth together. *He's na letting this go. Fine, let's try a different tactic.*

"Mr. Levins," she said in her most sultry tone, "I'm flattered you've been checking up on me. But you don' need to resort to asking others when"—she batted her eyelashes—"I'd be happy to tell you all you'd like to know. Privately."

"Muireall Ainsley!" Mother pressed her hand over her heart, then looked to Matthew. "I don' know what has gotten into her. Rest assured, her father and I certainly don' condone such forward behavior."

Mr. Levins shook his head. "'Tis no problem, Lady Oliver. I'm glad my future bride is eager to *deepen* our acquaintance." He winked at Muireall, and she took a sharp breath to stave off a wave of nausea.

Laura Oliver leaned back, so appalled at the suggestive display that her mouth fell open, but no sound came out. She turned to her husband, who wasn't nearly as uncertain.

"Don' be so hasty in claiming ownership o' her, *lad*," Laird Oliver snapped. "Until my daughter accepts an official proposal from you, yer just a suitor. Nothing more." He swiped his hand through the air. "And even if you were formally betrothed, there are still certain measures o' propriety that must be upheld. Is that clear?"

"Aye, sir." Matthew smiled roguishly.

Muireall glared at her dinner companion, silently asking, *What are you up to?*

The tacksman lifted his eyebrows and held out his hands as if to say, *Nothing. I don' know why you'd assume such a thing.*

"Well, let's move on to more appropriate topics o' discussion, then," Father grumbled, staring the two young people down until they lowered their gazes in acquiescence.

The conversation shifted to lighter subjects after that, but Muireall remained on edge for the rest of the meal, watching Mr. Levins for any sign of what he was trying to do.

When dinner came to a close, she asked the gentleman, "Why don' we take a stroll around the garden since you showed such interest in it before? I'd love to show you what I've been working on."

Father tossed his napkin on the table, his mouth twitching as if his smile were about to fall off. "You know what? I think you've had quite enough time together fer one evening. 'Twould be best if you took yer leave, Mr. Levins."

The tacksman rolled his lips together, irritation sparking in his eyes before it dissolved behind a curtain of civility. "Forgive me, laird. I didn' realize yer hospitality was so short-lived."

Laird Oliver's countenance darkened, but before he could reply, Muireall rose to her feet. "That sounds like an excellent idea, Father. Let me show you out, Mr. Levins." She took Matthew's arm and urged him out the door.

As soon as they were in the foyer, Muireall dropped the man's arm. "What do you want?"

He huffed as if he couldn't believe she'd ask such a ridiculous question. "You already know what I want. I want to marry you."

"That's exactly the opposite o' what you told me before. I thought you wanted a way to get out o' marrying me. Mr. Mendes is the answer to that. Why aren' you happy about it?"

He paused. "I may na like you as a person, but that doesn' mean I want a foreigner taking what's rightfully mine." His eyes raked boldly over her form.

Fiery indignation took hold of Muireall's spirit. "I am na yers."

Matthew grabbed her chin between his fingers, tightening his grip when she tried to pull away. "That may be true now, but Rigmore House belongs to Everton, na to some viscount who wants to play in a tavern."

She shoved his hand away. "Rigmore House is *my* home, na Mr. Mendes's." Her lips peeled back in a snarl. "And certainly na yers."

Matthew's eyes narrowed. "Are you sure you want go this route? All it takes is one word, and yer parents will throw out that precious servant o' yers so fast you won' even be able to say goodbye."

Muireall's spine stiffened, but she kept her face from betraying her fear. "And what if I were to tell my father about the extra money you've been squeezing out o' yer tenants?"

The man's confidence wavered. "How do you know about that?" His voice was low, threatening.

But she knew she had him cornered. She held up her fingernails, carefully inspecting each one as Matthew waited for her to respond. *Let him squirm a bit now that I have the upper hand.*

Finally, she stretched up to his ear and whispered, "Yer na the only one who knows what goes on in this village."

Many months ago, Anne had made some disparaging comments about Mr. Levins's taxes on his tenants. Muireall had put on a pretense of concern and easily extracted the full story from her loose-lipped servant, tucking the information away to use at her discretion. *And now 'tis coming in handy. Thank you very much, Anne.*

When she leaned away, Matthew's eyes no longer gleamed with contempt. Instead, he regarded her with a reluctant respect.

Muireall smirked. *You underestimated me. I'm much more than a simple annoyance. I could make yer life very difficult.*

He opened his mouth to speak.

"Muireall, let the gentleman leave." Mother appeared in the foyer, her lip curl on full display.

Mr. Levins's face twisted at the interruption, his hands clenching into fists. "This isn' over," he hissed at Muireall, then stormed out of the house.

Ugh, what a horrid man. Using Niall against me was a low blow. What am I going to do if he changes his mind and decides to tell my parents what he knows?

Laura came up on Muireall's right side, her long skirts swishing as she walked. The younger woman braced herself for the rebuke she knew was coming, keeping her eyes fixed on the front door.

She didn't have to wait long.

"I don' know what I witnessed back there, but if you know what's good fer you"—Laura glared until Muireall made eye contact—"you'll behave in a manner befitting yer position from now on."

Mother's gaze moved to Muireall's cheek, which seemed to burn anew under her scrutiny. "Is that understood?"

"Aye, Mother." Muireall bowed her head, then took her leave, eager to escape the charged atmosphere.

When she closed the bedroom door behind her, she slid to the floor in a heap, her carefully curated mask falling from her face.

What a night. She brushed her fingertips across her collarbone, then checked her heartbeat. Still racing.

As it had been ever since Mr. Levins had started talking about her "dedication" to the estate.

Nay, that's na quite right. 'Twas before that. Muireall's brow furrowed as she tried to recall what had set it off.

She froze. *'Twas the moment Niall touched me.*

Warmth rushed through her at the memory, but with it, came a startling revelation: *If Mr. Levins had made the claim I've gotten too close to Niall, he wouldn' have been wrong.*

Muireall could barely admit it, even to herself, but somewhere along the line, her relationship with the troublesome servant had become something she'd never expected—a friendship.

She slowly touched her cheek. Or perhaps worse.

Crossing the Threshold

The following day, Niall mostly kept to himself, eating his meals as quickly as he could in between attending church and working in the garden. He tried to keep his focus on the tasks before him—weeding, pruning, watering. Physical labor wasn't his favorite pastime, but at least it made sense.

Far more than the feelings trying to take control of his mind.

Last night had done something to him. Though he couldn't explain it, a surge of protectiveness had nearly overwhelmed him at the sight of Lady Oliver striking her daughter's face, too powerful to just ignore. He'd witnessed the older woman's cruelty and disregard for Muireall plenty of times, but never before had it bothered him to the point of madness.

Nothing short of madness could explain the way he'd behaved at dinner.

I could have lost my position had anyone seen me touching Mistress Oliver. Or calling her by her first name. Niall winced in disgust. *What was I thinking?*

He wrenched a thick weed from the dirt, his hand flying back as the root broke free. He tossed the plant aside and wiped some sweat from his brow. He'd been working almost nonstop all day, and now the sun was low in the sky.

If Muireall didn't show up soon, perhaps he'd go to Everton Inn to visit with the Burgesses. He'd already eaten dinner, but he'd happily make room for a plate of Adaira's cooking. Her food was undoubtedly the best in the village, no matter what Jeane Martin claimed.

They wouldn' turn me away if I stopped by. He'd been invited over for tea a few times now. And while it had been very awkward—especially with John incessantly glaring at him—the Burgesses had said they'd like to have him over for dinner soon.

Niall's heart warmed. *Well, this seems as good a night as any.* He brushed off his hands.

Soft footfalls caught his attention. The young mistress stood a few feet away in a pale-yellow dress, her expression aloof.

"Mistress Oliver," Niall greeted, his lips curving up into a smile before he could stop himself. "I wasn' sure you were coming tonight. Look, yer primrose has been growing."

He gestured to the plant, but she didn't even glance at it.

"You told me we'd have to go at night to find a kelpie, so I came."

"Did anyone see you leave?"

She shook her head. "I told my parents I wasn' feeling well and needed to retire early." There was a hardness to the woman's voice, almost as if she was angry with him.

Niall frowned. *Did I upset her last night? She seemed grateful when I distracted everyone from Mr. Levins's question. Or did something else happen after I left?* He'd avoided asking Gilbert any questions about how the rest of the dinner had gone, despite the curiosity burning within him.

He reached toward her. "Is something wr—" He broke off when Muireall stepped back.

He lowered his hand, confusion and hurt sweeping through him. The memory of when he'd first offered to help her flitted through his mind. He'd frightened her then, too.

After all we've been through, I thought . . .

Muireall's eyes drifted from his almost guiltily, but she said nothing.

What? What did you think? asked a sharp voice inside him. *That she trusted you? That yer silly attempt to comfort her last night was actually worth something? The only reason she's here right now is because you agreed to help her find the two remaining treasures. Otherwise, she would never spend time with a servant.*

Niall's shoulders sagged as he recalled how she'd treated him in those first weeks after he'd arrived. It wasn't until they'd struck their bargain that she'd even deigned to talk to him.

His gaze wandered over the woman's face, taking in her long eyelashes, full lips, and slight, upturned nose. Then he looked down at his plain clothes and dirt-covered shoes that were a size too big, his confidence shriveling. *Maybe I am just fooling myself.*

"Well, are you ready to go? If we're careful, we should be able to avoid being seen." Her tone was clipped, impatient.

"Aye, let's go," he replied, burying his feelings so deep even he couldn't reach them.

Once they'd decided how they were going to retrieve the bridle, the pair fell silent, moving through the village like ghosts. They split up just before Loch Isla came into view, with Muireall pressing ahead while Niall held back. The plan was simple: Muireall would draw the kelpie out, and while it was focused on her, Niall would attack. He would have to be quick, for kelpies were strong and cunning.

While Niall had never personally encountered one before, he'd heard plenty of stories about these despicable creatures that could shift between horse and something close to human. Unlike most magical beings, kelpies didn't discriminate between friend and food. Anything that moved was prey, whether it be animal, human, or another creature of magic— even other kelpies could fall victim to their ravenous appetites.

But kelpies had one weakness: their need for mates. All kelpies were male, and thus, unable to reproduce among themselves. Humans and horses were both viable partners, but they preferred humans since they were easier to subdue.

Niall's heart was in his throat as he peeked out at Muireall from behind a nearby tree. He'd wanted to approach the loch together, but Muireall had insisted their odds would be better if they had the element of surprise.

I never should have agreed to this.

The redhead walked leisurely along the bank, her expression more carefree than Niall had seen it in days. He wondered if she was as nervous as he was on the inside. She certainly should be. If he was too slow in getting to her, she could easily be dragged down to the loch's shadowy depths and taken to the kelpie's underwater domain, a place where Niall had little hope of reaching her.

The iron knife burned in his trouser pocket as he waited, watching the loch for any sign of life. After about half an hour, Niall started to worry he'd been wrong, that maybe the hoof prints at the water's edge hadn't belonged to a kelpie, after all. Muireall, too, seemed dispirited and eventually sat down on a fallen tree trunk. She stared out at the water, bright in the moonlight, then rose again and started to head in Niall's direction.

Niall stepped out from his hiding place, wishing he had something encouraging to say. If there wasn't a kelpie in this loch, they'd have to go searching beyond Everton, and coming up with a good excuse to leave town would be difficult.

Ripples appeared in the center of the loch. Niall ducked back behind the tree before daring another peek at the water. Muireall spun around, her body going stiff.

A tall, wet figure emerged from the loch, long strands of black hair clinging to his lanky body. His skin had a bluish tinge, much like that of a drowned corpse. Nails that were more like claws extended from his fingers. Over his body, he wore a drenched brown tunic, which did nothing to disguise the hooves at the bottom of his legs.

"Y-Yer . . ." Muireall trembled, more frightened than Niall had ever seen her.

Something uncontrollable rose up within him, and he lunged out of his hiding place, knife held high.

The kelpie snarled at Niall's approach, his black eyes narrowing in rage. "Leannan na mara." His voice was like the hiss of a snake, soft yet full of spite. "She's mine."

He grabbed Muireall around the waist and turned back to the loch.

Niall flew forward, reaching the pair as the water came up to waist level. "Let her go!"

He stabbed wildly at the kelpie, but the creature leaned away as the knife arced toward him. The blade sliced across the kelpie's arm, leaving a trail of blood in its wake.

The kelpie howled, then shoved Muireall away before launching himself at Niall.

"Watch out," Muireall cried, but it was too late. The kelpie dug his long nails into Niall's chest, then pulled Niall toward the middle of the loch.

Niall stabbed at the creature again, but the kelpie grasped his wrists, keeping the knife from reaching its destination. The two pushed against each other, but neither could gain the upper hand.

"Let's see how you enjoy drowning," the kelpie said with a sneer, then yanked Niall forward as his own body fell back, plunging them both into the watery depths.

***

"Niall!"

Panic tore through Muireall's chest as she watched the water horse pull Niall under. She tried to follow them, but as soon as the water reached her neck, her body seized up, trembling uncontrollably.

Tis happening all over again, she realized, gasping for breath. She hadn't even hesitated to charge in after her servant, but now, memories seized her mind:

Fighting the tide's grip as it sought to sweep her out to sea.

Choking and sputtering as water dipped into her lungs.

Longing to reach her brother, to pull him back to safety—but not if it meant facing the monster that had dragged him out there.

"Alastair, come back!"

Muireall shivered, goose bumps breaking out over her arms as she peered into the dark water, praying for a miracle.

Seconds later, a figure burst to the surface, then another swiftly behind him. Niall whirled around to the kelpie, driving his knife into the creature's bloated skin even as it tried to slam his head under the water.

Its answering shriek echoed through Muireall's skull, shaking her free of her paralysis. She screamed, drawing the kelpie's attention.

With a menacing smile, it swam toward her, its black hair flowing behind it like seaweed. Muireall hurried back toward the shore, but her limbs were heavy as she plodded through the cool water. She sensed it just behind her, felt its nails graze her leg—

A great splash made her already-rapid heart jolt with terror, but when she looked back, there was nothing behind her except ripples. She ran forward, not turning again until both her feet were on the shore.

A dark, sinuous shape rose up from the water—a horse as black as night. Malice burned in its luminous eyes, its nostrils flaring as it bucked in all directions.

And there, straddling its back, sat Niall, straining against the beast's wild movements with a golden bridle in his hands.

He's got it! He's found the bridle!

Niall pulled at the bridle, his face tight with concentration, but the kelpie refused to surrender. It galloped across the loch, its hooves moving over the water as smoothly as dry ground.

Where's the knife?

Both of Niall's hands were wrapped around the bridle, the dagger nowhere to be seen. Even as Muireall scanned the shoreline, she knew she wouldn't find it there. It had to be somewhere at the bottom of the loch.

And Muireall couldn't swim.

"Niall, the knife!" she cried, unsure if her voice could even be heard above the kelpie's whinnies.

Her servant's head whipped toward her, his eyes widening in the split second before the kelpie changed direction.

And locked its fearsome gaze on Muireall.

"Get out o' here!" Niall yanked on the bridle, his voice cracking in desperation.

The kelpie bucked once more, this time sending Niall flying backward. The young man's body smacked against the water, then disappeared from sight.

The kelpie whirled around and dove headfirst after him, sliding under the water without a sound.

The loch went perfectly still, and all Muireall could hear was her own blood rushing through her ears. She tried to call out, but fear strangled her voice. She pressed her hand to her chest, her fingers digging into the folds of her dress.

Niall? Niall!

After what felt like hours, her servant's thin form broke through the surface, coughing even as he swung around with his knife raised.

He's alive! Muireall's lungs filled with air, and she nearly cried out in relief.

Niall stayed still for a few seconds, but when the kelpie didn't reappear, he lowered his arm and swam toward shore. His strokes were slow, pained, as though it was all he could do to keep moving.

Once he'd gotten to the shallows, Muireall bounded into the water and grabbed his arm, nearly knocking the man over. "Is it dead?"

He nodded, a tired smile coming over his face.

Muireall smiled back, but before she could say more, he slumped against her, his energy depleted. Muireall swayed, bracing her foot as best she could in the soft mud. The two of them made their way back to the shore and flopped to the ground.

"Niall, are you all right?" she ventured, relief warring with concern as she awaited his answer. Cuts lined the man's arms and neck. Most appeared to have come from the kelpie's claws, but a few looked like bite marks. His shirt and trousers were in a similar state, exposing skin in several places.

The servant panted with exertion, the movement revealing a small section of his chest, and Muireall quickly averted her eyes.

Niall held up his hand, extending a golden bridle to her. "I got it," he said with a weak grin.

Irritation surged through Muireall's body, and she shoved him away, sending him straight onto his backside.

When he landed with a grunt, she rushed to help him back up. "I'm so sorry."

Niall grimaced, gingerly touching his left hip. "I know things didn' go exactly as planned, but can you na take yer anger out on me right now?" His tone was playful yet slightly hurt.

"I said I was sorry," she replied, her words harsher than she intended.

Niall's expression sharpened, his eyes glittering with displeasure. "What is wrong with you?" His voice was an ominous rumble now. "Is it that hard to show me kindness after I nearly *died* getting this fer you?" He held up the bridle again.

Muireall's jaw tightened even as guilt fluttered in her chest. "Watch yer tongue, servant."

Something flashed across the man's face, gone too quickly to discern it. "Oh, that's right. I forgot I'm just a servant, so my life must na matter to you," he said mockingly. "My apologies, yer Highness." He gave her a clumsy bow.

"Don' be ridiculous. O' course yer life matters."

An instinct warned her they were wandering into dangerous territory and that if this discussion carried on much longer, they'd pass over a threshold they couldn't come back from. What that threshold could be, though, she had no idea.

Niall scoffed. "But only as long as I'm still helping you, right?"

His arrogance was too much, and something inside Muireall snapped. Throwing caution to the wind, she asked, "Is there a point to this?"

Niall sprang forward, placing his hands on her shoulders as he closed the distance between them. His breath was warm against her face, his nose inches from hers. "After all this time," he said huskily, "am I still just a servant to you?"

His captivating eyes riveted Muireall to the spot, her heart hammering against her ribs. *Have his eyes always been this beautiful?*

She opened her mouth, but his nearness was so overwhelming she couldn't recall his question. "What?"

Niall's gaze darted to her lips, making Muireall's stomach swirl with anticipation. He leaned closer until his mouth just barely brushed hers, then pulled back with hopeful, probing eyes.

Muireall had never felt something so soft, so enticing. All she wanted to do was lean forward and—

She lurched out of his grasp and threw her hands out in front of her. "What are you doing? Don' touch me!"

Niall winced and ducked his head. "Forgive me, mistress. I . . . I lost myself fer a moment there." His voice was low with a distinct note of pain.

"I should say so," she said, but the words came out breathless. "How dare you kiss me. I—" She touched her tingling lips, a delightful shiver running through her, then shook her head in disgust.

What am I doing? I can' just let him get away with this. He needs to know how upset I am.

"I'm na someone you can just do that to." Muireall attempted to speak matter-of-factly. "You and me aren'—we're na—" Her pulse leaped as his eyes slid to hers, disarming her sense of reason once again.

His mouth spread in a devastating grin. "Na what?"

She gulped, cheeks burning even as the man's teasing tone tugged at her, drawing her in.

With a gasp, she spun away. She was too frazzled to explain right now; she'd try again another time. "We better head back," she said, her voice raw. "Are you well enough to walk?"

"To Rigmore House?" He laughed in disbelief. "Na likely."

She didn't want to turn around, didn't want to look him in the eye again, but her conscience compelled her. Despite his indecent behavior, he'd helped her, and she wasn't going to leave him behind.

Muireall took a deep breath and tentatively turned. "Then where to?"

"Get me to Drulea Cottage," he said, his dark eyes stony. Gone was the fire that had lit them only moments before, a fact Muireall found oddly disappointing. "Briony will let me stay there."

Something coiled in Muireall's gut. Several adults in the village used each other's first names, but unless a higher-class person was speaking to someone of the lower class, such informality was usually reserved for dear friends.

And lovers.

Adaira allows everyone to call her by her first name, she reminded herself.

But that's just her personality, she argued. *No one thinks anything o' it.*

Mistress Fairborn, on the other hand, had such a bad reputation that any perceived friendliness toward her could easily result in unfounded rumors.

Rumors . . . A hazy memory darted through Muireall's mind. She'd heard of Niall Moreland when he'd first come to the village, but she'd had no interest in making his acquaintance then. That hadn't stopped Anne from gossiping about him the morning after Johnsmas though.

"I saw the most interesting thing at the dance, my lady," Anne said as she helped Muireall into her clothes. *"Before the storm started, I mean. That handsome stranger with the long dark hair—I think his name is Mr. Moreland—was dancing with Briony Fairborn, and you'll never guess what he did."*

Muireall rolled her eyes, annoyed by the maid's wagging tongue. She hadn't attended the gathering for Johnsmas, nor did she wish to hear what she'd missed.

With a squeal, Anne whispered, "He kissed her! Right on the ear. I saw it, I did. That Mistress Fairborn really has all the newcomers in town besotted with her. Several o' the sailors were watching her, too, and Mr. Rendall told me he saw her and Mr. Mendes sitting way too close together out at Cramer's Field na long ago."

The rest of the memory drifted from Muireall's mind; she wished now that she'd asked Anne for more details. *Could Niall and Briony Fairborn have been in a secret relationship? I know she's with Mr. Mendes now, but that only tells me what Briony's feelings are, na Niall's.*

Drulea Cottage was the place where Niall had taken Muireall after the fairy dance, too. At best, that meant he trusted her. At worst—

She swallowed, not wanting to think about that. She nodded to the servant. "All right. Then let's go."

She spun on her heel and started walking, but when she didn't hear him behind her, she looked over her shoulder. "Aren' you coming?"

Niall glowered. "Did you forget what happened a few minutes ago? I'm going to need some help."

"Didn' seem to slow you down when you were kissing me," she said, then snapped her mouth shut as her face turned a vivid scarlet. She hurried to the man's side and put his arm over her shoulder, ducking her head to avoid his eye. She was grateful when he didn't respond, but she felt his stare all the way to the midwife's house.

When they arrived, Muireall had Niall sit down and lean against the cottage. It seemed the walk hadn't been good for him; sweat was dripping down his face, and he was breathing heavily.

"Niall? Are you all right?"

The man slouched forward, his arms landing on his knees before he fell to the side, unconscious.

"Niall!" Muireall banged on the door, terror seizing her.

The midwife grumbled from within, "Oh, who is it this time? I see now why Dr. Sherwin was so moody. Can' it wait until—" She broke off as she opened the door. Concern filled her golden eyes as she took in Muireall and Niall, then she scowled. "Why does this scene look so familiar?"

An Impossible, Unfathomable Thing

Once the two women had gotten Niall onto the nearest bed, Briony's eyes went from the scratches on the man's arms to a dark spot on his gray tunic. That hadn't been there before.

Muireall's hand shot forward, but when her fingers came away from the cloth, they were stained with blood. She gasped and turned to Briony. "You have to help him."

The midwife remained calm in the face of Muireall's rising anxiety, her tone commanding as she said, "Help me take off his shirt."

"What?" Muireall's voice was almost a shriek. "Are you mad? I couldn' possibly—"

The midwife scowled. "Mistress Oliver, this is no time fer decorum. If you want to help Niall, either assist me or get out."

Muireall flew into action, gently pulling off the man's right sleeve. Her cheeks burned with heat, but she tried not to think about the impropriety and focus instead on what needed to be done.

A deep gash across Niall's stomach was the source of the blood, and once his shirt was off, Briony wrapped a bandage around the wound. Similar cuts went across his torso, crisscrossing in random arrangements.

Muireall's heart went out to him, each mark a reminder of the danger he'd put himself in for her sake. Her unease lessened as she watched the midwife expertly clean his wounds. All the negative feelings she'd felt about coming here dissipated. Briony had been the right person to go to; she saw that now.

She tried not to, but she couldn't help noticing the man's attractive form, from his angular face, relaxed in sleep, to his long, lean torso. *Has he always been this good-looking?*

"How did this happen? What hurt him?" Briony didn't look up from her task.

Muireall hesitated, unsure if she should tell the whole truth.

"I need to know," Briony said with authority.

"'Twas . . . a kelpie," she confessed. She told herself it was right to be honest even as guilt pricked at her insides. It might make a difference in the way Niall's wounds would be treated. And if Niall hadn't wanted Briony to find out, he shouldn't have told Muireall to take him to Drulea Cottage.

The midwife's hand stilled for a fraction of a second, then she bandaged up the rest of Niall's cuts. The fact that she didn't question Muireall's sanity for giving such a response seemed evidence enough that she believed her.

"He should be fine," Briony said when she was done. "Kelpie wounds don' require any special care."

Muireall didn't ask why she knew that. Part of her was afraid to find out the answer.

"What about that one?" She pointed to a spot at the top of Niall's chest. She'd been trying not to look too closely before, but she realized now that this wound didn't look like the others. Unlike the kelpie's long thin scratches, this one was wider and had a curved shape. It didn't seem to have bled at all either.

Briony slowly rose back up to her full height. "I need to get more bandages in case he bleeds through these. Unfortunately, they're down at Dr. Sherwin's old office. Keep an eye on him while I'm gone." She slipped around Muireall and vanished out the door.

Muireall frowned, her eyes straying back to the strange wound on Niall's chest. *Did I imagine it, or did Briony's face change when I asked about that mark? And why didn' she answer me?*

Perhaps it didn't come from tonight.

But if that's the case, what could have made it?

Candlelight flickered over the man's half-naked form, creating shadows on his pale skin. Muireall brushed his hair away from his eyes, her lips curved in a soft smile. She'd never had someone risk so much for her before. Or pay so dearly for it.

Gratitude bubbled up inside her, along with something else she dared not name. "Thank you," she whispered.

"Yer welcome, Princess," Niall replied. He opened his eyes, chuckling as she drew back in surprise.

"Niall!" She smacked the man's shoulder.

He grunted. "I do hope this isn' becoming a habit." He rubbed his shoulder, then wagged his eyebrows at her.

Muireall glared, her lips twitching as she held back a grin.

Niall laughed again, then raised his arm to scratch the back of his head, drawing her eye to his wrist.

And the cuts she'd found the day he'd pricked his finger on the rosebush.

She couldn't help but note how similar they were to the kelpie's claw marks, though none were nearly as deep.

"Niall?"

"Hmm?" The man didn't seem embarrassed by his half-naked state, a fact that made her own embarrassment even worse.

"You don' have to tell me, but . . . the scratches on yer wrist—were they really just an accident?"

Niall slowly lowered his arm, his expression turning tentative as he looked down at the marks. "Na exactly."

That same vulnerable quality had returned to his voice, but this time, Muireall hoped he would trust her enough to tell her what had happened. Scratches like that weren't caused by simply brushing up against something sharp. Something—or someone—had hurt him.

"What was it?"

"'Twas . . . my own doing. I—I didn' mean to, na really. I just . . ."

"Just what?"

He sighed, then smiled sheepishly. "I get nightmares sometimes, and afterward, I'll wake up and find marks like these." He held out his hands, making her realize the cuts weren't confined to just one wrist—both were covered in dozens of tiny scratches.

"You do this in yer sleep?" Her voice broke a bit.

What horrors would drive him to harm himself?

Niall shrugged as if it weren't of any consequence. "Aye, but—" He paused. "Huh. Now that I think about it, I haven' had any nightmares in a while." He examined his wrists again, a warm smile spreading over his face. "Looks like they're healing up pretty well."

Muireall grinned in return, though concern remained in her eyes. "Do you think you'll have nightmares tonight because o' the kelpie?"

He shook his head. "I . . ." He let out a short chuckle, almost as if he couldn't believe it himself. "I'm na sure why, but I think I'm all right now."

"Well, just to be safe"—she turned away and pulled out an herb from her pocket[26]—"put this under yer pillow." She placed it in his hand.

Niall frowned. "What is this?"

Muireall tucked a strand of hair behind her ear. "'Tis lavender. It helps relax the mind, so you can have a better sleep."

"And you carry it with you?"

"Aye, and what's so wrong with that?" she snapped, unable to keep from getting defensive. "'Tis coming in handy now, isn' it? If you don' want it, I can take it ba—"

Niall moved his hand out of reach, his lips pinched in annoyance. "I didn' say I didn' want it." His expression softened. "Do you get nightmares, too?"

Muireall took a breath to deny it, then changed her mind. "Sometimes."

Niall didn't respond; it seemed he was waiting for her to say more.

---

[26] A cloth bag women wore under their petticoats or aprons.

"If it doesn' work, you could ask Mistress Fairborn fer some juniper leaves and see if those work better," Muireall added.

Maybe one day she would tell Niall about her past, but that day hadn't come yet.

Niall's eyes filled with understanding, but for once, he was gracious enough not to point out her blatant change in topic. He gave her an almost imperceptible nod, then glanced around. "By the way, where did Briony go?"

That same sharp feeling she'd sensed earlier twisted in Muireall's stomach for a second time. *There he goes, calling her "Briony" again. It really doesn' make sense fer him to be so familiar with her. Just who is she to him?*

"She went into town to get more bandages," she said casually, trying to ignore the emotions churning within her.

'Tis na my business what he thinks o' her. Niall and I aren' in the sort o' relationship where it matters how close he is to another woman. He can do as he pleases. It makes no difference to me.

But that kiss . . . Did it mean nothing to him?

Muireall's heart fluttered at the memory, and she groaned inwardly, irritated with herself. *If only I could simply ask him and rid myself o' this curiosity.*

But doing so would make him think she was interested in him, and she certainly didn't want him to give the wrong impression.

Niall closed his eyes, seemingly satisfied with her answer. And perfectly content to lie in Briony Fairborn's bed. Muireall's left hand closed into a fist.

"Thank you fer bringing me here, mistress."

"Muireall," she bit out, jealousy loosing her tongue before she could stop it.

The man opened his eyes. "What?"

She drew in a quick breath, her cheeks warming. But as his eyes met hers, her embarrassment faded away. "Muireall," she repeated, more firmly this time. "After what you did fer me tonight, I believe you've earned the right to use my first name."

The side of Niall's mouth lifted into a smirk. "Oh, I have? Almost getting eaten by a kelpie was all it took?"

Muireall laughed, a light, ebullient sound that filled the room and eased some of the tension in the air. The two of them spoke more easily after that, smiling and teasing each other with a camaraderie that hadn't been there in the past. Though Muireall wasn't about to admit it aloud, their encounter with the kelpie had indeed changed something between them. And where there had once been a clear boundary between mistress and servant, something far more nebulous now stood in its place.

When Briony returned, Muireall reluctantly bid the two of them good night, then made the long trek back to Rigmore House. The estate was perfectly quiet as she crept inside and slipped into her bedroom. But despite the silence, Muireall's heart was still thundering in her chest, and she wasn't sure she'd be able to calm down enough to go to sleep.

As she undressed and got into bed, the events of the night replayed through her mind. Almost being taken by the kelpie had easily been the most terrifying experience of her life. She shuddered just thinking about how the monster had nearly gotten her. *If I'd tried to get the bridle alone, I never would have made it. Thank goodness Niall was there.*

And then to kiss me . . . what could have possessed him to do that? Muireall's pulse spiked at the memory, but she pushed it away.

It had been a mistake; Niall had said as much already, so there was no point in dwelling on it.

In the morneen, I'll go back to Drulea Cottage to make sure he's all right. He lost a lot o' blood—

Muireall's eyes flew open. *Does that mean he won' be able to help me find the last treasure?*

She clucked her tongue. *Shame on me fer thinking about that at a time like this. After what I just put him through, I should try to get the cloak by myself. I did fine with the trow. A banshee isn'—*

Muireall shook her head, Mr. McLaren's wild stories of wailing women whirling through her mind. *All right, maybe I can' handle it on my own. But it won' hurt me to wait until Niall recovers. I still have time before the full moon.*

She closed her eyes, letting her mind drift, so she could get some much-needed rest. But as sleep took her, her final thought wasn't of the night's danger or the future's uncertainty—it was of how soft Niall's lips had felt against her own.

***

Niall waited until he could hear Briony's soft snores before he slowly rose from the bed. His body ached, but he couldn't afford to waste an opportunity like this. He tiptoed through the house, checking every drawer, every cupboard, every place where the midwife's sealskin might be hidden.

When he entered Briony's bedroom, he paused as he loomed over her sleeping form. Her black hair was splayed out across the pillow, her face relaxed. She'd been so kind as she'd tended to him tonight; it reminded him of how she'd treated him when he'd first come to Everton. Back when he'd simply been the lad she'd rescued. Back when she'd believed the best of him.

Niall bit down on his tongue, hating the nostalgia welling up inside him. It would be so easy to take her life right now. Then he could search the rest of the cottage without fear of being discovered. He pulled out the dagger in his pocket and ran his finger down the blade.

So easy . . . A drop of blood appeared on his finger.

He put the knife away, aggravated by his own carelessness. He'd lost far too much blood already tonight.

He looked down at Briony again. *If it hadn' been fer her and Muireall* . . .

He swallowed and turned away, his stomach lurching as a wave of guilt overtook him. He scolded himself for getting distracted, then continued his search.

I have to find the sealskin first; only then can I get rid o' Briony. He kept as quiet as he could, ignoring the way his body protested. And there, under the bed, he finally found his prize.

Niall's fingers trembled with anticipation. He reached out—

CREAK!

Niall leaned back from the floorboard, but it was too late. Briony started to stir. He pushed himself up to his feet and

173

darted back to the bed. He'd just thrown the blanket over his lower half when candlelight appeared under the door.

"Niall?" Briony whispered as she came inside. "Are you awake?"

He stretched as though he was just waking. "Briony? What's wrong?"

"I thought I heard a noise. I wanted to make sure you were well." The woman's eyes were bloodshot, and her hair was all askew. She held up the candle to his torso and gasped.

"You've reopened one o' yer wounds. You'll need a new bandage." She quickly retrieved one, then gingerly removed the bloody cloths around his middle.

Niall winced, pain shooting through him at the slightest pressure on his abdomen, but Briony's touch was gentle, soothing. He looked away, not saying a word as she worked. He'd just tried to kill her, yet here she was, nursing him.

A fact that was far more painful than any wound the kelpie had inflicted.

Once Briony had finished, she reminded Niall to lie still and that if he needed anything, he could call for her. He nodded, an uncomfortable tightness in his chest.

She stood up to leave, but as she did, he blurted, "Briony?"

"Aye?" she replied, arms full of his bloody bandages.

"Why did you save me?"

She tilted her head to the side, seemingly confused at his question. "Because you came to me fer help."

"But—but why?" Niall sputtered. "After everything that's happened between us, why bother? Aren' you . . . . aren' you afraid I might na really be safe to be around? That I might just be pretending? Wouldn' it have been better to just let me die?"

Briony leaned forward, her golden eyes studying him. "Part o' me *is* afraid yer na being honest with us, that you've got some scheme in the back o' yer mind. How could someone change so much in such a short span o' time?" She paused. "As fer yer other question, I've contemplated much more than just letting you die. I've killed you in my mind dozens o' times."

Niall grimaced, fear slithering down his spine at her cold honesty. "Then why aren' I dead?"

"At first, I didn' kill you fer William's sake. I didn' want to be the cause o' him losing more family. But then . . ." Briony smiled, her gaze drifting from his. "What you said before about na taking advantage o' Mistress Oliver—I don' know why, but when you told me that, I could tell you were being sincere."

When her eyes returned to his, they radiated with so much goodness Niall almost couldn't bear it. "And if you had learned to care about one human's wellbeing, that meant there was hope fer everyone else, too."

Niall sat speechless, his thoughts and feelings tumbling like waves upon the sand, each one breaking upon the other too quickly to grab hold of it before it drifted away.

"Well, goodnight, Niall," Briony said, then strode out of the room.

"Goodnight," he replied weakly, his shoulders caving inward. He settled back down in the bed and tried to relax.

He didn't dare sneak into Briony's room again. He knew where the sealskin was now; that was the important thing. He needed to wait until he'd regained more of his strength before he tried anything else.

Maybe I shouldn' even bother. Maybe I should just leave Briony alo—

He cut off the rest of the thought, searching for anything else to occupy his mind. His eyes landed on his wrists. His sleeves had slid up a bit, exposing the thin red scars on his skin. He rolled over and took in a deep breath of lavender, his heart warming at Muireall's kind gift.

It was true that he'd stopped having nightmares of late, but he'd lied about not knowing the reason. He had a pretty good inkling what was responsible.

Or rather, who.

The memory of Muireall's mouth returned, stealing his attention. A light smile broke over his cheeks. The touch of her lips had been tantalizing, and it had been nearly impossible to pull back and wait for her response.

But he hadn't wanted to force himself on her. The attraction between them—he'd needed to know if she'd felt it, too.

Her rejection had stung, but he'd kept himself from dwelling on it too much. Until now, in the quiet of this empty room, when the hurt spilled over him anew.

He scoffed at himself. *Why am I so upset? 'Tis na like the kiss really meant anything. She just made me so angry I lost control o' myself.*

Aye, that's what happened. 'Twas a lapse in judgment, a silly impulse, like I told Muireall.

Was it? whispered a second voice in his mind. *Or was it simply the first time you couldn' stop yerself from doing something you've wanted to do fer weeks?*

Niall ground his teeth. He hadn't wanted to admit it, but his thoughts *had* been straying in that direction for a while now. Muireall had always been attractive, but at some point, he'd become far too aware of the curve of her hips, the brightness of her eyes, the scent of her hair.

I've always been aware o' those things. Any man would be. I'm just . . . Just—

Niall dropped the argument with a sigh. He was past the point of self-deception. *How did I na see it when 'tis so obvious?*

The way Muireall's music had captivated him, the rage he'd felt when Lady Oliver had slapped her, his strange desire to please her with the Scottish primrose—they were all signs he should have recognized sooner.

And then tonight, when the kelpie had appeared and she'd gotten so scared, he'd lost all sense of reason and jumped out of his hiding place sooner than he'd intended.

It all added up to one impossible, unfathomable thing, and he'd been so foolish he hadn't noticed it until he'd crossed the line and done the unthinkable. Such a mistake could have resulted in him losing his position, and as a result, losing his only chance to return to the sea.

But why is that na what I'm most concerned about right now?

He knew he should be ashamed for forgetting his purpose in coming here. He'd gotten distracted a few times when he'd first arrived, but it had never taken him long to refocus on his priorities.

Steal the sealskin, kill his enemies, rescue William—those were the goals that had kept Niall going up until now.

But they weren't enough for him anymore, not when he'd had his entire world flipped upside-down by a beautiful, maddening, fascinating redhead who made him feel more alive than the sea ever had.

Somehow . . . I've fallen in love with her. I've fallen in love with the very enemy I came to destroy.

Niall ran his hands down his face. After the night he'd just had, he hadn't expected that simple confession to be the thing that frightened him most of all.

Family Ties

"Muireall Oliver, why are you still in bed?" Laura's voice was sharp in her daughter's ear. "Up, up!"

The young woman groaned as she forced her body into a sitting position. She ran her hand through her hair, still not fully awake. *Why does my back hurt so much?*

"What is it, Mother?" she asked impatiently, eyes still closed. Laura only woke her personally when something important was going on.

"Don' use that tone with me. The viscount is coming fer tea, so you need to get ready."

Muireall's eyes flew open. She jumped out of bed, discarding her fatigue like a well-worn coat. "Where's Anne?"

Mother huffed in disgust. "She's busy taking care o' something that new servant should have been doing. Fer some reason, Hamish can' find him." She sucked her teeth. "Honestly, after that horrendous behavior at dinner the other night, you'd think he'd know better than to shirk his duties. I'm about ready to tell him he's finished here."

"Nay, Mother, you can'!"

Laura's eyes widened in surprise, but Muireall plowed forward before her mother could say anything. "Niall injured himself while he was working yesterday, and Briony Fairborn is treating him."

"Injured himself?" Laura raised a cynical eyebrow. "Why wasn' Hamish aware o' this?"

"Because . . ." Muireall's mouth opened and closed like a fish's. "Briony came by last night and told me herself."

"Briony Fairborn came here? Are you—"

The door opened, and Bessie poked her head inside, effectively cutting off the Olivers' conversation. Her face was apologetic as she said, "Lady Oliver, Mistress Oliver, Mr. Mendes is here."

"What?" Mother turned from the door and shook her finger at Muireall. "Hurry up and get dressed. I'll entertain him until yer ready."

Muireall nodded and moved toward her wardrobe.

"And, daughter? You best na do anything to embarrass me this time. Don' think I've forgotten about *yer* behavior at dinner either."

Muireall scrunched her shoulders but didn't answer. She sensed her mother watching her, waiting for a reply, but she had more important things to do than placate the ill-tempered woman.

After a few seconds, the door slammed shut, and Muireall breathed a little more easily.

Until she had to face Mr. Mendes.

When she entered the sitting room a short while later, the young viscount was waiting with a genial smile. Laura greeted Muireall from a nearby chair, her tone sickeningly sweet, and gestured for her to join Mr. Mendes on the couch. Muireall sat down uneasily, folding her hands in her lap.

The viscount nodded his head. "I'm glad to see you looking well, Mistress Oliver. Yer mother told me you've been suffering from headaches recently, and that's why you haven' been able to visit."

"She did?" Muireall's voice was an incredulous squeak, but she resisted the urge to glare at her deceitful mother.

Mr. Mendes took a sip of his tea, but Muireall would have almost sworn he was grinning behind his cup. "Aye. She also conveyed her disappointment that I hadn't come to call on you before now."

This time, Muireall did shoot Laura a dark look. *What are you doing? How is insulting him going to earn his affection?*

Lady Oliver innocently lifted her perfectly sculpted eyebrows.

"But," Mr. Mendes continued, "I can honestly say I've come to remedy that situation. Mistress Oliver, would you care to join me for dinner at the inn tonight?"

Muireall eyed the gentleman with confusion. *I thought you wanted to marry Briony. Why would you invite me fer a meal?*

"Well, what are you waiting fer, Muireall?" Lady Oliver said. "We accept, good sir. My daughter and I would be honored to join you."

Mr. Mendes's mouth morphed into a slight frown. "Oh, dear. I'm not quite sure how to say this, but the invitation was for Mistress Oliver alone."

Lady Oliver's cheeks flooded with color, her expression shifting from happiness to utter embarrassment. Muireall had never seen the woman so flustered.

"My apologies." Laura bowed her head humbly, but Muireall could see the rage simmering just beneath her dignified appearance. It was there, in the way her lip quivered, teetering on the edge of curling. And there, in the way she squeezed her hands together as if she were imagining squeezing the viscount's neck.

Muireall almost laughed, for it wasn't often society dictated Lady Oliver accept a refusal with grace. Even though Mr. Mendes was a foreigner, he outranked her, and therefore, could get away with a lot.

She caught him watching her from the corner of her eye, and when she glanced his way, he sent her a wink. *What is he up to?*

"So, mistress, I'm still waiting fer yer answer. Can I expect you at about six o' clock?"

"Oh." She'd forgotten his request in the midst of her amusement. "A-Aye, you can."

"Excellent." He took another sip of tea, then set the cup back on its saucer. "In that case, I'd better head back and let Mistress Burgess know. Thank you so much for your hospitality, Lady Oliver." He rose from his seat, seemingly oblivious to the animosity radiating off his hostess.

"O' course, Viscount," Laura said through her teeth. "Until next time."

Once the man was gone, Lady Oliver's facade came down. She stomped her feet a few times and let out a tiny scream. "What a boorish man. How dare he treat me so callously. If he wants to marry you, he needs to be respectful o' his future mother-in-law. The nerve!" She turned to her daughter. "You make sure he realizes that quickly."

With that said, Laura whirled out of the room like a tornado, barking at every servant she happened to pass. Muireall winced, grateful she had other plans for her evening.

***

"Uncle?"

Niall opened his eyes. William stood beside the bed, his expression riddled with worry. Niall smiled. "Good morneen, lad."

The boy tentatively smiled in return, but it quickly dissolved into a concerned frown. "Uncle Niall, are you well?"

Niall grimaced as he sat up in the bed, but he quickly masked his pain with a light chuckle. "O' course I am. I've been through a lot worse than this."

"Indeed you have," rumbled a deep voice. Niall's good mood soured as John entered the room. The farmer stopped at the foot of the bed, his face unclear. "What sort o' trouble did you get yerself into this time?"

Niall rolled his eyes. "Na that 'tis any o' yer business, but I was helping Mistress Oliver obtain a rare . . . item." He gestured to his injured chest. "The task simply proved more difficult than I'd expected."

"I would say so." John homed in on the man's bandaged torso, and Niall almost cringed. The farmer's gaze pierced a bit too deeply, almost as if he could see Niall for what he truly was.

"To what do I owe the pleasure o' this visit?" Niall lifted his mouth into a friendly grin.

John's eyes flicked away, his jaw clenching with annoyance. "We're simply here to check on you. When Mistress Fairborn told us you were severely injured, William wanted to see how you were feeling."

The boy nodded. "Mistress Briony wouldn' tell us what happened, only that you were hurt. What was it? Did you get into a fight? Did you go through the Veil and make one o' the fairies angry?"

John's face twitched, the only sign that he cared about his brother-in-law's answer.

Niall took a deep breath—which he regretted when a wave of pain hit him—then said, "Nay, I didn'."

"Then what did this to you? Was it a sea-trow? A finman?" As William spoke, he came closer and closer. Niall grunted when the boy leaned too hard against his side.

"Oh, I'm sorry," William exclaimed, jumping back.

"The lad wouldn' stop asking questions, so I thought 'twas only right to go straight to the source," John said, his voice still gruff but slightly amused. Then his face darkened, and he put a protective hand on William's shoulder. "If Everton is no longer safe fer my family, I need to know about it."

Niall shook his head. "There's no need to worry. 'Twas a kelpie that did this, but he's na going to be a problem anymore." He grabbed the glass of water Briony had set on the table beside his bed.

Willliam's eyes went wide. "You mean you—"

He inclined his head, making the boy gasp.

"Were you frightened?"

Niall paused, considering his nephew's question. "Aye, I suppose I was."

Not for himself—he'd taken on plenty of magical folk before—but for Muireall. When that kelpie had grabbed her, Niall's vision had gone red, and he'd nearly lost his mind.

If anything had happened to her . . . His heart clenched, and he took a drink to distract himself.

"Best be more careful," John muttered, his words almost too soft to make out.

Niall spewed his water all over the floor. His eyes snapped to the farmer's, searching for a sign that he'd heard him wrong.

"What?" John crossed his arms defensively, his face bright red. "You were right in what you said before. No matter what's happened between us, yer still family."

The man's words triggered memories of warmth and laughter, visions of the life Niall had known long ago—

But that had been before John had stolen Elene away. Before Mother and Father had tried desperately to get her back. And before John had murdered Mother and Elene to keep his wife from returning home.

How dare you call me family when yer the reason mine is gone. Niall's hand twitched as he tried to suppress the anger in his heart. If he'd still been a selkie, he'd no doubt the sky would be in an uproar right now. But as a leannan na mara, the heavens no longer felt his pain.

Didn' think you had it in you, his father's voice whispered in the back of his mind, *but it seems you've won them over. Well done.* He could almost hear Callum applauding.

Niall's anger disappeared, replaced by a swell of pride. He *had* done it. Somehow, he'd tricked everyone into believing he'd really changed. Even his cynical brother-in-law, the one Niall had thought he'd never convince.

Yet the victory felt hollow somehow, lacking.

When Niall didn't answer, John coughed as if that would dispel the tension in the room. "And in the spirit o' family, I'd like to invite you fer dinner this evening."

William blinked his dark eyes, eagerly waiting for his uncle's answer.

Niall bit the inside of his cheek. He'd been trying to gain the Burgesses' trust for weeks now; by all accounts, he should accept the invitation without hesitation. It might mean earning the chance to spend time with William alone.

Yet, something about this was making his stomach turn.

"I don' think I should be moving all that much," he said weakly. "I'm na—"

"Then we can have dinner here," William interjected.

"I don' know if Briony would want to feed that many people. Besides, isn' Mr. Mendes staying at the inn right now, too?"

"Oh, I'm sure he wouldn' mind coming here instead," called a new voice.

Briony stood in the doorway, a bright smile on her face. "As fer me, I'd be glad to host." She nodded to John. "You and Adaira are always so welcoming; I'd be delighted to have you over fer a change."

The farmer's mouth twisted as he considered her suggestion. "I don' know. . . ."

"Please, Da'! Please," William begged, nearly jumping up and down. "Mum won' mind."

John soon surrendered to the power of his son's pleading, and plans were set for the Burgesses and Mr. Mendes to return to Drulea Cottage that evening.

But as John and William left, John's words bounced around Niall's mind: *No matter what's happened between us, yer still family.*

Niall leaned over the side of the bed and heaved.

Briony raced into the room. "Niall! Are you all right?"

He lay back down. "I think I just need some rest."

"If yer na up fer dinner tonight, we can do it another time."

Niall opened his mouth, about to accept her offer of escape, then shook his head. He smiled, though there was no true joy behind it. "Nay, I've been waiting fer this since I first got here."

"Waiting fer what?"

"To be part o' a family again."

A Betrothal

Niall's nap did little to settle his stomach, for it remained in knots as the evening drew nearer. Questions about the past were spinning through his mind, doubts and fears trying to pull down the truths he'd clung to with all his heart.

John admitted to being responsible fer Mum and Elene's deaths, but what if there's more to the story? What if he's na as terrible o' a person as I thought? Father claimed human beings were merciless monsters, but Muireall has proven that's na the case. What if John isn' as bad as I thought either?

Impossible! John tricked Elene into turning her back on her own kind and then killed her when she realized she'd made a mistake.

But no matter how much he tried, he couldn't make William's song fit with that narrative. It simply didn't make sense.

And what about what John said before? Niall thought back to the night he'd discovered the farmer was his brother-in-law. He still remembered John's words as clearly as if they'd been spoken only yesterday: *"I didn' force her to stay here. She did so o' her own free will."*

Niall clenched his jaw. He had to get to the bottom of this, once and for all.

When the Burgesses arrived, Briony happily ushered them inside. Adaira and William smiled excitedly, and John nodded to Niall in greeting.

"What's this?" Briony asked, pointing at the dish Adaira was trying to hide behind her back.

The innkeeper laughed sheepishly and handed the dish over. "Dearie, I know you wanted to make food fer us, but I couldn' resist bringing something o' my own."

Briony pulled the cover off, sending a delicious aroma into the air. "Peach pie?" She smiled. "A perfect choice."

Adaira grinned, then skipped over to where Niall sat at the dining table. Chicken, bannock[27], and vegetables had been set out only a few minutes before.

"I'm so glad we're finally doing this," she whispered to him. "William and I have been after John about it fer a long time."

Adaira's sincerity was difficult to endure, but Niall forced himself to smile back. She was rather hard to dislike, even if she had been a big reason why William had betrayed him.

"I appreciate yer efforts."

"I know you didn' know him fer long, but my father was a challenging man, too." She patted Niall's arm empathetically before taking a seat next to her husband.

He resisted the impulse to retort that their fathers weren't similar at all, that Adaira didn't understand anything. But the woman had shown herself wiser than she seemed. Maybe she wasn't completely wrong.

Na completely wrong? asked a voice inside him. *What have you done with Niall, son o' Callum? Has being in the human village made you forget what it means to be loyal?*

A few minutes later, Mr. Mendes joined them, adding to the cottage's tense atmosphere. Or maybe it was just the anxiety in Niall's own heart.

He glared at the new guest's right ankle. When the two of them had fought the last time he had been here, Niall had targeted that ankle specifically, knowing Mr. Mendes had recently broken it. To see it now, back at full strength, was most displeasing. He unconsciously rolled his shoulders, phantom pain appearing where the foreigner had stabbed him.

Mr. Mendes cleared his throat, and Niall lifted his eyes. The blond man's face was closed off, betraying nothing of his true emotions. "Good evening."

---

[27] A traditional Scottish bread made from oatmeal or barley flour.

There was nothing confrontational, nothing malicious in his tone or words, but Niall snapped, "Is it good?"

He glanced around the table at his dinner companions, unable to keep up this silly charade any longer. "How could it be when I'm surrounded by people who either hate me"—he stared at John—"tried to kill me"—his gaze moved on to Mr. Mendes—"or . . ."—his eyes trailed over to Briony—"both?"

Briony scowled and opened her mouth, but John spoke up first. "We all have quite the history, don' we?" He looked at each person in turn, his expression full of regret rather than bitterness.

"Oh, don' act like you've gotten over what happened," Niall said. "Out o' everyone, you have the most reason to despise me. After all, I tried to steal yer son from you. And I would have succeeded"—he turned his head toward Adaira—"if *you* hadn' gotten in the way."

The brunette blinked in surprise, but then her face crumpled with pity. And that just enraged him more.

"Stop it! Stop looking at me like that, all o' you!" He tried to get out of his seat, but pain shot through him as soon as he moved. He grunted and fell back into his chair.

"Uncle, are you all right?" William came to his side.

"Save yer concern." His voice was softer now but no less resentful. He turned away from the boy and refocused on John. "Tell me what happened the day Elene died. The truth."

The farmer sighed and nodded. "Very well."

With choked words, John recounted the day of his wife's passing, starting first when he'd discovered her missing, then describing the terrible event that had led to her and Mother's deaths. Such remorse coated the man's tongue that by the time he'd finished, Niall's fiery anger had been smothered, and all that was left was a chilling understanding.

"Yer saying 'twas an accident, then?" His voice trembled. "You . . . you were trying to protect her?"

His head was pounding, his mind screaming that it was a lie. But his heart was telling him something different.

"Aye, I was so desperate to save her. I . . ." John swallowed, unshed tears shining in the candlelight. "I should have told you sooner. I'm sorry."

Niall sucked in a breath. "Yer apologizing to *me*? After what I did to William? And the humans who died when I tried to destroy the village?"

The farmer's blue eyes were calculating as they assessed him, making him feel as small as an insect. And as helpless.

"Niall, we were yer enemies before. And from what Ellie told me, yer parents taught you humans were to be feared— and hated. As fer trying to kidnap William, I really believe that on some level, you thought you were saving him."

I was saving him, part of Niall wanted to say. *And once Briony is dead, I'll finish what I started. William won' be able to stop me, and once he knows what 'tis like to live amongst selkies, he'll never want to see another human again.* That was what he had been telling himself since he'd arrived; his brother-in-law wasn't going to shake his resolve.

And yet, that was exactly what was happening. No matter what Callum claimed, Niall knew without a shadow of a doubt that John was telling the truth about Elene's death.

Where does that leave me?

"Just like I was trying to do the day Ellie died," John added.

Niall clamped his eyes shut, tears pressing against his eyelids. "D-Don' compare me to you."

"I know this is hard to accept, but 'tis the truth. I hope you'll believe me, but in the meantime, I'm tired o' this wall between us, so . . . let me take the first step in tearing it down."

"And how do you plan to do that?" he bit out, eyes still closed.

"By forgiving you."

Niall froze, unable to fight the truth any longer. The world around him went hazy, his mind tugging him inward. He found himself standing at a closed door.

His deepest beliefs dwelt on the other side.

He slowly opened the door and stepped through, letting his worst memories cascade over him: the deaths of his mother and sister, Briony's betrayal, the loss of his sealskin, his exile.

So much hurt, so much pain—all because of the humans.

They're murderers, thieves, untrustworthy, whispered a cynical voice in his heart. *They've taken so much from you. Don' allow them to fool you again. Even their young are evil to their core. Remember?*

Niall watched his younger self run from a band of human children who had attacked him simply because he was different from them.

He winced at the memory, his instincts telling him to turn away.

Then another voice gently whispered, "Wait. Look again."

Niall forced himself to watch the scene once more, except this time, he watched it with new eyes.

And what he saw was almost more than he could bear.

The children's behavior had been wrong—there was no question of that—but it hadn't been driven by hatred. It had been motivated by the very same emotion that had driven him that day: fear.

We're na so different, after all, are we?

Niall slowly opened his eyes, letting his tears fall openly down his face. He looked around the table. The very same people peered back, human and selkie alike.

But instead of feeling rage at the sight of them, he felt only shame. These weren't monsters to be feared or weaklings to be exploited. They were just like him, with hopes and dreams and fears and struggles. Their lives might look different from his, but that didn't give him the right to use them as he pleased.

Niall had wronged them—all of them. And up until now, he'd still been wronging them, for he'd pretended to have had a change of heart when he'd really just been biding his time.

He met John's eye and said steadily, "I don' deserve yer forgiveness." His gaze swept around the room. "I've hurt all o' you too deeply. There's no way you could forgive me."

William launched himself at Niall, wrapping his small arms around him in a tight embrace. Niall ignored the pain in his chest and hugged the boy back, warmth filling his heart. Adaira soon joined in, whispering sweet words of comfort until John cleared his throat.

The three of them pulled away from each other, anxiously waiting to hear what he would say. He stood just behind Adaira, his mouth a firm line.

"Da'?" William asked.

John's lips lifted ever so slightly, and he clapped Niall on the shoulder. "Welcome to the family."

A knock sounded at the door.

***

Just before Muireall left for the inn, Hamish delivered a letter to her. *Is it about Niall? Has his health gotten worse?* She opened it with trembling fingers.

Dear Mistress Muireall Oliver, Maid of Harray,

I hope this letter finds you well. My deepest apologies, but I must ask that we postpone our dinner plans. I was recently informed that we are to dine at Drulea Cottage this evening. Again, I deeply regret inconveniencing you, and I assure you I will reach out soon to reschedule.

Sincerely,

Mr. Santiago Mendes

Muireall pressed the letter to her chest, her stomach clenched tight. Mother would be appalled to find out she had—in Mother's mind—failed yet again at catching the viscount's attention. It didn't matter that she had never wanted his attention in the first place.

She scanned the hallway, empty save for the butler and herself.

"Mistress?" Hamish asked, his eyebrows raised in polite concern.

"Does anyone else know you delivered this?" Muireall tried to keep the anxiety out of her voice.

"Nay, my lady."

"Then let's keep it that way."

The butler nodded before marching off, a strange glint in his eye.

Muireall hid the letter in her side table. *There, that fixes one thing. But I can' have Mother finding out about this. . . . What do I do?*

"Muireall, are you almost ready?" Laura's shrill voice just outside the door sent Muireall's pulse leaping with dread.

"Aye, Mother," she called. She came out of the room with a grin. "I'll just be leaving, then." As she slid past her mother, Laura's hand gripped her wrist.

"Remember, daughter, the family is counting on you."

Muireall swallowed and gave her a quick nod before dashing out the front door.

Almost as soon as she'd started up the path toward Drulea Cottage, she regretted it. "This is so inappropriate!" she mumbled to herself. "What am I even going to say? 'I'm sorry to intrude, Briony, but do you have room fer one more person? My parents will be so disappointed if they find out my dinner with Mr. Mendes got postponed.'"

The Calhouns passed her on the street, puzzled expressions on their faces.

Muireall rubbed her temples, embarrassed at getting caught talking to herself. *Ugh, that won' work.*

But I can' go home now. . . .

I'll just pretend I never saw the letter, she decided. She lifted her head, confidence restored.

And that will give me the perfect excuse to check on Niall, too, she thought, the knowledge adding a spring to her step.

When she got to the cottage and knocked on the door, Briony opened it with a surprised frown. "Mistress Oliver?"

"I know this is unexpected, but would it be all right if . . ." She spotted the Burgesses and Mr. Mendes inside.

Mr. Mendes rose to his feet and strode over, chagrin all over his features. "Mistress Oliver, did you not receive my letter?"

"I'm afraid I didn'."

"Then how did you know to come here?"

"Well, when I went to the inn and no one was there, I figured you must be meeting here." She smiled broadly, hoping no one would see through her lie.

Briony seemed hesitant, but Mr. Mendes quickly pulled her inside, saying something about how he was so sorry to have confused her and they would love for her to join them.

The Burgesses all greeted her genially, though they'd seemed tense when the door had first opened. Almost as if the conversation she'd interrupted hadn't been going well.

Muireall didn't spend much time thinking about that, though, for her gaze soon landed on her servant, who sat stiffly in one of the chairs. "Niall!"

She flew to his side, overcome with worry. His eyes were red, and there was a distinct flush to his cheeks. "Are you well? Did you have any nightmares last night? Is it all right fer you to be out o' bed yet?"

"I'm fine, mistress. Truly." His tone was sharp, almost embarrassed. He brushed her hand off his arm.

But she wasn't going to be dismissed that easily. *He should be resting right now, na pretending he's fine. Just because he wants to look strong doesn' mean he should neglect his health.*

"Niall, you need to be careful, so you don' reopen yer wounds from last ni—"

He grabbed her hand and met her eyes for the first time. "I'm all right, Muireall," he whispered, giving her a lopsided grin. "You don' need to worry about me so much."

She smiled back in relief. "Good. I need you to recover quickly. The garden needs you."

He quirked an eyebrow, mischief dancing in his gaze. "Only the garden?"

Butterflies fluttered in her stomach as his expression shifted from playful to sincere. She wanted to look away but found she couldn't, not when he was staring at her like that.

Could it be that I actually—

Mr. Burgess cleared his throat.

Muireall dropped Niall's hand and sat in the empty chair beside him, heat flooding her face. *They all saw us holding hands, didn' they? What will they think now? Surely they won' draw the wrong conclusion—*

Is it the wrong conclusion? She peeked at the others, dreading the judgment she knew she would find.

To her shock, no one was looking at her with disdain. Mr. Mendes, Mr. Burgess, and William simply seemed curious, whereas Adaira's eyes were crinkled in amusement. When she glanced at Briony, though, her fear returned.

Why does she look so worried?

"Shall we eat?" Mr. Burgess said.

Briony turned and grinned, instantly reverting to a happy hostess once more. "Aye, let's do that."

But Muireall noted how her smile didn't reach her eyes.

Mr. Mendes said the blessing, and everyone began eating. After a few minutes of light conversation, Muireall's anxiety abated, and she started to enjoy herself. Unlike meals at home, tonight's company was pleasant and friendly, and she didn't have to watch everything she said. There were no harsh words, no backhanded compliments, no icy silences—this was something she could get used to.

Until Adaira ruined it.

"Cousin, I had no idea you and Niall were so close," she remarked, her lips curving into a smirk.

"What? We're na—" Muireall's eyes flicked to Niall, only to find him watching her with a strange expression. *What should I say?*

"We're . . . friends," she settled on, ignoring the way her servant's mouth tightened.

A mouth that had felt far too soft against her own.

She swallowed and dropped her gaze, hoping no one would notice the heat in her cheeks.

"Friends? But I thought—" William turned to Niall. "Uncle, aren' you in love with her?"

Muireall ducked her head, fingers grasping her skirts. *Did he really just ask that? He should know better than to ask such a personal question!* Her pulse quickened, a sudden urge to flee coming over her. She nearly did just that, except something inside her held her back.

She didn't want to leave without first hearing Niall's answer.

Muireall released her grip on her dress and peeked up.

He was grimacing, a panicked look in his dark eyes.

Disappointment blew over her heart. *He's going to deny it. He doesn' think o' me that way. I'm just a stained-glass window to him, pretty to look at but nothing more. Na someone he could want to be with—*

His gaze locked with hers, and the fear that had been swirling in his eyes only seconds before vanished, giving way to something far more frightening. His lips parted.

"M-Mr. Mendes!" Muireall blurted. Everyone jumped, but she plowed forward, her voice squeaking, "I wanted to ask why you invited me fer dinner before. My mother thought yer invitation meant I still had a chance with you, but I know that's na the case."

The viscount's eyes darted to Briony for a second before flitting away. He slowly chewed the carrots in his mouth, his expression guarded. When the seconds stretched on and no one spoke, he chuckled. "That's a . . ." He scratched at the back of his neck. "That's a good question. I—"

"Oh, I can' take this," Adaira cut in. She grasped Briony's hand and declared, "Two nights ago, Mr. Mendes asked fer my blessing."

The midwife's jaw dropped. "Blessing fer . . ."

"Why, to marry you, silly."

Mr. Mendes's ears turned red. "Mistress Burgess, I wanted to ask her privately—"

Adaira waved her hand. "Nonsense. Who wouldn' want to be asked in front o' family and friends? And how many times have I told you to call me Adaira?"

Both the viscount and Briony glared at their presumptuous friend, but Mr. Mendes's annoyance abated within seconds, replaced by a firm resolve. He stood and walked around the table to kneel beside the midwife, his eyes somber.

"Amorzinho[28], I've loved you since the day you took me to Cramer's Field and told me trusting someone was worth the risk of getting hurt. Being with you has taught me just how important it is to let people close, and if you're willing, I'd like to show the rest of the world just how much you mean to me. Will you marry me?"

Muireall waited for Briony to die of embarrassment, as she would have in the face of such a public declaration, but instead, pure elation shone in the midwife's eyes. Briony confidently placed one hand on Mr. Mendes's jaw and said evenly, "Aye, I will."

After that, everything seemed to happen all at once. Mr. Burgess and his son broke into applause, exclaiming their

---

[28] Sweetheart.

congratulations to the happy couple, Adaira burst into happy tears, saying she'd been praying for this day for such a long time, and the newly engaged couple embraced each other with far more intimacy than Muireall thought proper.

Still, there was something to be said for their courage. She wished she had more of that.

Shortly afterward, Mr. Mendes turned to her, his hand clasped in his fiancée's. "I wanted to tell you I was going to propose tomorrow, so you didn't need to worry about your parents anymore. But it seems things didn't go quite the way I planned." He raised an eyebrow at Adaira, but the innkeeper just grinned innocently.

"Well, I wish you both a wonderful, happy life together," Muireall said, surprised to find she actually meant it. The two of them weren't a conventional couple by any means, but their love for each other was pure—anyone could see that.

Without meaning to, her thoughts strayed to the man next to her, curious about his reaction to the betrothal. *Is he happy fer them, too, or does he still have feelings fer Briony?*

She watched as he whispered something to his nephew. An easygoing smile was on his face, but that could just be an act. *How does he really feel about all this? And what was he about to say before I cut him off?*

He seemed to sense her watching him and turned. His smile disappeared, replaced by—

Muireall's heart skipped a beat. If she wasn't mistaken, that was yearning in his eyes.

Yearning . . . fer me? Was William right?

Something brushed against her hand, and she looked down with a gasp.

Niall's fingers ran over hers again, then he took her hand in his.

She peered up at him, unable to form a single coherent thought. his lips twitched with amusement. And hope.

Come see me in the morneen, he mouthed.

All right, Muireall mouthed back, still holding his hand.

What am I doing? This is far worse than Briony and Mr. Mendes's embrace earlier—at least they're engaged. Niall and I—we're na even courting. And he's my servant! 'Tis na even logical fer me to like him.

And yet . . . I do.

Powerless

Once dinner was over, Muireall left with the Burgesses and Mr. Mendes since they all had to go the same direction. As the group walked, she hung toward the back, feeling like an outsider even though they'd just spent the evening together. William and the men chatted amiably, oblivious to her distance, but Adaira slowed until Muireall had no choice but to walk beside her. She had a funny look on her face, making Muireall uneasy.

The laird's daughter turned away and ran her fingers through her hair, trying to look preoccupied.

"Adaira?" John asked when he realized his wife was no longer next to him. He spun around. "Are you coming?"

"Go on ahead," her cousin replied. "I'd like to talk to Muireall fer a bit."

He nodded, then hurried to catch back up with his son and Mr. Mendes.

Once they were relatively alone, Adaira turned to Muireall. "Cousin, we need to talk."

She hesitantly met her eye. "What about?"

Why am I so nervous? This is just Adaira. I don' have any reason to feel nervous.

Then she thought back to the way Adaira had been smirking earlier while talking about Niall, and her stomach flipped. *That's what this is about, isn' it? I don' know that I'm ready to talk about it yet. I only just realized it fer myself. Can' she see how uncomfortable I am?*

But Adaira either didn't see or didn't care, for her next words were: "How do you feel about what Niall said?"

"I don' know what yer talking about." Muireall locked her fingers together, wishing she could think of something else to talk about but drawing a blank.

Her cousin glared. "Don' be coy."

Muireall dropped her hands. "Fine. How do I feel about it? I . . ." She pressed her lips into a thin line. "I'm terrified, all right?"

"Why?"

"Because we could never work out." She gestured down the hill toward Rigmore House. "My parents—they would never allow a servant to inherit their estate."

"Then you do have feelings fer him?"

Muireall stared at the ground, unwilling to say it out loud.

"Don' be ashamed, dearie. 'Tis a completely natural thing."

"Na between a noblewoman and a servant!" She stopped walking and wiped at her suddenly wet cheeks. "What am I going to do?"

Adaira squeezed her shoulder. "Shhh, 'tis all right."

"But 'tis na!" Muireall cast off her cousin's hand and began to pace. "Niall is far from a suitable match. He's a commoner—and a poor one at that. And that's na even the worst part, is it?" She gave Adaira a knowing look.

A thread of nervousness came into Adaira's voice as she replied, "What do you mean?"

Muireall groaned. "Let's stop pretending, shall we? I already know Niall isn' human"—Adaira's mouth fell open, but she continued—"and so do you. That's why you warned me to stay away from him before, isn' it?"

The innkeeper's voice shook as she said, "How did you find out?"

Muireall hesitated. But Adaira knew so much now— enough to ruin her—that keeping secrets no longer felt like a priority. And she was so tired of shutting everyone out. It was time to let someone in.

She sighed and started at the beginning, from the moment her parents had told her she had to choose a husband by her next birthday. As she spoke, a weight slowly lifted from her chest, and by the time she was finished, she realized just how much of a toll this secret had been taking on her. It felt so nice to finally share this burden with someone else, someone she hoped she could trust.

" . . . Now, all that's left is the banshee's cloak. Then Niall and I can go back through the Veil, give the treasures to the Fairy Prince, and he'll grant me my favor."

Adaira had been quiet as Muireall had spoken—very unlike her usual, bubbly self. She took her cousin's hands now, her expression pained. "I know yer parents are difficult, but you should have just told them you didn' want to get married, na gotten yerself tangled up with fairies and trows and everything else you just said."

Muireall snatched her hands away. "What do you know?" She winced and shut her eyes, regretting the harshness in her voice.

She opened her eyes and spoke again, softly this time. "I tried to tell my parents, but they wouldn' listen to me."

Adaira's smile was open and understanding. "I know what 'tis like to have a parent like that. But at the end o' the day, you need to make the choices that are best fer *you*, regardless o' what everyone else thinks."

"And I am. I'm taking control o' my own destiny."

Her cousin raised her eyebrows, impatience flashing on her face. "Are you? You just said you were too afraid to stand up to yer parents, so you made a deal with a dangerous magical being who promised to fix yer problem if you did as he wished. That doesn' sound like someone who's in control."

Muireall started to refute the woman's words, but then an idea blossomed in her mind, one that brushed away her anxiety. "Adaira, what if . . . what if I change my deal with the fairies just the slightest bit?"

Adaira tilted her head. "How so?"

"Instead o' just having my parents stop pushing me to get married, what if they were to accept Niall as a suitor? Wouldn' that solve everything?"

The innkeeper grimaced. "What's going to happen when yer parents do something else you don' like? Are you going to run back to the Fair Folk fer help again? And what about

Niall? It sounds like he nearly lost his life fighting that kelpie, yet you want to put him through more. You just said you had feelings fer him."

"I didn' say that! I—" She broke off, for there wasn't a point in arguing such a minute thing. Not when she did, indeed, have feelings for the man. "Aye, I have feelings fer him. And that's why I can' afford na to follow through with this. There's still over a week before the full moon, plenty o' time fer Niall to recover"—

Adaira drew in a breath, but Muireall held up her hand.

—"and if he can' come, that's all right, too. I'll figure it out on my own."

Compassion filled Adaira's eyes. "Yer treading a dangerous path, dearie. I just hope you know what yer doing."

***

Muireall gently closed the door behind her, sighing in exhaustion. It had been a long day, and she was ready to crawl under her blankets and rest.

"Did you have a good time?" asked Mother.

Muireall started, not having noticed her in the shadows. "Mother! I didn' think you'd still be awake now. Why aren' you in bed?"

Laura slinked over, a dangerous smile on her face. "I was waiting fer you, o' course. I wanted to hear about how yer dinner with the viscount went."

"Oh." Muireall hesitated, her eyes sliding back and forth. "'Twas a nice evening. He's very respectable. I think he enjoyed my company."

Mother's grin transformed into a scowl. "Liar! You didn' have dinner with Mr. Mendes tonight. Tell me where you've really been."

Muireall flinched back from the angry woman. "But, Mother, I did, just like I told you—"

Laura slapped her across the face with the back of her hand, the force sending Muireall to the floor.

Muireall's muscles quivered as she slowly returned to her feet. "Don' touch me," she hissed. "I told you the truth. I don' understand why yer doing this."

Mother pulled out a piece of paper from her pocket and let it fall. As it drifted to the floor, Muireall's eyes widened at the words scrawled across the top: *Dear Mistress Muireall Oliver, Maid of Harray . . .*

The note landed softly, mockingly, as if its contents were of no consequence.

"W-Where did you get that?"

Laura scoffed. "That hardly matters. What does matter is where you really spent the evening."

"I—I—"

"You spent it with that servant, didn' you?"

"What?"

Mother threw her hands up in the air. "Oh, you can stop pretending. Did you think I was blind, daughter? I could tell he was besotted with you the night Mr. Levins came over. As any young man should be. I didn' say anything then because I thought 'twas only one-sided." She clucked her tongue in disappointment. "You can' imagine how dismayed I was when I found out the truth. *My* daughter, intimate with a servant." She shuddered with revulsion.

Muireall shrank into herself, unable to think of a single word to defend herself.

Wait, how does she know about Niall and me?

Mother huffed as if this were all a terrible inconvenience. "Naturally, my first inclination was to disown you. Such a horrid excuse fer a daughter could never be expected to inherit the family estate. 'Twould be an affront to society. But you got lucky, lass, and that's na to be yer fate, after all."

"'Tis na?"

Mother smiled, a real smile this time. "After receiving this devastating news, Mr. Levins gave me a most generous offer."

Muireall's legs nearly gave out. "Mr. Levins?"

He's the one behind all this? Does that mean he saw Niall kiss me?

"He agreed to cover up this terrible scandal on the condition that you marry him."

She stood frozen, her worst fears realized. "And what about Mr. Moreland?"

Mother curled her lip. "That fool will be thrown out o' Everton as soon as he drags his lazy body back to our doorstep."

"But, Mother . . ." Muireall felt weak, her head spinning out of control. "I still need his help—"

"Silence, you insolent bairn," Laura snapped. "Yer confined to yer quarters until yer birthday celebration where we'll announce yer betrothal to Mr. Levins. Now, go on up to yer room and think about how you can thank Mr. Levins fer giving you another chance."

Muireall scurried off in defeat, her throat tight. It was over, everything she'd been trying to do. If she was locked in her room until her birthday, she'd lose her chance to get the banshee's cloak.

And Niall was going to be sent away forever. *How can this be when I was so close?*

She gritted her teeth, rage coursing through her. *How did Mr. Levins get hold o' that letter? The only people who saw it were me and—*

Hamish.

He's the one spying fer Mr. Levins.

The anger rushed out of her, hopelessness spreading across her body. Her eyes flew to the window, the almost-full moon looking more distant than normal.

I knew Hamish didn' like me, but to betray me like this—

She took a deep, calming breath. There was comfort in knowing one's enemies. It made the world less frightening.

But knowing and being able to do something about it were two different things.

And right now, Muireall felt more powerless than ever.

New Plans

The sun seemed especially brilliant as Niall opened his eyes the following morning. Birdsong filled his ears, and his heart felt lighter than it had in ages. Life was full of possibilities, and happiness was finally within reach.

"Welcome to the family." Niall basked in the warmth of that statement. It held such promise, such hope. Though he and the Burgesses had a complicated and painful history, they were moving forward now.

Together.

But what about Father? He risked so much to give me this chance. How can I waste it? Niall swallowed, his mind shooting straight back to the day he'd returned home after losing his sealskin. It had taken almost all of his strength to reach the islet where his herd gathered during the warm months, but he'd rowed his stolen boat without ceasing, knowing his very life depended on it. For if Briony had discovered he was still alive, there was not a single doubt in Niall's mind that she would have ended him right there.

***

Just a wee bit farther, Niall told himself each time a wave of dizziness threatened to overtake him. *Then Father will help me.*

Blood pooled from his open wounds with every heave of the oars, staining the floorboards red. Mr. Mendes had struck him twice with Mr. McLaren's dagger: once in his right shoulder and once in his chest, dangerously close to his heart. He also bore bite marks on his hand and leg, painful reminders of Briony's treachery.

When the islet finally came into view, he nearly cried with joy. Once his oars struck sand, he tumbled out of the boat, his vision spotty from blood loss.

A dark shape loomed in the distance, slowly coming closer. *Someone from the herd!* He reached out his hand. "H-Help me . . ."

Instead of assistance, though, angry growls answered him. He drew back in surprise. "'Tis me, Niall," he whimpered.

Some part of him knew he should have expected this. He was worse than an outsider now that his sealskin was gone.

But right now, he lacked the strength to consider it for long. He lacked the strength to even take another step forward. "Please," he cried, but then his eyelids fluttered closed, and darkness fell.

When he woke, someone was pressing a bowl of water to his lips. He blinked a few times, still disoriented. The face above him was familiar, comforting. *Who—*

"Haldis?"

"Shh," the woman cooed. "Drink this. You've been feverish fer the last few days, and yer body is very weak."

Niall swallowed the water, then took in his surroundings. He was on a makeshift bed inside the shallow cave where the herd often gathered while in human form, but besides Haldis, he was completely alone. He glanced down at himself, noting the dressings across his chest.

He sighed, relieved that Haldis had been the one to find him. She was an older selkie whose mate had been killed by humans long ago. Rather than allowing herself to be consumed by bitterness, though, she had remained an integral part of the herd and taken to tending those who were wounded. She was a grandmother-like figure to several of the younger selkies, Niall included.

"'Tis good to see you." He looked past her to the cave opening, half-expecting someone to walk in. "Where's Father? Does he know I'm here?"

Haldis's dark eyes narrowed in disapproval. "Callum was out hunting when you arrived yesterday. He——" Her gaze fell away from him. "As far as I know, he hasn' been informed o' yer . . . situation."

Anxiety stirred in his heart. He hadn't been thinking clearly when he'd come here yesterday. Now that he'd lost his sealskin, this place could no longer be his home.

Not when his presence was a threat to the entire herd.

For while Niall had lost his powers and become a leannan na mara, he still had the ability to reclaim his former status. But the only way to do that was to kill another selkie and steal their pelt for himself. As a means of protection, magical law dictated that a leannan na mara had to be expunged from his herd in one of two ways—execution or exile.

Which one will Father choose?

"Why are you tending to me, Haldis?" Niall asked.

The older woman looked down her nose at him in such a way that he felt like a child about to be reprimanded.

"I took an oath the day Danr died that I would do all in my power to help those suffering because o' humans. You know that." She pointed to his shoulder. "And after what happened to my mate, did you think I wouldn' recognize yer wounds? I know the humans' handiwork when I see it."

Niall smiled gratefully, glad that at least someone was on his side. Haldis was an esteemed member of the community. *Maybe she can convince Father to be merciful toward me.*

Haldis's finger slid from his shoulder and pressed on his injured hand. "This mark, though, was na made by any human."

He leaned away from her, not wanting to discuss Briony's betrayal. He still could barely comprehend it himself. Never would he have thought a fellow selkie would attack him.

And fer what? To save a human? He gripped the bed tightly, hatred coiling around his heart. *I will have my vengeance, one way or another—*

A snarl cut off his thoughts. Niall looked up as Callum stormed into the cave. Before he could brace himself, the older man shoved him onto the cold ground.

"You disgrace! Can' you do anything right?" Father hovered over him, fists clenched, entire body quaking with fury. "I've already lost yer mother and"—his voice cracked with despair—"sister. How could you be so careless?"

Hot tears spilled down Niall's cheeks, his shame billowing over. "I . . . I was trying to save Briony."

Anger blazed anew in Callum's eyes. "Einar's daughter? How many times have I told you that lass is no better than a human? She's poisoned with the same madness that stole Elene from us."

Niall shuddered beneath his steely gaze. "I see that now. She . . . she's the one who did this to me. After I tried to rescue her, she burned up my sealskin and made me"—he gestured to himself in disgust—"this. I should have listened to you, Father. I'm sorry."

"Apologies fix nothing." Callum exhaled and ran his hand down his face. When he next spoke, his voice was calmer, though no less wounded. "You know as well as I that you have no place here now. To harbor a leannan na mara is a crime punishable by death."

There it was: the ultimatum he'd known was coming.

Niall hung his head. "Will you have me executed, then?"

"That remains to be seen." Callum started to leave.

"You should know—without Briony, Everton is defenseless! The humans have no idea we're out here. If the herd was to come together, we could easily take them down."

Callum paused but didn't turn. "I won' risk the herd's safety over a personal vendetta. Na even fer you."

". . . What if 'twas na fer me?"

"What do you mean?"

Niall let out a bitter laugh. "Father, I found the man who killed Mother and Elene: John Burgess. He's there in Everton."

When Callum spun around, his gaze seeking, Niall suppressed a scowl. Father always had loved Elene more.

"Tell me everything."

As Niall explained what had happened—his discovery of John and William's identities, Briony's decision to side with the humans, facing off with Einar's murderer, and his eventual defeat—he watched the calculating expression on his father's face. Unlike Niall, Callum never did anything without carefully thinking it through first. It was yet another reason why the two of them struggled to get along.

But right now, Niall was grateful for his father's meticulous nature. He'd tried to solve things his way, and that hadn't worked. Perhaps his father could come up with a better strategy.

When Niall finished, Callum was silent for a long time. Then he nodded and said, "I see. I must go."

"Go? But, Father—" Niall tried to get up, then moaned as pain tore through him.

"I'll be back as soon as I can." With that, Callum swept out of the cave, leaving Niall to wonder what on earth he could be planning.

For the next several days, Haldis was Niall's only company. The rest of the herd kept their distance, whispering among themselves as they passed in and out of the cave. They all knew what he was now; the scent of a leannan na mara was unmistakable to seal-folk, but so far, none had tried to kill him. Niall spent most of the time sleeping, which seemed better than being awake when, at any moment, his next breath could be his last.

On the morning Callum finally returned, his eyes were bright. "I've found a solution, son."

Hope stirred in Niall's chest. "What is it? I'll do anything, Father."

Callum clasped his hand. The moment their skin touched, a burst of power shot up Niall's arm.

"What—" Niall pulled away, shivers running through his body. "What did you do?"

"Give me back yer hand."

His eyes narrowed. "Nay, na until you tell me what this is."

Father's lips flattened with impatience. "I went to King Daegan and convinced him to part with a bit o' magic. Now, you can make one fairy deal with the person o' yer choice. Use it wisely."

"You went to the Fair Folk? But they're treacherous! You . . ." His mouth opened and closed several times. "After everything that happened with Daegan's daughter, how could you . . ."

He trailed off at his father's somber expression, understanding coming over him. Fairy magic was dangerous; Callum would never have turned to it unless it was the only way. "You did it fer me. What did you promise him?"

Father's gaze darted toward the cave's entrance, then he leaned close. "That doesn' matter. Use this to help you reclaim what you lost. Get yer revenge on Einar's daughter and become a selkie again." He held out his hand for the second time.

As soon as Niall took it, magic coursed through him. He grimaced as its icy tendrils settled into his veins.

"Father, are you all right?" he asked when he noticed Callum wincing. He grasped his father's shoulder and felt a hint of power lingering under Callum's skin.

The older man waved his concern away with a quick, "I'm fine," but his voice was strained.

"The magic. You kept some fer yerself?"

"I kept enough to sense when you've completed yer deal. That will let me know when to come find you." Father's mouth stretched into a menacing grin. "Then we can finish tearing Everton apart together."

***

Niall pressed his fingers to his temples as the memory faded. His father had expelled him from the herd as soon as Niall was well enough to travel, with the promise to reunite once Briony was out of the way.

He would be devastated if he knew Niall had decided to give up on their plan. But Niall couldn't continue with it, not after everything he'd found out. *John, William, all these people here deserve the chance to live. Even Briony.*

Father said he'd be able to sense it once I completed my deal. What's he going to do when he comes here and sees I'm still a leannan na mara? Will he even listen to me if I try to explain?

"Have a good rest?" Briony asked as she came into the room with a cup of tea.

He tucked his worries aside and schooled his expression into something friendlier. "Aye, and you?"

Briony's eyes twinkled, a dazzling smile coming over her face. "Aye, I did."

"That smile isn' from the good sleep you had, though, is it?" Niall waggled his eyebrows, then took a sip of tea. "I'd say it has more to do with what happened *before* you went to bed."

She rolled her eyes. "Don' tease. Last night was . . . eventful, that's fer sure."

"I wonder if Mr. Mendes would like to hear you describe it that way."

Briony glared. "You had quite the night, too." Her face softened. "I'm glad you've reconciled with the Burgesses. 'Twas good fer all sides. But this thing with Mistress Oliver—"

"Are you really going to criticize my taste? Or are you just upset that I've moved on from you?" Niall quipped.

"I told you before that it wasn' a good idea."

He wiped the amusement off his face. "And I told *you* before that I wasn' going to hurt her. I meant it. I thought you wanted me to start over."

"But na with her! There are so many reasons why it would never work out. Don' you know?"

"I've faced impossible odds before."

"This is more than that. Even if her parents were completely different people and welcomed you with open arms, it still wouldn' work."

"Why na?"

"Because if you want to have a relationship with her, you need to trust her with yer past. And I don' think yer ready to do that."

"I . . ." Niall looked down into his cup. The steaming liquid swirled, making him realize his hand was shaking. He stilled, then raised his eyes, his jaw set. "That's my affair, na yers."

"As protector o' Everton—"

"That doesn' apply to matters o' the heart, Briony. And I do believe yer taking this self-appointed 'protector' role a wee bit too seriously."

She growled. "Better to take things too seriously than na seriously enough."

Niall turned away from her, effectively ending the conversation. He'd figure out how to make things work with Muireall, one way or another.

A short while later, Briony left to check on some sick neighbors, but she promised to return soon. Niall was supposed to be resting, but there was no way he could do that, not when Muireall hadn't yet arrived.

But when morning came and went without a single visitor, he started to get nervous. *What's taking her so long? Was she unable to get a moment to herself?*

Or did my confession frighten her off?

Niall's heart lurched. *She didn' react well when I kissed her. Maybe I'm going too fast.*

I better go apologize. He threw off his blankets and pushed himself to his feet. He froze as pain rippled across his torso. Once it had subsided to a dull ache, he took a slow step, then another.

"Where do you think yer going?" Briony cried. She stood in the doorway, hands on her hips.

"I just wanted to get some water."

Her golden eyes cut straight through his lie. "I'm na a fool, Niall. Were you going to try to go to Rigmore House by yerself?"

"Muireall was supposed to meet me this morneen. I need to—"

She shook her head. "You need to get back in that bed before I make you."

Niall stuck out his lips but complied. He held back a wince as he lay down. "Would you go check on her fer me?"

Briony pursed her lips, still looking slightly annoyed. "All right, so long as you promise to stay here."

He smiled and nodded. "Thank you."

***

Muireall paced the floor. She'd barely slept last night, her mind whirling as she'd tried to come up with a plan to get herself out of this.

Anne softly knocked on the door before slipping inside with a tray full of food.

Muireall took one look at it before scoffing. "I'm na even allowed to leave my room fer meals?"

The maid trembled as she set the tray down on the little table in the middle of the room. "Lady Oliver said you'd had quite the ordeal and needed yer rest, so I was to bring this to you here."

"Is that so? Well, you can tell my mother she can' keep me locked up in here. I won' be a prisoner in my own home." She shook her head. "Nay, I can' say that; otherwise, she'll treat me even worse than this. I—" She broke off with a frustrated howl.

Anne threw her hands over her ears. "Please don' scream, my lady. I didn' mean to upset you."

"I'm sorry, Anne." Muireall gently pulled the maid's arms down. "I'm na angry with you."

The girl gaped. "Yer . . . yer na?"

The disbelief in her voice crushed Muireall's heart. *Just how much have I mistreated you over the years? And I don' have any idea how to make it up to you. . . .*

There's no time fer that now, the more rational side of her brain reminded her. *I have to figure out a way to get out o' here.*

"Listen"—she took the girl's hands in hers—"I know I haven' been a very kind mistress. But right now, I desperately need yer help to escape."

Anne stared back at her, hesitant, fearful. Maybe too fearful. Muireall knew that expression well. It was the same one she made when thinking about her mother's imminent wrath.

She dropped Anne's hands and took a step back, shoulders falling. *I can' ask this o' her. If she gets caught, her whole family will suffer.*

"Anne, I . . . I shouldn' have said anything. You don' need to—"

"I'll do it," the girl whispered. Her voice was low, but it resonated with courage.

"A-Are you sure? You do realize that if you get caught, you'll most likely be sent away. And even if you aren', you could be shunned."

Anne lifted her chin, rebellion sparkling in her blue eyes. "I know. I know what Lady Oliver does to anyone who crosses her. Including you, my lady." Her voice was louder this time but still just as steady.

Muireall gazed at her in surprise. All this time, she'd thought Anne was hardly more than a frightened bird, eager to spread gossip among her friends but lacking any sort of backbone. Now she saw a completely different person before her.

I've never been so glad to be wrong.

"All right then," she said with a conspiratorial grin. "In that case, the first thing I need you to do is send a few messages fer me."

A Wounded Creature

Muireall smiled at the knock on the door. She hadn't had any guests in the last few days, save for Anne, who'd shared the news that Lady Oliver was telling everyone Muireall was too ill for visitors. Not even Briony Fairborn had been allowed to see her, and she'd put up such a fuss that Muireall had heard the shouting all the way from her bedroom.

There was one person Lady Oliver wouldn't keep from visiting Muireall though. The very person Muireall was eager to see.

"You may enter." She kept her face relaxed as Matthew Levins marched into the room, despite the anxiety leaping in her stomach. If she was going to make this work, she needed to be convincing.

Matthew's expression was arrogant. "Have you decided to concede?"

She slowly sipped her tea, making him wait as long as she could without being openly impolite. The terrible man deserved far worse. "Aye, indeed, I have."

The tacksman's smirk grew. "Excellent to hear. However, you could have said as much in yer letter. Why invite me here?"

Muireall puckered her lips into a delicate pout. "I'm na sure yer aware, but I've been confined to my room until our engagement is formally announced at my birthday celebration. . . ."

She glanced up, searching for a trace of sympathy on his face, but Matthew was unmoved. She sniffled, her face crumpling further. "But since I've agreed to become yer *bride*"—she tried not to gag on the word—"I hoped you would be kind enough to go fer a walk with me. I'm sure Mother and Father wouldn' mind this small allowance."

At least, she prayed they wouldn't. *Mother did say she wanted me to think o' a way to thank Mr. Levins fer giving me another chance.*

Matthew crossed his arms. When he spoke, his voice was full of contempt. "You asked me here because you wanted an excuse to get out o' the house?" He snorted. "And here I thought you were *almost* an equal adversary. Turns out yer just a spoiled bairn willing to make herself pathetic in front o' her enemy just to relieve her own boredom. How disappointing."

Muireall dug her fingernails into her skirts, barely keeping herself from lashing out. "Perhaps I am. But would you help me, anyway?" she asked in a purposefully high-pitched tone, batting her eyelashes at him.

He looked away in disgust. "I'd rather spend as little time with you as possible, so nay, I believe I'll just go home."

She threw up her hand as he turned to leave. "Wait!" She dropped the charming laird's daughter act. "There's something else I need to tell you. Something I'm sure you don' want to risk other ears hearing." She looked pointedly at the open door behind him.

Matthew's eyes narrowed with skepticism, but after a moment, he gave a sharp nod. "Fine. But it better be worth it."

She rose, a coy smile on her face. "My dear Mr. Levins, I assure you 'twill be."

Once the pair was outside, Muireall guided her intended into the garden. "No one will disturb us here."

He glanced at the beautiful flowers, his wrinkled nose declaring how unimpressed he was by the display.

Just another reason Niall would make a far better partner. You have absolutely no sense o' taste. Muireall walked lackadaisically, playing the part of a simpering fool quite effectively.

"So, what was it you wanted to say?" he asked. "I hope 'tis na another threat. After what you did, any complaints about my business dealings will fall on deaf ears."

"That *is* something I've been curious about. How did you find out about Niall and me?"

The tacksman rolled his eyes. "I saw him kiss you up at Loch Isla the other night."

"Ah, I wondered if that had been the case."

She hid a contemptuous grin. *If only you'd witnessed what happened just prior to that, I'm sure our kiss wouldn' have seemed nearly so important. How delightful 'twould have been to see the horror on yer face.*

Her lips turned down. "Why were you at Loch Isla so late? You couldn' have had yer sheep with you, or we would have noticed."

For the first time, Matthew's superior attitude fell away. "I was just . . . I like to go there sometimes to be alone." His eyes became distant, wistful. But just as quickly, they hardened to stone, and he snapped, "We've strayed from the purpose o' this conversation. Do you have something to tell me or na?"

They'd just reached the far side of the garden. Out of view of anyone potentially observing them from the windows.

Muireall grinned triumphantly at her companion. "Oh, I just wanted an excuse to get out o' the house." She winked before tearing off, leaving Matthew standing there with his mouth open.

Mother and Father will be furious, but it can' be avoided. I hope Niall got my message.

Even if he hadn't, she couldn't wait any longer. Tonight was the full moon, so she had to get the banshee's cloak today. She sped over the grass, wind whipping through her wavy hair. She hadn't run like this since she was a child, but propriety was the last thing on her mind right then.

How will it work when the Fair Folk grant my favor, anyway? Will Mother and Father just forget about their plan to make me marry Mr. Levins? Will they tell me they're sorry fer forcing me into this?

Muireall almost laughed. She doubted even fairy magic could make her parents apologize for something.

She skidded to a stop at the docks, scanning the area for any sign of Niall.

He's na here yet. How long should I wait? She hesitantly wandered out onto the nearest dock, her eyes locking on the blue water that stretched out as far as she could see.

She swallowed, anxiety starting to build in her gut. She hadn't been this close to the ocean in a long time, and now she was about to go out on it. *Am I ready fer this?*

"Agassi?"

Muireall turned as the merchant from the market—Mr. Park, she thought his name was—strolled up from one of the ships. He wore similar attire to what he'd had on the last time she'd seen him—long, flowing robes of red and white this time—and a large black hat with a string of beads. His brown eyes were puzzled, his brow furrowed with concern.

"Mr. Park." Muireall smiled politely, and the man gave her a quick bow in return. "There's no need fer that, sir. I'm na royalty."

He chuckled a bit. "That's simply how we greet each other where I'm from. I must admit I was a bit too surprised last time, and I forgot to do so."

She cocked her head to the side. "What were you so surprised about?"

Mr. Park pulled at his sleeves, his gaze drifting away from her. "Oh, nothing much."

Muireall remembered the strange figurines he'd had on display at his stall. At the time, she'd marveled at their intricacy and beauty, but she hadn't fully considered their significance. "Because Niall was there?" she guessed.

Mr. Park's eyes briefly widened before he smiled and shook his head. "That's not it at all, agassi. I was simply not feeling well that day. If you'll excuse me." He bowed again and started to walk past her.

"Because you knew he wasn' human, right?"

Mr. Park went stiff. Slowly, he turned around and met her stare, his countenance grave. "If you also know it, you should know it is not safe to be near him." His tone was adamant.

"He's na dangerous, Mr. Park. I trust him."

"Then you're a fool, agassi. A wounded creature is to be feared above all others."

"Wounded?"

He frowned. "I thought you—" His breath caught, understanding filling his eyes. He motioned for her to follow him. "Let's discuss this somewhere we won't be overheard."

He led her to a mysterious ship floating at the end of the dock. Muireall gawked at the fearsome dragon's head jutting out of the end and the spiked roof-like covering stretching over the top. Two square sails blew in the breeze, and a white flag with intricate black symbols fluttered at its rear.

Fear—slippery and cold—flooded Muireall's belly. *This doesn' look like a merchant vessel. It looks like a warship.*

Why on earth would Father allow someone like Mr. Park to stay here?

Just as the thought entered her mind, a ray of sunlight struck her eyes. She blinked a few times, but when her vision was restored, the warship was gone, and an unassuming merchant ship like the ones that passed through frequently sat in its place.

Muireall stood motionless for a few seconds, her heart racing. *What just happened?*

"Are you coming, agassi?" Mr. Park asked with a warm smile.

She swallowed, her instincts telling her to run. *That was magic I just witnessed, wasn' it? There's some sort o' illusion over this ship to make it appear normal.*

Mr. Park held out his hand to help her onto the ship, his smile still in place.

He may na be all he seems, but he hasn' done anything to harm me. I need to find out what he knows.

Muireall kept her head high as she accepted the merchant's offer and stepped aboard the strange vessel.

Once they were inside, Mr. Park guided her past a row of cannons to a closed-off room at the back. She hesitated when he opened the door and gestured for her to go inside.

With a tender, compassionate expression, he said, "I assure you, agassi, you have nothing to fear from me."

Muireall threw her shoulders back with a huff and sauntered inside, hating that he'd seen through her bravado.

Several paintings hung from the walls, each depicting scenes in the countryside, and a white porcelain vase sat in the corner. There was a low table in the center of the room, but rather than chairs, two decorative cushions were positioned on either side of it.

Muireall pointed to the paintings. "Are these pictures o' where yer from?"

The merchant didn't answer and instead directed her to the small table. Once they were both seated, he said, "You don't know what he is, do you?"

Muireall fidgeted with her skirts. "I know he's a leannan na mara, but I don' know anything beyond that. What did you mean when you said he was wounded?"

Mr. Park ran his finger along the edge of the table, hesitant to speak. When he finally responded, his voice was low, as if saying the words quietly would give them less power. "A leannan na mara is a selkie who no longer has a sealskin."

A . . . selkie? Muireall's heart nearly stopped. She glanced out the window at the sea, pain shooting through her skull. She shut her eyes, trying to push away the memories pressing against her consciousness.

Her voice was an incredulous whisper as she replied, "Nay, yer lying."

Mr. Park's face softened. "I'm sorry, agassi. When the two of you came to my stall that day, I recognized him in an instant. I haven't come across any others of his kind personally, but from what I've heard, they're not a being you want to get entangled with."

How does he know what a leannan na mara is? Muireall knew she should tread carefully here; she didn't know this man, didn't know if his words could be trusted. But her curiosity was too great.

If Niall used to be a selkie, that means it could have been him who—

She rubbed her arms, suddenly freezing with cold. The thought was too absurd. She couldn't believe she'd even considered it. *Niall is a good person. He would never—*

"What makes them so dangerous?" she asked. She had to keep calm, had to keep from letting her emotions run rampant. Gathering information was a wise course of action. It was something to focus on besides the sinking feeling in her heart.

"The sea is a selkie's deepest love. To be parted from it is far from easy. It's a bit like having one's soul ripped in two or like seeing a loved one die right in front of you." Mr. Park's expression darkened. "As you can imagine, grief over such a loss is often all-consuming. Many times, a leannan na mara will take his rage out on everyone he can. They may not have selkie abilities anymore, but they're very intelligent beings who shouldn't be underestimated."

As he spoke, Muireall sat silently, past conversations whirring through her mind.

"I get nightmares sometimes, and afterward, I'll wake up and find marks like these."

"Niall has suffered a great deal o' loss, and he has more reason fer bitterness than you can imagine."

"I am but a shadow o' a memory, one amongst countless lovers the sea has rejected."

Nay, it can' be. . . .

But the truth was staring her straight in the face. If Mr. Park was right, that meant Niall used to be a selkie, the same type of creature that had killed Alastair.

Tears slid down Muireall's cheeks as images filled her mind, visions of the moment she'd tried so hard to forget.

And this time, she didn't have the strength to oppose them.

***

"Alastair, I don' want to do this. Let's just go home," the young girl complained as she and her brother walked along the beach just outside of town. Muireall was only seven years old, and since Alastair was already fourteen, it wasn't often they played together anymore. She was grateful for the chance to spend time with her brother today, but she was nervous about his choice of activity.

"Na until I teach you how to swim," Alastair said with a grin.

Muireall huffed but nodded. There was no talking Alastair out of something once he'd set his mind to it. She didn't know why he thought today was the day to teach her how to swim.

221

She would have much rather gone shopping at the market or exploring in the woods.

"This looks like a good spot," he said, stopping just past some rocks.

She glanced around, but she didn't see why this particular place was any better than where they'd been before. In fact, this was a pretty secluded area; it didn't seem very safe.

"Come on. 'Twill be fun," Alastair called as he hurried into the water.

The waves were small today, almost like they were inviting her in, but Muireall wasn't convinced. The ocean had always given her an uneasy feeling in the pit of her stomach. Too many fishermen had lost their lives in it, and those who returned often told stories of monstrous creatures lurking in its depths.

"Why do I need to know how to do this again?" She hesitantly followed, glad that her brother stopped once the water reached his knees. With their stark height difference and the strong undertow around here, that was deep enough in her mind.

Alastair rolled his eyes. "Because we live on an island," he drawled, giving her a look like she was stupid.

"What does that have to do with knowing how to swim?"

"What happens if you fall out o' a boat? Or what if you want to play in the water with yer friends and the tide pulls you out to sea?"

Muireall grumbled in annoyance, but she did see his point. Alastair always seemed to make good points. *But why do I usually get punished after I go along with him?*

"Won' you be here to make sure I stay safe, anyway?"

Her brother may not have been the nicest person, but if there was one thing she was positive of, it was that he would do anything to protect her.

Alastair's green eyes dimmed. "I may na always be here. That's why you need to know how to do it by yerself."

He got like this sometimes—all moody and vague. Mum said it was because he was remembering what had happened to him the year before, the day he'd almost gotten pulled into the ocean by a group of seals. Muireall hadn't been there when it had happened, and Alastair refused to talk about it, but the other bairns who'd been there said it had been the scariest thing they'd ever seen. Three massive grey seals had come out of nowhere, growling and snarling like they'd gone mad. Most of the bairns had run away as soon as they'd seen them but not Alastair. He hadn't been scared.

He'd paid the price for that mistake.

"What do I do now?" she asked as she stood in front of her brother.

He reached out and lifted her at the waist. "First, just get used to how it feels to float. Then we'll start working on the swimming part."

Muireall nodded, anxious but trusting that Alastair knew what he was doing.

As she started to lean back, a cry pierced the air. The two of them turned to see a small seal that lay a few yards down the beach. It hadn't been there a few minutes ago, and from the way it was moving its front fins, it seemed wounded.

"Aw, the poor thing's hurt," Muireall said. "Do you think we can help it?"

She looked to her brother, but rather than pity, something darker gleamed in his face. "Alastair?"

He let go of her, his gaze on the seal. "I'll be right back."

He walked out of the water and made his way toward a stick, his stride cautious but purposeful. Once it was in his grasp, he turned to the seal with a wicked smile.

"Alastair, what are you doing?"

He didn't answer, his focus still on the animal before him. He slowly lifted the stick, then charged.

"Don'! Stop!" Muireall pushed her way toward them, trying to reach her brother before he hurt the defenseless creature, but the seal rolled out of the way just as Alastair's stick slammed into the sand. The lad took another swing, but the seal slid backward into the water.

She had almost gotten to them when the seal disappeared beneath a wave. Alastair continued to pursue it, moving farther away from the shore.

"Alastair!" she cried, going as far as she dared even as her brother kept trying to find the seal.

Soon, he was up to his waist and still going deeper, striking the water over and over with his stick.

The seal's head popped out of the water, then latched onto Alastair's sleeve. With a triumphant growl, it pulled the boy backward.

Alastair screamed as he fought to keep his footing, then turned to his sister.

"Take my hand!" Muireall reached out, desperation giving her the courage to go deeper.

A new wave began to form, rolling in her direction.

The two siblings locked eyes. In that moment, Muireall's senses seemed to heighten, picking up everything around them—the frantic beating in her chest, the sea spray stinging her eyes, the sudden weightlessness of her feet slipping—

Alastair opened his mouth just as the wave crested over the top of Muireall's head, drowning out her brother's words. The girl tumbled backward, water filling her lungs as she sank beneath the surface.

She didn't know how long she was under, but her next thought was of a strange shape blocking the sun. She blinked a few times as her vision began to clear.

She lurched back with a shriek. The seal—monster—was right above her, its black eyes watching her curiously. She leaped to her feet, stumbling a few times, then raced across the sand toward town.

After running for a bit without hearing any sounds of pursuit, Muireall paused and turned around.

Where did it go? The seal had been right at the edge of the waves' reach just a moment ago. But now, there was no sign of it.

Her heart began to slow, and her thoughts returned to her brother. "Alastair? Alastair!" She scanned the water, waiting for him to resurface.

He has to be here somewhere!

When her search led nowhere, she dropped to the ground. *If I wait long enough, he'll come up. He has to.*

But the longer Muireall waited, the more her hope dried up. Salty tears mingled with the sand and seawater on her cheeks, but she paid them no mind. She sat there unmoving for minutes, hours, years it seemed, unable to accept what was becoming plain to see.

Alastair was not coming back.

It was only once the sun had started to dip in the sky that Muireall realized she was shivering. It was September, and the days were growing cold again. She needed to get home and change into dry clothes.

What will I tell Mum and Da'? Alastair was their favorite child, their firstborn and heir. It would destroy them to find out he was gone.

I won' tell them anything, she decided. *They'll hear about it eventually. Just na from me.*

To a seven-year-old, this made plenty of sense. When she got home, she hurried to her room, bathed, and changed clothes before her parents even noticed she'd returned. Only the servant who prepared her bath was privy to the knowledge that the young mistress had been drenched with seawater, and Muireall threatened to have the woman thrown out if spoke a word about it.

The following morning, it was Mr. McLaren who told the Olivers the devastating news: Alastair's body had washed up on shore. According to the village doctor, he'd drowned sometime the day before.

Parents held their children a little tighter after that, warning their sons and daughters never to go to the beach alone. Muireall's mother and father clung to her more, too, not letting her stray far from their watchful eyes. At first, she gladly accepted their newfound attachment, happy they were finally noticing her now that her brother was gone.

Until their grip became so suffocating, she almost envied Alastair.

Then she'd remember that creature's terrifying gaze, and a shudder would pass through her.

She'd realized later that it must have been no ordinary seal that had attacked him. This creature had been far smarter than any animal. It had acted wounded, then drawn Alastair away from the safety of the beach, so it could drag him to his death.

From what she'd read in her books and heard in Mr. McLaren's stories, the creature that had killed her brother had to have been a selkie.

And she was the only one who knew the truth.

***

As Muireall came back to the present, trembling with anxiety, someone grabbed her hand. "Agassi, are you all right?"

She opened her eyes, not remembering when she'd closed them.

Mr. Park dropped her hand, his cheeks flushed. "I . . . got you some tea." He gestured to two small cups on the table in front of her.

She swallowed. "Thank you, sir." Fear and doubt swirled in her mind, making it difficult to think. She grabbed the closer cup and quickly drank, hoping the warm liquid would help her regain some semblance of control. But as she set the cup back down, her hand was still shaking.

Mr. Park pursed his lips, an unasked question hovering in the air. He opened his mouth, then closed it and took a sip of tea. "You and I don't know each other, but I assure you that everything I've said is the truth."

"How can I know that?" Muireall snapped.

He opened his hands. "What reason have I to lie?"

"What reason have you to tell the truth?"

"A general sense of responsibility for the humans I encounter," he replied, pride shining in his eyes.

Muireall also noted a hint of subterfuge in his voice, though, as if he wasn't telling her quite everything.

"Most people aren't aware of the magical beings around them," he continued. "Most can't be trusted with such knowledge."

"And yet you thought 'twas wise to tell me?"

Mr. Park raised an eyebrow. "You're the one who admitted your friend isn't human."

She conceded his point with a slight nod. She took a deep breath, feeling her nerves settle down. Things weren't as bad as she'd thought. She just needed to look at this logically, and everything would be fine.

Mr. Park only told me what Niall used to be. He's obviously biased against Niall's kind; he doesn' know Niall like I do. 'Tis just a coincidence that Niall is the same kind o' creature as the one that killed Alastair.

"I appreciate you sharing this information with me, but"—she confidently met the merchant's eye—"it doesn' change anything."

His mouth fell open. "But, agassi, did you not hear what I just said?"

"I don' know what you have against my servant or his kind, but Niall Moreland saved my life."

Mr. Park crossed his arms. "Was he the one to endanger it in the first place?"

Muireall rose to her feet, her face a rosy red. "As I said, I trust him. Now, thank you fer the tea, but I really must be going."

She marched off, her outward poise belying the icy chill in her heart.

Ruthless

Niall hastened down the path, Muireall's letter bouncing around his mind. As soon as Anne had delivered it to Drulea Cottage, Briony had read out the short message: "Dear Mistress Fairborn, please tell Niall to meet me at the dock around one o' clock."

Far too short. No word about how she was doing. No word about why she hadn't shown up the other day either.

Briony had tried visiting her, but Lady Oliver had claimed Muireall was too ill for company. Not that that made any sense when Briony was acting as the town doctor until a suitable replacement could be found.

What if she's hurt? A vision of Lady Oliver striking her Muireall's cheek flashed through his mind, and he walked a little faster.

Settle down. Settle down, Niall. You'll be seeing her soon, and if she's well enough to go hunting fer the banshee's cloak, she must be fine.

And once all this is over, the two o' us will have a chance to be together.

His eyes crinkled at the corners. Though he'd been afraid of his feelings before, Muireall's response the other night had given him hope. Enough hope to stop running from the truth anymore.

Besides, he wasn't about to let that troublesome Portuguese merchant outdo him. If Mr. Mendes was confident enough to declare his love, Niall certainly was, too.

As he arrived at the dock, Muireall emerged from the ship at the end. Her movements were rigid, and she held herself with the same arrogant air she always did.

Niall smiled. *She's fine. 'Twas foolish o' me to worry*. He opened his mouth to call out to her—

Muireall's shoulders slumped, her face crumpling as if she was about to cry.

He raced the rest of the way to her, his feet pounding against the wooden boards. "Muireall!"

The woman's head shot up, her eyes going wide for a split second before she grinned at him. "Niall." Her voice was shaky, her smile weak.

Niall swept her into his arms, unsure what had upset her but wanting to do what he could to comfort her. She hesitated to return the hug at first, then melted into his embrace as if she'd lost all her strength.

"What's wrong?" he whispered against her hair, reveling in the feel of her body against his.

She slowly pulled away, a little more color in her cheeks. She shook her head. "'Tis nothing. I just . . ." She glanced at the ship behind her. "I was worried you wouldn' make it."

"I was worried, too, when you didn' meet me at Briony's house." He tried not to sound angry, but a hint of bitterness scorched his tongue.

"I'm sorry about that. My mother has been keeping me locked away in my room. She"—Muireall dropped her gaze— "found out about you and me."

Niall blinked. "What? How?"

"Mr. Levins saw us while we were up at Loch Isla. Saw us kissing, anyway. But don' worry." Her voice grew a bit stronger. "I've thought o' a way to make things work out. All I have to do is ask Prince Aodhàn to change my parents' opinions o' you, then everything will be fine."

He cocked his head to the side, his lips twitching with amusement. "And what do you want their opinions to be?"

"I . . ." Muireall's voice dropped to a whisper. "I want them to see you as a potential suitor. If . . . that's what you want, too."

Warmth spread through Niall's chest. It wasn't exactly the confession he'd been hoping for, but it was enough for now.

She wants to be with me, too.

Muireall shifted in place before finally peeking up at him. "Is it what you want?"

Niall's gaze roamed over her face, his mouth spreading into a smirk. *You know how I feel. Stop pretending you don'.*

He waited, fully expecting her to admit she was only teasing him. *Everything I've done up to this point makes it obvious. Yer feelings are the only ones that have been a mystery. There's no way you could still be unsu—*

He frowned. "You don' know?"

When Muireall's eyes narrowed in irritation, he knew he'd made a mistake. "Wait. Don' answer that," he blurted, not wanting this to turn into an argument that would leave them both angry.

"Don' cut me off," she snapped, putting her hands on her hips.

"You cut me off the other night, so 'tis only fair," he said before he could stop himself.

"What? When did I do that?"

She doesn' remember? How could she— He raked his fingers through his hair, wishing she wasn't so infuriating. *Why does she have to make everything difficult?*

That's part o' why you love her, he reminded himself.

Niall closed his eyes and groaned inwardly. Then his lips curled up. *We make quite the pair, don' we?*

He opened his eyes again, his anger subsiding as he peered down at the woman before him. "I'll tell you exactly when: the moment William asked me how I felt about you."

Muireall's arms dropped to her sides, her mouth falling open.

Well, that's one way to get her to be quiet. Niall's gaze drifted to her lips, and he leaned closer. *I can think o' better ways tho—*

He stopped, his mouth just a hairsbreadth from hers, and pulled back. *I don' want this to end the same way it did the last time I kissed her. She's waiting fer me to make things clear. Fine, here goes.*

"When I first agreed to help you, I was only interested in what I could get out o' it. Somewhere along the way, though, it

turned into doing it fer yer sake. I felt bad fer you and didn'
want you to be stuck in a loveless marriage. But then . . ." His
brow furrowed. "I saw what yer mother did to you before the
dinner"—

Muireall grimaced, her eyes skittering away for a second
before returning to his.

—"and something happened to me. I've never felt so
enraged fer someone, so protective o' them." The words slid
off his tongue, soft and sincere. "I thought I'd gone mad fer a
moment; otherwise, why would I be reckless enough to—" His
gaze flicked to her cheek, and judging by the blush spreading
over it, he knew she knew *exactly* what he was referring to.

"You've always been reckless," she whispered, a tiny smile
on her beautiful face.

He winked, loving the way her blush deepened. "True. But
this—this was something different. Something *more*."

He enjoyed teasing her, but he hoped she could tell now
that he was being completely serious. "I've been in love before;
at least, I thought I was. . . ." He trailed off, dark memories
encroaching on his thoughts.

"With Briony Fairborn?"

Niall continued on as if she hadn't said anything, though
he knew his lack of denial was confirmation enough. "I realize
now that what I felt before was only a taste, a shadow. Even
the sea herself, captivating as she is, never ensnared my heart
as you have. And I know fer certain there's no hope o' ever
getting it back."

His eyes met hers, a deep chuckle rumbling in his throat.
"I suppose one o' the rumors about you turned out to be true,
after all. You are indeed the most ruthless woman I've ever
met."

***

Muireall stood absolutely still, Niall's words ringing in her ears.
He can' mean that. . . . Did I hear him right?

The man's closeness was intoxicating, but she resisted the
desire to press in closer and instead studied his face. *Is he trying
to fool me? Could he have some sort o' hidden motive behind all this?*

But there was no lie in his beautiful eyes, dark as obsidian yet glowing with a fiery love Muireall could no longer ignore.

The world around them faded, no longer important, no longer worth noticing. Memories wove through her mind of moments they'd shared, all leading up to this precise point in time:

"Just who do you think you are, traipsing across my property?"

"I know I'm just a servant, and we didn' meet on the best o' terms, but if there's anything I can do to help . . ."

"Stay with me, and you'll be safe."

"What if I gave you a position that would make it easier to be alone together?"

"Don' lie to me, Muireall. You may fool everyone else but na me."

"After all this time, am I still just a servant to you?"

"Muireall? You did hear me, right?" Niall's voice was soft, tentative, as if he feared she would reject him. Again.

Oh, Niall, you poor fool. What have I put you through? She placed her hand along his jaw, his skin smooth beneath her fingers. He closed his eyes and leaned into her touch.

She smiled, joy billowing up in her heart. Somehow, Niall had slipped past her defenses. Past her facades. Then he'd done something she wouldn't have thought possible: he'd found the real person hiding behind all that and brought her out into the light.

But it still wasn't enough to fully quell the fear inside her.

Niall had taken a step forward, bravely declaring his love. Muireall wished she could be so bold, but everyone she'd opened her heart up to had either hurt her or left her. *What if this ends the same way?*

Still, he deserves an answer, and I can' bear to push him away again.

Muireall did the only thing she could think of: shot forward and pressed her lips to his.

Niall only hesitated for a second before wrapping his arms around her and pulling her against his chest. Her knees buckled as euphoria overtook her, but Niall held her steady, his hands cradling her back. Pleasure radiated through her body as the kiss grew more fervent, their mouths moving in unison with their beating hearts.

Only when the need to breathe became urgent did the two pull apart, panting as they stared at each other in shocked silence.

Muireall's gaze went to Niall's swollen lips, wanting nothing more than to taste them again but knowing they still had a task to complete.

He gave her a lopsided grin, then playfully tugged at a strand of her hair. "I've been wanting to do that fer far too long."

She hunched her shoulders, embarrassment creeping in. "'Twas na that long ago you . . ."

"Perhaps, but you didn' kiss me back last time." His eyes twinkled, and he held out his hand.

She hesitantly took it, his touch sending another jolt through her. Her fears seemed so silly, so needless now. Maybe she could let them go. She squeezed Niall's hand, smiling up at him.

"Now, are you ready to go get that cloak?"

A line appeared on her forehead. "Aren' you forgetting something?"

Niall shook his head, eyes wide with confusion. "What would that be?"

Muireall gestured to the boats.

"Oh. I knew that." He strode toward one of them, but she scurried after him and grabbed his arm.

"Na that one." She giggled and turned him toward Mr. Buchanan's boat. It was the smallest one at the dock, barely large enough to be called a fishing boat, and she had no idea when it had last been used. The cobwebs all over it were far from comforting. "That one."

I hope Anne delivered that letter.

Niall hopped into the boat and grabbed the oars. Muireall climbed in more cautiously, holding her arms out as it rocked under her weight.

When she sat down, her heart fluttered, reminding her of the imminent danger should she tumble out. *'Tis fine. Don' overreact. Even if I did fall, Niall would get me out. He used to be a selkie, after all, so he must be a good swimmer.*

She grabbed the side of the boat and peered at the islets in the distance. There were almost twenty of them, and none were guaranteed to hold the banshee's lair.

What if we don' find it in time?

Nay, we have to. Failure isn' an option. We will find the banshee's home. We will get the cloak. And we will take the three treasures to the Prince.

She frowned. "Niall?"

"Hmm?" He kept the same, steady rhythm, his arms moving back and forth seemingly without effort.

"How are we going to get the cloak? We didn' have time to make a plan."

"I was wondering when you'd ask about that. Na to worry. I've got it all figured out."

When he didn't explain further, Muireall scoffed. "And? What is it?"

"Since you did such a good job last time, I'm sending you in again as bait." He threw the words out casually, as if they were of no consequence.

"What?"

Niall grinned. "I'm only teasing. I'm sure you've heard about the meaning behind banshees' terrible wails, but what you probably don' know is that those wails are especially painful fer my kind."

"Why is that?"

He shrugged. "Don' know."

"Can banshees be reasoned with? Or are they more like kelpies?" Muireall resisted the urge to shudder as she recounted their encounter with the dreadful water horse.

"They can, but . . ." He drew his eyebrows together.

"Is there something yer na telling me?"

"Banshees are fairly merciless, and they have the ability to see the deaths o' everyone you care about, past and future. So, 'tis in our best interest to avoid speaking with her if possible." Nervousness danced in his eyes.

Is he afraid o' being forced to relive his sister's death?

She nodded. "All right. What's yer plan, then?"

"I'm hoping she won' be home."

Muireall opened her mouth to insult Niall's intelligence, but he quickly continued, "Banshees take great pains to keep people from stumbling into their abodes. Even if she hasn' heard about yer deal with the Prince, there will be no fooling her into thinking we're there by chance. When we get close to the entrance, I want you to duck out o' sight while I get her attention. As soon as yer hidden, cover yer ears. She'll probably start wailing right away, but when she does, I'll try to knock her out, so you can grab the cloak. We'll be gone before she wakes up."

She gave him a look of disbelief.

"I know how it sounds, but I'm stronger than a banshee, and we'll have surprise on our side."

"But you just said banshee wails are extremely painful fer you. What if you can' handle it?"

"I appreciate the concern, Princess, but I'll be fine." Niall tapped her nose, then resumed rowing.

"Have you ever heard a banshee wail before?"

"What a silly question. I'm a leannan na mara, remember?" His dark eyes left hers, and he said no more.

Muireall chewed on her lip, watching the shoreline as they cut around Everton's edge and made their way toward one of the islets.

I need another plan in case this one fails.

A few minutes later, she asked, "When we get there, how will we know we've found the banshee's lair? What do they live in?"

"Oh, did I na mention it before? In caves."

The Truth

As Muireall stepped onto the shore, she inhaled a deep breath of salty air. *This is it. The final treasure.* Freedom was so close she could almost taste it; her heart nearly leaped with anticipation.

But the task at hand could still prove challenging, so she staunched her joy and stayed vigilant. Niall, too, had dropped his nonchalant attitude and had his iron knife clenched in his hand.

The islet they'd come to was rocky with only a few hardy grasses here and there. The ground was uneven, with several hills and severe drop-offs that made it necessary to carefully watch one's step. There also seemed to be no source of fresh water and hardly any cover from a storm.

In short, a terrible place to live.

Is there even a cave here? Muireall didn't see anything remotely suggesting one, but perhaps she'd spot something once they'd gotten over this hill.

The second hill was the same, as was the third.

After an hour of walking without even getting halfway across the islet, she swiped at her brow. This place had seemed so small when the boat had docked. *How could it be this—*

Her eyes darted to Niall, who seemed to already know what she was about to ask. "Magic. The islet has been made to look peedie[29] to anyone passing by. We must be in the right place."

---

[29] Small.

They spent the next several minutes wandering until they finally came upon an unassuming cave nestled against a steep hill. They'd started on the outer rim of the island, the sea close by on their right. Muireall would have preferred going more inland, but Niall had insisted on staying near the ocean, at least to start with.

Muireall lifted her eyebrows at her companion. "That hole is where the banshee lives? I don' believe it."

"Haven' you learned by now that looks can be deceiving?"

She gave the cave a second glance, trying not to let her skepticism cloud her judgment. Her red locks swayed in the wind coming from the entrance, almost as if it were beckoning them nearer.

Wind? Muireall's senses went on alert, her eyes swerving in all directions.

A raspy voice whispered, "What pretty wee thieves have come to my doorstep."

Niall threw his arm in front of Muireall and pulled out his dagger, gaze sweeping the sky.

A keening shriek pierced the air just before the banshee flew out of hiding. Muireall clapped her hands over her ears, gritting her teeth to hold back a cry. Such an unearthly sound should never be uttered; it ricocheted through her like a hammer striking metal.

The creature hovered in the air directly above them, her hands resting at the sides of her black cloak as she continued her vocal assault. Her appearance was every bit as horrifying as the stories described: stringy white hair strewn about an ashen, wrinkled face; pale blue eyes that gleamed with hatred; claw-like nails at the tips of long, gaunt fingers; and a pure white dress.

Muireall's hands began to tremble, but she fought to control herself. She had to; otherwise—

Niall howled beside her, throwing himself to the ground. Blood dripped from his fingers as he covered his ears to block out the banshee's wail.

What do I do? We didn' even get to put Niall's plan into motion. He said na to engage with her, but—

The word "plan" jogged Muireall's memory. *Sorry, Niall, but I'm going to have to go with my idea now.*

"Stop!" she shouted at the creature. "Please, I need to speak with you."

Niall won' have to worry about reliving his sister's death if I'm the one doing the talking.

The banshee's cry died away, but suspicion remained in her eyes. "Speak with me?" She giggled, a disjointed, chilling sound that felt like insects crawling down Muireall's back.

Still, it was better than the screaming.

The banshee zoomed forward, stopping only a few inches from Muireall. "All right." She opened her mouth in a wide, ominous smile that displayed two rows of perfect white teeth. "I'm listening."

Niall slowly rose to his feet, wiping his bloody hands on his trousers. "We've come to—"

"Na you," the banshee sneered, dismissing him with a gust of wind that sent him flying off the side of the cliff.

"Niall!" Muireall sprinted to the cliff's edge just as he hit the water with a loud splash.

"Oh, he'll be fine," the banshee said, clucking her tongue. She waved her hand, summoning a second wind that carried Muireall deep into the cave before depositing her into a high-backed chair.

Muireall sat motionless for several seconds, trying to get her bearings. *Niall didn' tell me banshees could control wind. We were in no way prepared fer this.*

She glanced up. *What in the—*

Her jaw dropped at the cave's furnishings, so lavish they rivaled those of Rigmore House. An elegant table with ten matching chairs sat upon an immaculate black-and-white fur rug. Tapestries bedecked the walls, woven with finer detail than any human hand could achieve. A roaring fire crackled in a large fireplace at the back of the room. Above the mantel hung the head of what appeared to be a giant green serpent, its mouth open wide as if it intended to devour her.

Muireall gulped, the fire's warmth powerless against the fear spreading through her veins.

The banshee appeared with a plate of biscuits, her hood pulled back from her face. She seemed far less gruesome now, almost grandmotherly. *If Grandmother never combed her hair a day in her life.*

The creature put the plate on the small table between them and sank into the chair across from her. "Now, what was it you wished to say?"

Muireall was at a loss for words. This wasn't at all what she'd been expecting. "I—I—"

"Do speak up, dear." The banshee snatched a biscuit off the plate, her thin lips lifting at the corners as she took a bite.

I was going to offer her wealth, but I see now that that would be a waste o' time. She has no lack o' material possessions.

Could there be a heart lurking beneath that ugly exterior? Maybe she's more like Lachlan than the kelpie?

Muireall took a deep breath. "You see, I need yer cloak."

"I gathered that," the banshee replied, her tone bored. "I may live in a cave, but that doesn' mean I'm completely oblivious to the outside world."

"Then you heard about my deal with the Fairy Prince."

"O' course I did. And since I'm the only banshee within twenty miles, I knew you'd be coming here sooner or later."

Muireall frowned, trying to gauge her mood. "Then yer na angry about it?"

The banshee laughed, the sound still discordant but slightly less grating this time. "Oh, dear"—her blue eyes hardened—"why ever would you think I'm na angry?"

A hand snaked out from behind the banshee's chair and gripped the creature's throat.

"Muireall, run!" Niall cried, his face emerging from the shadows.

Muireall jumped to her feet, tearing out of the cave. She'd almost made it into the sunlight when an unseen force yanked her backward.

"Na so fast, dear."

She landed straight back in the chair she'd just left, except this time, Niall sat motionless in one beside her, and the banshee stood a few feet away. Muireall turned to Niall, her heart falling at his defeated expression.

The banshee clapped a few times, her smile mocking. "Congratulations. You two are undoubtedly the most foolish visitors I've had in quite some time. Especially you, leannan na mara. I would have thought you would be wise enough na to—"

She threw a hand over her shocked mouth. "Wait. You couldn' be Callum's son, could you?"

Niall looked away, but he didn't deny her claim.

Muireall's head swiveled between them. *Callum . . . that's the same name the Fairy Prince used. Does every magical being know who Niall's father is?*

The banshee rose a few inches into the air, eyes glinting with mischief. "I've heard all kinds o' things about you. Want to hear them?"

"We're only here fer the cloak," Muireall said curtly. "Is there any way we can convince you to part with it and let us go?"

"Let you go?" The banshee tapped her lip. "Hmm, that doesn' sound like much fun. I don' get guests often. I should enjoy it while I can, wouldn' you say?" She flew closer until she was almost in Muireall's face.

The redhead tried not to gag, but the creature's stench was so wretched she had to turn her head. It reminded her of rotting flesh.

"Did he tell you about my special gifts?" the banshee whispered in her ear, giggling manically.

Muireall peeked at Niall, hoping he was working on some solution to get them out of this mess. *Keep her talking,* he mouthed.

"N-Nay, he didn'," she said, returning her attention to the banshee.

"Well, besides what I've already shown you, there's one more talent I'm blessed with. But most people don' particularly like it."

"I'd love to hear about it."

"Truly?" The hag lit up with delight. "Whenever I look into someone's eyes, I can see the deaths o' all their loved ones."

Even though she'd known what the banshee would say, Muireall's stomach still dropped. "That *is* quite the talent."

The banshee basked in the praise. "It truly should be appreciated more. I don' know why the humans I visit are so upset whenever they see me. I'm only trying to help them, so they don' waste the time they have left."

In a way, it made sense, but there was also a mad quality to her words that made Muireall wonder if the banshee's goal was truly so altruistic. She certainly seemed to be reveling in their fear.

Niall better hurry with whatever he's doing. Muireall didn't dare check and risk losing the banshee's attention.

"Should I show you?"

Muireall pressed her head back into her chair. "That's all right. I'd rather na know about sad things before they happen."

"Oh, it doesn' have to be about *future* deaths." The banshee's ghostly finger trailed along Muireall's chin, cold as ice and delicate as a feather. "You've already lost someone dear to you."

Her gaze snapped to Niall, who had managed to get all but his right leg free from the chair. "But you know all about that, don' you?"

He stiffened, and for a second, Muireall thought it was because of the banshee's magic.

Then she saw the shame in his eyes.

"Niall . . . what is she talking about?"

He frowned and shook his head. "I have no ide—"

"Enough lies," the banshee cut in. "Should you wish to leave with my cloak"—she clasped the edge of the hood—"only the truth shall suffice."

Hope blossomed in Muireall's chest. *We still have a chance to make it out o' here and get the cloak to the Prince! But what could she mean?*

Niall slowly turned until he was facing the two women. He glared at the hag and said through gritted teeth, "There is no truth to tell. Now, let us go."

"Wrong answer." The banshee flicked her wrist, and a wind slammed him against the cave wall.

"Stop! Don' hurt him. Please!"

The creature whirled toward Muireall, her blue eyes flat. "You wouldn' be saying that if you knew what he'd done." She nodded to Niall. "Do you want to tell her, or should I?"

Niall growled, his body trembling with rage. If he'd not been held firmly in place, he looked like he would have torn the banshee apart.

"Ah, me, then." She spun back to Muireall and pointed at the leannan na mara. "He killed him."

Muireall's heart skipped. "What are you talking about? Niall would never—"

"Oh, this is more entertaining than I thought 'twould be," she tittered. "And I haven' even gotten to the best part. Don' you want to know who 'twas?"

"Nay, stop it," Muireall cried, stomach tightening with apprehension. "I don' want to hear another word."

"Then 'tis a good thing I don' particularly care what you want." The banshee flew forward and leaned close to her ear. "He killed Alastair."

A Fool and a Monster

Muireall closed her eyes. It was a good thing she was already sitting; otherwise, she would have surely lost her footing. *That can' be right. Niall would never do something like that. Could never do something like that . . . right?*

He must be absolutely furious. To have someone accuse him o' something like that—I'm surprised he isn' shouting already.

She opened her eyes, turned to the man she loved, and—

All the breath whooshed out of her lungs, for in the instant before Niall's eyes ripped away from hers, she saw something glittering there that she never should have seen: guilt.

Nay, it can' be. That doesn' make any sense. Why would he feel guilty unless he had . . . unless he . . .

I must be mistaken.

"Niall, look at me." Her voice was almost a whimper. When he didn't respond, she screeched, "Look at me!"

He winced but didn't turn her way.

As the echoes of her cry faded, the truth finally started to sink in. There was no reason for him to keep quiet, no reason to allow such a horrible claim to be made without protest.

Unless it was true.

Unless Niall really had killed Alastair.

That's why he didn' want to talk to the banshee, Muireall realized. *Na because he didn' want to relive his sister's death. Because he didn' want the truth to come out about Alastair's.*

Tears gathered in her eyes. *How could I have been so stupid?* She'd learned long ago not to let anyone close enough to see her weak spots. The mask she'd worn day in and day out may have kept her alone, but it had also kept her safe.

But I let his handsome smirk and disregard fer the rules trick me into lowering my guard. She scoffed inwardly. *And he turned out to be exactly whom I was trying to protect myself from.* As the truth sank deeper, it felt like shards of glass embedding themselves in her broken heart.

But when he said he loved me, it seemed like he really meant—

Her brother's scream resounded in her ears before she could finish the thought. A cascade of emotions overtook her—fear, helplessness, grief—everything she'd felt the day Alastair died. She'd just been a small child then, incapable of fully understanding what was happening.

But she was grown now and no longer had the luxury of ignorance. She knew exactly what had been done to her brother.

And who was responsible.

Muireall blinked back her tears, hatred blazing through her being. She glared at the monster beside her, recognizing now that she'd been deceived. Niall might have claimed he loved her, but only people were capable of love.

A tinkling laugh reminded her of the banshee's presence, and she turned to the vile hag.

"This has been such a delight. Perhaps I should have guests more often." The banshee paused, then raised her eyebrows when no one responded. "Nay? All right, time to go."

The force holding Muireall and Niall in place vanished.

"To thank you fer the entertainment"—the banshee giggled again—"I'll let you both leave with yer lives still intact." She beamed like she was being unbelievably generous.

"With the cloak?" Niall asked, his voice low and pained.

The sound of it made Muireall grit her teeth. *How dare he think he still has the right to speak!*

But he's right that I need the cloak if I'm going to—

Wait. Her heart clenched, the dream she'd been holding onto so preciously collapsing in on itself. *I can' ask the Prince to*

246

make my parents change their minds about Niall. Na when he's even worse than they already think he is. To think I wanted to use fairy magic to make my parents accept the man who murdered their son. What a horrible daughter I've turned out to be.

The banshee's voice flitted through the air, pulling Muireall out of her self-deprecating thoughts. "Nay, that shall be staying with me"—she winked at Niall— "since you were a liar to the end. And black *is* my favorite color." She twirled dramatically, the cloak fanning out around her.

Muireall broke out in a cold sweat. *I may na want Niall anymore, but that doesn' mean I want to accept my parents' choice. I can' marry Matthew!* "But I have to ha—"

"Farewell!" The banshee waved, and Muireall and Niall flew through the air, only to be dumped on the ground at the cave's entrance.

Muireall groaned as she picked up Niall's discarded dagger and pulled herself to her feet. *The banshee was far too powerful fer the likes o' me. There's no way I'm going to get her cloak.* She almost turned to Niall, but the very idea of asking him for help made her sick to her stomach. She peered up at the sky, noting the sun's position, then started trudging back toward the boat. *Good thing I had another idea in case I couldn' get the cloak.*

She felt Niall's presence behind her, but she ignored him. She didn't want to talk to him, didn't want to think about him right now. Not when everything she'd been striving for had just gone up in smoke. Not when looking at him might make her fall apart.

I'm losing daylight. I have to get back to Everton, so I can cross the Veil by the time the moon rises.

"Muireall, let me explain!"

She swallowed but kept walking. She had no time to waste, especially not on—

"Princess, please," he begged, his voice broken and desperate.

Before Muireall could stop herself, she'd spun around, her heart in her throat.

Niall's dark eyes were wet with unshed tears, but she folded her arms, determined not to let herself be moved. She wasn't going to be fooled a second time.

"From what I can tell, there's nothing to explain," she said stonily.

"But I—"

She cut him off before he could say something that might tug at her shattered heart. "I don' want to hear it. I have to go."

She dropped her gaze, done with this conversation. Done with him.

"I meant what I said about loving you."

Muireall froze, blood rushing through her ears. *I need to go. I have to get back to the Prince. I don' need answers from him. I don' need—*

Her lips moved of their own accord, her eyes lifting to his. "Did you know who I was the day we met?"

Niall grimaced, then gave her a sharp nod.

"You knew . . ." Her breath was shaky. "And yet you still tried to get close to me, to use me fer—fer what?"

He licked his lips. "I . . . It doesn' matter why I came here because everything's changed. I'm na the same person I was back then."

"Na the same person?" Muireall scoffed, anger billowing up inside her until it was too much to contain. With it, out spilled the questions she'd been trying not to ask. "So, what were you before? Someone who toyed with human lives fer sheer amusement? Is that what I am to you—just a game?" She was practically screaming now, but she didn't care. In that moment, she didn't care if the whole world heard her.

Niall grabbed her hand, his eyes pleading. "O' course na. You brought joy back into my life after I thought I'd lost everything."

Muireall pulled out of his grip. "D-Don' touch me."

If he touched her, she might forget her anger. Her hatred. And she couldn't do that.

So, she asked the only question that really mattered: "Why did you kill Alastair?"

"You have to understand." He ran his hand through his hair, his eyes sliding back and forth before returning to hers. "All my life, I was taught humans were treacherous. And even though selkies possess far greater power, we're weak when we're in our seal form. Only the very brave or very foolish ever go near them."

"I don' believe this. . . . Are you trying to tell me 'twas bravery that led you to murder my brother? That you thought you were protecting other selkies from a threat?" The notion was so ridiculous she almost snorted in derision.

She waited for him to backtrack, but instead, a grim smile played at the man's lips, and when he spoke, his voice rang with challenge. "That's exactly what I was doing."

Muireall's grip tightened on the dagger, and before she knew what she was doing, she'd sliced a thin line across Niall's cheek. "I was a fool fer trusting you when yer nothing more than a monster. Don' ever speak to me again."

***

Niall reared back, his face roaring with heat. But that pain was nothing compared to the betrayal in Muireall's tear-stained eyes.

I'm so sorry. His heart reached out to her, his strongest desire to ease her pain, but she had made it clear she wouldn't accept his comfort or explanations, so he swallowed his words and stepped back.

Regret burned in his chest as she stormed off, but he made no attempt to stop her. She had every right to be furious with him, every right to never want to see him again. After what he'd done, he deserved far worse.

As she disappeared from view, Niall sank to the ground and closed his eyes, telling himself he wouldn't follow, that he would respect her wishes and stay away.

But something prickled at the back of his mind. Something important—

A memory rammed against his thoughts: *"If I were to fail, what sort o' payment would the Prince want?"*

"Oh, something trivial. I'm sure you've got plenty o' things at home that would do, so don' worry about it."

Niall sprang to his feet and broke into a run. Muireall had no idea that had been another lie. Aodhàn wouldn't demand a trinket as payment. He would enslave her for the rest of her life.

And 'tis all thanks to my cowardice in the banshee's cave. If only I'd been brave enough to tell her the truth, then she wouldn' be in this mess. She'd have known about Alastair, but at least she'd have the cloak right now.

I have to tell her what she's walking into, so she can run. I can keep her out o' Aodhàn's reach. It won' be the best life, but at least she won' be a slave. There's nothing else I can—

Niall slowed. *Nay, that's na true. There is one other thing I can do.* He swerved to the left, the brittle grass crackling under his shoes. The sun was dipping in the sky; the full moon would be rising soon. He had to hurry.

A cliff stretched out before him, showcasing the gorgeous blue sea that he'd once loved above all else. His former lover smiled at him, her waves cresting coyly. Niall dove headfirst into the water, but his heart wasn't swayed by the ocean's tender embrace. Instead, one solitary thought filled him, fueling him with strength and purpose.

I have to save her.

Changing the Terms

Muireall didn't wait for Niall to catch up before she hopped into Bernard's boat. But when she glimpsed storm clouds gathering in the sky, pity pricked her heart. *Am I really just going to leave him here?*

She grabbed the oars and started rowing. *Aye, that's exactly what I'm going to do. After what he did to Alastair, he can stay here and die, fer all I care.*

The trip felt so much longer than it had the first time, and the farther Muireall went, the angrier she became. Angrier at Niall but also at herself.

The signs were all there; I just chose na to see them. When I told Lachlan my song was fer Alastair, didn' Niall's face darken? Mr. Park warned me, too, but I pushed his concerns aside. And didn' Adaira and Mr. Burgess tell me to stay away from him?

Muireall's anger turned to a new target. *After dinner the other night, why didn' Adaira tell me about Alastair? Even though she didn' approve o' my deal with the fairies, she didn' seem opposed to us being together. In fact, she seemed happy about it! Is it possible she didn' know?*

O' course, that must be it. She would never want me to be with the monster who killed my brother. . . .

Her earliest memories of Alastair came to the forefront of her mind: playing together, laughing as they got into mischief, watching the stars at night—

Then the scenes shifted as the two of them grew older: Alastair threatening Briony whenever she was nearby, knocking

Ewan to the ground, excluding Muireall from playing with his friends—

She shook her head a few times, breaking off the train of thought. *Stop it, Muireall. Don' be looking fer something to justify what Niall did. Alastair had his flaws, but he loved me. And there's nothing he could have done to deserve death.*

Once she was back in Everton, she moved cautiously through the streets, wondering if her parents had sent anyone out to look for her. Only a few people were around, most having already returned to their homes for the evening. She inclined her head to those she passed, hoping no one would find her presence odd. Steven McLaren scowled as he walked by, and Muireall forced herself to keep a steady, easy pace. *If that old fool notices anything amiss, he'll get me into trouble fer sure.*

As soon as Mr. McLaren was gone, she ducked behind the church and heaved a sigh. Her relief grew tenfold when she spotted a bag tucked against the side of the building.

She opened it, smiling at the sight of the treasures within. *Bless you, Anne.* There was even the sapphire necklace she'd asked the maid to place there in the event that she couldn't obtain the cloak.

Surely Prince Aodhàn will accept this instead. He seemed to know Niall—and harbor a grudge toward him. Once I tell him I was betrayed, will he be merciful and give me the favor, anyway?

The memory of the Prince's heartless gaze sent a tremor through her. Mercy didn't seem like something he commonly bestowed.

The moon was already rising; she didn't have time to delay. Muireall slung the bag over her shoulder and set off, grateful for the growing dark. Walking through town was one thing; she'd hardly be able to explain if someone saw her sneaking off into the woods.

***

Niall stepped through the Veil. This time, there was no dance, no merriment as he passed into the clearing. Instead of revelers, four guards stood on either side of the fairy ring, their gazes cool and unnerving. Their silver armor, crafted from beithir[30] scales, was nigh unbreakable and covered their bodies in an eerie glow.

They'd been waiting for him.

Niall threw his shoulders back, not one to be intimidated, then paused. *Right now, 'tis probably better to appear as pitiful as possible.*

He hunched over a bit, lowering his eyes as he said, "Please inform Prince Aodhàn that I need an audience with him."

The nearest one, a fairy with blond hair and dark eyes, turned his long nose up before marching away to relay the message.

Within a few minutes, the guard returned, his expression revealing nothing.

Will he see me? I know his sister and I have had our disagreements, but Aodhàn didn' seem too hostile last time.

The guard nodded, the movement so slight Niall almost missed it. "Make it quick."

He smiled graciously and followed as the fairy led him across the clearing. His heart ached as he trod over the grass where he and Muireall had danced, the memory bittersweet now.

If only I'd known then what I know now, I would have held her closer.

The moon shone brightly upon them, lighting the way to the Prince's throne at the clearing's edge, where three guards stood at attention. It wasn't Aodhàn's true throne, just the seat reserved for him when he came here, to Glanadh Rionnagach. His real throne was at Mullach Solais Na Gealaich, the Prince's summer home, not far from here. Niall had only seen it once, and it had been quite the spectacle. The seat in which Aodhàn now sat, though beautiful, was lackluster in comparison.

The Prince's mouth was a hard line as Niall approached, his blue eyes curious. He wore a black suit similar to his attire last time, but this one featured a delicate silver leaf pattern that reflected the light. The thin circlet atop his head was

---

[30] A large Scottish serpent said to have a venomous sting.

superfluous, for any who gazed upon him instantly recognized his royal aura.

And if they chose to ignore it, Aodhàn would quickly make an example of them.

Once Niall was a few feet from the throne, he pressed his face to the floor, a more respectful gesture than necessary, but one he hoped would sway the Prince to grant his request. "Yer Highness, thank you fer granting me an audience with you tonight."

"Don' waste time on ceremony, leannan na mara. Why are you here when yer mistress is na? Does she na realize what tonight is?"

He slowly raised his head. "Oh, she does. I came here on my own because I wished to make a deal with you."

Aodhàn sucked his teeth. "Yer mistress has already made a deal with me. Why should I agree to another?" He leaned forward in his chair, his eyes flashing. "Or are you here because she couldn' achieve her goal?"

Niall winced. "How wise you are, yer Highness. That is indeed why I'm here."

"Flattery is most unbecoming on you. One would almost think you had no practice at it." Niall opened his mouth, but the Prince continued in the same mocking tone, "And I hardly think I am the best person on which you should hone yer skills. Do keep the rest o' yer lies to yerself until you can sound more sincere."

Niall clenched his jaw, trying to contain his anger. "Fine. In that case, just give me a wee bit more time before you throw me out."

Aodhàn leaned back, his face portraying mild interest. "Very well. Yer human mistress couldn' collect the banshee's cloak. I assume you want to change the terms o' the deal, so she can still receive my favor."

"That's correct."

"And what would you give me in exchange? I doubt you possess anything o' value." His eyes passed over the leannan na mara dismissively.

"I offer my life."

The fairy paused, then arched a smooth eyebrow. "To do with as I wish?"

Niall bowed his head, gulping at the Prince's malicious tone.

"Even if I should choose to end it right now?"

He glanced up, instinct telling him to back out, but the Prince was already signaling the guards. He slumped forward in defeat, his pulse racing. "So long as you give Muireall what was agreed upon."

All went silent.

Niall wondered how long he should wait for the Prince to consider the proposal, but just as he was about to speak again, the fairy said, "How could you be so predictable?"

His head shot back up, his brow furrowing at the Prince's incredulous expression. "What are you talking about? How could you know what I would do?"

His eyes widened, the truth hitting him like a punch to the gut. "You set Muireall up to fail"—he pointed an accusing finger—"didn' you? The banshee—she was far too prepared when we got there. You warned her we were coming."

The Prince's lips lifted in a vicious grin, confirming his suspicions.

"But why?" he demanded. "Why do it? Muireall has no quarrel with the Fair Folk."

"Oh, it had nothing to do with her."

Niall faltered. "Then you did it simply because I was helping her."

I'm so sorry, Muireall. Being with me has cursed you more than I realized.

"You've worked it all out, then?" Aodhàn taunted.

What I would give to break his perfect teeth.

"Na quite, yer Highness." Niall met the Prince's eye, his anger making it impossible to feign respect any longer. "What I still don' understand is why you went to all the trouble o' sabotaging me. Since my kind is so *inferior* to yers, you should have known I wouldn' succeed."

Rather than being offended like Niall had expected, the Prince threw back his head in a laugh. "Yer arrogance is so amusing. 'Tis almost a pity I promised to give you away."

"Give me away? Wha—"

"I accept yer offer, Niall, son o' Callum," Aodhàn declared, his voice echoing with power.

A brilliant streak of silver light shot out from the Prince's hand toward Niall. When it reached him, it stretched over his body and transformed into ice-cold chains.

Niall grunted and tried to wrench himself free, but it was useless. The chains held his arms against his torso in a vice grip far too strong for mere force to break. Magic had placed them there; only magic could remove them.

"You know"—the fairy's tone bordered on gleeful now—"when she told me you would do this, I didn' believe her. You may be a leannan na mara, but I thought you had *some* self-respect. How could you be this pathetic?"

"She?"

A new figure flew into the clearing, then slinked up to the right side of the throne. Her golden dress sparkled in the moonlight, hugging her body's curves and highlighting the iridescent flecks of her yellow-green wings. She leaned against the side of the throne and gave Niall a lazy smile.

It had been a long time since he'd last lain eyes on that smile, but seeing it now made his soul seize with dread.

Aoife's brilliant blue eyes, so like her brother's, were full of sadistic pleasure as she stared down at him. "Miss me?"

In Need of a Friend

Muireall's stomach was in knots as she stepped into the fairy ring. The chirping insects dulled, and she barely had time to close her eyes before her surroundings shifted. She'd only done this once before, and that had been with Niall at her side. *What if I don' end up in the same place this time?*

What if the Prince doesn' uphold his end o' the deal?

The clearing materialized in less than a heartbeat, and before Muireall could even collect her bearings, someone grabbed her arms.

"Let go o' me!" She tried to pull free, but the man—fairy—holding her was too strong. Two more armored fairies stood nearby, their faces as passive as the one holding her. She gave up struggling almost immediately and said, "I'm here to see the Prince."

"Did you bring the treasures?" The guard's voice was sharp, cutting through the air like glass.

"I—" Muireall's cheeks reddened, and she glanced down at her bag. "I have enough."

He didn't look impressed, but he let go of her arms and took a step back. "Follow me."

They crossed the clearing, but rather than returning to the throne she'd seen last time, they took a hard left. Ahead of them rose a green hillock with a wide opening at its center, similar in shape to Lachlan's knoll but on a much larger scale. Blazing torches sat on either side of the entrance, but instead of inviting her in, their presence sent a sudden chill down her spine.

Muireall swallowed, forcing herself to enter even as her senses screamed at her to flee. More torches lit the path before them, casting frightening shadows that seemed to sway with a life of their own. An unsettling aura hung over this place, pressing heavily on her shoulders like it meant to suffocate her. The guard marched wordlessly, his steps echoing in her ears as he turned this way and that down what felt like a labyrinth of passageways.

She tripped over her feet several times in the dark maze, her heart pounding as she tried to keep track of each turn they took.

Finally, they came to a closed door. The guard knocked once.

"Enter," called the Prince's unmistakable voice, and the door swung open.

A large room stretched before her, its walls bathed in moonlight, thanks to a generous opening in the ceiling. Muireall had a passing thought that she should have noticed a hole like that from outside, but then she wondered if anything in here was real or simply an illusion meant to impress her.

If that's the case, 'tis certainly working.

The Prince sat leisurely upon a throne that was even more elaborate than the one from the clearing, his mouth stretched in a devilish smile that made her legs wobble.

Keep it together, Muireall. You just have to convince him to take the necklace instead; then all will be well. She lowered her head in a respectful bow.

"Ah, the human lass," he remarked casually. "I was wondering if you would show up tonight."

"We made a deal, didn' we?" Muireall's voice was hard, belying her inner fear. She painstakingly opened her satchel, first taking out the fiddle, then the bridle.

The Prince's eyes sparkled with greed. "Wonderful. Wonderful. And the cloak?"

She hesitated, hand hovering over the necklace. "I wasn' able to get the third treasure, I'm afraid."

The fairy's expression darkened. "Then why return at all?"

"I was hoping we could work out something else instead." She slowly pulled out the necklace. "This heirloom has been in my family fer six generations. I'm sure someone with yer good taste can appreciate its value."

Aodhàn flicked his wrist, the motion making the necklace float through the air and land in his hand. His eyes barely glanced at the jewelry before hardening in displeasure. "You thought something this worthless could compare to a banshee's cloak?"

Muireall shuddered before she could stop herself. "I . . ."

The Prince flung the necklace to the ground. The ominous gleam in his eyes shifted, giving way to a cordial grin. "Luckily fer you, I've received something else that will suffice."

"Something else?"

"Come forward and receive yer reward." The Prince held out his hand.

She cocked her head to the side. *Is this some sort o' trick? Should I ask fer more details about what the reward is first?*

Prince Aodhàn was smiling now, but his unpredictable mood swings could prove deadly. *I better accept it before he changes his mind.*

Muireall reached forward, and when their fingers touched, a bolt of energy shot through her. She yelped and jumped away. "What was that?"

"That was yer end o' the deal. When you return home, you won' need to worry about yer parents forcing you to marry. The thought has completely left their minds."

"Truly?"

When the Prince nodded, she pressed her hand to her heart, a weight lifting from her chest. *That will be enough, right? I don' need to alter the terms.*

She started to turn away, then paused. "Wait. I don' understand. Why don' I owe you? I didn' bring the banshee's cloak."

"I was hoping you'd ask." Prince Aodhàn inclined his head toward something just behind her.

Muireall spun around and gasped. Niall stood a short distance away, armored fairies on either side of him. His wrists were shackled, and he sported a large purple bruise on his left cheek. He stared at her, his eyes brimming with tears.

"Niall!" Muireall lifted her foot to run to him, then stopped. She turned to the Prince. "What's the meaning o' this?"

The fairy's sneer sent a wave of panic through her. "Niall came to me and gave me an offer I couldn' refuse." His eyes flicked to the prisoner. "His life"—he looked back to her—"fer yers."

Muireall wrapped her arms around herself. *What? He . . . took my place?* New emotions stirred within her, wrestling for dominance in her withered heart.

So, that's what Lachlan meant when he said I'd be indebted to the Prince if I broke the deal? I'd owe him my life?

Niall lied to me. Again. Betrayal gripped her, numbing her insides.

She felt Niall's eyes on her, but she refused to look at him again. She lifted her head to the Prince. "Then I suppose this concludes our meeting." She curtsied.

"Don' you care what's going to happen to him?"

She swallowed down a sudden lump in her throat. "Na at all. Thank you fer yer time, yer Highness."

Muireall forced herself to turn and walk away, but as she did, Prince Aodhàn's laughter filled her ears. "Niall, it seems yer selfless act was fer naught. Humans are such fickle beings. I almost feel sorry fer what my sister is about to do to you. She's been waiting a long time to repay you."

Muireall hesitated. *His sister?* She whirled around, Niall's dark eyes still on her.

Are you going to be all right? Her mouth started to form the words—

"Hurry up now," the Prince ordered. A burst of silver light shot from his hand, sending Muireall careening back through the mound's dark passageways so quickly she had to close her eyes to avoid being sick. She tripped as the magical force abated, falling forward onto her hands.

With a grunt, she pushed herself back up and brushed off. She was back at the fairy ring, the same three guards standing around her.

One unsheathed his sword and pointed it at her. "Leave."

Muireall lurched backward on instinct, landing straight in the fairy ring.

Once she was back in Everton, she paced at the edge of Cramer's Field, trying to figure out what to do. Despite what she'd said before, her heart was wracked with worry.

It doesn' matter what happens to Niall, she reminded herself. *He deserves it. He killed Alastair. Whatever the Prince's sister is going to do to him doesn' concern me.*

With that in mind, Muireall stalked off, not slowing until she reached Rigmore House. Once there, she took a quick breath and slipped soundlessly inside. The Fairy Prince may have said her troubles were over, but she'd believe that when she saw it. She tiptoed up to her room and opened the door, nearly jumping in fright at the sight of her father within.

Joseph put his hands on his hips, forehead creased. "Where have you been, lass? I've been so concerned."

"I . . ." Muireall peered at her father, puzzled. In all her life, he'd never waited for her in her room before. It had always been her going to him when they had a conflict to resolve. *And when has he ever said he was concerned about me?*

"I'm sorry. I didn' mean to cause alarm. I know I was supposed to stay here until the ball, but I needed some fresh air."

Father patted her arm. "You must be nervous about morn. 'Tis na every day you get a title passed to you."

Muireall drew back. "A title? Yer passing it to me without even waiting fer me to get married?"

When Joseph's eyes filled with confusion, she realized she'd made a mistake. *That's something I should already know, isn' it?*

She chuckled sheepishly and covered her mouth. "What am I saying? How could I forget?" She pretended to yawn. "I must be more tired than I thought."

Father nodded, accepting her words, though a trace of curiosity lingered in his eyes. "You had me worried there fer a moment." He grinned. "You should get some rest."

Muireall turned away as he started to leave, but then he called, "Daughter?"

She spun around. "Aye?"

Joseph's eyes crinkled up. "I'm very proud o' you."

Once he was gone, Muireall sat on her bed, reeling with shock, both over his words and what was to come tomorrow. *If he's passing the lairdship to me, that means I'll be in charge o' the workings o' the estate. Me, Muireall. Na Matthew or anyone else, just me.*

But the happiness surging through her was short-lived, for within a few seconds, her mind was conjuring up the traitorous leannan na mara she'd abandoned.

Nay, na abandoned. Just . . .

She smacked her pillow a few times, hating the guilt still gnawing at her. *I need to get some sleep, like Father said. Everything will be clear in the morneen.*

But as she climbed into bed, she wasn't so sure she believed it.

***

Niall hung his head as the guards marched him back to his cell, his spirit broken. Other prisoners snickered and mocked him as he passed by. Most appeared to be Fair Folk, judging by their wings and ears, but a few elves and brownies also eyed him from the shadows. Once the guards had deposited him in his cell and removed his shackles, they walked off, eager to be rid of him.

He sank to the floor with a sigh. Soon, Aoife would return to take him to her home. He wasn't sure exactly what awaited him, but based on their conversation earlier, it would be far from pleasant:

"You already got yer revenge," he said with more bluster than he felt. "What more do you want from me?"

Princess Aoife scowled from the other side of the cell, her petite hands curling into fists. "Do you truly think losing yer voice fer a month is payment enough fer what you did?" She ran her fingers through her silvery-blond tresses. "My betrothed left me at the altar!"

Niall scoffed. "'Tis hardly my problem he was so vain as to leave you just because yer hair fell out."

She shot a bolt of magic at him, knocking him flat on his back.

262

He touched a tender spot on his head as he slowly stood back up.
"Yer Highness, that almost stings."

She growled and leaned in as far as she could, her eyes mere slits. "By
the time I'm done with you, you'll be wishing I was that tame."

"Why na just do it now, then?"

Aoife pulled back, regaining her composure. "I'd rather na make a
mess in my brother's home. 'Twould na be polite, you know. But don'
worry . . ." She slid her finger along the cell bars, slowly, teasingly. "I'll be
back once everything is prepared."

Niall shook his head, his body tenser than a bowstring.
Aoife wasn't one to make empty threats. Whatever she had in
store would either kill him or make death seem like mercy.

Muireall will be all right now. That's what's important, he told
himself. *And I deserve far worse than this.*

"Yer nothing more than a monster," her voice whispered for the
thousandth time that day. The words still pierced him no
matter how many times he replayed them. All his life, he'd
thought humans were the monsters, but now he knew he'd
been wrong all along. *I am a monster. How could I be anything else*
when I murdered the brother o' the woman I love?

He slammed his fist against the floor, hating himself. *When*
I saw her crying that day, I should have just left her alone. Then we never
would have gotten close, and I never would have broken her heart.

But then you'd have continued on with yer plan and killed her, his
conscience pointed out. *Along with everyone else in Everton. At least*
now the village will be sa—

He gasped and pressed his fingers to his wrist, trying to
sense the magical bond that had tied him to Muireall ever since
they'd made their arrangement. But to his horror, no spark of
magic flowed through his blood.

My contract with Muireall—is it complete now even though I never
got my favor from her?

But if 'tis, that means—

His father's words crashed into him: *"I kept enough to sense*
when you've completed yer deal. That will let me know to come find you.
Then we can finish tearing Everton apart together."

Niall grasped the cell bars, pulling at them like a madman.
As soon as his hands made contact, fairy magic shot through

his body, zapping him with such a heavy burst of pain that he yelped and let go.

I should have known better. He scanned the room for any sign of a way out. Though Aodhàn had put an enchantment on the bars, the prince was cocky, cocky enough that he might have overlooked something.

When Niall's search proved fruitless, he called to the guards at the entrance, "I need to speak to his Highness!"

No one responded, so he cried out a few more times, his voice growing louder and louder. Finally, footsteps echoed through the prison, and a guard appeared at his door.

"Oh, good," he said with a wry grin. "I was beginning to think you all were hard o' hearing. One would think that with ears like those, you'd be better at it."

The guard—a tall fairy with black hair and amber eyes— bared his teeth and placed a hand on the hilt of his sword. "Make another sound, and I will gladly run you through."

Niall raised his hands palm up. The guards who'd brought him here had already roughed him up when he'd mocked their uniforms, and this fellow didn't look like he was playing around. Still, he couldn't resist poking at him a little more. "As fun as that sounds, I doubt the Princess would be very happy if you did that."

The fairy snorted, his jaw clenching in rage. He gripped his sword tighter, then let out an angry breath and stepped back. "You better be glad yer under her protection."

"Whatever could I have done to earn such aggression?" Niall asked, placing a hand over his heart.

"A leannan na mara need na ask why."

Niall's eyes narrowed as he felt his own temper flare. "You don' know a thing about me."

The guard smirked. "Everyone knows what you did to the Princess. And even if we didn'"—his smile widened— "someone inept enough to lose his sealskin isn' worth keeping alive."

It took every ounce of self-control not to punch the guard right in the face. And the smug fairy knew it.

"I need to talk to his Highness," Niall grumbled.

"The Prince isn' taking any more audiences today."

"I have information he'll want to know." The lie spun smoothly off his tongue. Anything would do as long as it got him out of this cell.

The guard didn't look convinced, but he replied, "And what would that be?"

"I can' tell *you.*"

The fairy shook his head. "Then as far as I'm concerned, this conversation never happened."

"When the Prince asks why I didn' tell him sooner, then, I'll make sure he knows 'twas yer fault."

Niall waved cheekily as the fairy stomped off, then turned, his shoulders slumping. *Well, that didn' work.*

His brow furrowed. He'd paid attention as they'd led him through the palace, mentally mapping out potential escape routes. But such thoughts were useless if he couldn't find a way out of this cell.

I never got my favor from Muireall, he reminded himself. *The deal can' be complete yet.* The thought brought a sliver of comfort, but he couldn't fully put his doubts to rest. Not until he saw Everton for himself.

A soft voice from the corner whispered, "You look like you could use a friend."

A Savior

The following morning, Muireall went through the motions of her daily routine, trying to figure out what had changed because of the Prince's deal. From what she could tell, her parents seemed to have forgotten everything about her relationship with Niall and were completely committed to passing off the lairdship to her. They were also very apologetic for having pushed her to marry Matthew. The servants, on the other hand, didn't seem to have been affected by the fairy magic and would stare in bafflement any time Laird or Lady Oliver made a peculiar comment about the upcoming ball.

Muireall was unsure how to feel, her heart and mind tugging her in two different directions as evening drew closer. She was relieved that her parents weren't disappointed in her any longer—in fact, she'd never seen them so proud—but knowing it was only because of fairy magic left a bad taste in her mouth.

Is this really what I want?

The guilt she'd been feeling since leaving Niall kept pressing on her, too. She tried to tell herself she'd been justified, that she should stop thinking about him and move on with her life, but the image of him standing there, broken and chained, haunted her thoughts.

"Twas truly lovely."

Her hand slipped on her harp strings, sending a shrill note through the air.

"Muireall? What's wrong?" Lady Oliver asked. She and Father sat across from her in the sitting room, their faces etched with concern. They'd asked her if she'd like to play a few songs for them before they got ready for the ball, and Muireall had been so flattered by their interest that she'd started playing without giving it much thought. But the song her fingers had gravitated to was none other than the one she'd played in her contest with Lachlan.

She slowly breathed in and out, overcome with emotion. That had been the first compliment Niall had given her, at least the first one that hadn't felt like an insult.

"I'm fine," she said weakly, then resumed playing, though her thoughts remained far away.

"Are you trying to tell me 'twas bravery that led you to murder my brother? That you thought you were protecting other selkies from a threat?" Her voice sounded strange in her head, her strained emotions making her sound like someone else.

Since when did I become someone no longer ruled by logic? Someone who let my heart dictate my actions? Muireall shook her head, disappointed with her weakness. Niall had even fooled her into believing it might not be weakness to let her feelings out, that by being vulnerable, she might actually be showing courage.

But anyone who claimed murdering a defenseless boy was brave clearly had no idea what real courage looked like.

Still, she couldn't help but wonder why he would have considered Alastair a threat. *Was it just because he was human?*

Nay, that can' be it because he only went after Alastair. He could have killed me, too, but instead he . . .

The color drained from her face as something tugged at the edge of her consciousness. A sliver of memory she'd sealed up since her brother's death.

Her instincts told her to back away, to shove it to the back of her mind without further examination. She'd done that countless times over the years, but this time, she hesitated. This time, she needed to know what it was she was trying not to remember.

When I started to drown, how did I end up back on the beach?

A vision of a small seal filled her mind, its black eyes peering at her as she lay flat on her back. She'd screamed as soon as she'd recognized it, but now its presence gave her pause. *The seal was right in front o' me when I woke up. Why? He had just killed Alastair, yet I was unharmed. . . .*

Fragments of memory began to surface: the seal's mouth wrapping around her arm, getting pulled through the water, a soft nose brushing her face.

Muireall gasped. *The seal—did it—did Niall . . .*

That's na possible.

But the memory continued to clear, and as it did, the truth became undeniable. Although Niall had indeed killed Alastair, after Muireall had slipped underwater, he hadn't just left her to die. He'd brought her back to the shore.

He'd saved her.

"Daughter, are you crying?"

Muireall came back to the present and lifted her hand to her face, only now noticing the moisture clinging to her eyelashes. She wiped at her tears. "I'm sorry. I wrote this fer Alastair, and I guess I was just feeling sentimental."

Laura made a soft cooing sound and clasped her hands together. "My sweet lad . . . if only he were still with us, he'd have been laird by now." She glanced at her husband, who nodded in agreement. "Then you wouldn' have to take on this burden, Muireall."

What is she saying? Surely na—

"I . . . I really don' think o' it like that. I'm—I'm honored to do this fer the family," she said weakly, a twinge of dread tightening her stomach.

"Oh, you don' need to pretend," Laura said with a laugh. "I know you'd much rather sit in that silly garden all day than do anything o' real value."

Muireall bit her lip to stop more tears from flowing. *She still doesn' think I'm good enough fer this? I thought . . .*

She turned to her father, but the man was silent. *Do you believe that, too, Father? You told me before that you were proud o' me.*

As he looked away from her desperate stare, a cold truth settled into her bones. *It doesn' really matter what he believes if he's unwilling to say anything against Mother, does it?*

Muireall rose to her feet, blinking several times. "Excuse me." She turned and walked out the door, her feet carrying her to the garden even as her tears spilled over and her vision blurred.

She sat down at the fountain, trying to focus on the trickling water rather than the deluge of emotions pressing in on her. *Even now, they still don' want me fer who I am. No one does.*

I thought using the fairy magic would help Mother and Father realize how capable I am. But even now, I'm still na good enough. And I don' think I ever will be.

A tiny voice whispered in her mind, *So, why bother trying anymore?*

She covered her face with her hands, grief cascading over her. She saw now that the life she'd wished for—a life where her parents truly accepted her just as she was—was nothing more than a fairytale, a dream she'd never achieve. She'd tried so hard to do what they wanted, *be* what they wanted, but it would never satisfy them. Perhaps Alastair could have, but Muireall would never be him.

Self-pity threatened to overtake her, but just as it descended, a new thought lit up her mind. *I don' want to be Alastair. I just want to be me.*

She cut off mid-sob, the revelation shocking her to her core. She grasped hold of it, watching as the thought fanned into a flame that forced the shadows in her mind to flee. *I just want to be me. Even if I'm na enough fer anyone else, I'm enough fer me.*

I'm enough.

Muireall wiped away her tears and stood, new strength flowing through her. A smile tickled the corners of her mouth, and she knew for the first time in her life that she was going to be fine. Regardless of her parents' opinions. Regardless of anyone's.

She didn't need them to accept herself anymore. Her own acceptance was enough.

The freedom I thought I was looking fer—I had access to it all along. Joy bubbled up inside her as that really sank in. All this striving for perfection, all her fear of not meeting her parents' expectations—such a huge weight had lifted off her that she wanted to laugh and cry and belt out her jubilation for all to hear.

But then her eyes landed on something she hadn't noticed before: a few feet away, the Scottish primrose was blooming, its violet flowers stretching up toward the sun.

Almost without meaning to, she plucked a few flowers and cradled them against her chest. They were so small, so fragile, yet powerful enough that she almost came undone all over again.

There was someone who wanted me just as I am. She sniffled, swallowing down a thick lump in her throat.

A footstep interrupted Muireall's reverie, and she whirled toward the sound. William stood at the garden's entrance, his features wracked with worry. "Have you seen Niall?"

She opened her mouth, but thunder rolled above them, drowning out her response. An immense cloud hung in the sky, stretching in all directions like long black fingers. *A storm? But the sky has been clear all—*

Wait. If Niall used to be a selkie, then that means—

She peered at the small boy with new eyes, understanding whipping through her. "William? Are you doing that?"

He paled. "You know I'm a . . ." His brows knit together, and he shook his head. "That's way too strong to be me. But 'tis someone's doing; that's fer sure."

Muireall's hands dug into her skirts, fear wracking her body.

William dashed over and tugged at her hand. "That's why I wanted to find Uncle Niall. Mistress, do you know where he is? No one will tell me, and I'm scared."

She stiffened at the boy's touch; she wished she could comfort him, but she was unsure how. "He's . . . he's gone."

"Gone?" asked a deep voice.

An older man stood just outside the garden, his dark eyes fixed on her. Damp black hair flecked with silver draped across his shoulders, and a wet shirt and trousers clung to his muscular frame. His expression was curious yet guarded, and his voice emanated with power.

Where did he come from? And why is he all wet?

Muireall held back a shudder as familiarity washed over her. When Niall had first come to Rigmore House, he'd been in a similar state. And from the confident way this stranger carried himself to his distinctive black eyes, he resembled Niall a little too much. "Who are—"

"My name is Callum." His gaze drifted from her to the boy cowering at her side. His expression softened, longing filling his eyes. "You look just like her. . . . You must be William. I'm . . ." His breath hitched. "I'm yer grandfather."

This is him, then. Niall's father. Muireall tried to keep her shock from showing on her face even as the lad gasped and burrowed deeper into her side. She wrapped her arm around him, keeping her attention on the intruder. She didn't know William that well, but she didn't want any harm to come to him. And since his parents were nowhere in sight, she'd just have to step into the role of protector until someone else could.

Callum looked between them, noting Muireall's defensive stance, then spread his mouth into a friendly grin. "Would you be so good as to tell me where Niall is?"

Muireall felt William's head shaking against her. "Don' tell him," he whispered.

Callum's eyes narrowed, and a bolt of lightning struck the ground a few feet away. Muireall jumped backward, pulling William along with her. The massive storm cloud above them grew a bit larger.

"Let's try this again. If you want to live, step away from my grandson and tell me where Niall is."

Muireall raised her hands. "Let's be reasonable about this. There's no need fer violence—"

A second bolt erupted from the sky, this one landing a hairsbreadth from Callum's feet.

"Get away from them," growled a female voice.

The three of them twisted around. Briony Fairborn was just a few feet away, wind whipping through her raven hair. With one hand raised to the sky and her golden eyes blazing, everything suddenly clicked into place.

She's the selkie Niall wanted to protect from my brother.

"You . . ." Callum's eyes widened in disbelief. "How are you here? Niall was supposed to kill you."

Muireall's blood ran cold. *What? Is that what Niall originally came here to do? He said it didn' matter why he came . . . . but if Callum*

A dangerous smile worked its way over Briony's face, her features transforming from unassuming and docile to predatory. "I guess he changed his mind."

Callum bared his teeth. "Impossible. But no matter. You'll be gone soon enough. As will anyone else who gets in my way." He lifted his arms, and a flood of lightning crashed around Briony, one bolt striking her leg.

She screamed and crumpled to the ground, clutching at her wound.

"Mistress Briony!" William cried. As one, he and Muireall leaped over the garden wall, then knelt at the woman's side.

"Briony, are you all right?" Muireall grabbed her arm and pulled her into a sitting position.

Briony coughed a few times, her face streaked with dirt. "I—I'm fine." She pressed her hand over her leg and shut her eyes, trembling with pain.

"No one hurts my friends." William stood up and raised his arm.

Callum's expression turned to alarm as giant hailstones came flying from the heavens. He covered his head as they pelted his arms, muttering curses.

Then, just as suddenly as it had appeared, the hail vanished.

William stared at his hands in dismay. "What . . ."

"Yer strong, lad, I'll give you that," Callum admitted, a touch of pride in his voice as he wiped some blood from his cheek. He smirked. "But yer no match fer a pureblood selkie."

"What about both o' us?" Briony challenged, shakily rising to her feet. She lifted her hands once more. William followed her lead, and soon, the cloud above their heads was larger than ever, churning with wind and fury.

Callum glanced upward, his dark eyes uncertain.

"Still feeling arrogant?" Though she was injured, Briony's voice was steady, steady enough that Muireall's fear dissipated. Callum may be stronger than Briony and William separately, but together, their power eclipsed his.

Callum's mouth twisted with anger. "This isn' over," he snarled, then turned and fled toward the beach.

Briony sighed and lowered her arms, her leg giving out as she collapsed.

Only Human

Niall tried not to jump as he whirled around. He'd been certain he was alone. *What sort o' being would Prince Aodhàn put me in here with?* Dreadful images rose up in his mind—

But the creature watching him from the corner was far from terrifying. In fact, if it weren't for her otherworldly beauty, he would have sworn she was human.

"Who are . . ." Niall analyzed his cellmate with a critical eye. Her features were young, petite, fairy-like, but no wings donned her back. Cuts and bruises lined her face, arms, and legs, signs she'd been treated with the same disregard he had. Despite that, her long blond hair still bore a healthy sheen, and a soft light radiated from her pale skin. A sleeveless green dress covered her torso, and her cracked feet were bare.

There was no webbing between her toes, so she couldn't be a selkie. Most selkies had dark hair, anyway.

Niall's gaze drifted back up to her face, and his breath caught.

The girl's eyes were large and curious, but that wasn't what had struck his attention. It was their color: a strange golden shade he'd only seen one time before.

A smile tugged at her pink lips, highlighting her innocent appearance. Rather than being disarmed by the movement, though, Niall stiffened even more. No innocent creature would be in this dungeon.

"Who are you?" he asked tersely, watching for any sign of deception.

"My name is Ynes," the girl said, her voice light and heavily accented, though Niall couldn't place its origins. Her golden eyes twinkled with mischief. "But that's not what you truly wish to know, is it, *leannan na mara*?"

Niall frowned; he didn't like being disadvantaged, and this woman seemed to be enjoying the fact that she knew his race while he didn't know hers. Common courtesy dictated magical beings reveal their true natures upon meeting; at least, that was the case in Scotland.

When he didn't answer, she wagged her eyebrows and continued, "All you need to know is if I'll help you escape."

"And will you?" he challenged, his patience running thin. He was in no mood for games. He had to get out of here fast if he was going to save Muireall—and the rest of Everton. "You seem just as trapped as I am."

Ynes smirked, the movement stretching a cut at the corner of her mouth. "Ah, but that's only for now. And since you'll be leaving soon, that will give us all the opportunity we need."

Niall's eyes narrowed, but he chuckled despite himself. Her confidence was admirable even if it turned out to be misplaced. "What did you have in mind?"

***

"Briony!" Muireall caught the woman as she fell, then slowly lowered her to the ground. Her eyes were closed, her skin pallid.

William cringed. "Is she . . ."

Muireall pressed her fingers to the midwife's throat. The pulse was weak, but it was definitely there. "Just passed out."

William smiled in relief. "Oh, good."

"Let's get her up to my room. You think you can help me?"

"Isn' yer room on the top floor?"

Muireall clicked her tongue. "Where are yer parents?"

"They're at home. Should I go get them?"

"Aye, please do that."

Soon after the lad was gone, Muireall glimpsed a lone figure approaching the estate. His steps were rapid, purposeful. *What is he doing here?*

"Mr. Park!" She waved her arms wildly until the man noticed her. He rushed over, the beads on his hat swinging back and forth.

"Agassi, what happened?" he asked as he took in the unconscious woman on the ground.

"Can you help me get her to my room?"

He nodded and picked Briony up in his arms as if she weighed almost nothing. Muireall directed him to her room, ignoring the confused gazes of the servants they passed.

Once Mr. Park had set Briony on the bed, he peered at the scorch mark at the bottom of her dress. "What caused this?"

"'Twas a lightning strike. I . . . She's the closest thing we have to a doctor. I don' know who to ask fer help."

The merchant nodded, then started pulling up Briony's dress.

"What are you doing?" Muireall grabbed his wrist.

"Allow me to check the wound." Mr. Park's voice was soft but authoritative.

She hesitated, unsure if she should trust him, then let go. "All right."

With careful movements, he shifted Briony's clothes until her shins were exposed. On her right leg lay a cluster of feathery red lines. The merchant pulled a small jar from his sleeve and opened it to reveal a white salve. He dabbed a bit on the wound, then placed the back of his hand on her forehead.

Once he was finished, he turned to Muireall and gave a quick bow. "Thank you for trusting me to help your friend."

"Why hasn' she woken up yet?"

"Being struck by lightning is often fatal"—

Muireall sucked in a breath.

—"for a human," he said pointedly. "But a selkie's body can withstand much more stress. She'll probably wake in the next few hours. When she does, tell her she needs to get lots of rest. She should be back to normal within about a week, I'd say."

Muireall was hardly surprised that Mr. Park knew Briony was a selkie. He'd known Niall was a leannan na mara right away. He probably already knew about William, too.

"Thank you so much fer yer help, Mr. Park." She licked her lips. "I must ask, though, what were you doing on the estate?"

"As soon as I saw the clouds forming, I knew there was trouble." His brown eyes flicked to Briony's sleeping form. "But it seems I wasn't fast enough. I apologize."

Muireall jerked her head back. "You knew the storm wasn' normal?"

Just who is this man? What is he?

"When you've seen the things I have, you start to get a sense for what's natural and what's not," he replied cryptically. "But tell me what happened."

She gestured to the nearest chair. Once they were both seated, she explained, "A selkie attacked us, but Briony and William managed to fend him off. Barely."

"Why did he attack?"

"He wanted to know where Niall is." At Mr. Park's questioning look, Muireall continued, "His name is Callum. He's Niall's father. When Briony showed up, he was shocked. He said . . . Niall was supposed to kill her."

She waited for the merchant's expression to change at this revelation, but his face remained unreadable.

"Did the selkie say he would return?"

She nodded.

"Hmm . . ." Mr. Park tapped his knuckle against his mouth, considering her words. "In that case, you should get as far away from here as you can."

"What? What about everyone else? Shouldn' we warn them how dangerous he is?"

"As I told you before, most people can't be trusted with the truth of what's around them."

"But when Callum comes back and still doesn' find Niall . . . He threatened to kill anyone who gets in his way. And what if he's na alone next time? The people here aren' prepared." She pointed to the sword hanging from his waist. She'd never seen him wield it, but she had a feeling he was quite adept. "Could you—"

Mr. Park snorted. "Maybe one or two, but I'm only human."

Well, that eliminates my theory that he was a magical creature. And if Briony won' be back to full strength fer several days . . .

She turned away with a frustrated groan. *Niall, how could you just leave me like this? You must have known yer father would be coming back, but you didn' even bother to tell me. This would be so much easier if you were he—*

Muireall swiveled back, her face brightening. "What if we could avoid a fight altogether?"

"What do you mean?"

"I'm saying"—a smile broke over her cheeks—"I'm going to give Callum what he wants. Or at least, part o' what he wants. But to do that, I'm going to need—"

The door flew open, and Adaira barreled inside. "Where is she?"

Muireall gestured to the bed, but the innkeeper was already bounding that direction. William, Mr. Burgess, and Mr. Mendes appeared behind her.

"My son told us about yer unexpected visitor," Mr. Burgess grumbled to Muireall as the others crowded around the bed. His eyes cut over to Mr. Park, then darkened with suspicion. "Why are you here?"

The foreign man held up his hands. "Only to help, I promise you," he said, but his tone was spiteful.

Muireall looked between the two, wondering at the animosity between them.

"Is Briony going to be all right?" Mr. Mendes asked, tenderly stroking the midwife's temple. The movement stirred Muireall's compassion, reminding her of her worry after Niall's fight with the kelpie.

"I examined the wound, and it looks like she'll be fine," Mr. Park supplied.

There was a collective sigh of relief, the tension evaporating like dew in the morning sun. Mr. Burgess smiled as his wife fussed with the sheets, concerned if her friend was warm enough, and Mr. Mendes shook Mr. Park's hand to thank him for his assistance.

William and Muireall, though, were far from calm as they exchanged a nervous glance. The two of them knew their troubles were far from over. Callum's threat still loomed, and like it or not, they would have to deal with it.

Muireall rubbed her forehead, wishing she didn't have to be the bearer of bad news. She'd grown surprisingly fond of the unlikely group. From what she'd seen, they were all good, genuine people. The last thing they deserved was more hardship thrust upon them.

"Unfortunately, it sounds like Callum intends to return," she announced.

As expected, the atmosphere of the room soured, but before anyone could speak up, she turned to Mr. Park. "I was actually just about to ask if you would help me get Niall back from the other side o' the Veil."

"The Veil? As in the Fairy Realm? Why would Niall be there?" Mr. Burgess cut in, his voice gruff and concerned.

Shame flooded Muireall's cheeks. Even though Niall had been dishonest with her, some of the blame for his imprisonment lay squarely on her shoulders; she saw that now. *But how can I tell them the truth? When I found out Niall had taken my place, I didn' even try to get him back. Instead, I walked away. I could have tried to barter with the Prince or told him I didn' want the deal anymore or—or something! Anything would have been better than just . . . leaving him to die. Now we're all in a predicament that perhaps could have been avoided if I'd na let my feelings get the best o' me.*

He must hate me.

Adaira floated to her side. "Is this because o' yer deal?" The words fell from her lips like a gentle rain. They bore no anger, no condemnation, just compassion and understanding.

Muireall choked up, tears dripping from her eyes. "You were right, Adaira. I . . ." She shook her head, struggling to speak. "We couldn' get the cloak, and"—bitterness loosened her tongue—"that *fool* never told me the price o' na completing a fairy deal is—is—" She shut her mouth, trying not to break down into sobs.

"Your life," Mr. Park finished.

"Then why are you here when Uncle Niall isn'?" William blurted, his lower lip quivering like he was about to cry, too.

"Because he took my place," Muireall whimpered. "Because . . ."

Thin arms wrapped around her back, and before she knew it, she was weeping against Adaira's shoulder. "There, there, dearie. Let it out."

She wasn't sure how long the two of them stood there, but when she finally pulled back, Adaira's answering smile was like a balm to her wounded soul. It seemed to say, *Aye, you've made mistakes, but so have we all. Forgive yerself, and let's move forward together.*

"So, what's yer answer, Mr. Park?" Mr. Burgess asked. Everyone turned to the foreigner expectantly.

He glanced around the room, then slowly shook his head. "I'm sorry. I truly am, but I'm not equipped to break a prisoner out of the fairies' custody. And even if I was"—his tone turned haughty—"it sounds like Niall deserves to be there. Now, I must take my leave. If all you've said is true, I need to get my ship away from here as soon as possible."

Muireall stomped over until she was directly in front of the stubborn merchant. "Did you na hear what I said before? He's looking fer his son, and he's na going to stop until he finds him."

Mr. Park scowled. "Do you know how I've managed to survive all this time? It wasn't with stupidity."

"When I sat across from you on yer ship, you told me you felt responsible fer the people around you. Now that a real threat is here, though, yer only interested in protecting yerself."

Guilt shimmered in the man's brown eyes, but his jaw remained hard. "Think what you wish."

"Well, if yer na going to help her, I will," called a weak voice.

Everyone spun around to Briony, who was sitting up in the bed.

"Briony!" Mr. Mendes was at her side in an instant, one hand cupping her face. "How are you feeling?"

She winced but pressed her mouth into a grin. "Definitely na my best, but I've survived worse. Help me up?"

"Agassi, you were just struck by lightning. You shouldn't be walking right now," Mr. Park said.

Briony sent the man a sharp glare. "I fail to see why I should heed yer counsel. If it were up to you, you'd let·the people o' this town—people who welcomed you in—perish, just to save yer own skin. Unlike you, I don' run when others are in danger."

"And that's one of the reasons why I love you." Mr. Mendes smiled, his eyes full of adoration as he helped her to her feet.

"You can count on us, too," Mr. Burgess added, one arm around his wife. "My brother-in-law may have gotten himself into this mess, but we're certainly going to help him out o' it."

Mr. Park wrinkled his brow, conflict skittering over his features. His fingers clenched the hilt of his sword, unclenched it, clenched it again. Finally, his hands fell to his sides. "Fine. I'll help you. But there's one thing you should know first."

A series of gasps went around the room as the man revealed his true nature.

Muireall did a double take, unsure if she could trust what her eyes were seeing. "I thought you said you were human."

"I lied."

Stealth Mission Gone Wrong

"Let's go," barked a guard.

Niall didn't move from the floor. Even when the fairy kicked at his feet, he stayed absolutely still, seemingly dead. *This had better work.*

The guard scoffed. "I don' have time fer this."

Niall's ears perked up as the cell door creaked open, but still, he maintained his position.

The guard squatted down and rolled him over onto his back. "On yer feet, leannan na mara." His breath was rancid, probably the result of too much fairy wine, and it took all of Niall's willpower not to cough. "On yer feet, or I'll—"

A sharp blow and grunt cut off the rest of his threat, then the guard was on the floor in a heap.

Niall opened his eyes and stood as Ynes strained to drag the fairy's unconscious body to the back of the cell. *Hmm, no superhuman strength*, he noted, not offering to help her. Instead, he quipped, "Couldn' you have done that a wee bit sooner? His breath was enough to make a man hurl."

The small woman huffed, then scanned the room. "Unless you'd like worse done to you, keep quiet," she said menacingly to the other prisoners.

"Take us with you," squeaked a brownie.

Ynes spat at the disobedient creature, a tongue of flame extending from her open mouth and striking the prisoner's chest. The brownie collapsed, the stench of burning flesh filling the air. Niall wrinkled his nose, unsure if the brownie was dead or simply unconscious.

"Anyone else want to try their luck?" Ynes hissed.

The other prisoners jumped back, shaking their heads as she stared each of them down.

"I'm glad na to be yer enemy." Niall chuckled.

She turned her piercing eyes on him, which seemed to be glowing more than before. "Our alliance ends here, leannan na mara. Stay out o' my way." She raced toward the jail's entrance.

"Hey, you promised—"

Her form winked out of view, leaving Niall to wonder again what sort of creature she was. Invisibility and fire-breath were handy gifts but rare among the magical community.

He shrugged, then darted out of the jail. Ynes had helped him escape his cell; it didn't matter much if she went back on her word about helping him get out of the mound. It was easier not to get caught if he was alone, anyway.

He came to a four-way intersection and tried to remember which way to go from here. *'Twas to the left, wasn' it?*

Before Niall could decide, footsteps approached from the right. he ducked into the left passageway, grateful for how it curved out of sight. He pressed his body against the wall, praying whoever it was would go a different direction.

When the footsteps dulled, he let out his breath, then surveyed the path ahead. The passage branched off into several tunnels, each just barely lit by torchlight. A few doors lined the walls, but they all looked exactly the same.

"Who's there?" rumbled a voice.

***

"Are you sure I can' come?" William asked for the third time.

The boy stood with his parents, Mr. Mendes, Briony, and Muireall at the edge of Torin Woods where Mr. Park had told them all to meet. The sun was drifting downward; evening would be upon them soon.

Along with the birthday ball Muireall would not be attending.

"Aye, son, I'm sure." Mr. Burgess nodded to his wife, who tightened her grip on the boy's shoulder and nodded back.

"Be careful," Adaira said.

Mr. Burgess cradled her face in his hands, then kissed her softly on the mouth. "Always, love."

An ache rose in Muireall's chest, so she turned away before her emotions could get the better of her. Except then she was facing Mr. Mendes just as he pulled Briony into a tight embrace. Muireall clenched her teeth, dropping her eyes to the ground.

"Is everyone ready?" Mr. Park asked as he joined the group. His gaze landed on Muireall, his mouth tilting in a knowing half-smile. "Something the matter, agassi?"

She scowled, then spun on her heel. "We better go. The Prince mentioned he would be giving Niall to his sister, so I don' know how long we have before Niall gets moved."

"You heard the lady," Adaira said.

Soon, Muireall and the men were tramping through the forest. Briony, Adaira, and William would stay behind at Drulea Cottage to keep an eye on the village. From there, they'd be able to spot Callum should he return.

Muireall found the fairy ring easily, but as she stood at its fringe, fear paralyzed her. Her knowledge of Niall's location made her essential to the operation, but they were about to go up against trained soldiers. She was embarrassingly unprepared and maybe more of a liability than an asset.

"Mistress Oliver, are you all right?" Mr. Mendes asked.

She took a deep, shaky breath. "Am I making a mistake? What if I'm just sending all o' us to our deaths?"

He squeezed her shoulder, his touch warm and comforting. "Mistress Oliver, you're not forcing any of us to be here. We all want to do what we can to protect Everton, and we all want to get Niall home safely."

She cocked her head, unconvinced. "Even though he tried to kill Briony?"

Mr. Mendes raised his eyebrows in surprise, but then his eyes creased as a wry grin came over his face. "You knew that?" When she didn't respond, he said, "And yet you're more desperate to get him back than any of us."

Muireall blushed, not wanting to divulge just how much she cared about the leannan na mara. She wasn't even entirely sure herself. Her feelings were still so muddled that when she finally faced him again, she wasn't sure if she'd punch him or kiss him.

"I don' know all the details o' what happened with him and Briony," she said softly, "but Niall told me he's na the person he used to be. And I . . ." She lifted her chin, embracing the faith in her heart. "I believe him."

Even if 'tis foolish, even if I may regret it later, I still choose to believe him.

Mr. Mendes assessed her slowly, his green eyes perceptive yet kind. Finally, he gave a crisp nod. "So do I."

She let out a relieved breath; she hadn't realized how much she'd needed someone to agree with her. Someone to tell her she wasn't just being naive or letting her feelings cloud her judgment. The fact that it was Mr. Mendes made it all the better, for unlike the Burgesses, he wasn't biased because of family ties. He had every reason not to trust Niall. And from what Muireall knew of Mr. Mendes, he wasn't the sort to be easily swayed. If he believed Niall had changed, it was almost certainly true.

"When all this is over, I'll tell you that story. It's quite interesting."

Muireall smiled, looking forward to the day when life was peaceful enough to sit and listen to a story again. To indulge in such a simple pleasure as gathering together with friends, for no reason except to enjoy each other's company—it was a luxury she'd never experienced before.

Friends . . . I suppose I have Niall to thank fer that, too.

Mr. Park and Mr. Burgess caught up with the pair and fanned around the fairy ring. The farmer's blue eyes were hard, resolute, yet pulsing with a sliver of fear. Out of all of them, he had the most to lose.

Mr. Mendes clapped him on the back. "I'll see you on the other side."

Mr. Burgess nodded, then lifted his foot—

"Wait!" Mr. Park pulled the farmer back before he could step into the circle.

Mr. Burgess threw his arms out, catching himself just before he toppled to the ground. "Why did you do that?"

Mr. Park ignored his cross tone and replied, "We need to all go through at the same time"—he drew his sword—"*and* have our weapons out."

Mr. Mendes pulled out a rapier with an ornately decorated pommel. Such a magnificent blade must be worth more than what many of her neighbors earned in a year, reminding Muireall that though Mr. Mendes didn't act the part, he was still undoubtedly noble. He held the sword confidently, giving the impression that though he'd had little reason to use it while he'd been here, he knew how to handle himself.

Mr. Park handed Mr. Burgess a long, double-edged sword identical to his own. "Thought you might need this."

The farmer took the blade with a half-hearted grunt, fumbling a bit as he moved it from side to side. He was clearly unused to such a weapon, but his motives were pure. Muireall had no doubt he would give up his life for the sake of his companions if such sacrifice was necessary.

Muireall unsheathed Niall's dagger, grateful she'd snatched it up after he'd dropped it at the banshee's cave. Light bounced off the blade as she turned it this way and that, her stomach churning at the thought of what she was about to use it for. *Can I really do this?*

Niall's crumpled look as he'd stood before her in chains flitted through her mind. Her grip tightened on the dagger, courage sparking in her veins as she remembered their purpose. It wouldn't make the task easier, but it did remind her that it was necessary. She would remedy her mistake in leaving Niall behind, no matter the difficulty.

Mr. Park surveyed the group, satisfaction gleaming in his dark gaze. "All right. *Now*, we can go."

The four of them stepped through. Muireall's head spun as the magic transported them to the Fairy Realm, colors and sounds shifting so quickly she couldn't comprehend them. She blinked a few times as the fairies' clearing appeared, hoping they'd arrived without anyone noticing—

The tip of a sword pressed against her chest. "Who are you?" asked a tall, dark-haired guard, his blue eyes narrowed in suspicion. Two more guards flanked him, swords lowered but ready to be wielded at a moment's notice.

"I—"

Her startled gasp was lost in the clang of metal against metal as Mr. Park's blade clashed with the nearest guard's. The dark-haired fairy pushed against him, straining, then Mr. Park jumped back, raising his sword in a defensive stance, his body poised to strike. The move was so flawless Muireall couldn't help but think he'd done this many times.

The other fairies lifted their swords, their expressions hard. "Am bu chòir dhuinn fios a leigeil don phrionnsa?[31]" one asked.

The leader shook his head, fuming. "Is urrainn dhuinn seo a làimhseachadh sinn fhìn.[32]"

Mr. Mendes and Mr. Burgess fanned out on either side of Mr. Park, blocking Muireall from view.

"We don't have to fight," Mr. Mendes said, his tone matter-of-fact. "Just tell us where Niall is."

Muireall peeked over Mr. Burgess's shoulder, then wished she hadn't. Mr. Park had warned her fairies were merciless, but now, peering into their cold, hard eyes, she believed him.

"This is His Majesty King Daegan's territory," the lead fairy replied, switching over to Scots English. "You have no right to be here."

"We're na leaving without him," Mr. Burgess growled.

"In that case . . ." As one, the guards threw themselves forward, their blades flashing in the sunlight.

Muireall stiffened, waiting for the fairies' swords to fall, but then Mr. Park advanced in a flurry of motion, his blade disarming one fairy, piercing another in the side, then hovering directly over the third's throat.

She gaped. While she was grateful Mr. Park was their ally, she couldn't help but feel frightened at how easily he'd vanquished their enemies. Mr. Mendes and Mr. Burgess

---

[31] Should we let the prince know?

[32] We can handle this ourselves.

seemed equally shocked, but Mr. Mendes at least had the good sense to point his rapier at the unarmed guard. The one Mr. Park had stabbed lay unconscious on the ground, blood seeping into the earth.

"Where is the leannan na mara?" Mr. Park asked, his voice sharper than the sword in his hand.

The fairy swallowed, a pinprick of blood beading on his neck at the sword's tip. "He's in the dungeon at Mullach Solais Na Gealaich," he sputtered, pointing in the direction of the mound Muireall had gone to before.

"And how do we find the dungeon once we're inside?"

"Take the third tunnel on the right, then keep going until you reach the double doors."

Mr. Park pulled away, then slammed the sword's pommel against his head. The fairy stumbled before collapsing to the ground.

Mr. Mendes frowned. "Mr. Park, I—"

The foreigner slid around him, then performed an identical move on the remaining fairy, sending his body to join the others.

Mr. Mendes's scowl deepened, and he looked like he was about to rebuke the man for his callousness, but Mr. Park jerked his head toward the other side of the clearing. "We need to move."

Muireall trailed after him, Mr. Burgess and Mr. Mendes on her heels. Mr. Park glided silently across the field, his black robes blending in with the darkening landscape. The rest of them weren't nearly so quiet, their feet pounding in time with Muireall's racing heart.

When they slipped inside the mound without incident, she breathed a little more easily. No alarms had been signaled so far; perhaps their stealth operation would succeed, after all.

But her relief was short-lived. They'd only barely turned down the third passage before a voice cried, "Intruders!"

Several fairies approached from around a bend in the tunnel, their swords drawn. Muireall narrowed her eyes, telling herself she could do this even as her arms trembled.

"Allow me." Mr. Park flew forward, his movements a blur, and before she knew it, all the fairies lay on the floor, unconscious or worse.

When he swiveled around, she arched an eyebrow. "I'm starting to think you could have done this single-handedly."

Mr. Park scowled, a sharp reply on his tongue—

A second group of fairies appeared before them, stealing his attention. He breezed toward the newcomers, his sword sweeping through the air. The guards tried to counter his attacks, but they were no match for the mysterious foreigner.

Before he'd finished them off, six more fairies emerged behind them. Mr. Mendes sprang into their midst, his movements slower than Mr. Park's but still very effective. Mr. Burgess quickly joined in, his brute strength making up for his lack of skill. For now.

Muireall clutched her dagger, sweat glistening on her temple as she stood in the middle. This was her chance to do her part to rescue Niall, yet here she remained, frozen.

Mr. Mendes flew backward as one of the fairies summoned a burst of magic. His body slammed against the wall, then slid to the floor in a heap.

Muireall shook off her hesitation and took a wild stab at the nearest fairy, her dagger finding a gap in his side where his armor came together.

He sucked in a breath, his eyes widening with disbelief and rage when they landed on his attacker. Muireall pulled out the dagger and stumbled backward.

"Yer going to regret that, human." He lunged at her, his sword cutting through the air.

She screamed and jumped to the side, avoiding his strike but falling to the ground in the process.

"Yer mine," he sneered.

She wished now that she'd had the strength to carry a sword of her own; maybe then she would have stood a chance of getting out alive.

Mr. Mendes's rapier was a welcome sight, meeting the fairy's blade as it descended toward her head. He quickly overpowered the guard, then thrust his blade into the fairy's chest.

Muireall turned away, bile rising in her throat. Nearby, Mr. Burgess was holding his own against a pair of fairies, but the final member of their party was nowhere to be seen.

"Where's Mr. Park?"

The only response she got was a slight downward turn of Mr. Mendes's mouth before he went to aid Mr. Burgess.

Three more fairies arrived on the scene, assessed the situation, then quickly moved to neutralize the men.

"We'll hold them off. Go find Niall," Mr. Mendes called, blocking a heavy blow before he'd even finished speaking.

Muireall scurried off, her wide, frightened eyes scanning the corridor for any sign of movement, any indicator that she might have to leap into another fight she might not survive.

I must be close now. Didn' the guard say 'twas at the end o' this tunnel? Double doors . . .

But when the passage came to an abrupt end with two open archways on either side, her chest tightened.

O' course he lied to us. Either that, or I took a wrong turn somewhere. She whirled around, panic overtaking her. *Are the walls closing in on me?*

She glanced warily over her shoulder. She could always turn back if need be, devise a new plan of action.

She took a deep breath. *Nay, I can' go back. The others are counting on me to find Niall.*

This passage looked vaguely familiar—and she tried to ignore the annoying possibility that that might just be because everything in here looked mostly the same—so perhaps she was close to the throne room.

She hurried down the left passageway, praying she'd chosen wisely. She'd always had a good sense of direction; if ever she'd needed it to pay off, now was the time.

She took a quick breath as her eyes landed on a figure down the hall. It was a dark-haired man, his back to her. His body was shrouded in shadows, but his bearing was so familiar her heart thudded to a halt.

N-Niall? She didn't dare speak the name aloud in case she was wrong. In case she was just seeing what she so desperately wished to see.

Despite her silence, the man seemed to sense her and spun around. She shrank back, pressing against the wall even as he stepped closer.

"... Muireall?"

Reunited

Niall slipped behind the nearest door, grateful to discover he'd stepped into a small storage room. Vats lined the walls, and the scent of wine filled the air. He tucked his body into the corner farthest from the door.

The voice had sounded fairly distant, and judging by how long it took for footsteps to reach his ears, he hoped the voice's owner hadn't seen where he'd gone. He held his breath as the footsteps grew louder, then stopped just outside the door. The doorknob began to turn—

"Arran, thig gu sgiobalta![33]" cried a male voice.

The doorknob stilled, a hairsbreadth from unlatching.

"Dè a th' ann?[34]" asked a second male voice, laced with irritation.

"Luchd-ionnsaigh—Feumaidh a Mhòrachd a h-uile duine aig an aon àm.[35]"

"Stiùir mi an sin.[36]"

The weight in Niall's chest died away as the two fairies marched off, and once they were gone, he let out a low chuckle. *It doesn' come any closer than that.*

---

[33] Arran, come quickly!
[34] What is it?
[35] Intruders—his Highness needs everyone at once.
[36] Lead me there.

But it wasn't over. Not yet. Not until he could look Muireall in the eye and know beyond a shadow of a doubt that she and the rest of Everton were safe.

He opened the door and padded down the empty corridor, pausing when he reached an intersection. Something tickled at the back of his neck, some vague sense that he was being watched, so he whirled around.

A small figure huddled against the wall, barely visible in the flickering firelight. He glimpsed a long dress, wavy hair, striking green eyes—

My mind must be playing tricks on me. It couldn' be her. After what he'd done, there was no way she would come back for him.

But her name was on his lips before he could stop himself, his heart propelling him forward. "Muireall?"

The person slowly stepped away from the wall, her features sharpening. Specks of dirt clung to her skirt, and she held a small dagger in her fist.

It is her!

Niall bounded the rest of the way to her, his heart nearly leaping from his chest. "Muireall, yer here." His hands tingled at his sides. All he wanted was to cling to her, to breathe in her scent and never let go.

But he couldn't, not when her final words were still echoing in his ears, cleaving his soul in two. *"I was the fool fer trusting you when yer nothing more than a monster."*

"Did you . . . come fer me?" he asked, his voice catching as it wavered between hope and despair.

The woman peered up at him with guarded eyes, as if she'd placed a curtain between them that prevented him from seeing her true feelings. How he longed to strip that barrier away and uncover what lay beneath, to look upon her without any more pretenses or lies, as they had at the docks before everything had fallen apart.

Nay, na quite. I was still lying to her then. Only now can she see past everything.

"Listen, Muireall"—he rubbed the back of his neck—"I'm so sorry fer na telling you the truth before. I should have been honest with you from the beginning. You deserved better than—"

"Nay, *you* listen," she interrupted, her tone firm. "I'm na here fer you, so get that out o' yer thick head right now. I'm here because yer mad father is looking fer you, and we didn' want him to hurt anyone else while trying to get to you."

Anyone else? He hurt someone? Then his mind snagged on another strange detail. "'We'?"

Muireall jerked her chin toward where she'd just come from. "There's no time." Then she was off, dashing down the tunnel without so much as checking to see if he was following.

***

Muireall's stomach quivered even as she tried to remain focused on the task at hand: getting back to the others, so they could all escape the Fairy Realm in one piece. But Niall was here—*right here*—at her side when she'd been so sure she'd never see him again. Her heart was screaming at her, begging her to tell him how worried she'd been. And how sorry she was that she'd left him behind.

Her more sensible side refused to give in to such feelings. *He lied to me*, she reminded herself. *And na only that but he also killed Alastair. I can' just let that go.*

But Niall told you before that he was different, that falling in love with you changed him, her heart argued.

Aye, but that doesn' excuse what he did. Nothing will.

They soon found Mr. Mendes and Mr. Burgess, still alive but cut and bruised in several places. Mr. Mendes's injuries didn't seem too severe, but Mr. Burgess's hand was pressed over a long gash on the left side of his torso, blood staining the edges of his fingers.

"There you are," the farmer said, beaming at the pair as though he wasn't in what looked like terrible pain. "Was wondering if Mistress Oliver would be able to find you."

"John? You—" Niall's warm expression faded as his eyes landed on the blond man at Mr. Burgess's side. He wrinkled his nose. "Yer here, too?"

Mr. Mendes let out a quiet chuckle. "Try not to look so excited." He said to Muireall, "Is Mr. Park not with you?"

"Mr. Park?" Niall frowned. "Don' tell me you brought the whole village, Princess."

Muireall ignored the jab, tucking away the tenderness that flared up within her at his use of that troublesome nickname. "We need to go now while we still can."

The group hurried out of the mound, their feet light. Just as they reached the clearing, a strange humming sound rose in the air. Muireall glanced over her shoulder, and her blood turned to ice.

A host of fairy soldiers hovered high in the air, many armed with bows and arrows. But that wasn't what frightened her the most—it was the enmity in their eyes. Enmity that made it clear they wouldn't be taking prisoners today.

"Watch out," she called as arrows rained down from the sky. The first few were near-misses, but the group was still too far from the fairy ring. Eventually, someone was going to get hit.

"Here!" cried a familiar voice. Mr. Park stood a short distance away at the edge of the clearing, his hand raised. Trees spread out on either side of him, but he was still in the fairies' direct line of sight.

Several arrows hit the ground around his feet. He lowered his hand and glowered at the approaching enemy as if daring them to loose another arrow.

Muireall and the others dashed over to him, breathing heavily. "How did you get here so fast?" she panted.

He gave her a flat look as if she were stupid, then urged them all to keep running. "You're almost back to the ring."

Muireall was about to do as he'd bidden, then paused, ducking as more arrows flew through the air. The soldiers would be upon them soon. "Are you na coming with us?"

Mr. Park's mouth lifted into a lopsided grin even as he shook his head. "I'll draw them away." He turned to leave.

"Wait, but—"

Niall grabbed her outstretched arm, pulling her out of the way as an arrow zinged past. "Let him go, Muireall. He knows what he's doing."

She frowned but let her arm drop, hating to abandon someone to such danger when it was her fault he'd even come here.

Niall released her arm and followed after Mr. Mendes and Mr. Burgess, but Muireall lingered, her eyes locked on Mr. Park.

"This way," the foreigner shouted as he ran straight at the soldiers, waving his sword back and forth. "Come after me!"

The fairies barely glanced at him before continuing toward the others, but then Mr. Park made an inhumanly high leap, his sword swiping at their legs.

One fairy cried out as the blade drew blood, grabbing at his leg with a look of sheer terror.

"Still going to ignore me?" Mr. Park taunted. He took a few steps back, his sword ready.

As soon as the angry soldiers swerved at him, he darted off, heading toward the forest. The fairies followed, drawing back their bowstrings to shoot again—

Muireall stiffened, for five of the soldiers had turned at the last second, their piercing eyes zeroing in on her.

Niall appeared and yanked her backward, jarring her from her stupor. "Move!"

The two of them charged across the clearing, soon catching up to Mr. Burgess, who was several yards behind Mr. Mendes. The farmer slowed without warning, clutching his injured side, and Muireall couldn't stop herself before she rammed into his back and sent the two of them careening to the ground. The heels of Muireall's hands took most of the impact, whereas Mr. Burgess slammed face-first into the dirt.

Mr. Mendes heard the collision and spun around. He and Niall moved to help Mr. Burgess, but then their eyes widened at something behind them.

An arrow whistled through the air, and the only thing Muireall had time to do was brace herself for the pain she knew was coming.

A few seconds passed, and she lifted her head, confused. *What in the— How did we get back here?*

No longer were they in the fairy clearing. Somehow, they'd arrived back at the edge of Torin Woods, not a fairy in sight.

Muireall glanced at the fairy ring around them. "I don' understand. . . ."

A soft chuckle drew her attention. To her right, a few inches from the fairy ring, stood Lachlan, hands on his hips. "I told you to come find me if you ran into trouble. Good thing you were so noisy I couldn' help but hear you come by." A smile tugged at the trow's gray lips, softening his hideous features.

"Lachlan! Did you . . ." She trailed off, still trying to wrap her head around what had just happened.

The trow's smile widened in understanding, and he snapped his fingers, just like he had when he'd summoned her clarsach.

"When you and yer friends didn' come back from the Fairy Realm, I got worried and went to make sure you were all right." His expression soured. "Lucky I got there when I did; otherwise—"

Muireall embraced the tiny creature, tears streaming down her face. "Thank you. Thank you."

When she pulled back, Lachlan's mouth opened and closed a few times, too shocked to respond.

"Aye, thank you . . . sir?" Mr. Mendes said uncertainly. He seemed to be trying not to flinch, despite his obvious discomfort with the strange being before them. Mr. Burgess, too, was visibly uneasy, but Muireall wasn't sure how much of that was because of his injury.

Lachlan shook himself, then grinned at Mr. Mendes. "Happy to help any friend o' Muireall's," he replied with a bow. His eyes narrowed at Niall. "Even you, I suppose."

Niall bared his teeth, but Muireall gave him a scathing look. *Lachlan just saved our lives; show a wee bit o' gratitude.*

The trow turned to her. "Well, you better get going. From what I hear, Callum and his herd are already on their way to the village."

"What? Did you hear anyth—"

Lachlan snapped his fingers again and vanished before she could finish.

Muireall groaned, then shared a tired look with Mr. Mendes and Mr. Burgess. The three of them had already been through quite the ordeal today, and the day's troubles were far from over.

"That wound needs tending to," she said to the farmer. His skin was turning a pasty white, and he looked like he could pass out at any moment.

He shook his head. "Later. I have to make sure my family is all right."

"But—"

"I'm fine, mistress," he interrupted, giving her a thin smile that wasn't convincing in the slightest.

"It could be a lot worse," grumbled a male voice.

Everyone turned as Mr. Park stumbled out of the fairy ring, slashes and blood all over his robes.

Muireall and Mr. Mendes rushed to his side and helped ease him to the ground. His breaths were ragged, and it seemed to be all he could do to keep himself from falling over.

"You made it back," Muireall said, giving him a hopeful smile.

"Barely. I shouldn't have let myself be swayed by your friend's courageous words. Next time I'll do better," he said with a dry smile that quickly turned into a grimace.

She scrutinized her friend. His face bore multiple cuts and bruises, none of which had been there when last she'd seen him. Her eyes narrowed on a particularly large stain on his torso. "How much o' that blood is yers?"

Mr. Park frowned at his robes. It almost looked as if he'd gone wading in the loch, they were so soaked. "Would you believe me if I said none?" When Muireall simply scowled, he added, "I'll be fine. This isn't the first fight I've gotten into. Though it will be the last one for those fairies." His face darkened as his eyes drifted back to the fairy ring.

The others stiffened. *He killed all o' them? At once?* From what Muireall remembered, there had been at least fifteen soldiers. A sense of awe fell over the group. Even Niall looked reasonably impressed.

"Let's get you and John to Drulea Cottage. Briony will take care o' you both," Mr. Mendes said finally. He nodded to Niall, who readily helped Mr. Burgess to his feet. Mr. Park had a more difficult time rising, but between Muireall and Mr.

Mendes's help, he, too, was able to make the trek to the midwife's home.

When they arrived, though, the place was deserted.

Betrayal of the Worst Kind

When no one came to the door, the group staggered into the empty house. As Niall helped John into a chair, his eyes swept around, scanning for signs of a struggle. But there was nothing broken, nothing strewn about. Everything was in its proper place, save for three cups of half-drunk tea on the table.

Mr. Mendes's mouth twisted as he lifted one of the teacups. "They probably just went to check on the inn," he said, but Niall could tell no one—not even Mr. Mendes—believed that.

Mr. Park started to swoon, so Muireall and Mr. Mendes helped him onto the bed in Briony's mother's old room. They found some bandages and did their best to wrap them around the man's wounds, wincing a few times at how deep they were. When they stepped back, both had blood on their hands.

Niall moved forward to look more closely at the unconscious foreigner, curious why he would risk his life for someone he barely knew. *Mr. Park better make it through this, so I can ask him.*

John shook his head, but the effort made him lose his balance and have to grab onto the table to keep from falling. "We have to get to the beach."

"*Yer* na going anywhere." Niall took the sword still clenched in the man's fist. John started to protest, but he cut him off. "You won' be able to help anyone in yer current state. You'd only be in the way. Stay here with Mr. Park. The rest o' us will go find them."

The farmer frowned, but Niall stared him down. "Please, John. Trust me. I'll find yer family and keep them safe."

His expression softened, then he gave a brisk nod. "Get going, then."

As the three of them turned to leave, John added, "And Niall, I do trust you'll take care o' *our* family."

The man's words cut him to the quick, reminding him of just how important these people had become, and to his surprise, he found himself blinking back tears. "I won' let you down," he promised, then joined the others outside.

The first thing he noticed when he stepped out was that the sky was no longer a cloudless blue. Instead, dark, angry clouds covered everything, looking ready to spill over at any moment. Thunder rolled in the distance, and gusts of wind sent chills down his spine, but he stood rooted to the spot.

"Niall, were you and yer father planning to . . . to . . ." Muireall trailed off, her eyes wide.

"We're too late," he whispered, almost to himself, unable to conceal his growing horror.

"Not yet. Look." Mr. Mendes pointed to a speck of clear sky near the beach, shining like a beacon in the growing darkness.

Briony and William.

The group raced down the hill, eager and terrified of what they would find. As their feet pounded against the dirt road, a large shape emerged from the sea, moving in the direction of the beach. It was difficult to make out clearly, but Niall knew in his gut what it was.

The herd. As soon as they get to the shore and cast off their skins, Briony and William won' stand a chance. They must have summoned the storm ahead o' time as a warning. Or perhaps to make it easier na to be spotted until 'tis too late.

Or perhaps . . . Father was trying to let me know he was coming.

He raced ahead, his strides reckless and desperate.

***

302

"We can' wait any longer," Briony called, her voice barely audible over the screeching wind. She stood with Adaira and William at the docks, their eyes fixed on the approaching selkies. She had been watching the unwelcome newcomers for several minutes now, her anxiety climbing as they drew nearer. There must have been at least fifteen of them, though it was difficult to tell when they swam so closely together. Their movements were perfectly synchronized, their heads bobbing above the water without fear.

She had felt them coming before she'd seen them. Niall had told her that pureblood selkies could sense each other, but since she wasn't fully selkie, she'd only ever felt twinges of familiarity when in other selkies' presence. Until now. Perhaps it was because she'd been learning how to control her powers, or perhaps it was because there were so many of them, but about an hour earlier, a sudden shock of awareness had run through her, making her nearly fall out of her chair. William must have felt it, too, for he'd cried out at the exact same time she had.

Briony swallowed, glancing from the seals to the cliffs behind her. Santiago still hadn't brought Niall back. If guarding Everton hadn't been so important, she would never have let him go without her, injured or not. The two of them had almost died too many times to take any more unnecessary risks, and Santiago was only human.

Have a wee bit o' faith, she told herself. *He and John can handle themselves, and they have Mr. Park along with them.*

She frowned, not feeling very reassured. Muireall might trust the foreigner, but she certainly didn't. He'd only been in town for a few weeks, and though he also clearly had a magical heritage, that didn't tell them anything about his motives.

"Perhaps I can stall them long enough fer the others to get here," she said softly.

"I hope you don' think yer going by yerself, dearie," Adaira said, hands on her hips.

Briony smiled at her headstrong friend. "You don' have any powers. You could get killed."

Adaira glared. "So could you. Besides, after all we've been through, there's no way I'm going to let you stand alone." She raised her chin in challenge.

"I'm coming, too," William said. "He's my grandfather. Maybe he'll listen to me."

Briony grimaced, not wanting to put them in more danger. But William had proven himself capable when he'd helped her fend off Callum's attack, and if talking civilly with the herd didn't work, she'd need his assistance again. And Adaira was just too stubborn to leave even if Briony tried to force her to.

She gave a sharp nod, and the three of them marched onto the beach, their expressions nervous but resolute.

The herd stopped only a few feet from the shore, eyes locked on Briony, Adaira, and William. One seal separated from the others, then went out of sight behind a large boulder. Callum soon emerged, now in human form, his sealskin wrapped around his middle.

"I promised to return," he bit out. The smile on his face was cold as he strode toward them.

Lightning struck near his foot, and he jerked back.

"Na any closer," Briony warned.

He tilted his head. "Do you really think you stand a chance against all o' us?"

"If yer so sure o' victory, why bother talking to us at all? I thought you wanted me dead." She hoped he wouldn't see through her attempt to stall them.

Callum's mouth twitched, then he gestured to the seals behind him. "I spoke to the herd, and since yer Einar's offspring, we're willing to offer you a place among us. *If* you give up this foolish attempt to protect the humans who killed yer father."

"That's a lie," Briony spat. "The real reason you haven' attacked yet is because you don' know where Niall is."

His eyes narrowed ever so slightly, confirming her suspicion. The selkies weren't trying to be generous. They were biding their time until Niall's whereabouts were known.

Callum shook his head. "And here I was trying to be reasonable and offer you a chance at a family."

"I already have one," Briony replied, her voice ringing with pride as her eyes flicked to Adaira and William. "And I won' let you harm it."

"Neither will I," Niall declared, stepping into view.

***

Niall's heart pounded as he stood face to face with his father. The eyes of the herd were on him, their gazes pricking at him like darts.

"Niall." Callum's face lit up with such joy it was like a punch to the gut. Niall wished with everything in him that he wasn't about to wrench it all away.

"Hello, Father," he replied, his voice cold, numb.

"Are you hurt anywhere?" Callum reached for his son, then drew back with a hiss. He stared at his fingers in horror, red burns already forming where he'd brushed against the iron sword in Niall's hand. Confusion knit his brow. "Why do you have that?"

Niall swallowed. "To stop you from hurting anyone here."

Disbelief spread across the older man's face. "What are you saying? I'm here to rescue you. We're all here. Why would you want to stop us?"

"Father, the people o' this town"—Niall's gaze swept over Briony, Adaira, and William, then to Muireall and Mr. Mendes, who'd arrived shortly after him—"don' deserve to die."

Callum shook his head, disbelief giving way to anger. "Don' deserve to die? These are the people responsible fer Einar's death. Fer Elene's and yer mother's. How could—"

He stiffened, then eyed Niall curiously. "Did Einar's daughter use her charmsong on you, son?"

Niall tightened his grip on his sword, sweat pouring down his back. When he'd grabbed the blade earlier, he'd been almost sure there was no way he'd need it. Now, he wasn't as confident. "Nay, she didn'."

"Then yer simply blinded because yer still in love with her," Father said, his tone biting and scornful.

"Nay, na her. I—"

305

A soft intake of breath made him turn, his eyes snapping to Muireall's. Doubt swirled in her gaze. *Nay, Muireall. I told you before—yer the only one I've ever truly loved. Please, believe me.*

As she stared back at him, the tiniest flicker of hope passed through her eyes. Niall's mouth lifted, and he turned back—

Father's fist crashed into his jaw, knocking him straight to the ground. He slowly got back on his feet, shame weighing down his limbs.

"Yer in love with a human now? Niall, how could you? After what happened to Elene and yer mother—" Callum broke off, overcome with emotion. The sky crackled above them, fueled further by his growing rage.

"I know it seems hard to believe," Niall said quickly, "but if you would just listen to me, I can explain everything."

Father's eyes became slits, his mouth stretching into a tight smile. "You don' need to explain anything. I've heard enough. I see now that you were right."

"What? I . . . I was?" Niall blinked several times, looking from the still-worsening storm back to his father.

Callum laughed bitterly. "Oh, aye, you were absolutely right." He wiped the smile off his face, his expression turning stony. "I only wish I'd believed you when you first told me Everton needed to be destroyed."

He threw his hand in the air, and lightning descended in a blinding flash. Niall didn't even have time to brace himself before unbearable heat surged through him, and an earsplitting howl tore out of his throat.

Time seemed to slow as he fell backward, his eyes taking in his surroundings: Briony leaping forward with her arms raised to protect him, Adaira screaming and covering William with her body, Mr. Mendes flying through the air, his sword aimed at Callum's heart.

But the only thought Niall could manage before he passed out was, *Where is Muireall?*

Taking a Stand

As soon as Callum's fist connected with Niall's jaw, Muireall knew they'd made a mistake. Callum wasn't going to accept that his son had changed, nor was he going to leave the people of Everton in peace.

Her eyes went from the seals to her sorely outnumbered group of friends. *Unless . . .*

She bolted off the beach, not waiting to see how Niall and Callum's conversation ended. She veered to the left, her breaths coming in great heaves. But she didn't slow down, not even when her lungs were screeching in agony, for she couldn't afford to waste a precious second.

Not when the fate of her entire village hung in the balance.

She cut around the side of Rigmore House to the door that led straight to the ballroom. Lights, music, and voices emanated from within.

Have they na noticed the storm brewing? Raindrops were already beginning to fall, and if Callum's punch was anything to go by, things were about to get much worse.

She grabbed the door handle, paused for a split second, then burst into the room.

The wind smashed the door against the wall, alerting everyone of her arrival. Donal McGuff and Nathaniel Levins lowered their fiddles, those on the dance floor slowed to a stop, and the chattering villagers went silent. Muireall's eyes swept over the crowd, her face flushing at her neighbors' inquisitive expressions.

"Muireall! We've all been waiting fer you," Laura exclaimed as she flitted over from the other side of the room. She eyed her daughter up and down, then crossed her arms over her bosom. A decadent red dress stretched over her ample figure, and a string of pearls dangled from her neck.

"That isn' the dress I picked out fer you," she snipped, her voice teetering between control and hysterics. She cast a glance around the ballroom, then let out a painfully fake giggle. "You certainly know how to make an entrance though. Doesn' she, Joseph?"

Father, who stood a few feet away, threw back a swig of ale, then joined his wife and daughter. He, too, looked nervous, but his anxiety seemed more directed at Lady Oliver than the guests. "Daughter, where have you been? The ball started almost an hour ago."

"Mother, Father, I need yer help," Muireall said evenly. She gulped, then raised her voice to address the crowd, "I need everyone's help. Everton is in danger."

"Danger? What are you talking about?" Father asked, one eyebrow raised.

She bit her lip. *Do I tell the truth or . . .*

Thunder crashed outside, causing several townsfolk to gasp as the wind and rain picked up. Muireall's heart sped up; they were running out of time.

"I know this sounds mad," she started, "but a group o' selkies has come ashore, and they mean to kill us. All o' us. Briony and a few others are out on the beach, doing what they can to stop them, but they're na strong enough on their own." She held up her dagger. "Those o' you with weapons need to come with me right now."

Laura stepped in front of her daughter, her cheeks sizzling with anger and embarrassment. "Selkies? Have you lost yer mind?" She swung around to the guests. "Please excuse my daughter. She must have had too much to drink. She doesn' know what she's—"

"Nay, I know exactly what I'm talking about," Muireall snapped, moving out from behind her mother. Her voice was shaky, but she wasn't about to let Laura silence her. Not anymore.

Mother turned to her, face frozen in shock. Muireall might have even laughed at the funny sight, were it not for her knees knocking together. Such public disregard of her mother's authority was far beyond anything she had dared before, and she knew as soon as Laura got a hold of herself, the older woman would do all she could to make Muireall regret it.

But that didn't matter right now. What mattered was protecting Everton.

And Niall.

Oh, Niall, I hope yer all right.

"You said Briony is out there?" Mistress McGuff asked.

Muireall swiveled toward her, noting the bewilderment on her neighbors' faces. Even without anyone voicing it, she could tell what they were thinking: *How could Briony Fairborn fight off selkies?*

But the answer to that was a secret Muireall wasn't at liberty to share, so all she said was, "Aye, she is. She's risking her life right now to keep all o' you safe. So, I ask—nay, *beg* you to please come help her."

When the only response she got was silence, Muireall's heart fell. She'd expected more of her neighbors. For all their talk of taking care of one another, prejudice seemed to have won out. She took a deep breath, preparing herself to charge back out into the storm.

"I'll go," Mr. McGuff said finally. Everyone looked at him in surprise, but the man's face didn't waver. "Briony Fairborn saved my wife when our house nearly burned to the ground. If she's in trouble, I'll do what I can to repay that debt."

"And I'll go," Daniel Calhoun called.

His wife, Freda, babe in her arms, gaped at him incredulously. "But, Daniel, what about—"

He silenced her with a firm head shake. "Without her, I would have lost both my wife and my daughter." His countenance softened as he peered at his healthy baby girl, then he looked pointedly around the room. "And so would many o' you."

About ten more men offered to help after that, with several mentioning times Briony had assisted them. The rest of the crowd parted in stunned silence as the volunteers stepped forward, ready to do what they could.

Muireall smiled, grateful her village hadn't let her down. She only prayed it would be enough to turn the tide. "Thank you all. Now, hurry. They may have already started their attack."

With that said, people poured out of the ballroom to retrieve their weapons, the party forgotten. Muireall moved toward the exit, but as she did, her mother stepped in front of her.

"Muireall Oliver, if you do this, you can consider yerself disowned from the family," Laura screeched, her eyes wild.

She paused, the harsh words ripping through her. *Mother wouldn' really do that . . . would she?* She gazed into Laura's eyes, searching for some sign of love within them.

But when all that shone back at her was rage, she knew her mother's threat was more than just words.

Take it back, whispered a frightened voice inside her. *Take it back, and everything will return to normal. If you don', you'll lose yer family. Yer home. Yer garden.*

Muireall clenched her teeth. *I refuse to go back to the way things were. No matter the cost. Call me a disgrace, throw me out, take away my inheritance—I'm na going to let Mother stop me anymore.*

Na when I'm trying to do what's right.

Instead of responding, she looked over her shoulder. Straight at her father. "Are you coming?"

Laird Oliver's eyes, still full of anxiety, slid from his daughter to his wife, giving Muireall all the answer she needed.

She let out a soft sigh and nodded in understanding. She'd expected as much, but that didn't make his silence any less painful.

With one final glance at her parents, Muireall lifted her chin, pushed her feelings aside, and darted back out into the storm, dagger in hand.

***

The first thing Niall was aware of as he came to was the sand caking his fingers. *Did I fall asleep on the beach?* Memories of

310

playing on the islet with Elene the night before filled his thoughts, and he smiled.

She must have left me here on purpose. She was often playing harmless tricks like that on him, but he didn't mind since he'd find some way to get her back later. Then the two of them would laugh and try to come up with some more mischief to get into. Mother and Father would scold them, but Niall knew they enjoyed their children's antics, even if they would never admit it.

Elene . . .

Something pressed at the edge of his consciousness, something urgent he needed to do, but he couldn't remember what it was. He'd much rather continue sleeping, his heart warm and content. Perhaps he'd forgotten a chore Father wanted him to complete, or maybe Mother needed—

"Niall, get up!" cried a voice above him.

His eyes shot open. Briony stood over him, hands outstretched toward the sky. Storm clouds swirled all around them, bolts of lightning blasting the ground in quick succession.

Niall's memories of his sister faded, the past falling away as he returned to the present.

He pulled himself to his feet, ignoring a dull ache at the back of his skull, and took stock of the situation. Mr. Mendes stood a short distance up the beach, swinging his sword as Callum maneuvered out of the way. William and Adaira were on Niall's left, frightened but uninjured. And the other selkies were—

Niall retrieved his sword and loped toward them, blocking the two nearest ones from the shore. They hissed and snarled, betrayal burning in their black eyes, but they didn't dare come closer while in seal form. Not when he held an iron blade that would burn them with a single touch.

Stay back. Please, he silently begged, not wanting to harm those he'd grown up swearing to protect.

But he knew without a shadow of a doubt that if they kept coming, he would do what he had to. He wasn't going to let them take innocent lives, and he certainly wasn't going to put Muireall in any more danger.

Muireall! He whirled around, but there was no sign of the beautiful redhead anywhere on the beach. *She should be here. Why isn' she here?*

The other selkies swam closer, forcing Niall to move back and forth, so none could slip past. Briony and William appeared on either side of him, calling down lightning and hail.

A few selkies cried out, unable to get out of the way before they were struck, then sank beneath the water. The rest dodged the onslaught by diving under the water, only to reemerge seconds later.

"We can' keep this up," Briony cried as one of her bolts struck a seal between the eyes.

"Do you have any other suggestions?" Niall snapped, swiping at the selkie nearest him. The seal just barely avoided the swing, then disappeared beneath the water. Niall bit back a curse, trying to figure out where it had swum off to.

"Enough o' this!" Callum bellowed.

Niall's gaze cut over to his father, who now bore a shallow wound on his arm. Mr. Mendes glanced up, still armed, as the sky directly above him crackled with thunder.

Briony raced toward her betrothed and threw out her hands, creating a shield just in time as lightning cascaded down.

But her departure created an opening for the other selkies, and soon, one got to the shore. As it started to peel back its pelt, Adaira leaped in from out of nowhere and stabbed it in the back with a knife. The seal shrieked, then came at her with its teeth.

Adaira fell backward, the knife slipping from her hand. Niall hurried to defend her, piercing the selkie in the side. The seal retreated to the water, but two more came forward to take its place.

"Thank you, Niall," Adaira whimpered, but he barely heard her, his arm rising and falling as he held the newcomers at bay. Each time his blade struck true, it felt like his heart was rending in two, but he didn't hesitate. Hesitation could mean the difference between life and death. A small part of him was grateful they were still in seal form; in the thick darkness, he couldn't tell exactly whom he was attacking.

"Have you seen Muireall?" he asked when he got the chance. The seals he'd been fighting had pulled back, one sporting a deep cut in its side. *Did Muireall get dragged off into the sea? Is she lying unconscious too far away fer me to see her?*

"She ran off earlier while you were talking to yer father," Adaira said with a brief shake of her head.

She left? He stumbled a bit. He shouldn't have been surprised. She wasn't trained to defend herself; she must have gone somewhere to hide.

But these are her friends—nay, family, he corrected himself, remembering Adaira and Muireall were cousins. *How could she abandon them?*

That thought was swiftly followed by another, far more vulnerable one: *How could she abandon me?*

Niall's heart clenched, and he berated himself for being such a fool. *O' course she doesn' love you. How could she after what you did? She told you before that she didn' cross the Veil fer yer sake. Just because she got upset when Father claimed you were in love with Briony doesn' mean she still has feelings fer you. It doesn' mean—*

He cut off his inner diatribe, his thoughts stolen away by an unearthly vision at the edge of the beach.

For there she stood, red hair streaming behind her, green eyes shining with a light that seemed to cast out the darkness looming over his soul. *Muireall? You came back.*

The hope rising within him evaporated as he caught sight of movement from the corner of his eye. Two selkies had come ashore while he was distracted, and now they were almost out of their sealskins.

Lightning struck the ground around him as they added their powers to the storm churning above. Niall swiped at one, knocking him on his side, then slammed his sword hilt into the back of his head.

"Don' test me," he threatened the two remaining selkies, a mated couple by the names of Firoz and Davina. He held his sword just above their heads.

The two shared a look, then Davina leaped at Niall's legs, knocking him to the ground. Firoz lifted his hand and called down a flood of rain on Niall's head, making him choke and cough.

Niall raised his sword, swinging blindly until he heard a sickening scream.

The rain abated, and he opened his eyes, his stomach turning at the sight of Firoz lying in a pool of blood while Davina wailed and cradled her mate's face in her hands.

Niall stared at his sword in horror. *What have I done?*

"You'll pay fer this, Niall." Davina's voice was raw. She raised her hand, her gaze flicking toward Muireall.

He spun around. "Get out o' here," he screeched. "It isn' safe. You have to—"

Before he could finish speaking, several men appeared behind her, some armed with pitchforks, others with swords and knives. The villagers' eyes widened at the scene before them, and a few looked like they wanted to turn back. Muireall said something to them; then, as one, they hurtled onto the beach, weapons raised.

The sound that came from Davina's throat was something between a shriek of terror and a roar of frustration. Niall swung toward her, his heart shuddering when he saw her pulling Firoz—fully in seal form now—back toward the sea. The selkie was injured but still breathing. For now.

Niall surveyed the rest of the beach, noting how the rest of the selkies were starting to retreat as well. William, Adaira, and Mr. Mendes stood at the water's edge, making sure none decided to change their minds. Father was still in the midst of battling Briony, but he seemed to be gaining the upper hand. The midwife was straining to maintain her shield as Callum's seemingly unending supply of wrath hurled bolt after bolt at her head.

Niall charged across the sand, then stepped in front of his friend. "'Tis over, Father."

Callum's expression faltered, but his assault continued. "'Tis na over until I rid the world o' those who stole my family from me. First Elene, then yer mother, and now you."

Niall's breath caught, a lump forming in his throat. "Father, I'm still right here."

Callum shook his head, and—if Niall wasn't mistaken— tears mingled with the rain on his cheeks. "Nay, yer na my son. My son would never stand against his own people."

"I would if it meant I was protecting the innocent."

Callum lowered his hands, relinquishing control over the storm. Niall's eyes went to Briony, smiling in relief when he saw she was still standing.

A humorless laugh drew his attention back to his father. "Innocent? Humans are never innocent. They're selfish, greedy thieves who think nothing o' killing our kind." Callum's words hummed with familiarity, reminding Niall of his own prejudice when he'd come to Everton's shore, intent on revenge.

Raised voices and pounding feet told Niall the townsfolk were closing in. If he didn't convince his father now, he'd lose his opportunity. *I have to make him see before he gets himself killed.*

"Some but na all," he countered. He took a step forward, reaching out. "Please, Father, don' make the same mistakes I did. We've both lost so much already."

"Grandfather, please!" William scurried up to Niall's side. Bruises dotted his face and arms, consequences of a fight he never should have been part of. "Mistress Briony is a good person. Don' hurt her!"

Callum's mouth quivered, and Niall knew he was seeing Elene in the boy's face, hearing her in his voice.

"Elene wouldn' want this, Father," Niall added. "Stop before 'tis too late."

Callum opened his mouth to speak, then his gaze shot to something behind them. "It seems Everton is more protected than I realized." His voice rumbled with betrayal, pain, and what sounded like a trace of regret. "Fer now."

With that, he withdrew, his seal form soon disappearing beneath the foam.

The Greatest Treasure

Three weeks later

"He said what?" Muireall asked.

"He said he saw a kelpie up at Loch Isla last night, but according to Gilbert, Mr. Levins had been drinking a lot," Anne eagerly replied, happy to share the latest gossip.

The village had been abuzz ever since the strange and terrible incident the night of Muireall's birthday. The night Everton had learned selkies were real. From that moment on, a sense of wonder had spread over the community, and the young people listened more intently to the fanciful stories of their elders. No longer were the old tales of trows, fairies, and selkies just yarns meant to amuse each other and scare the children; now, they were potential—if not probable—truth.

A few had been bold enough to ask Briony Fairborn about the incident, whom many claimed had singlehandedly thwarted the selkies' attack with such powerful magic she couldn't possibly be human, but the midwife had only answered their questions with riddles none could understand. The bravest bairns had gone up to Drulea Cottage in secret in the hopes of seeing her perform magic again, but Briony somehow always managed to discover them, no matter how well they hid.

Muireall Oliver, for her part, had said very little of what had happened that fateful night, but most knew better than to ask her. She was still a "living statue" in the eyes of her neighbors. That nickname seemed to be wearing off a bit, though, especially since she had started spending many of her evenings at Everton Inn or Drulea Cottage with the Burgesses and Mistress Fairborn.

There was also talk that she and Lady Oliver were still locked in a dispute, and Lady Oliver's threat to disinherit her daughter would soon come to fruition.

But those were all just rumors, for Muireall was much too tight-lipped to allow her private affairs to become common knowledge. Only a select few knew the truth of what she had been going through, and she trusted them to keep her secrets safe.

Another source of intrigue was Niall Moreland's abrupt departure from Rigmore House and subsequent relocation to Everton Inn. Though everyone now knew he was the brother of Mr. Burgess's late wife, it didn't make sense why he'd suddenly given up his position as the Olivers' gardener. A few servants whispered that he'd had an affair with none other than the young mistress, herself, but Muireall's cold demeanor made this seem unlikely.

And no one had been brazen enough to ask her outright so far.

"I better get going, Anne. The Burgesses are expecting me fer dinner," Muireall said after a few more minutes of chatting. "Thank you fer keeping me informed."

The young maid smiled in response. A friendship had bloomed between them in the last few weeks, one Muireall was exceedingly grateful for. Between her mother's icy silence as she waited for her to apologize and her father's pleading for her to heed her mother, it was nice to spend time with someone so easy to get along with.

Especially with how tenuous things were between her and Niall.

Heaviness settled in her chest. She didn't want to think about him. That wish proved impossible, though, when she arrived at Everton Inn, and he was the one who answered the door.

"Good evening," she said stiffly, not meeting his eye.

"Aye." His voice was a mixture of awkwardness and something else Muireall couldn't identify.

The two had hardly spoken since the selkie attack and only then in terse sentences that were so stilted Muireall wasn't sure how much longer she could keep it up.

Her bitterness toward Niall had subsided the moment he had walked out on the beach and declared his allegiance to the people of Everton. Anyone brave enough to do that deserved a second chance.

But every time she'd tried to open up to him, her mind would recall the pain in his eyes as he'd watched his father disappear into the sea foam. The memory always made her tongue stick to the roof of her mouth before she could get a word out.

Not because she believed Niall had made the wrong decision. It was because she knew firsthand how agonizing it was for parents to turn their backs on you. And if what he had told her was true, falling in love with her had been the greatest catalyst for his shift in loyalty.

She'd told herself that didn't make it her fault, that their decisions were still their own, but she still couldn't shake a sense of guilt for the role she'd played in destroying the relationship between a father and son.

William, who seemed oblivious to Niall's distress, mentioned Callum often, and each time he did, Niall retreated a little further into his shell. How Muireall longed to reach out and draw him back, to tell him someone still loved him and that he'd done the right thing, but she feared her efforts would only make things worse. And she didn't think she could handle another rejection right now.

She didn't say any more as Niall stepped aside to allow her entrance, but internally, she was scoffing at herself. *How ironic that I finally realize I love him when I've lost the nerve to even look him in the eye.*

She was soon distracted from her melancholy by Adaira's boisterous welcome. Her husband and son were already seated at the table, and within a few minutes, Mr. Mendes and Briony emerged from the inn's back door, their faces flushed. With a knowing twinkle in her eye, her cousin shared how excited she was for Briony and Mr. Mendes's wedding the following week, and her enthusiasm was so potent Muireall couldn't help but smile along with her.

Just as everyone started eating, someone knocked on the door. Adaira leaped to her feet, eager to welcome in whomever it was, but she returned a few seconds later with a perplexed expression.

"Who was it, dear?" Mr. Burgess asked, a half-eaten biscuit in his right hand.

Adaira shook her head and plopped back into her seat next to William. "There was no one there."

As she went back to eating her soup, Muireall shared a concerned look with Niall, who sat across from her. "You don' think the Fair Folk . . ."

Her voice petered off, but from the flash in his eyes, she knew he understood what she was asking.

In the aftermath of the selkies' attack, it seemed no one else had noticed how strange it was that the fairies hadn't come looking for Niall yet. Perhaps the others thought the Prince simply didn't care about his escaped prisoner. If they'd met Prince Aodhàn, though, Muireall suspected they wouldn't be nearly so nonchalant. The thought of that fairy's cold smile still made her legs go weak.

"'Tis possible . . ." Niall murmured, rising from his chair to go see for himself.

Muireall took a sip of soup, but at the sound of hushed voices in the foyer, she darted out, her heart racing with fear.

But rather than finding a fairy at the front door, the figure she found with Niall was none other than Lachlan, whose pointed nose was raised in indignation.

"Where is she, you great buffoon? You know I can make you tell me if I wish," the trow threatened, curving his finger in Niall's direction.

"Lachlan!" she greeted, a smile breaking out over her face.

The trow's features softened as she came into the room, but anxiety danced in his red eyes. "Muireall, you can' know how glad I am to see you."

"Is something wrong?" she asked, catching the urgency in his tone.

"Aye, unfortunately, there is." His gaze passed from her to Niall. "Princess Aoife has placed a bounty on yer head."

She gasped at the same time Niall said, "Wait, why were you looking fer Muireall, then? Shouldn' you have been trying to find me?"

Lachlan scoffed. "I don' particularly care what happens to you, leannan na mara. 'Tis Muireall I'm concerned about."

She swallowed. "Are they after me, too?"

"Nay, but anyone who's around this one"—he sent Niall a quick glare—"isn' safe."

Niall crossed his arms, seemingly more offended by Lachlan's comments than the very real danger he'd just been informed of.

"Can fairies cross the Veil any time they like?" Muireall looked between the two of them.

"Aye, but fairy law dictates they must be discreet. If too many humans find out about their existence, they'll start crossing the Veil into the Fairy Realm and cause all kinds o' trouble," Niall explained. "I've been careful na to go near any fairy rings since I've gotten back, and I've been staying close to John and William instead o' going anywhere alone. If a fairy came after me, there's almost no way he could do it without being noticed."

"From what I've heard, the price Princess Aoife is offering is high enough that it won' be long before discretion doesn' matter anymore, law or no law." The trow glanced at Niall. "The best thing you can do is get out o' here as quickly as possible and hope no one follows you."

Leave? All the blood left Muireall's face. Her eyes shot to Niall, hoping he'd see how desperately she wanted him to stay, but before their gazes met, Lachlan grasped her hands.

"And fer yer own sake, you need to stay away from him. I don' want you getting yerself into trouble again. You have a promise to keep, you know."

She winced. She'd forgotten about that. She didn't feel anywhere near equipped for such a responsibility. "About that promise . . . would it be all right if I transferred it to a friend o' mine?"

When Lachlan's face hardened, fear trickled down her spine. The trow's kind nature had made it easy to stop thinking of him as dangerous, but perhaps she'd been naïve. *Will he hurt me if I don' keep my word?*

"I just—I want to make sure yer well cared fer," she clarified, "and I'm na sure I'm the best person fer that. After all, I'm just a human."

She almost laughed at her own words. *What a statement.* Before meeting Niall, she never would have thought her humanity could be a disadvantage. Now she knew better.

The trow considered her proposal, his mouth a firm line. "And whom would you be referring to?"

"Briony Fairborn, the . . . selkie."

"Oh, I know about Briony Fairborn," Lachlan murmured cryptically. He said to Niall, "She's a bit more than a selkie, though, isn' she?"

Niall tilted his head to the side, puzzled.

The trow turned back to Muireall. "All right. I'll accept the change."

"Thank you. As fer yer advice . . ." Her gaze flicked to Niall, who was watching her anxiously. He looked away as soon as their eyes met, leaving her wondering what he could be thinking. ". . . I'll have to think about it," she mumbled.

Lachlan huffed in disapproval, but he nodded. "I shall take my leave, then." He snapped his fingers and vanished in the blink of an eye.

"What was that?" William asked, appearing from the dining room. His father and Adaira were just behind him, both wearing identical expressions of shock.

"That was my friend, Lachlan." Muireall gave them a small smile. "He's a trow."

The inn erupted into questions after that, mostly from William, but the adults made their fair share of inquiries as well. Muireall did her best to answer everyone as they returned to the table and resumed their meal, but her mind was elsewhere. She shot a few subtle glances at Niall, hoping he'd give her some sort of indication that he wasn't really going to leave, but he didn't look up from his food or engage with anyone for the remainder of dinner.

"Thank you fer the delicious meal. I better return home now," she said once everyone had finished. Her eyes slid to Niall one last time, just in case he might have something to say, but he didn't react to her statement.

With a sigh, she rose from her chair.

"Niall, you'd best walk her back," Adaira said, her tone making it more of a command than a request. "'Tis already dark, and I don' want my cousin losing her way." She sent Muireall a conspiratorial wink.

Niall stiffened, and for a second, Muireall thought he was going to refuse. But then he reluctantly stood and moved toward her, his gaze lowered. "All right. I'll be back soon."

Her heart sank. *There's so much we need to talk about. 'Twill take too long fer you to be back "soon," won' it? Or do you na plan to speak to me still?*

As the two glided out the door and into the night, Muireall's stomach was in knots. *Should I speak up first, or should I wait fer him to broach the topic?*

Chirping crickets masked their footfalls, and a breeze sent a shiver through her body. *Perhaps 'tis more the silence than the air making me cold,* she thought, adjusting her arisaid[37] around her shoulders.

Just when Muireall finally took a deep breath to speak, Niall said, "So, are you truly going to heed the trow's advice?"

She started at his voice, the dulcet sound sending shivers through her body. Her lips tilted up, for she'd sorely missed their talks. She stole a peek at him, but his quizzical expression gave her pause.

Wait, he asked me something. What was it? Warmth flooded her cheeks as his question came back to her. "Ah, about staying away from you? I suppose that depends . . ."

He's worried about me staying away from him? Does that mean he still cares? Muireall's fingers twitched as she debated reaching for his hand. *Would he shy away from me?*

"Depends on what?" he asked, his words a gentle caress.

Her breath quickened, and she lifted her eyes to his. For the first time in what felt like forever, he didn't look away.

---

[37] A draped garment traditionally worn in Scotland.

They had abandoned the pretense of walking back to Rigmore House by this point, and they stood motionless just outside the church. Anyone might see them here, but Muireall couldn't care less about that right now. All that mattered was the man standing in front of her, the man she was terrified might disappear at any moment.

"On if yer going to leave me." Her blood went cold, and she dropped her gaze. "I mean, if yer going to leave Everton. I don' know why I said it like that. I—"

She wrung her hands, her mouth going dry. *How could I make such an embarrassing mistake? He doesn' want to be with me anymore. How could he after—*

"Muireall."

Niall's voice drew her from her thoughts. She lifted her head, her breath catching as something flared in his dark eyes. He took a step toward her.

"Niall, what are you doing?" Her pulse raced. He was far closer than was proper. One more step, and she'd be able to lean forward and kiss him.

One more step, and she doubted she'd have the self-control not to.

"Do you want me to leave?" His voice was soft, sensual, and altogether impossible to resist.

"Never."

The answer burst through her lips before she could stop it. She had a brief moment of panic, not used to feeling so exposed, but she bit down the urge to take it back. Maybe Niall still loved her; maybe he didn't, but if he was about to leave, she was going to be honest while she had the chance. "I . . . I love you, Niall, and I—"

She choked, tears filling her eyes. "I can' bear the thought o' parting from you. Na again."

Almost before she'd finished speaking, Niall's fingers were at her chin, tilting it up as his lips folded over hers.

Muireall didn't respond at first, shock holding her in place, but then a searing heat ran through her veins, and her mouth moved in turn. His hands grasped her shoulders, crushing her against him as the kiss deepened. Her doubts and uncertainties melted away, replaced by the joyous realization that her hopes were more than just a fantasy.

He doesn' hate me. He still loves me, too.

Niall pulled back, panting, and rested his forehead against hers. "Took you long enough to say something."

Muireall blinked a few times, dizzy from his kiss, then stepped out of his embrace with a frown. "Me? I've been waiting fer you all this time."

His eyebrows knitted together. "Why would you be waiting fer me? Yer the one who told me never to speak to you again."

"That was before I came and rescued you from the Fairy Realm," she pointed out, her words clipped, "which I never heard a thank you fer, by the way."

He scoffed. "I would have gotten out on my own even if you hadn' come."

"Is that so? Well, in that case, perhaps 'twould be better if you did just leave since you clearly don' appreciate me." Muireall spun on her heel and tried to stomp off, but Niall grabbed her wrist.

"Calm down, Princess, calm down." His condescending tone only made her angrier. He tried to swing her toward him, but she pulled out of his grip.

"How can I calm down when yer being so rude?"

Niall laughed, the sound light and teasing. "When have I ever been rude to the woman I love?"

"'When haven' you' is the better question. O' all the—"

He pecked her lips, sending a flurry of sparks through her.

A blush worked its way up her neck, but she clung desperately to her anger even as she felt it slipping away. "Now, don' you try to distract me, Niall Moreland."

"I wouldn' dream o' it." His face turned somber. "But Lachlan's words aren' to be taken lightly. Staying here puts everyone in danger. Too much danger."

"What are you saying?"

Niall took her hands in his, his eyes somewhere between hopeful and sad. "I know Mr. Park is planning to leave as soon as Briony and Santiago's wedding is over. Said something about taking his ship south. I'm sure he'd allow me to go with him if I asked."

Muireall trembled, not wanting to believe what she was hearing. She shook her head. "Nay, nay, you can'. Were you na listening to what I said? You can' leave me."

The right side of his mouth curled up, a hint of playfulness returning. "Who said anything about leaving you?"

"You . . . you want me to go with you?"

Niall nodded, staying silent as he waited for her response.

Muireall didn't say anything for a long moment, her thoughts spinning in all directions. She knew her mother's patience in waiting for an apology would run out soon. When that happened, Laura's threat to disown her would become a reality. No matter how much Mother valued appearances, control was still more important.

But now that Muireall had tasted freedom, she wasn't about to go back in her mother's cage.

Once that truth sank in, Laura would turn her out, reputation or no reputation. Muireall would be left penniless, forced to rely upon her cousin, Adaira, to survive. Rigmore House would become a thing of her past, a place she was no longer welcome.

But leaving all of Everton behind was another thing entirely.

As she considered the offer, she waited for fear to spread over her heart. She'd always been a homebody, preferring the familiarity of her garden over venturing somewhere new, but to her surprise, the thought of traveling to a far-off place sent a thrill of anticipation through her veins.

But my flowers . . . Images of her roses, azaleas, and lilies flooded her mind. Her garden had been her joy and sanctuary for so many years. The one place where she could be herself. Not her parents' perfect daughter, not her servants' young mistress, just Muireall. *Can I bear to say goodbye to it?*

Niall squeezed her hand, sending a shock up her arm. A smile tugged at her lips as she moved her focus—and her eyes—to what she'd be gaining, rather than what she'd be leaving behind.

And suddenly, all her reservations faded away.

For although her garden had been her haven, she realized she no longer needed it as she once had. She could be "just Muireall" wherever she went.

And there was nowhere she'd rather be than at Niall's side.

There was just one more thing they needed to get straight.

"Niall Moreland, as much as I love you, unmarried men and women don' travel together," she told him, her lips pursed.

With a wink that nearly made her knees buckle, he replied, "I'm na asking you to."

Muireall leaned forward, her nose brushing his. "That sounds suspiciously like a proposal."

"Mistress Oliver, I thought you knew better than to make assumptions." He pulled back slightly and raised his eyebrows.

She wrapped her arms around his neck. "If you keep talking, I might change my mind."

His wide eyes had her stifling a laugh. "You better na. 'Twill hurt my pride too much if I let Rigmore House's greatest treasure slip from my grasp."

Muireall's face lit up at the compliment, her heart nearly bursting. "Hmm . . . in that case, you'd better kiss me again."

"As you command, Princess."

Epilogue

Despite the festive occasion, Mr. Park's gaze returned to the perimeter again and again, scanning for potential threats. The sun had set hours ago, but the large bonfire in the center of Mary's Hill gave the villagers enough light to continue dancing long into the night. It was foolhardy to have the wedding celebration out here, so close to the Fairy Realm's entrance, but no other location in Everton could fit such a multitude of people.

None except the Olivers' ballroom, and since Laird and Lady Oliver vehemently opposed the day's nuptials, there was no way they would have allowed the villagers to use the space, anyway.

Mr. Park watched both brides twirl with their respective grooms, their faces glowing with delight. A fiddler stood nearby, strumming a happy tune that drew in even the most reluctant of dancers. Everyone seemed carefree tonight, the worries of human life forgotten in the midst of the celebration.

Little did they know, a stranger had snuck into their midst.

Mr. Park slunk up to the newcomer at the edge of the clearing and subtly drew his blade before placing it against her back. "What business have you here?"

The woman hissed and spun around so quickly he barely had time to react. He raised his sword threateningly, ready to use it if needed.

Now that he could see her clearly, though, he wondered just how much of a threat she could be. With her petite frame and no visible weapons, she appeared practically defenseless. He couldn't make out the tips of her ears from under her blond hair, but a fairy could have easily used magic to conceal their true form. Even so, the unsettling way she moved gave him the distinct impression he wasn't dealing with one of the Fair Folk.

This visitor was something else entirely.

The stranger's head swung from side to side in an undulating, almost serpentine manner as she assessed him. Her eyes suddenly flashed yellow, her lips peeling back into a snarl. "I hardly need answer you, gumiho."

Mr. Park lost his grip on his sword, catching it just before it clattered against the ground. By the time he'd gotten his bearings and looked back up, the stranger was gone.

Author's Note

And that's a wrap! I hope you loved the characters and world of Everton. As of right now, I am in the process of creating a prequel novella told from the perspective of Everton's own mad fisherman, Vincent McLaren. This novella will be a special gift for my website members. Become a website member for free at www.clairekohlerbooks.com. Joining will also give you access to my monthly newsletter, where you'll get inside information about all my upcoming releases.

If you enjoyed *The Treasure of Rigmore House*, be sure to leave a review. As an indie author, your reviews are invaluable to me, and I love hearing what my readers think. Thank you for coming with me on this journey, and I can't wait to share my next story with you soon.

www.ingramcontent.com/pod-product-compliance
Lightning Source LLC
Chambersburg PA
CBHW021212310726
48971CB00006B/1535